CHRISTIAN AND PLIABLE IN THE SLOUGH OF DESPOND.

Page 63.

THE
PILGRIM'S PROGRESS.

BY JOHN BUNYAN.

WITH

ONE HUNDRED AND SEVENTY ILLUSTRATIONS

AND A LIFE OF THE AUTHOR.

PUBLISHED BY THE

CHARLES FOSTER PUBLISHING CO.,

No. 716 Sansom Street,

PHILADELPHIA, PA.

THE LIONS IN THE PATH.

LIST OF ILLUSTRATIONS.

LORD HATE-GOOD.

Page 158.

List of Illustrations.

GREAT-HEART.

Page 300.

List of Illustrations.

OLD HONEST.

Page 346.

List of Illustrations.

List of Illustrations.

INTRODUCTION.

HE "PILGRIM'S PROGRESS" is, without question, of all uninspired volumes, the most extraordinary book in the English language. Regard being had to the condition of its author, and the circumstances connected with its production, to its widespread popularity, and its suitableness for readers of every class, there is none to compare with it.

The acceptance which the Pilgrim's Progress has met, from the first, is altogether unparalleled, and time shows no abatement in its popularity. Among all the competitors for public favor which have since issued from the press, it retains its pre-eminence.

There is scarcely a known language into which it has not been translated. Wherever English is spoken it is familiar as a household word. It appears in all forms and is read by all classes. Richly illustrated and elegantly bound it adorns the parlor tables of the wealthy. Well thumbed and sometimes tattered, as if from constant usage, it lies upon the shelf or window-sill of the poor.

Children are entranced with the interest of the story; its tranquil or gloomy scenes, its pictures of danger and conflict—of triumph and despair. Men too illiterate to account for the fascination, are attracted to its pages, and learned men who may have but little sympathy with its religious purpose, feel the spell of its genius, and are compelled to admire for the beauty or the awfulness of its creations, its vivid embodiments, its clear insight, keen satire, and terse Saxon style.

The young Christian, just starting on his course, reads it for guidance and encouragement in his own conflicts and perils ; and the aged saint lingering for a while on the river's brink, before the messenger summons him into the presence of the King, testifies to the accuracy with which it pictures the serene and mellowed joys of the land of Beulah.

It is wonderful that any man should have written a book of such universal and enduring popularity. More wonderful still that it should have been written in prison by an uneducated tinker,—written spontaneously, not as an effort, but as a relief from mental fulness—as the thoughts came crowding up in all their freshness, in an untrained, but singularly original and fertile mind.

Time would fail and space forbids us to expatiate further on the beauties of the book. The more we study it, the more do we feel how much it deserves its match-less popularity, and the more cordially do we commend it to the careful perusal of all readers.

LIFE OF

JOHN BUNYAN.

BIRTHPLACE OF BUNYAN AT ELSTOW, ENGLAND.

15

John Bunyan

16

THE LIFE OF JOHN BUNYAN.

JOHN BUNYAN has faithfully recorded his own spiritual history. Had he dreamed of being "forever known," and taking his place among those who may be called immortals of the earth, he would probably have introduced more details of his temporal circumstances, and the events of his life. But, glorious dreamer as he was, this never entered into his imaginations.

Less concerning him than might have been expected has been preserved by those of his own sect; and it is now not likely that anything more should be recovered from oblivion. The village of Elstow, England, which is within a mile of Bedford, was his birthplace, 1628 the year of his birth; and his descent, to use his own words, "of a low inconsiderable generation; my father's house," he says, "being of that rank that is meanest and most despised of all the families in the land."

It is stated in a history of Bedfordshire, that he was bred to the business of a brazier, and worked as a journeyman in Bedford: but the Braziers' Company would not deem itself more honored now if it could show the name of John Bunyan upon its rolls, than it would have felt disparaged then by any such fellowship; for he was, as his own statement implies, of a generation of tinkers, born and bred to that calling, as his father had been before him. Wherefore this should have been so mean and despised a calling is not however apparent, when it was not followed as a vagabond employment, but, as in this case, exercised by one who had a settled habitation, and who, mean as his condition was, was nevertheless able to put his son to school, in an age when very few of the poor were taught to read and write. The boy learned both, "according to the rate of other poor men's children," but soon lost what little he had been taught, "even," he says, "almost utterly."

Some pains, also, it may be presumed, his parents took in impressing him with a sense of his religious duties ; otherwise, when in his boyhood he became a proficient in cursing and swearing above his fellows, he would not have been visited by such dreams and such guilty feelings as he has described. "Often," he says, "after I had spent this and the other day in sin, I have in my bed been greatly afflicted, while asleep, with the apprehensions of devils and wicked spirits, who still, as I then thought, labored to draw me away with them."

His waking reflections were not less terrible than these fearful visions of the night ; and these, he says, "when I was only a child, but nine or ten years old, did so distress my soul, that then, in the midst of my many sports and childish vanities, amidst my vain companions, I was often much cast down, and afflicted in my mind therewith ; yet could I not let go my sins. Yea, I was also then so overcome with despair of life and heaven, that I should often wish, either there had been no hell, or that I had been a devil, supposing they were only tormentors ; that if it must needs be that I went thither, I might be rather a tormentor, than be tormented myself."

These feelings, when he approached toward manhood, recurred, as might be expected, less frequently, and with less force ; but though he represents himself as having been what he calls a town sinner, he was never so given over to a reprobate mind, as to be wholly free from them. For though he became so far hardened in profligacy that he could "take pleasure in the vileness of his companions," yet the sense of right and wrong was not extinguished in him, and it shocked him if at any time he saw those who pretended to be religious, act in a manner unworthy of their profession.

Some providential escapes, during this part of his life, he looked back upon afterwards, as so many judgments mixed with mercy. Once he fell into a creek of the sea, once out of a boat into the river Ouse, near Bedford, and each time was narrowly saved from drowning. One day an adder crossed his path ; he stunned it with a stick, then forced open its mouth with the stick, and plucked out the tongue, which he supposed to be the sting, with his fingers, "by which act," he says, "had not God been merciful unto me, I might by my desperateness have brought myself to my end." If this indeed were an adder, and not a harmless snake, his escape from the fangs was more remarkable than he was himself aware of. A circumstance which was likely to impress him more deeply, occurred in the eighteenth year of his age, when, being a soldier in the Parliament's army, he was drawn out to go to the siege of Leicester. One of the same company wished to go in his stead; Bunyan consented to exchange with him; and the volunteer substitute, standing sentinel one day at the siege, was shot through the head with a musket ball.

Some serious thoughts this would have awakened in a harder heart than Bunyan's; but his heart never was hardened. The self-accusations of such a man are to be received with some distrust,—not of his sincerity, but of his sober judgment. It should seem that he ran headlong into the boisterous vices which prove fatal to so many of the ignorant and brutal, for want of that necessary and wholesome and restrictive discipline which it is the duty of a government to provide; but he was not led into those habitual sins which infix a deeper stain.

"Had not a miracle of precious grace prevented, I had laid myself open," he says, "even to the stroke of those laws which bring some to disgrace and open shame before the face of the world." That grace he had. He was no drunkard; for, if he had been, he would loudly have proclaimed it: and, on another point, we have his own solemn declaration, in which he replies to those who slandered him as leading a licentious life with women. "I call on them," he says, "when they have used to the utmost of their endeavors, and made the fullest inquiry that they can, to prove this charge against me."

Bunyan married presently after his substitute had been killed at the siege of Leicester, probably, therefore, before he was nineteen. This he might have counted among his mercies, as he has counted it that he was led "to light upon a wife," whose father, as she often told him, was a godly man, who had been used to reprove vice, both in his own house and among his neighbors, and had lived a strict and holy life, both in word and deed. There was no imprudence in this early marriage, though they "came together as poor as poor might be, not having so much household stuff as a dish or spoon betwixt them both;" for Bunyan had a trade to which he could trust, and the young woman had been trained up in the way she should go.

She brought him for her portion two books, which her father had left her at his death. *The Plain Man's Pathway to Heaven* was one; the other was Bayly, Bishop of Bangor's *Practice of Piety*. These books he sometimes read with her; and they did not, he says, reach his heart to awaken it, yet they did beget within him some desires to reform his careless life, and made him fall in eagerly with the religion of the times, go to church twice a day with the foremost, and there very devoutly say and sing as others did ; yet, according to his own account, retaining his wicked life.

One day the minister preached against Sabbath-breaking, and Bunyan, who used especially to follow his sports on Sundays, fell in conscience under that sermon, verily believing it was intended for him, and feeling what guilt was, which he could not remember that he had ever felt before.

THE WIFE OF BUNYAN PERSUADES HIM TO READ HER BOOKS.

Home he went, with a great burden upon his spirit ; but dinner removed that burden ; his animal spirits recovered from their depression ; he shook the sermon out of his mind ; and away he went, with great delight, to his old sports.

The Puritans, notwithstanding the outcry which they had raised against what is called the Book of Sports, found it necessary to tolerate such recreations on the Sabbath ; but it is more remarkable to find a married man engaged in games which are now only practised by boys. Dinner had for a time prevailed over that morning's sermon, but it was only for a time ; the dinner sat easy upon him—the sermon did not ; and, in the midst of a game of tip-cat, as he was about to strike the cat from the hole, it seemed to him as if a voice from heaven suddenly darted into his soul, and said, Wilt thou leave thy sins, and go to heaven ? or have thy sins and go to hell ? "At this," he continues, "I was put to an exceeding maze ; wherefore, leaving my cat upon the ground, I looked up to heaven, and was as if I had, with the eyes of my understanding, seen the Lord Jesus looking down upon me, as being very hotly displeased with me, and as if he did severely threaten me with some grievous punishment for these and other ungodly practices.''

The voice he believed was from heaven ; and it may be inferred, from his relation, that though he was sensible the vision was only seen with the mind's eye, he deemed it not the less real. The effect was to fasten upon his spirit a sudden and dreadful conclusion, that it was too late for him to turn away from his wickedness, for Christ would not forgive him. He felt his heart sink in despair ; and this insane reasoning passed in his mind, '' My state is surely miserable,—miserable if I leave my sins, and but miserable if I follow them. I can but be damned ; and if I must be so, I had as good be damned for many sins, as be damned for few.'' Thus he says, '' I stood in the midst of my play, before all that were present, but yet I told them nothing ; but having made this conclusion, I returned desperately to my sport again. And I well remember that presently this kind of despair did so possess my soul, that I was persuaded I could never attain to other comfort than what I should get in sin ; for heaven was gone already, so that on that I must not think. Wherefore I found within me great desire to take my fill of sin, still studying what sin was yet to be committed, that I might taste the sweetness of it,—lest I should die before I had my desires. In these things, I protest before God, I lie not ; neither do I frame this sort of speech : these were really, strongly, and with all my heart, my desires. The good Lord, whose mercy is unsearchable, forgive me my transgressions !''

When thus faithfully describing the state of his feelings, at that time, Bunyan was not conscious that he exaggerated the character of his offences. Yet, in another part of his writings, he qualifies those offences more truly, where he speaks of himself as having been addicted to '' all manner of youthful vanities ;'' and this relation itself is accompanied with a remark, that it is a usual temptation to the devil, '' to overrun the spirits with a scurvy and seared frame of heart, and benumbing of conscience ;'' so that, though there be not much guilt attending the poor creatures who are thus tempted, '' yet they continually have a secret conclusion within them, that there is no hope for them.'' This state lasted with him little more than a month ; it then happened, that, as he stood at a neighbor's shop-window, '' cursing and swearing, and playing the madman,'' after his wonted manner, the woman of the house heard him ; and though she was, he says, a very loose and ungodly wretch, she told him that he made her tremble to hear him ; '' that he was the ungodliest fellow for swearing that ever she heard in all her life ; and that, by thus doing, he was able to spoil all the youth in the whole town, if they came but in his company.''

The reproof came with more effect than if it had come from a better person. It silenced him, and put him to secret shame ; and that, too, as he thought, "before the God of heaven ; wherefore," he says, "while I stood there, and hanging down my head, I wished with all my heart that I might be a little child again, that my father might learn me to speak without this wicked way of swearing ; for, thought I, I am so accustomed to it, that it is in vain for me to think of a reformation."

From that hour, however, the reformation of this, the chief sin to which he was addicted, began. Even to his own wonder it took place, and he who till then had not known how to speak unless he put an oath before and another behind to make his words have authority, discovered that he could speak better and more pleasantly without such expletives than he had ever done before.

Soon afterwards he fell in company with a poor man who talked to him concerning religion and the scriptures, in a manner which took his attention, and sent him to his Bible. He began to take pleasure in reading it, especially the historical parts ; the Epistles he says he "could not away with, being as yet ignorant both of the corruption of our nature and of the want and worth of Christ to save us." And this produced such a change in his whole deportment, that his neighbors took him to be a new man, and were amazed at his conversation from prodigious profaneness

BUNYAN READS HIS BIBLE.

to a moral and religious life. They began to speak well of him, both to his face and behind his back, and he was well pleased at having obtained, and, as he thought, deserved, their good opinion. And yet, he says, "I was nothing but a poor painted hypocrite,—I did all I did either to be seen of, or to be well spoken of, by men. I knew not Christ, nor Grace, nor Faith, nor Hope ; and as I have well seen since, had I then died, my state had been most fearful."

One day when he was tinkering in the streets of Bedford, he overheard three poor women, who, as they sat at a door in the sunshine, were conversing about their own spiritual state.   He was himself "a brisk talker in the matter of religion;" but these persons were, in their discourse, "far above his reach."   Their talk was about a new birth,—how they were convinced of their miserable state by nature,—how God had visited their souls with his love in the Lord Jesus,—with what words and promises they had been refreshed and supported against the temptations of

BUNYAN LISTENS TO THE WOMEN.

the Devil,—how they had been afflicted under the assaults of the enemy, and how they had been borne up; and of their own wretchedness of heart, and of their unbelief, and the insufficiency of their own righteousness. "Methought," says Bunyan, "they spake, as if you did make them speak. They spake with such pleasantness of Scripture language, and with such appearance of grace in all they said, that they were to me as if they had found a new world, as if they were 'people that dwelt alone, and were not to be reckoned among their neighbors.'"

He felt his own heart shake as he heard them ; and when he turned away, and went about his employment again, their talk went with him, for he had heard enough to convince him that he "wanted the true tokens of a true godly man," and to convince him also of the blessed condition of him that was indeed one.

He made it his business, therefore, frequently to seek the conversation of these women. They were members of a small Baptist congregation which a Kentish man, John Gifford by name, had formed at Bedford. The first effect of his conversation with them was that he began to look into the Bible with new eyes, and "indeed was never out of it," either by reading or meditation.

He now took delight in St. Paul's Epistles, which before he "could not away with ;" and the first strong impression which they made upon him was that he wanted the gifts of wisdom and knowledge of which the Apostle speaks, and was doubtful whether he had faith or not ; yet this was a doubt which he could not bear, being certain that if he were without faith, he must perish. Being " put to his plunge" about this, and not as yet consulting with any one, he conceived that the only means by which he could be certified was by trying to work a miracle, a delusion which he says the tempter enforced and strengthened by urging upon him those texts of Scripture that seemed to look that way.

One day, as he was between Elstow and Bedford, the temptation was hot upon him that he should put this to the proof by saying "to the puddles that were in the road, *be dry ;* and to the dry places, *be ye puddles !* And truly one time I was going to say so, indeed, but, just as I was about to speak, this thought came in my mind, 'But go under yonder hedge and pray first that God would make you able.' But when I had concluded to pray, this came hot upon me, that if I prayed and came again, and tried to do it, and yet did nothing notwithstanding, then to be sure I had no faith, but was a castaway, and lost. Nay, thought I, if it be so, I will not try yet, but will stay a little longer."

About this time the happiness of his poor acquaintance whom he believed to be in a sanctified state was presented to him, he says, in a kind of vision,—that is, it became the subject of a reverie, a waking dream,—in which the germ of the " Pilgrim's Progress " may plainly be perceived.

"I saw," he says, "as if they were on the sunny side of some high mountain, there refreshing themselves with the pleasant beams of the sun, while I was shivering and shrinking in the cold, afflicted with frost, snow, and dark clouds. Methought also, betwixt me and them I saw a wall that did compass about this mountain. Now through this wall my soul did greatly desire to pass ; concluding that if I could, I would even go into the very midst of them, and there also comfort myself with the heat of their sun. About this wall I thought myself to go again and again, still praying as I went, to see if I could find some way or passage, by which I might enter therein ; but none could I find for some time. At last I saw, as it were, a narrow gap, like a little doorway, in the wall, through which I attempted to pass. Now the passage being very straight and narrow, I made many efforts to get in, but all in vain, even until I was well nigh quite beat out by striving to get in.

"At last, with great striving, methought I at first did get in my head ; and after that, by a sideling striving, my shoulders, and my whole body : then was I exceeding glad, went and sat down in the midst of them, and so was comforted with the light and heat of their sun. Now the Mountain and Wall, &c., was thus made out to me. The Mountain signified the Church of the Living God ; the Sun that shone thereon, the comfortable shining of his merciful Face on them that were within ; the Wall, I thought, was the Word, that did make separation between the Christians and the World : and the Gap which was in the Wall, I thought, was Jesus Christ, who is the Way to God the Father. But forasmuch as the passage was wonderful narrow, even so narrow that I could not but with great difficulty enter in thereat, it showed me that none could enter into life but those that were in downright earnest ; and unless, also, they left that wicked World behind them ; for here was only room for Body and Soul, but not for Body and Soul and Sin."

When Bunyan finally passed from his unsettled condition of mind into a state of happy feeling, his reason was nearly overthrown by the transition. "I had two or three times," he says, "at or about my deliverance from temptation, such strange apprehensions of the Grace of God that I could hardly bear up under it. It was so out of measure amazing when I thought it could reach me, that I do think if that sense of it had abode long upon me, it would have made me uncapable of business."

He had not, however, yet attained to that self-control which belongs to a sane mind : for after he had formally been admitted into fellowship with Gifford's little congregation, and had been by him baptized accordingly, by immersion, probably in the river Ouse (for the Baptists at that time sought rather than shunned publicity on such occasions), he was for nearly a year pestered with strange and villanous thoughts whenever he communicated at the meeting.

These, however, left him. When threatened with consumption at one time, he was delivered from the fear of dissolution, by faith, and the strong desire of entering upon eternal life ; and in another illness, when the thought of approaching death for a while overcame him, "behold," he says, "as I was in the midst of those fears, the words of the Angels carrying Lazarus into Abraham's bosom, darted in upon me, as who should say, 'so shall it be with thee when thou dost leave this world !' This did

sweetly revive my spirits, and help me to hope in God ; which, when I had with comfort mused on a while, that Word fell with great weight upon my mind, 'Oh, Death,
where is thy sting?   Oh, Grave, where is thy victory?'   At this I became both well
in body and mind at once ; for my sickness did presently vanish, and I walked comfortably in my work for God again.''

When, the year after Gifford's death, a resolution was passed by the meeting that
"some of the brethren (one at a time) to whom the Lord may have given a gift, be
called forth and encouraged to speak a word in the church for mutual edification,''
Bunyan was one of the persons so called upon.

"Some,'' he says, "of the most able of the Saints with us,—I say, the most able
for judgment and holiness of life,—as they conceived, did perceive that God had
counted me worthy to understand something of His will in His holy and blessed
Word ; and had given me utterance in some measure to express, what I saw, to others
for edification.   Therefore they desired me, and that with much earnestness, that I
would be willing at some times to take in hand in one of the meetings to speak a
word of exhortation unto them.   The which, though at first it did much dash and
abash my spirit, yet being still by them desired and entreated, I consented to their
request ; and did twice, at two several assemblies (but in private), though with much
weakness and infirmity, discover my gift amongst them ; at which they not only
seemed to be, but did solemnly protest, as in the sight of the great God, they were
both affected and comforted, and gave thanks to the Father of Mercies for the grace
bestowed on me.''

In those days the supply of public news came so slowly, and was so scanty when
it came, that even the proceedings of so humble an individual as Bunyan became matter of considerable attention in the town of Bedford.   His example drew many to the
Baptist Meeting, from curiosity to discover what had affected him there, and produced
such a change in his conversation.

" When I went out to seek the Bread of Life, some of them,'' he says, "would follow, and the rest be put into a muse at home.   Yea, almost all the town, at first, at
times would go out to hear at the place where I found good.   Yea, young and old for
a while had some reformation on them : also, some of them perceiving that God had
mercy upon me, came crying to Him for mercy too.''

Bunyan was not one of those enthusiasts who thrust themselves forward, in confident reliance upon what they suppose to be an inward call.   He entered upon his
probation with diffidence and fear, not daring " to make use of his gift in a public
way ;'' and gradually acquired a trust in himself, and a consciousness of his own
qualifications, when some of those who went into the country to disseminate their
principles and make converts, took him in their company.

Exercising himself thus as occasion offered, he was encouraged by the approba-
tion with which others heard him : and in no long time, "after some solemn prayer,
with fasting," he was "more particularly called forth, and appointed to a more
ordinary and public preaching, not only to and amongst them that believed, but also
to offer the Gospel to those who had not yet received the faith thereof."

The Bedford meeting had at this time its regular minister, whose name was John
Burton ; so that what Bunyan received was a roving commission to itinerate in the
villages round about, and in this he was so much employed, that when in the ensuing
year he was nominated for a deacon of the congregation, they declined electing him
to that office, on the ground that he was too much engaged to attend to it.   Having
in previous training overcome his first diffidence, he now "felt in his mind a secret
pricking forward" to this ministry ; not "for desire of vain glory," for he was even
at that time "sorely afflicted" concerning his own eternal state, but because the
Scriptures encouraged him, by texts which ran continually in his mind, whereby "I
was made," he says, "to see that the Holy Ghost never intended that men who have
gifts and abilities should bury them in the earth, but rather did command and stir
up such to the exercise of their gift, and also did command those that were apt and
ready, so to do."

Those gifts he had, and could not but be conscious of them.   He had also the
reputation of possessing them, so that people came by hundreds to hear him from all
parts round about, though "upon divers accounts"—some to marvel, and some perhaps to mock ; but some also to listen, and to be "touched with a conviction that
they needed a Saviour."   "But I first," he says, "could not believe that God should
speak by me to the heart of any man, still counting myself unworthy ; yet those
who were thus touched would love me and have a particular respect for me : and
though I did put it from me that they should be awakened by me, still they would
confess it, and affirm it before the saints of God.   They would also bless God for me
(unworthy wretch that I am !), and count me God's instrument that showed to them
the way of salvation.   Wherefore seeing them in both their words and deeds to be so
constant, but also in their hearts so earnestly pressing after the knowledge of Jesus
Christ, rejoicing that ever God did send me where they were ; then I began to conclude it might be so that God had owned in His work such a foolish one as I, and
then came that word of God to my heart with much sweet refreshment, 'the blessing
of them that were ready to perish is come upon me ; yea, I caused the widow's heart
to sing for joy.'" (Job xxix. 13.)

When he first began to preach, Bunyan endeavored to work upon his hearers by
alarming them.   He dealt chiefly in comminations, and dwelt upon the dreadful doc-

trine that the curse of God "lays hold on all men as they come into the world, because of sin."

"This part of my work," says he, "I fulfilled with great sense : for the terrors of the law, and guilt for my transgressions, lay heavy upon my conscience. I preached what I felt,—what I smartingly did feel, even that under which my poor soul did groan and tremble to astonishment. Indeed, I have been as one sent to them from the dead. I went myself in chains, to preach to them in chains ; and carried that fire in my own conscience, that I persuaded them to be aware of. I can truly say, that when I have been to preach, I have gone full of guilt and terror even to the pulpit-door ; and there it hath been taken off, and I have been at liberty in my mind until I have done my work ; and then immediately, even before I could get down the pulpit-stairs, I have been as bad as I was before. Yet God carried me on ; but surely with a strong hand, for neither guilt nor hell could take me off my work." This is a case like that of the fiery old soldier John Haime, who was one of Wesley's first lay preachers.

When he was in a happier state of mind, he took a different and better course, "still preaching what he saw and felt." He then labored "to hold forth our Lord and Saviour" in all his offices, relations, and benefits, unto the world ; and "to remove those false supports and props on which the world doth lean, and by them fall and perish.'

While he was thus usefully employed, "the Doctors and Priests of the country," he says, "began to open wide against him," and in the year 1657 an indictment was preferred against him at the assizes for preaching at Eaton ; for though this was in the golden days of Oliver Cromwell, the same writer who tells us that "in those days there was no persecution," observes that "the Presbyterian ministers who were then in possession of the livings, could not bear with the preaching of an illiterate tinker and an unordained minister."

But the Presbyterians were not the only clergy who had intruded into the benefices of their loyal brethren, or retained those which were lawfully their own by conforming to the times and deserting the Church in whose service they were ordained.

There was a full proportion of Independents among these incumbents, and some Baptists also. And that there was much more persecution during the Protectorate than Cromwell would have allowed, if he could have prevented it, may be seen by the history of the Quakers,—to say nothing of the Papists, against whom the penal laws remained in full force,—nor of the Church of England.

The simple truth is, all parties were agreed in the one Catholic opinion that certain doctrines are not to be tolerated. They differed as to what those doctrines were ; and they differed also as to the degree in which they held the principle of intolerance, and the extent to which they practiced it. The Papists, true to their creed, proclaimed it without reserve or limit, and burnt all heretics wherever they had power to do so. The Protestants, therefore, tolerated no Papists where they were strong enough to maintain the ascendancy which they had won. The Church of England would have silenced all sectaries. It failed in the attempt, being betrayed by many of its own members ; and then the Sectaries overthrew the Church, put the Primate to death, ejected all the Clergy who adhered to their principles, imprisoned some, deported others, and prohibited even the private and domestic use of the Liturgy.

The very Baptists of Bunyan's congregation, and at a time too when Bunyan was their pastor, interdicted a " dearly beloved sister " from communicating with a church of which her son-in-law was minister, because he was not a Baptist ; and they excluded a brother "because in a great assembly of the church of England he was profanely *bishopt*, after the antichristian order of that generation, to the great profanation of God's order, and heart-breaking of his Christian brethren.''

The Independents flogged and hanged the Quakers : and the Quakers prophesied in the gall of bitterness against all other communities, and condemned them to the bottomless pit, in hearty belief and jubilant expectation that the sentence would be carried into full effect by the Devil and his Angels.

Those troubles came on a few months only after the Restoration, Bunyan being one of the first persons after that event who was punished for nonconformity.

The nation was in a most unquiet state. There was a restless, rancorous, implacable party, who would have renewed the civil war, for the sake of again trying the experiment of a Commonwealth, which had so completely and miserably failed when the power was in their hands. They looked to Ludlow as their General ; and Algernon Sydney took the first opportunity of soliciting for them men from Holland and money from France. The political enthusiasts who were engaged in such schemes counted upon the sectaries for support.

Even among the sober sects there were men who, at the cost of a rebellion, would gladly have again thrown down the Church Establishment, for the hope of setting up their own system during the anarchy that must ensue. Among the wilder, some were eager to proclaim King Jesus, and take possession of the earth, as being the Saints to whom it was promised : and some (a few years later), less in hope of effecting their republican projects than in despair and vengeance, conspired to burn London. They were discovered, tried, convicted, and executed. They confessed their intention ; they named the day which had been appointed for carrying it into effect, because an astrological scheme had shown it to be a lucky one for this design ; and on that very day the fire of London broke out.

In such times the Government was rendered suspicious by the constant sense of danger, and was led as much by fear as by resentment to severities which are explained by the necessity of self-defence,—not justified by it, when they fall upon the innocent, or even upon the less guilty.

A warrant was issued against Bunyan, as if he had been a dangerous person, because he went about preaching. This office was deemed (and well it might be) incompatible with his calling. He was known to be hostile to the restored Church; and probably it might be remembered that he had served in the Parliament's army.

Accordingly, he was arrested at a place called Samsell, in Bedfordshire, at a meeting in a private house. He was aware of this intention, but neither chose to put off the meeting, nor to escape, lest such conduct on his part should make "an ill savor in the country," and because he was resolved "to see the utmost of what they could say or do to him." So he was taken before the Justice, Wingate by name, who had issued the warrant.

Wingate asked him why he did not content himself with following his calling, instead of breaking the law; and Bunyan replied that he could both follow his calling and preach the Word too. He was then required to find sureties. They were ready; and, being called in, were told they were bound to keep him from preaching, otherwise their bonds would be forfeited.

Upon this Bunyan declared that he would not desist from speaking the word of God. While his mittimus was making, in consequence of this determination, one whom he calls an old enemy of the truth, entered into discourse with him, and said he had read of one Alexander the coppersmith who troubled the apostles,—"aiming 'tis like at me," says Bunyan, "because I was a tinker; to which I answered that I also had read of Priests and Pharisees that had their hands in the blood of our Lord." Aye, was the rejoinder, and you are one of those Pharisees, for you make long prayers to devour widows' houses.

"I answered," says Bunyan, "that if he had got no more by preaching and praying than I had done, he would not be so rich as now he was." This ended in his committal to Bedford jail, there to remain till the quarter sessions. He was offered his liberty if he would promise not to call the people together, but no such promise would he make; and when he was told that none but poor, simple, ignorant people came to hear him, he replied that such had most need of teaching, and therefore it was his duty to go on in that work.

It appears, however, that after a few days he listened to his friends, and would have given bond for his appearance at the sessions; but the magistrate to whom they applied was afraid to take it. "Whereat," says Bunyan, "I was not at all daunted, but rather glad, and saw evidently that the Lord had heard me. For before I went down to the justice, I begged of God that if I might do more good by being at liberty than in prison, that then I might be set at liberty, but if not—His will be done; for I was not altogether without hope but that my imprisonment might be an awakening to the saints in the country. Therefore, I could not tell which to choose; only I in that manner did commit the thing to God. And verily, at my return I did meet my God sweetly in the prison again, comforting of me, and satisfying of me that it was His will and mind that I should be there."

Some seven weeks after this the sessions were held, and John Bunyan was indicted as a person who "devilishly and perniciously abstained from coming to Church to

BEDFORD JAIL.

hear divine service, and who was a common upholder of several unlawful meetings and conventicles, to the great disturbance and distraction of the good subjects of this kingdom."

He answered that as to the first part of this, he was a common frequenter of the Church of God: but being demanded whether he attended the parish Church, he replied that he did not, and for this reason, that he was not commanded so to do in the word of God. "We were commanded there to pray, but with the spirit, not by the Common Prayer-Book, the prayers in that book being made by other men, and not by the motion of the Holy Spirit within our own hearts." And as to the Lord's Prayer, said he, "there are very few that can, in the spirit, say the two first words of that prayer; that is, that can call God their father, as knowing what it is to be born again,

and as having experience that they are begotten of the Spirit of God ; which if they
do not, all is but babbling."

Having persuaded himself by these arguments, Bunyan used them as if they had
been strong ones. "Show me," he said, "the place in the Epistles where the Common Prayer-Book is written, or one text of Scripture that commands me to read it,
and I will use it. But yet, notwithstanding, they that have a mind to use it, they
have their liberty ; that is, I would not keep them from it. But for our parts, we can
pray to God without it. Blessed be his name !" But the Sectaries had kept their
countrymen from it, while they had the power ; and Bunyan himself in his sphere
labored to dissuade them from it.

Men who are called in question for their opinions, may be expected to under or
over estimate them at such times, according as caution or temerity may predominate
in their dispositions. In none of Bunyan's writings does he appear so little reasonable, or so little tolerant, as upon these examinations. He was a brave man—a bold
one,—and believed himself to be an injured one,—standing up against persecution ;
for he knew that by his preaching, evident and certain good was done ; but that there
was any evil in his way of doing it, or likely to arise from it, was a thought which,
if it had arisen in his own mind, he would immediately have ascribed to the sugges-
tion of Satan.

Some further disputation ensued. "We were told," he said, "to exhort one
another daily, while it is called to-day :" but the Justice replied he ought not to
preach. In rejoinder, he offered to prove that it was lawful for him and such as him
to preach, and quoted the Apostle's words, "as every man hath received that gift,
even so let him minister the same unto another."

"Let me a little open that Scripture to you," said the magistrate : "*As every man
hath received his gift;* that is, as every man hath received a trade, so let him follow
it. If any man have received a gift of tinkering, as thou hast done, let him follow
his tinkering. And so other men their trades, and the divine his calling."

But John insisted that spiritual gifts were intended in this passage. The magistrate said men might exhort if they pleased in their families, but not otherwise. John
answered, "if it were lawful to do good to some, it was lawful to do good to more.
If it were a good thing to exhort our families, it was good to exhort others. And if
it were held a sin for them to meet together and seek the face of God, and exhort one
another to follow Christ, he would sin still." They were now at a point. "You confess the indictment, then ?" said the magistrate. He made answer : "This I confess :
We have had many meetings together, both to pray to God, and to exhort one another ; and we had the sweet comforting presence of the Lord among us for our

encouragement. Blessed be His name! There I confess myself guilty, and no otherwise.''

Then said the magistrate : '' Hear your judgment. You must be had back again to prison, and there lie for three months following ; and at three months' end, if you do not submit to go to Church to hear divine service, and leave your preaching, you must be banished the realm. And if after such a day as shall be appointed you to be gone, you shall be found in this realm, or be found to come over again without special license from the king, you must stretch by the neck for it. I tell you plainly.''

Bunyan resolutely answered that '' if he were out of prison to-day, he would preach the Gospel again to-morrow, by the help of God !''

Back, therefore, he was taken ; ''and I can truly say,'' he says, '' I bless the Lord for it ; that my heart was sweetly refreshed in the time of my examination, and also afterwards at my returning to the prison, so that I found Christ's words more than bare trifles, where He saith, ' He will give you a mouth and wisdom which all your adversaries shall not be able to gainsay nor resist.' '' (Luke xxi. 15.) Three months elapsed, and the Clerk of the Peace then went to him, by desire of the magistrate, to see if he could be persuaded to obedience. But Bunyan insisted that the law being intended against those who designed to do evil in their meetings, did not apply to him.

He was told that he might exhort his neighbors in private discourse, if he did not call together an assembly of people. This he might do, and do much good thereby, without breaking the law. '' But,'' said Bunyan, '' if I may do good to one, why not to two?—and if to two, why not to four?—and so to eight, and so on?'' '' Aye,'' said the Clerk, ''and to a hundred, I warrant you !'' '' Yes,'' Bunyan answered, '' I think I should not be forbidden to do as much good as I can.''

They then began to discuss the question whether under pretence of doing good, harm might not be done, by seducing the people ; and Bunyan allowed that there might be many who designed the destruction of the Government. Let them, he said, be punished ; and let him be punished, also, should he do any thing not becoming a man and a Christian. If error or heresy could be proved upon him, he would disown it, even in the market-place ; but to the truth he would stand to the last drop of his blood. Bound in conscience he held himself to obey all righteous laws, whether there were a king or not ; and if he offended against them, patiently to bear the penalty. And to cut off all occasion of suspicion as touching the harmlessness of his doctrines, he would willingly give any one the notes of all his sermons, for he sincerely desired to live in peace, and to submit to the present authority.

'' But there are two ways of obeying,'' he observed ; ''the one to do that which I

3

in my conscience do believe that I am bound to do, actively ; and where I can not obey actively, there I am willing to lie down, and to suffer what they shall do unto me." And here the interview ended, Bunyan thanking him for his " civil and meek discoursing," and breathing a wish that they might meet in Heaven.

Shortly afterwards the Coronation took place, and the proclamation which allowed persons to sue out a pardon during twelve months from that day, had the effect of suspending the proceedings against him, if any further were intended.

When the assizes came, his wife presented a petition to the Judges that they would impartially take his case into consideration. Sir Matthew Hale was one of these Judges, and expressed a wish to serve her if he could, but a fear that he could do her no good ; and being assured by one of the Justices that Bunyan had been con- victed, and was a hot-spirited fellow, he waived the matter. But the High Sheriff encouraged the poor woman to make another effort for her husband before they left

BUNYAN'S WIFE BEFORE JUDGE HALE.

the town ; and accordingly, " with a bashed face and a trembling heart," she entered the Swan Chamber, where the two Judges and many magistrates and gentry of the country were in com- pany together.

Trembling, however, as she was, Elizabeth Bunyan had imbibed some- thing of her husband's spirit. She had been to London to petition the House of Lords in his behalf, and had been told by one whom she calls Lord

Barkwood, that they could do nothing, but that his releasement was committed to the Judges at these next assizes ; and now I am come to you, she said, and you give neither releasement nor relief. And she complained to Hale that her husband was kept unlawfully in prison, for the indictment was false, and he was clapped up be- fore there were any proclamations against the meetings.

One of the Judges then said he had been lawfully convicted. "It is false," re- plied the woman ; "for when they said to him, 'Do you confess the indictment?' he said only this, that he had been at several meetings, both when there was preach- ing the Word and prayer, and that they had God's presence among them." "Will your husband leave preaching?" said Judge Twisden. "If he will do so, send for him." "My Lord," said she, "he dares not leave preaching, as long as he can speak."

Sir Matthew himself was not likely to be favorably impressed by this sort of pleading. But he listened sadly when she told him that there were four small children by the former wife, one of them blind ; and that they had nothing to live upon while their father was in prison, but the charity of good people ; "Alas, poor woman !" said Hale. But Twisden said poverty was her cloak, for he understood her husband was better maintained by running up and down a-preaching. than by following his calling. Sir Matthew asked what was his calling, and was told he was a tinker. "Yes," observed the wife, "and because he is a tinker and a poor man, therefore he is despised and cannot have justice."

The scene ended in Sir Matthew mildly telling her he was sorry he could do her no good ; that what her husband had said was taken for a conviction ; and that there was no other course for her than either to apply to the king, or sue out his pardon, or get a writ of error, which would be the cheapest. She urged them to send for Bunyan, that he might speak for himself. His presence, however, would rather have confirmed those in their opinions who said there was not such another pestilent fellow in the country, than have moved the Judges in his favor.

Elizabeth Bunyan concludes her account by saying : "This I remember, that though I was somewhat timorous at my first entrance into the chamber, yet before I went out I could not but break forth into tears ; not so much because they were so hard-hearted against me and my husband, but to think what a sad account such poor creatures will have to give at the coming of the Lord !"

No further steps for procuring his release were taken at this time, either because the means for defraying the legal expenses could not be raised, or, which is quite as probable, because it was certain that Bunyan, thinking himself in conscience bound to preach in defiance of the law, would soon have made his case worse than it then was. For he had fortunately a friend in the jailer, and was somewhat like a prisoner at large, being allowed to go whither he would, and return when he thought proper.

He attended the meetings of the congregation to which he belonged ; he was employed by them to visit disorderly members ; he was often out in the night ; and it is said that many of the Baptist congregations in Bedfordshire owe their origin to his midnight preaching. "I followed my wonted course," he says, "taking all occasions to visit the people of God, exhorting them to be steadfast in the faith of Jesus Christ, and to take heed that they touch not the Common Prayer. So far did this liberty extend that he went "to see the Christians at London,"—an indiscretion which cost the jailer a severe reproof, and had nearly cost him his place ; and which compelled him to withhold any further indulgence of this kind ; "so," says Bunyan, "that I must not now look out of the door." "They charged me," he adds, "that I went thither to plot and raise divisions and make insurrections, which, God knows, was a slander."

It was slanderous to charge him with plotting, or with traitorous intentions ; but in raising divisions he was, beyond all doubt, actively and heartily engaged. The man who distinguished a handful of Baptists in London as *the Christians* of that great metropolis, and who, when let out by favor from his prison, exhorted the people of God, as he calls them, to take heed that they touch not the Common Prayer-Book, was not employed in promoting unity, nor in making good subjects, however good his intentions, however orthodox his creed, however sincere and fervent his piety. Peace might be on his lips, and zeal for the salvation of others in his heart ; but he was certainly at that time no preacher of good will, nor of Christian charity.

And without reference to human laws, it may be affirmed that the circumstances which removed this high-minded and hot-minded man from a course of dangerous activity, in which he was as little likely to acquire a tolerant spirit as to impart it, and placed him in confinement, where his understanding had leisure to ripen and to cool, was no less favorable for his moral and religious nature than it has ultimately proved to his usefulness and his fame.

It would be wronging him here were the touching expression of his feelings, when compelled to leave his wife and little ones, to be withheld.

"I found myself," he says, "a man encompassed with infirmities. The parting with my wife and poor children, hath often been to me, in this place, as the pulling the flesh from the bones ; and that not only because I am somewhat too fond of these great mercies, but also because I should have often brought to my mind the many hardships, miseries, and wants, that my poor family was like to meet with, should I be taken from them ; especially my poor blind child, who lay nearer my heart than all besides.

" Oh, the thoughts of the hardships I thought my poor blind one might go under would break my heart to pieces ! Poor child ! thought I, what sorrow art thou like to have for thy portion in this world ! Thou must be beaten ; must beg ; suffer hunger, cold, nakedness, and a thousand calamities, though I can not now endure the wind should blow upon thee ! But, yet, recalling myself, thought I, I must venture you all with God, though it goeth to the quick to leave you ! Oh, I saw in this condition I was as a man who was pulling down his house upon the heads of his wife and children : yet, thought I, I must do it, I must do it ! And now I thought on those two milch-kine that were to carry the Ark of God into another country, and to leave their calves behind them." (1 Sam. vi. 10.)

These fears passed away when he found that no further proceedings were intended against him. But his worldly occupation was gone, for there was an end of tinkering as well as of his ministerial itinerancy.

" He was as effectually called away from his pots and kettles," says Mr. Ivimy, in his "History of the Baptists," "as the Apostles were from mending their nets." He learned, therefore, to make tagged thread-laces, and by this means supported his family. They lost the comfort of his presence; but in other respects their condition was not worsened by his imprisonment, which indeed was likely to render them objects of kindness as well as of compassion to their neighbors.

BUNYAN PARTING FROM HIS WIFE AND CHILDREN.

In an age when the state of English prisons was disgraceful to a Christian people, and the treatment of prisoners not unfrequently most inhuman, Bunyan was fortunate in the place of his confinement and in the disposition of his jailer, who is said to have committed the management of the prison to his care, knowing how entirely he might be trusted. He had the society there of some who were suffering for the same cause: he had his Bible and his Book of Martyrs; and he had leisure to brood over his own thoughts. The fever of his enthusiasm had spent itself; the asperity of his opinions was softened as his mind enlarged ; and the " Pilgrim's Progress " was one of the fruits of his imprisonment, But before that work is spoken of more particularly, it will be convenient to pursue the story of his life to its close.

He remained a prisoner twelve years.   But it appears that during the last four of those years he regularly attended the Baptist Meeting, his name being always in the records ; and in the eleventh year the congregation chose him for their pastor ; " he at the same time accepted the invitation, and gave himself up to serve Christ and His Church in that charge, and received of the Elders the right hand of fellowship."

The more recent historian of the Baptists says, " how he could exercise his pastoral office in preaching among them, while he continued a prisoner in the jail, we are at a loss to conceive."   Unquestionably only by being a prisoner at large, and having the liberty of the town while he was lodged in the prison.   There is a print in which he is represented as pursued by a rabble to his own door ; but there is no allusion to any such outrage in any part of his works.

In his own neighborhood, where he had always lived, it is most unlikely to have happened.   His character had by this time obtained respect, his books had attracted notice, and Dr. Barlow, then Bishop of Lincoln, and other Churchmen, are said to have pitied "his hard and unreasonable sufferings, so far as to stand very much his friends in procuring his enlargement."   How this was effected is not known.

From the time of his release from prison his life appears to have passed smoothly. His congregation and his other friends bought ground and built a Meeting-House

for him, and there he continued to preach before large audiences. Every year he used to visit London, where his reputation was so great that if a day's notice were given, the Meeting-House in Southwark, at which he generally preached, would not hold half the people that attended. Three thousand persons have been gathered together there ; and not less than twelve hundred on week

BUNYAN'S RESIDENCE AFTER HIS RELEASE FROM PRISON.

days, and dark winter mornings at seven o'clock.   He used also to preach in the surrounding counties.   The Baptist congregation at Hitchen is supposed to have been founded by him.

Their meetings were held at first about three miles from that town, in a wood near the village of Preston, Bunyan standing in a pit, or hollow, and the people round about on the sloping sides. "A chimney-corner at a house in the same wood is still looked upon with veneration, as having been the place of his refreshment." About five miles from Hitchen was a famous Puritan preaching-place called Bendish. It had been a malt-house, was very low, and thatched, and ran in two directions, a large square pulpit standing in the angles; and adjoining the pulpit was a high pew, in which ministers sat out of sight of informers, and from which, in case of alarm, they could escape into an adjacent lane.

The building being much decayed, this meeting was removed in 1787 to a place called Coleman Green; and the pulpit, which was there held to be the only remaining one in which Bunyan had preached, was with a commendable feeling carefully removed thither. But another "true pulpit" is shown in London in the Jewin Street Meeting.

It is said that Owen greatly admired his preaching; and that being asked by King Charles the Second "how a learned man, such as he was, could sit and listen to an illiterate tinker," he replied, "May it please your majesty, could I possess that tinker's abilities for preaching, I would most gladly relinquish all my learning."

Little has been recorded of Bunyan during the sixteen years between his enlargement and his death. It appears that besides his yearly visit to London, he made stated circuits into other parts of England; that he exerted himself to relieve the temporal wants of those who were suffering as nonconformist under oppressive laws; that he administered diligently to the sick and afflicted, and successfully employed his influence in reconciling differences among "professors of the gospel," and thus prevented "many disgraceful and burdensome litigations."

One of his biographers thinks it highly probable that he did not escape trouble in the latter part of Charles the Second's reign, "as the justices of Bedford were so zealous in the cause of persecution;" but it is much more probable that in a place where so much indulgence had been shown him during the latter years of his imprisonment, he was let alone; and there can be little doubt but that if he had undergone any further vexation for the same causes, a full account of it would have been preserved.

At Bedford, where he was liked as well as known, he was evidently favored; in other places he would be exposed to the same risk as other nonconforming preachers; and there is a tradition among the Baptists at Reading that he sometimes went through that town dressed like a carter, and with a long whip in his hand to avoid detection. Reading was a place where he was well known. The house in which the Baptists met for worship was in a lane there; and from the back door they had a bridge over a branch of the river Kennett, whereby in case of alarm they might escape.

In a visit to that place he contracted the disease which brought him to the grave. A friend of his who resided there had resolved to disinherit his son ; the young man requested Bunyan to interfere in his behalf ; he did so with good success, and it was his last labor of love ; for, returning to London on horseback through heavy rain, a fever ensued, which, after ten days, proved fatal.

He died at the house of his friend Mr. Stradwick, a grocer, at the sign of the Star, on Snow Hill ; and was buried in that friend's vault in Bunhill Fields burial-ground, which the Community regard as their sacred ground,—and especially for his sake. It is said that many have made it their desire to be interred as near as possible to the spot where his remains are deposited. His age and the date of his decease are thus recorded in his epitaph :—

MR. JOHN BUNYAN,

Author of the Pilgrim's Progress,

ob. 12 Aug. 1688, æt. 60.

The Pilgrim's Progress now is finished,
And Death has laid him in his earthly bed.

BUNYAN'S TOMB.

His earliest biographer says, that "though by reason of the many losses he sustained by imprisonment and spoil, his chargeable sickness, &c., his earthly treasure swelled not to excess, yet he always had sufficient to live decently and creditably." But all that Bunyan had to lose by "spoil" was his occupation as a tinker, which, fortunately for him and the world, was put an end to earlier than in the course of his Preacher's progress he could otherwise have cast it off.

That progress raised him to a station of respectability and comfort ; and he was too wise and too religious a man to desire riches either for himself or his children. When a wealthy London citizen offered to take one of his sons as an apprentice without a premium, he declined the friendly and advantageous offer, saying, " God did not send me to advance my family, but to preach the Gospel." No doubt he saw something in the business itself, or in the way of life to which it led, unfavorable to the moral character.

Three children survived him ; there were none by the second marriage. The blind daughter, the only one whom it might have troubled him to leave with a scanty provision, happily died before him. He is said to have kept up " a very strict discipline in his family, in prayer, and exhortations." Such strictness of discipline did not in this case produce any ill effect ; for, according to what little is known of his children, they went on in the way they had been trained. His eldest son was forty-five years a member of the Bedford Meeting : he preached there occasionally, and was employed in visiting the disorderly members ; he was therefore in good repute for discretion, as well as for his religious character.

The names of other descendants are in the books of the same meeting. In the burial-ground belonging to it his great-granddaughter Hannah Bunyan was interred in 1770, at the age of 76 ; and with her all that is related of his posterity ends.

A description of his character and person was drawn by his first biographer. " He appeared, in countenance," says that friend, " to be of a stern and rough temper ; but in his conversation mild and affable : not given to loquacity or much discourse in company, unless some urgent occasion required it ; observing never to boast of himself or his parts, but rather seem low in his own eyes, and submit himself to the judgment of others ; abhorring lying and swearing ; being just in all that lay in his power to his word ; not seeming to revenge injuries ; loving to reconcile differences, and make friendship with all.

" He had a sharp, quick eye, accomplished with an excellent discerning of persons, being of good judgment and quick wit. As for his person, he was tall of stature ; strong-boned, though not corpulent ; somewhat of a ruddy face, with sparkling eyes ; wearing his hair on his upper lip, after the old British fashion ; his hair reddish, but in his latter days time had sprinkled it with gray ; his nose well set, but not declining or bending, and his mouth moderate large ; his forehead something high, and his habit always plain and modest."

" And thus have we impartially described the internal and external parts of a person who had tried the smiles and frowns of Time, not puffed up in prosperity, nor shaken in adversity, always holding the golden mean."

It remains now to speak of that work which has made the name of Bunyan famous.

It is not known in what year the Pilgrim's Progress was first published, no copy of the first edition having as yet been discovered. The second is in the British Museum: it is "with additions," and its date is 1678; but as the book is known to have been written during Bunyan's imprisonment, which terminated in 1672, it was probably published before his release, or at least immediately after it.

POPULARITY OF THE PILGRIM'S PROGRESS.

The earliest which I have been able to obtain, is the Eighth edition, printed for Nathaniel Ponder, in London "at the Peacock in the Poultry, near the Church, 1682;" for whom also the ninth was published in 1684 and the tenth in 1685. All of these no doubt were large editions.

This noted eighth edition is "with additions;" but there is no reason to suppose that they were "new ones, never made before," for the ninth and tenth bear the same promise, and contain no alteration whatever. One passage of considerable length was added after the second edition,—the whole scene between Mr. Byends and his three friends, and their subsequent discourse with Christian and Faithful. It appears to have been written with reference to some particular case ; and in Bunyan's circle the name of the person intended was probably well known.

The rapidity with which these editions succeeded one another, and the demand for pictures to illustrate them, are not the only proofs of the popularity which the Pilgrim's Progress obtained before the second part was published. In the verses prefixed to that part, Bunyan complains of dishonest imitators.

> *   *   *   "Some have, of late, to counterfeit
> My Pilgrim, to their own, my title set ;
> Yea, others, half my name, and title too,
> Have stitched to their books, to make them do."

[It is proper to say here that in versifying, as is evident to readers of his works, Bunyan was attempting an art which he had never learnt, and for which he had no aptitude—but in prose he wrote as he conversed, using the plain straightforward language of common life.]

These interlopers may very likely have given Bunyan an additional inducement to prepare a second part himself. It appeared in 1684, with this notice on the back of the title page : "I appoint Mr. Nathaniel Ponder, but no other, to print this book. John Bunyan. January 1, 1684." No additions or alterations were made in this part, though the author lived more than four years after its publication.

Disraeli, from whose works the best-informed reader may learn much, and who in the temper of his writings, as well as in the research which they display, may be a useful model for succeeding authors, calls Bunyan "the Spenser of the people."

He is, indeed, the Prince of Allegorists in prose. The allegory is never lost sight of in the first part : in the second it is not so uniformly preserved ; parties who begin their pilgrimage in childhood, grow up upon the way, pass through the stage of courtship, marry and are given in marriage, have children and dispose of their children. Yet to most readers this second part is as delightful as the first ; and Bunyan had perhaps more pleasure in composing it not only because he was chewing the cud of his old inventions, but because there can be no doubt that he complimented the friends whom he delighted to honor, by giving them a place among the persons of his tale.

We may be sure that Mr. Valiant-for-the-Truth, Old Honest of the Town of Stupidity, Mr. Despondency and his daughter Muchafraid, and their companions, were well known in "Bishop Bunyan's" diocese; and if no real characters were designed by him in those who are less favorably introduced as turning back on their journey, striking into by-paths, or slumbering by the way, likenesses would be discovered where none were intended.

THE PILGRIM'S PROGRESS

FROM

THIS WORLD TO THAT WHICH IS TO COME.

THE FIRST PART.

45

THE AUTHOR'S APOLOGY FOR HIS BOOK.

WHEN at the first I took my pen in hand,
Thus for to write, I did not understand
That I at all should make a little book
In such a mode ; nay, I had undertook
To make another ; which when almost done,
Before I was aware, I this begun.

    And thus it was : I, writing of the way
And race of saints in this our gospel-day,
Fell suddenly into an allegory
About their journey, and the way to glory,
In more than twenty things, which I set down :
This done, I twenty more had in my crown ;
And they again began to multiply,
Like sparks that from the coals of fire do fly.
Nay then, thought I, if that you breed so fast,
I'll put you by yourselves, lest you at last
Should prove *ad infinitum*, and eat out
The book that I already am about.

    Well so I did ; but yet I did not think
To show to all the world my pen and ink
In such a mode ; I only thought to make
I knew not what ; nor did I undertake
Thereby to please my neighbor ; no, not I ;
I did it mine own self to gratify.
    Neither did I but vacant seasons spend
In this my scribble ; nor did I intend
But to divert myself, in doing this,
From worser thoughts which make me do amiss.

    Thus I set pen to paper with delight,
And quickly had my thoughts in black and white.

For having now my method by the end,
Still as I pulled, it came; and so I penned
It down; until at last it came to be,
For length and breadth, the bigness which you see.

Well, when I had thus put my ends together,
I showed them others, that I might see whether
They would condemn them, or them justify;
And some said, Let them live: some, Let them die;
Some said, John, print it; others said, Not so;
Some said, It might do good; others said, No.

Now was I in a strait, and did not see
Which was the best thing to be done by me:
At last I thought, Since you are thus divided,
I print it will; and so the case decided.
For, thought I, some I see would have it done,
Though others in that channel do not run:
To prove, then, who advised for the best,
Thus I thought fit to put it to the test.

I further thought, if now I did deny
Those that would have it thus to gratify,
I did not know but hinder them I might
Of that which would to them be great delight;
For those which were not for its coming forth,
I said to them, *Offend you I am loath;*
Yet, since your brethren, pleased with it be,
Forbear to judge, till you do further see.

If that thou wilt not read, let it alone;
Some love the meat, some love to pick the bone;
Yea, that I might them better palliate,
I did too with them thus expostulate:

May I not write in such a style as this?
In such a method too, and yet not miss
My end, thy good? Why may it not be done?
Dark clouds bring waters, when the bright bring none.
Yea, dark or bright, if they their silver drops
Cause to descend, the earth, by yielding crops,
Gives praise to both, and carpeth not at either,
But treasures up the fruit they yield together;
Yea, so commixes both, that in their fruit
None can distinguish this from that; they suit

Her well when hungry ; but, if she be full,
She spews out both, and makes their blessing null.

You see the ways the fisherman doth take
To catch the fish ; what engines doth he make!
Behold ! how he engageth all his wits ;
Also his snares, lines, angles, hooks, and nets :
Yet fish there be, that neither hook nor line,
Nor snare, not net, nor engine, can make thine :
They must be groped for, and be tickled too,
Or they will not be catched, whate'er you do.
How does the fowler seek to catch his game?
By divers means, all which one cannot name :
His guns, his nets, his lime-twigs, light, and bell :
He creeps, he goes, he stands ; yea, who can tell
Of all his postures ? Yet there's none of these
Will make him master of what fowls he please.
Yea, he must pipe and whistle to catch *this*,
Yet, if he does so, *that* bird he will miss.

If that a pearl may in a toad's head dwell,
And may be found too in an oyster shell:
If things that promise nothing, do contain
What better is than gold, who will disdain,
That have an inkling of it, there to look,
That they may find it ? Now, my little book
(Though void of all these paintings, that may make
It with this or the other man to take)
Is not without those things that do excel
What do in brave but empty notions dwell.

"*Well, yet I am not fully satisfied
That this your book will stand, when soundly tried.*"

Why, what's the matter? "*It is dark !* " What though?
"*But it is feigned.*" What of that ? I trow
Some men, by feigned words, as dark as mine,
Make truth to spangle, and its rays to shine!
"*But they want solidness.*" Speak, man, thy mind!
"*They drown the weak ; metaphors make us blind.*"

Solidity, indeed, becomes the pen
Of him that writeth things divine to men:
But must I needs want solidness, because
By metaphors I speak ? Were not God's laws,

His gospel laws, in olden time held forth
By shadows, types, and metaphors? Yet loath
Will any sober man be to find fault
With them, lest he be found for to assault
The Highest Wisdom. No, he rather stoops,
And seeks to find out what by pins and loops,
By calves, and sheep, by heifers and by rams,
By birds and herbs, and by the blood of lambs,
God speaketh to him; and happy is he
That finds the light and grace that in them be.

Be not too forward, therefore, to conclude
That I want solidness, that I am rude:
All things solid in show, not solid be;
All things in parable despise not we,
Lest things most hurtful lightly we receive,
And things that good are, of our souls bereave.
My dark and cloudy words, they do but hold
The truth, as cabinets enclose the gold.

The prophets used much by metaphors
To set forth truth; yea, whoso considers
Christ, his apostles too, shall plainly see
That truths to this day in such mantles be.

Am I afraid to say, that holy writ,
Which for its style and phrase puts down all wit,
Is everywhere so full of all these things,
(Dark figures, allegories,) yet there springs
From that same book, that lustre, and those rays
Of light, that turns our darkest nights to days.

Come, let my carper to his life now look,
And find there darker lines than in my book
He findeth any; yea, and let him know,
That in his best things there are worse lines too.

May we but stand before impartial men,
To his poor one I dare adventure ten,
That they will take my meaning in these lines
Far better than his lies in silver shrines.
Come, truth, although in swaddling-clouts I find,
Informs the judgment, rectifies the mind;
Pleases the understanding, makes the will
Submit; the memory too it doth fill

With what doth our imagination please;
Likewise it tends our troubles to appease.

Sound words, I know, Timothy is to use,
And old wives' fables he is to refuse;
But yet grave Paul him nowhere did forbid
The use of parables; in which lay hid
That gold, those pearls, and precious stones, that were
Worth digging for, and that with greatest care.

Let me add one word more: O man of God,
Art thou offended? Dost thou wish I had
Put forth my matter in another dress?
Or that I had in things been more express?
To those that are my betters, as is fit,
Three things let me propound, then I submit:

1. I find not that I am denied the use
Of this my method, so I no abuse
Put on the words, things, readers, or be rude
In handling figure or similitude,
In application; but all that I may
Seek the advance of truth, this or that way.
Denied, did I say? Nay, I have leave,
(Examples too, and that from them that have
God better pleased, by their words or ways,
Than any man that breatheth now-a-days,)
Thus to express my mind, thus to declare
Things unto thee that excellentest are.

2. I find that men (as high as trees) will write
Dialogue-wise; yet no man doth them slight
For writing so: indeed, if they abuse
Truth, cursed be they, and the craft they use
To that intent; but yet let truth be free
To make her sallies upon thee and me,
Which way it pleases God; for who knows how,
Better than He that taught us first to plough,
To guide our minds and pens for his design?
And He makes base things usher in divine.

3. I find that holy writ, in many places,
Hath semblance with this method, where the cases
Do call for one thing to set forth another:
Use it I may then, and yet nothing smother

Truth's golden beams : nay, by this method may
Make it cast forth its rays as light as day.

　And now, before I do put up my pen,
I'll show the profit of my book ; and then
Commit both me and it unto that Hand
That pulls the strong down, and makes weak ones stand.

　This book it chalketh out before thine eyes
The man that seeks the everlasting prize :
It shows you whence he comes, whither he goes ;
What he leaves undone ; also what he does :
It also shows you how he runs and runs,
Till he unto the Gate of Glory comes.

　It shows, too, who set out for life amain,
As if the lasting crown they would obtain.
Here also you may see the reason why
They lose their labor, and like fools do die.

　This book will make a traveller of thee
If by its counsel thou wilt ruled be ;
It will direct thee to the Holy Land,
If thou wilt its direction understand :
Yea, it will make the slothful active be ;
The blind also delightful things to see.

　Art thou for something rare and profitable?
Or wouldst thou see a truth within a fable?
Art thou forgetful ? Wouldst thou remember
From New-year's day to the last of December?
Then read my fancies ; they will stick like burs,
And may be, to the helpless, comforters.

　This book is writ in such a dialect
As may the minds of listless men affect :
It seems a novelty, and yet contains
Nothing but sound and honest gospel strains.

　Wouldst thou divert thyself from melancholy?
Wouldst thou be pleasant, yet be far from folly?
Wouldst thou read riddles and their explanation?
Or else be drowned in thy contemplation?
Dost thou love picking meat ? or wouldst thou see
A man i' the clouds, and hear him speak to thee?

Wouldst thou be in a dream, and yet not sleep?
Or wouldst thou in a moment laugh and weep?
Wouldst thou lose thyself and catch no harm,
And find thyself again without a charm?
Wouldst read thyself, and read thou know'st not what,
And yet know whether thou art blest or not,
By reading the same lines?　O then come hither!
And lay my book, thy head, and heart together.

JOHN BUNYAN.

THE JAIL.—BUNYAN SLEEPS.

THE
PILGRIM'S PROGRESS.

CHAPTER I.

AS I walked through the wilderness of this world, I lighted on a certain place where was a den,* and laid me down in that place to sleep ; and as I slept, I dreamed a dream.

* Bedford Jail, in which the author was a prisoner for conscience' sake.

I dreamed, and behold, I saw a man clothed with rags standing in a certain place, with his face from his own house, a book in his hand, and a great burden upon his back.[1]* I looked and saw him open the book, and read therein ; and as he read, he wept and trembled : and not being able longer to contain, he brake out with a lamentable cry, saying, "What shall I do?"[2]

In this plight, therefore, he went home and refrained himself as long as he could, that his wife and children should not perceive his distress ; but he could not be silent long, because that his trouble increased.

Wherefore at length he broke his mind to his wife and children : and thus he began to talk to them. O, my dear wife, said he, and you the children of my bowels, I, your dear friend, am in myself undone by reason of a burden that lieth hard upon me ; moreover, I am for certain informed that this our city will be burned with fire from heaven ; in which fearful overthrow, both myself, with thee my wife, and you my sweet babes shall miserably come to ruin, except (the which yet I see not) some way of escape can be found whereby we may be delivered.

CHRISTIAN READING HIS BOOK.

At this his relations were sore amazed; not for that they believed that what he had said to them was true, but because they thought that some frenzy distemper had got into his head; there-

* See notes at the end.

fore, it drawing towards night, and they hoping that sleep might settle his brains, with all haste they got him to bed.

But the night was as troublesome to him as the day; wherefore, instead

CHRISTIAN TALKS TO HIS WIFE AND CHILDREN.

of sleeping, he spent it in sighs and tears. So when the morning was come, they would know how he did. He told them, Worse and worse; he also set to talking to them again; but they began to be hardened.

They also thought to drive away his distemper by harsh and surly carriage to him; sometimes they would deride, sometimes they would chide, and sometimes they would quite neglect him. Wherefore he began to retire himself to his chamber to pray for and pity them, and also to condole his own misery; he would also walk solitarily in the fields, sometimes reading, and sometimes praying: and thus for some days he spent his time.

Now I saw, upon a time, when he was walking in the fields, that he was (as he was wont) reading in his book, and greatly distressed in his

CHRISTIAN RETIRES TO HIS ROOM.

mind; and as he read, he burst out, as he had done before, crying, "What shall I do to be saved?"

I saw also that he looked this way, and that way, as if he would run; yet he stood still because (as I perceived) he could not tell which way to go. I looked then, and saw a man named Evangelist coming to him, and he asked, Wherefore dost thou cry?

He answered, Sir, I perceive, by the book in my hand, that I am condemned to die, and after that to come to judgment;[4] and I find that I am not willing to do the first,[5] nor able to do the second.[6]

Then said Evangelist, Why not willing to die, since this life is attended with so many evils? The man answered, Because I fear that this burden that is upon my back will sink me lower than the grave, and I shall fall into Tophet.[7]   And sir, if I be not fit to go to prison, I am not fit to go to judgment, and from thence to execution; and the thoughts of these things make me cry.

Cast into Hell.

EVANGELIST POINTS THE WAY TO THE WICKET GATE.

Then said Evangelist, If this be thy condition, why standest thou still? He answered, Because I know not whither to go. Then he gave him a parchment roll, and there was written within, Flee from the wrath to come.[8]

The man therefore read it, and, looking upon Evangelist very carefully, said, Whither must I fly? Then said Evangelist, pointing with his finger over a very wide field, Do you see yonder wicket gate?[9] The man said, No.

Then said the other, Do you see yonder shining light?[10] He said, I think I do. Then said Evangelist, Keep that light in your eye, and go up directly thereto, so shalt thou see the gate; at which, when thou knockest, it shall be told thee what thou shalt do. So I saw in my dream that the man began to run. Now he had not run far from his own door when his wife and children, perceiving it, began to cry after him to return; but the man put his fingers in his ears and ran on, crying, Life! life! eternal life![11] So he looked not behind him,[12] but fled towards the middle of the plain.

CHRISTIAN FLIES FROM DESTRUCTION.

The neighbors also came out to see him run;[13] and as he ran, some mocked, others threatened, and some cried after him to return; and among those that did so, there were two that resolved to fetch him back by force. The name of the one was Obstinate, and the name of the other Pliable. Now by this time the man was got a good distance from them, but, however, they were resolved to pursue him, which they did, and in a little time they overtook him.

Then said the man, Neighbors, wherefore are ye come? They said, To persuade you to go back with us. But he said, That can by no means be : you dwell, said he, in the city of Destruction, the place also where I was born : I see it to be so ; and dying there, sooner or later you will sink lower than the grave, into a place that burns with fire and brimstone : be content, good neighbors, and go along with me.

OBST. What, said Obstinate, and leave our friends and our comforts behind us !

CHR. Yes, said Christian (for that was his name), because that ALL which you shall forsake is not worthy to be compared with a little of that which I am seeking to enjoy ;[14] and if you will go along with me, and hold it, you shall fare as I myself ; for there, where I go, is enough and to spare.[15] Come away, and prove my words.

OBST. What are the things you seek, since you leave all the world to find them?

CHR. I seek an inheritance incorruptible, undefiled, and that fadeth not away ;[16] and it is laid up in heaven, and safe there,[17] to be bestowed, at the time appointed, on them that diligently seek it. Read it so, if you will, in my book.

OBST. Tush, said Obstinate, away with your book : will you go back with us or no?

CHR. No, not I, said the other, because I have laid my hand to the plough.[18]

OBST. Come then, neighbor Pliable, let us turn again, and go home without him: there is a company of these crazy-headed coxcombs, that when they take a fancy by the end, are wiser in their own eyes than seven men that can render a reason.

PLI. Then said Pliable, Don't revile ; if what good Christian says is true, the things he looks after are better than ours : my heart inclines to go with my neighbor.

OBST. What, more fools still ! Be ruled by me, and go back ; who knows whither such a brain-sick fellow will lead you? Go back, go back, and be wise.

CHR. Nay, but do thou come with thy neighbor Pliable ; there are such things to be had which I spoke of, and many more glories besides. If you believe not me, read here in this book ; and for the truth of what is expressed therein, behold, all is confirmed by the blood of Him that made it.[19]

PLI. Well, neighbor Obstinate, said Pliable, I begin to come to a point; I intend to go along with this good man, and to cast in my lot with him; but, my good companion, do you know the way to this desired place?

CHR. I am directed by a man, whose name is Evangelist, to speed me

OBSTINATE TURNS BACK.

to a little gate that is before us, where we shall receive instructions about the way.

PLI. Come then, good neighbor, let us be going. Then they went both together.

OBST. And I will go back to my place, said Obstinate: I will be no companion of such misled, fantastical fellows.

Now I saw in my dream, that when Obstinate was gone back, Christian and Pliable went talking over the plain; and thus they began their discourse.

CHR. Come, neighbor Pliable, how do you do? I am glad you are persuaded to go along with me. Had even Obstinate himself but felt what I have felt of the powers and terrors of what is yet unseen, he would not thus lightly have given us the back.

PLI. Come, neighbor Christian, since there are none but us two here, tell me now further, what things are, and how to be enjoyed, whither we are going.

CHR. I can better conceive of them with my mind, than speak of them with my tongue: but yet, since you are desirous to know, I will read of them in my book.

PLI. And do you think that the words of your book are certainly true?

CHR. Yes, verily; for it was made by him that cannot lie.[20]

PLI. Well said; what things are they?

CHR. There is an endless kingdom to be inhabited, and everlasting life to be given us, that we may inhabit the kingdom forever.[21]

PLI. Well said; and what else?

CHR. There are crowns of glory to be given us; and garments that will make us shine like the sun in the firmament of heaven.[22]

PLI. This is very pleasant; and what else?

CHR. There shall be no more crying, nor sorrow; for he that is owner of the place will wipe all tears from our eyes.[23]

PLI. And what company shall we have there?

CHR. There we shall be with seraphims and cherubims:[24] creatures that will dazzle your eyes to look on them. There also you shall meet with thousands and ten thousands that have gone before us to that place; none of them are hurtful, but loving and holy; every·one walking in the sight of God, and standing in his presence with acceptance forever. In a word, there we shall see the elders with their golden crowns;[25] there we shall see the holy virgins with their golden harps;[26] there we shall see men, that by the world were cut in pieces, burnt in flames, eaten of beasts, drowned in the seas, for the love they bare to the Lord of the place;[27] all well, and clothed with immortality as with a garment.[28]

PLI. The hearing of this is enough to ravish one's heart. But are these things to be enjoyed? How shall we get to be sharers thereof?

CHR. The Lord, the governor of the country, hath recorded that in this book;[29] the substance of which is, if we be truly willing to have it, he will bestow it upon us freely.

PLI. Well, my good companion, glad I am to hear of these things: come on, let us mend our pace.

CHR. I cannot go as fast as I would, by reason of this burden that is on my back.

CHRISTIAN AND PLIABLE IN THE SLOUGH OF DESPOND.

Now I saw in my dream that just as they had ended this talk, they drew nigh to a very miry slough that was in the midst of the plain: and they being heedless, did both fall suddenly into the bog. The name of the slough was Despond. Here, therefore, they wallowed for a time, being grievously bedaubed with dirt; and Christian, because of the burden that was on his back, began to sink in the mire.

PLI. Then said Pliable, Ah, neighbor Christian, where are you now?

CHR. Truly, said Christian, I do not know.

PLI. At this Pliable began to be offended, and angrily said to his fellow, Is this the happiness you have told me all this while of? If we have such ill speed at our first setting out, what may we expect between this and our journey's end? May I get out again with my life, you shall possess the brave country alone for me. And with that he gave a desperate struggle or two, and got out of the mire on that side of the slough which was next to his own house: so away he went, and Christian saw him no more.

Wherefore Christian was left to tumble in the Slough of Despond alone; but still he endeavored to struggle to that side of the slough that was farthest from his own house, and next to the wicket gate; the which he did, but could not get out because of the burden that was upon his back : but I beheld in my dream, that a man came to him, whose name was Help, and asked him what he did there.

CHR. Sir, said Christian, I was bid to go this way by a man called Evangelist, who directed me also to yonder gate, that I might escape the wrath to come. And as I was going thither, I fell in here.

HELP. But why did not you look for the steps?

CHR. Fear followed me so hard that I fled the next way, and fell in.

HELP. Then said he, Give me thine hand: so he gave him his hand, and he drew him out,[30] and he set him upon sound ground, and bid him go on his way.

Then I stepped to him that plucked him out, and said, Sir, wherefore, since over this place is the way from the city of Destruction to yonder gate, is it, that this plat is not mended, that poor travellers might go thither with more security? And he said unto me, This miry slough is such a place as cannot be mended: it is the descent whither the scum and filth that attends conviction for sin doth continually run, and therefore it is called the Slough of Despond; for still, as the sinner is awakened about his lost condition, there arise in his soul many fears and doubts, and discouraging apprehensions, which all of them get together, and settle in this place: and this is the reason of the badness of this ground.

Yet it is not the pleasure of the King that this place should remain so bad.[31] His laborers also have, by the direction of his Majesty's surveyors, been for above these sixteen hundred years employed about this patch of ground, if perhaps it might have been mended: yea, and to my knowledge, said he, there have been swallowed up at least twenty thousand cartloads, yea, millions of wholesome instructions, that have at all seasons been brought from all places of the King's dominions (and they that can tell, say, they are the best materials to make good ground of the place), if so be it might have been mended; but it is the Slough of Despond still, and so will be when they have done what they can.

HELP DRAWS CHRISTIAN OUT OF THE SLOUGH OF DESPOND.

True, there are, by the direction of the Lawgiver, certain good and substantial steps, placed even through the very midst of this slough; but at such times as this place doth much spew out its filth, as it doth against change of weather, these steps are hardly seen: or if they be, men, through the dizziness of their heads, step beside, and then they are be-mired to purpose, notwithstanding the steps be there: but the ground is good when they are once got in at the gate.[32]

PLIABLE'S RETURN TO HIS OWN HOUSE.

Now I saw in my dream, that by this time Pliable was got home to his house. So his neighbors came to visit him; and some of them called him wise man for coming back, and some called him fool for hazarding him-self with Christian: others again did mock at his cowardliness, saying, Surely, since you began to venture, I would not have been so base as to

5

have given out for a few difficulties. So Pliable sat sneaking among them. But at last he got more confidence, and then they all turned their tales, and began to deride poor Christian behind his back. And thus much concerning Pliable.

Now as Christian was walking solitarily by himself, he espied one afar off come crossing over the field to meet him; and their hap was to meet just as they were crossing the way of each other.

The gentleman's name that met him was Mr. Worldly Wiseman: he dwelt in the town of Carnal Policy, a very great town, and also hard by from whence Christian came. This man then, meeting with Christian, and having some inkling* of him (for Christian's setting
*Slight knowledge.   forth from the city of Destruction was much noised abroad, not only in the town where he dwelt, but also it began to be the town-talk in some other places)—Mr. Worldly Wiseman, therefore, having some guess of him, by beholding his laborious going, by observing his sighs and groans, and the like, began thus to enter into some talk with Christian.

WORLD. How now, good fellow, whither away after this burdened manner?

CHR. A burdened manner indeed, as ever I think poor creature had! And whereas you ask me, Whither away? I tell you, sir, I am going to yonder wicket-gate before me ; for there, as I am informed, I shall be put into a way to be rid of my heavy burden.

WORLD. Hast thou a wife and children?

CHR. Yes ; but I am so laden with this burden, that I cannot take that pleasure in them as formerly : methinks I am as if I had none.[33]

WORLD. Wilt thou hearken to me, if I give thee counsel?

CHR. If it be good, I will ; for I stand in need of good counsel.

WORLD. I would advise thee, then, that thou with all speed get thyself rid of thy burden ; for thou wilt never be settled in thy mind till then : nor canst thou enjoy the benefits of the blessings which God hath bestowed upon thee till then.

CHR. That is that which I seek for, even to be rid of this heavy burden : but get it off myself I cannot, nor is there any man in our country that can take it off my shoulders ; therefore I am going this way, as I told you, that I may be rid of my burden.

WORLD. Who bid thee go this way to be rid of thy burden?

CHR. A man that appeared to me to be a very great and honorable person : his name, as I remember, is Evangelist.

WORLD. I beshrew* him for his counsel! There is not a more dangerous and troublesome way in the world than

* Hope that he may suffer.

MR. WORLDLY WISEMAN.

is that into which he hath directed thee; and that thou shalt find, if thou wilt be ruled by his counsel. Thou hast met with something, as I perceive, already ; for I see the dirt of the Slough of Despond is upon thee : but that slough is the beginning of the sorrows that do attend those that go on in that way.   Hear me : I am older than thou : thou art like to meet with, in the way which thou goest, wearisomeness, painfulness, hunger, perils, nakedness, sword, lions, dragons, darkness, and, in a word, death, and what not.   These things are certainly true, having been confirmed by many testimonies.   And should a man so carelessly cast away himself, by giving heed to a stranger ?

CHR. Why, sir, this burden on my back is more terrible to me than all these things which you have mentioned : nay, methinks I care not what I meet with in the way, if so be I can also meet with deliverance from my burden.

WORLD. How camest thou by thy burden at first ?

CHR. By reading this book in my hand.

WORLD. I thought so ; and it has happened unto thee as to other weak men, who, meddling with things too high for them, do suddenly fall into thy distractions ; which distractions do not only unman men, as thine I perceive have done thee, but they run them upon desperate ventures, to obtain they know not what.

CHR. I know what I would obtain ; it is ease from my heavy burden.

WORLD. But why wilt thou seek for ease this way, seeing so many dangers attend it ? especially since (hadst thou but patience to hear me) I could direct thee to the obtaining of what thou desirest, without the dangers that thou in this way wilt run thyself into.   Yea, and the remedy is at hand.   Besides, I will add, that, instead of those dangers, thou shalt meet with much safety, friendship, and content.

CHR. Sir, I pray open this secret to me.

WORLD. Why, in yonder village (the village is named Morality) there dwells a gentleman whose name is Legality, a very judicious man, and a man of a very good name, that has skill to help men off with such burdens as thine is from their shoulders ; yea, to my knowledge, he hath done a great deal of good this way ; aye, and besides, he hath skill to cure those that are somewhat crazed in their wits with their burdens.   To him, as I said, thou mayest go, and be helped presently.   His house is not quite a mile from this place ; and if he should not be at home himself, he hath a pretty young man, his son, whose name is Civility, that can do it (to speak on) as well as the old gentleman himself : there, I say, thou mayest be eased of thy burden ; and if thou art not minded to go back to thy former habitation (as indeed I would not wish thee), thou mayest send for thy wife and children to this village, where there are houses now standing empty, one of which thou mayest have at a reasonable rate : provision is there also cheap and good ; and that which will make thy life the more happy is, to be sure there thou shalt live by honest neighbors, in credit and good fashion.

Now was Christian somewhat at a stand ; but presently he concluded, If this be true which this gentleman hath said, my wisest course is to take his advice : and with that he thus further spake.

CHR. Sir, which is my way to this honest man's house?

WORLD. Do you see yonder high hill?

CHR. Yes, very well.

WORLD. By that hill you must go, and the first house you come at is his.

So Christian turned out of his way to go to Mr. Legality's house for help : but, behold, when he was got now hard by the hill, it seemed so high, and also that side of it that was next the wayside did hang so much over, that Christian was afraid to venture farther, lest the hill should fall on his head ; wherefore there he stood still, and wotted not what to do. Also his burden now seemed heavier to him than while he was in his way. There came also flashes of fire,[34] out of the hill, that made Christian afraid that he should be burnt : here therefore, he did sweat and quake for fear.[35] And now he began to be sorry that he had taken Mr. Worldly Wiseman's counsel ; and with that he saw Evangelist coming to meet him, at the sight also of whom he began to blush with shame. So Evangelist drew nearer and nearer ; and coming up to him, he looked upon him, with a severe and dreadful countenance, and thus began to reason with Christian.

EVAN. What dost thou here, Christian? said he: at which words Christian knew not what to answer; wherefore at present he stood speechless before him. Then said Evangelist further, Art not thou the man that I found crying without the walls of the city of Destruction?

CHR. Yes, dear sir, I am the man.

EVAN. Did not I direct thee the way to the little wicket-gate?

CHR. Yes, dear sir, said Christian.

EVAN. How is it, then, thou art so quickly turned aside? For thou art now out of thy way.

CHR. I met with a gentleman so soon as I had got over the Slough of

Despond, who persuaded me that I might, in the village before me, find a man that could take off my burden.

EVAN. What was he?

CHR. He looked like a gentleman, and talked much to me, and got me at last to yield: so I came hither: but when I beheld this hill, and how it hangs over the way, I suddenly made a stand, lest it should fall on my head.

EVAN. What said that gentleman to you?

CHR. Why, he asked me whither I was going; and I told him.

EVAN. And what said he then?

CHR. He asked me if I had a family; and I told him. But, said I, I am so laden with the burden that is on my back, that I cannot take pleasure in them as formerly.

EVAN. And what said he then?

CHR. He bid me with speed get rid of my burden; and I told him it was ease that I sought. And, said I, I am therefore going to yonder gate, to receive further direction how I may get to the place of deliverance. So he said that he would show me a better way, and short, not so attended with difficulties as the way, sir, that you set me in; which way, said he, will direct you to a gentleman's house that hath skill to take off these burdens: so I believed him, and turned out of that way into this, if haply I might be soon eased of my burden. But when I came to this place, and beheld things as they are, I stopped, for fear (as I said) of danger: but I now know not what to do.

EVAN. Then said Evangelist, Stand still a little, that I show thee the words of God. So he stood trembling. Then said Evangelist, See that ye refuse not Him that speaketh; for if they escaped not who refused him that spake on earth, much more shall we not escape, if we turn away from Him that speaketh from heaven.[36] He said, moreover, Now the just shall live by faith; but if any man draw back, my soul shall have no pleasure in him.[37] He also did thus apply them: Thou art the man that art running into this misery: thou hast begun to reject the council of the Most High, and to draw back thy foot from the way of peace, even almost to the hazarding of thy perdition.

Then Christian fell down at his feet as dead, crying, Woe is me, for I am undone! At the sight of which Evangelist caught him by the right hand, saying, All manner of sin and blasphemies shall be forgiven unto men.[38] Be not faithless, but believing.[39] Then did Christian again a little revive, and stood up trembling, as at first, before Evangelist.

CHRISTIAN BENEATH MOUNT SINAI.

71

Then Evangelist proceeded, saying, Give more earnest heed to the things that I shall tell thee. I will now show thee who it was that deluded thee, and who it was also to whom he sent thee. The man that met thee is one Worldly Wiseman, and rightly is he so called ; partly because he savoreth only the doctrine of this world,[40] (therefore he always goes to the town of Morality to church) ; and because he is of this carnal temper, therefore he seeketh to pervert my ways though right. Now there are three things in this man's counsel that thou must utterly abhor.

1. His turning thee out of the way.

2. His laboring to render the cross odious to thee.

3. And his setting thy feet in that way that leadeth unto the administration of death.

First, Thou must abhor his turning thee out of the way ; yea, and thine own consenting thereto : because this is to reject the counsel of God for the sake of the counsel of a Worldly Wiseman. The Lord says, "Strive to enter in at the strait gate,"[41] the gate to which I send thee ; "for strait is the gate that leadeth unto life, and few there be that find it."[42] From this little wicket-gate, and from the way thereto, hath this wicked man turned thee, to the bringing of thee almost to destruction : hate, therefore, his turning thee out of the way, and abhor thyself for hearkening to him.

Secondly, Thou must abhor his laboring to render the cross odious unto thee ; for thou art to prefer it before the treasures of Egypt.[43] Besides, the King of glory hath told thee, that he that will save his life shall lose it. And he that comes after him, and hates not his father, and mother, and wife, and children, and brethren, and sisters, yea, and his own life also, he can not be his disciple.[44] I say, therefore, for man to labor to persuade thee that that shall be thy death, without which, THE TRUTH hath said thou canst not have eternal life, this doctrine thou must abhor.

Thirdly, Thou must hate his setting of thy feet in the way that leadeth to the ministration of death. And for this thou must consider to whom he sent thee, and also how unable that person was to deliver thee from thy burden.

He to whom thou wast sent for ease, being by name Legality, is the son of the bondwoman which now is, and is in bondage with her children,[45] and is, in a mystery, this Mount Sinai, which thou hast feared will fall on thy head. Now if she with her children are in bondage, how canst thou expect by them to be made free? This Legality, therefore, is not able to set thee free from thy burden.

No man was as yet ever rid of his burden by him; no, nor ever is like to be: ye can not be justified by the works of the law; for by the deeds of the law no man living can be rid of his burden.

Therefore Mr. Worldly Wiseman is an alien, and Mr. Legality is a cheat; and for his son Civility, notwithstanding his simpering looks, he is but a hypocrite, and can not help thee. Believe me, there is nothing in all this noise that thou hast heard of these sottish men, but a design to

beguile thee of thy salvation, by turning thee from the way in which I set thee. After this, Evangelist called aloud to the heavens for confirmation of what he had said; and with that there came words and fire out of the mountain under which poor Christian stood, which made the hair of his flesh stand up.

The words were pronounced; As many as are of the works of the law, are under the curse; for it is written, Cursed is every one that continueth not in all things which are written in the book of the law to do them.[46]

Now Christian looked for nothing but death,

FIRE COMES OUT OF THE MOUNTAIN.

and began to cry out lamentably, even cursing the time in which he met with Mr. Worldly Wiseman; still calling himself a thousand fools for hearkening to his counsel. He also was greatly ashamed to think that this gentleman's arguments, flowing only from the flesh, should have the prevalency with him so far as to cause him to forsake the right way. This done, he applied himself again to Evangelist in words and sense as follows.

CHR. Sir, what think you? Is there any hope? May I now go back, and go up to the wicket-gate? Shall I not be abandoned for this, and sent back from thence ashamed? I am sorry I have hearkened to this man's counsel; but may my sins be forgiven?

EVAN. Then said Evangelist to him, Thy sin is very great, for by it thou hast committed two evils: thou hast forsaken the way that is good, to tread in forbidden paths. Yet will the man at the gate receive thee, for he has good-will for men; only, said he, take heed thou turn not aside again, lest thou perish from the way, when his wrath is kindled but a little. [47]

CHAPTER II.

THEN did Christian address himself to go back ; and Evangelist, after he had kissed him, gave him one smile, and bid him God speed ; so he went on with haste, neither spake he to any man by the way ; nor if any man asked him, would he vouchsafe them an answer. He went like one that was all the while treading on forbidden ground, and could by no means think himself safe, till again he was got into the way which he had left to follow Mr. Worldly Wiseman's counsel. So, in process of time, Christian got up to the gate. Now, over the gate there was written, " Knock, and it shall be opened unto you." [48]

He knocked, therefore, more than once or twice, saying,

> "May I now enter here? Will he within
> Open to sorry me, though I have been
> An undeserving rebel? Then shall I
> Not fail to sing his lasting praise on high."

At last there came a grave person to the gate, named Goodwill, who asked who was there, and whence he came, and what he would have.

CHR. Here is a poor burdened sinner. I come from the city of Destruction, but am going to Mount Zion, that I may be delivered from the wrath to come. I would therefore, sir, since I am informed that by this gate is the way thither, know if you are willing to let me in.

GOOD. I am willing with all my heart, said he ; and with that he opened the gate.

So when Christian was stepping in, the other gave him a pull. Then said Christian, What means that? The other told him, A little distance from this gate there is erected a strong castle, of which Beelzebub is the captain ; from whence both he and they that are with him shoot arrows at those that come up to this gate, if haply they may die before they can enter in. Then said Christian, I rejoice and tremble. So when he was got in, the man at the gate asked him who directed him thither.

CHR. Evangelist bid me come hither and knock, as I did: and he said, that you, sir, would tell me what I must do.

GOOD. An open door is set before thee, and no man can shut it.

CHR. Now I begin to reap the benefit of my hazards.

GOOD. But how is it that you came alone?

CHRISTIAN KNOCKING AT THE GATE.

CHR. Because none of my neighbors saw their danger as I saw mine.

GOOD. Did any of them know of your coming?

CHR. Yes, my wife and children saw me at the first, and called after me to turn again: also some of my neighbors stood crying and calling after me to return; but I put my fingers in my ears, and so came on my way.

GOOD. But did none of them follow you, to persuade you to go back?

CHR. Yes, both Obstinate and Pliable; but when they saw that they could not prevail, Obstinate went railing back, but Pliable came with me a little way.

GOOD. But why did he not come through?

CHR. We indeed came both together until we came to the Slough of Despond, into the which we also suddenly fell. And then was my neighbor Pliable discouraged, and would not venture farther. Wherefore, getting out again on the side next to his own house, he told me I should possess the brave country alone for him; so he went his way, and I came mine; he after Obstinate, and I to this gate.

GOOD. Then said Goodwill, Alas, poor man; is the celestial glory of so small esteem with him, that he counteth it not worth running the hazards of a few difficulties to obtain it?

CHR. Truly, said Christian, I have said the truth of Pliable, and if I should also say the truth of myself, it will appear there is no betterment betwixt him and myself. It is true, he went back to his own house, but I also turned aside to go into the way of death, being persuaded thereto by the carnal arguments of one Mr. Worldly Wiseman.

GOOD-WILL. Oh! did he light upon you? What! he would have had you seek for ease at the hands of Mr. Legality. They are, both of them, a very cheat. But did you take his counsel?

CHR. Yes, as far as I durst; I went to find out Mr. Legality, until I thought the mountain that stands by his house would have fallen upon my head; wherefore, there I was forced to stop.

GOOD-WILL. That mountain has been the death of many, and will be the death of many more; it is well you escaped being by it dashed in pieces.

CHR. Why, truly, I do not know what had become of me there, had not Evangelist happily met me again, as I was musing in the midst of my dumps; but it was God's mercy that he came to me again, for else I had never come hither. But now I am come, such a one as I am, more fit, indeed, for death, by that mountain, than thus to stand talking with my Lord; but, oh, what a favor is this to me that yet I am admitted entrance here!

GOOD-WILL. We make no objections against any, notwithstanding all that they have done before they came hither. They are in no wise cast out,[49] and therefore, good Christian, come a little way with me, and I will teach thee about the way thou must go. Look before thee; dost thou see this narrow way? THAT is the way thou must go; it was cast up by the patriarchs, prophets, Christ, and his Apostles; and it is as straight as a rule can make it. This is the way thou must go.

CHR. But, said Christian, are there no turnings or windings, by which a stranger may lose his way?

GOOD-WILL. Yes, there are many ways butt down upon this, and they are crooked and wide. But thus thou mayest distinguish the right from the wrong, the right one only being straight and narrow.[50]

Then I saw in my dream, that Christian asked him further if he could not help him off with his burden that was upon his back; for as yet he had not got rid thereof, nor could he by any means get it off without help.

He told him, As to thy burden, be content to bear it, until thou comest to the place of deliverance; for there it will fall from thy back of itself.

Then Christian began to gird up his loins, and to address himself to his journey. So the other told him, That by the time he was gone some distance from the gate, he would come at the house of the Interpreter, at whose door he should knock, and he would show him excellent things. Then Christian took his leave of his friend, and he again bid him God-speed.

Then he went on till he came to the house of the Interpreter, where he knocked over and over; at last one came to the door, and asked who was there.

CHR. Sir, here is a traveller, who was bid by an acquaintance of the good-man of this house to call here for my profit; I would therefore speak with the master of the house. So he called for the master of the house, who, after a little time, came to Christian, and asked him what he would have.

CHR. Sir, said Christian, I am a man that am come from the City of Destruction, and am going to the Mount Zion; and I was told by the man that stands at the gate, at the head of this way, that if I called here, you would show me excellent things, such as would be a help to me in my journey.

INTER. Then said the Interpreter, Come in; I will show that which will be profitable to thee. So he commanded his man to light the candle,

GOOD-WILL SHOWS CHRISTIAN THE WAY.

GOD'S MINISTER.

and bid Christian follow him : so he had him into a private room, and
bid his man open a door ; the which when he had done, Christian saw

the picture of a very grave person hang up against the wall ; and this was the fashion of it. It had eyes lifted up to heaven, the best of books in his hand, the law of truth was written upon his lips, the world was behind his back. It stood as if it pleaded with men, and a crown of gold did hang over his head.

CHR. Then, said Christian, What meaneth this?

INTER. The man whose picture this is, is one of a thousand, he can beget children,[51] travail in birth with children,[52] and nurse them himself when they are born. And whereas thou seest him with his eyes lift up to heaven, the best of books in his hand, and the law of truth writ on his lips, it is to show thee that his work is to know and unfold dark things to sinners ; even as also thou seest him stand as if he pleaded with man ; and whereas thou seest the world as cast behind him, and that a crown hangs over his head, that is to show thee that slighting and despising the things that are present, for the love that he hath to his Master's service, he is sure in the world that comes next to have glory for his reward.

Now, said the Interpreter, I have showed thee this picture first, because the man whose picture this is, is the only man whom the Lord of the place, whither thou art going, hath authorized to be thy guide in all difficult places thou mayest meet with in the way ; wherefore, take good heed to what I have showed thee, and bear well in thy mind what thou hast seen, lest in thy journey thou meet with some that pretend to lead thee right, but their way goes down to death.

Then he took him by the hand, and led him into a very large parlor that was full of dust, because never swept; the which after he had reviewed a little while, the Interpreter called for a man to sweep.

Now, when he began to sweep, the dust began so abundantly to fly about, that Christian had almost therewith been choked. Then said the Interpreter to a damsel that stood by, Bring hither the water, and sprinkle the room; the which, when she had done, it was swept and cleansed with pleasure.

CHR. Then said Christian, What means this?

The Interpreter answered, This parlor is the heart of a man that was never sanctified by the sweet grace of the gospel; the dust is his original sin and inward corruptions, that have defiled the whole man. He that began to sweep at first, is the Law; but she that brought water and did sprinkle it, is the Gospel.

Now, whereas thou sawest, that so soon as the first began to sweep, the

6

dust did so fly about that the room by him could not be cleansed, but that thou wast almost choked therewith; this is to show thee, that the law, instead of cleansing the heart (by its working) from sin, doth revive, put strength into, and increase it in the soul, even as it doth discover and forbid it, for it doth not give power to subdue.[53]

INTERPRETER SHOWS CHRISTIAN THE ROOM FULL OF DUST.

Again, as thou sawest the damsel sprinkle the room with water, upon which it was cleansed with pleasure; this is to show thee, that when the gospel comes in the sweet and precious influences thereof to the heart, then, I say, even as thou sawest the damsel lay the dust by sprinkling the floor with water, so is sin vanquished and subdued, and the soul made clean through the faith of it, and consequently fit for the King of glory to inhabit.[54]

I saw, moreover, in my dream, that the Interpreter took him by the hand, and had him into a little room, where sat two little children, each one in his chair. The name of the eldest was Passion, and the name of the other Patience. Passion seemed to be much discontented; but Patience was very quiet.

Then Christian asked, What is the reason of the discontent of Passion? The Interpreter answered, The Governor of them would have him stay

PASSION AND PATIENCE.

for his best things till the beginning of the next year : but he will have all now ; but Patience is willing to wait.

Then I saw that one came to Passion, and brought him a bag of treasure, and poured it down at his feet, the which he took up and rejoiced therein, and withal laughed Patience to scorn. But I beheld but a while, and he had lavished all away and had nothing left him but rags.

CHR. Then said Christian to the Interpreter, Expound this matter more fully to me.

INTER. So he said, these two lads are figures : Passion, of the men of this world ; and Patience, of the men of that which is to come ; for as here thou seest, Passion will have all now this year, that is to say, in this world ; so are the men of this world : they must have all their good things now, they cannot stay till next year, that is, until the next world, for their portion of good.

That proverb, "A bird in the hand is worth two in the bush," is of more authority with them than are all the Divine testimonies of the good of the world to come. But as thou sawest that he had quickly lavished all away, and had presently left him nothing but rags ; so will it be with all such men at the end of this world.

CHR. Then said Christian, Now I see that Patience has the best wisdom, and that upon many accounts. First, because he stays for the best things. Second, and also because he will have the glory of his, when the other has nothing but rags.

INTER. Nay, you may add another, to wit, the glory of the next world will never wear out ; but these are suddenly gone. Therefore Passion had not so much reason to laugh at Patience, because he had his good things first, as Patience will have to laugh at Passion, because he had his best things last ; for first must give place to last, because last must have his time to come ; but last gives place to nothing ; for there is not another to succeed.

He, therefore, that hath his portion first, must needs have a time to spend it; but he that hath his portion last, must have it lastingly; therefore it is said of Dives, "Thou in thy lifetime receivedst thy good things, and likewise Lazarus evil things ; but now he is comforted, and thou art tormented." [55]

CHR. Then I perceive it is not best to covet things that are now; but to wait for things to come.

INTER. You say the truth : "For the things which are seen *are* temporal; but the things which are not seen *are* eternal" [56] But though this be so, yet since things present and our fleshly appetite are such near neighbors one to another ; and again, because things to come, and carnal sense, are such strangers one to another ; therefore it is that the first of these so suddenly fall into amity, and that distance is so continued between the second.

Then I saw in my dream that the Interpreter took Christian by the hand, and led him into a place where was a fire burning against a wall, and one standing by it, always casting much water upon it, to quench it; yet did the fire burn higher and hotter.

Then said Christian, What means this?

The Interpreter answered, This fire is the work of grace that is wrought in the heart; he that casts water upon it, to extinguish it and put it out, is the Devil; but in that thou seest the fire notwithstanding burn higher and hotter, thou shalt also see the reason of that. So he had him about to the backside of the wall, where he saw a man with a vessel of oil in his hand, of the which he did also continually cast, but secretly, into the fire.

Then said Christian, What means this?

The Interpreter answered, This is Christ, who continually with the oil of his grace, maintains the work already begun in the heart: by the means of which, notwithstanding what the devil can do, the souls of his people prove gracious still.[57] And in that thou sawest that the man stood behind the wall to maintain the fire, that is to teach thee that it is hard for the tempted to see how this work of grace is maintained in the soul.

I saw also, that the Interpreter took him again by the hand, and led him into a pleasant place, where was builded a stately palace, beautiful to behold; at the sight of which Christian was greatly delighted. He saw also, upon the top thereof, certain persons walking, who were clothed all in gold.

Then said Christian, May we go in thither?

Then the Interpreter took him, and led him up towards the door of the palace; and behold, at the door stood a great company of men, as desirous to go in, but durst not. There also sat a man at a little distance from the door, at a table-side, with a book and his inkhorn before him, to take the name of him that should enter therein; he saw also that in the door-way stood many men in armor to keep it, being resolved to do the men that would enter what hurt and mischief they could.

Now was Christian somewhat in amaze. At last, when every man started back for fear of the armed men, Christian saw a man of a very stout countenance come up to the man that sat there to write, saying, Set down my name, Sir: the which when he had done, he saw the man draw his sword, and put an helmet upon his head, and rush toward the door upon the armed men, who laid upon him with deadly force; but the man not at all discouraged, fell to cutting and hacking most fiercely.

So after he had received and given many wounds to those that attempted to keep him out, he cut his way through them all,[58] and pressed forward into the palace, at which there was a pleasant voice heard from those that were within, even of those that walked upon the top of the palace, saying—

"Come in, come in,
Eternal glory thou shalt win."

So he went in, and was clothed with such garments as they. Then Christian smiled and said, I think verily I know the meaning of this.

Now, said Christian, let me go hence. Nay, stay, said the Interpreter, till I have showed thee a little more, and after that thou shalt go on thy

THE MAN OF STOUT COUNTENANCE FIGHTS HIS WAY INTO THE PALACE.

way. So he took him by the hand again, and led him into a very dark room, where there sat a man in an iron cage.

Now the man, to look on, seemed very sad; he sat with his eyes looking down to the ground, his hands folded together, and he sighed as if he would break his heart. Then said Christian, What means this? At which the Interpreter bid him talk with the man.

Then said Christian to the man, What art thou? The man answered, I am what I was not once.

CHR. What wast thou once?

MAN. The man said, I was once a fair and flourishing professor, both in mine own eyes, and also in the eyes of others ; I once was, as I thought, fair for the Celestial City, and had then even joy at the thoughts that I should get thither.[59]

CHR. Well, but what art thou now?

THE MAN IN THE CAGE.

MAN. I am now a man of Despair, and am shut up in it, as in this iron cage. I cannot get out. Oh, now I cannot !

CHR. But how camest thou in this condition?

MAN. I left off to watch and be sober ; I laid the reins upon the neck of my lusts ; I sinned against the light of the Word and the goodness of God; I have grieved the Spirit, and he is gone; I tempted the devil, and he is come to me; I have provoked God to anger, and he has left me: I have so hardened my heart, that I cannot repent.

Then said Christian to the Interpreter, But is there no hope for such a man as this? Ask him, said the Interpreter. Nay, said Christian, pray, Sir, do you.

INTER. Then said the Interpreter, Is there no hope, but you must be kept in the iron cage of despair?

MAN. No, none at all.

INTER. Why, the Son of the Blessed is very pitiful.

MAN. I have crucified him to myself afresh;[60] I have despised his person;[61] I have despised his righteousness; I have "counted his blood an unholy thing;" I have "done despite to the Spirit of Grace."[62] Therefore I have shut myself out of all the promises, and there now remains to me nothing but threatenings, dreadful threatenings, fearful threatenings of certain judgment and fiery indignation, which shall devour me as an adversary.

INTER. For what did you bring yourself into this condition?

MAN. For the lusts, pleasures, and profits of this world; in the enjoyment of which I did then promise myself much delight; but now every one of those things also bite me, and gnaw me like a burning worm.

INTER. But canst thou not now repent and turn?

MAN. God hath denied me repentance. His Word gives me no encouragement to believe; yea, himself hath shut me up in this iron cage; nor can all the men in the world let me out. Oh eternity! eternity! how shall I grapple with the misery that I must meet with in eternity!

INTER. Then said the Interpreter to Christian, Let this man's misery be remembered by thee, and be an everlasting caution to thee.

CHR. Well, said Christian, this is fearful! God help me to watch and be sober, and to pray that I may shun the cause of this man's misery! Sir, is it not time for me to go on my way now?

INTER. Tarry till I shall show thee one thing more, and then thou shalt go on thy way.

So he took Christian by the hand again, and led him into a chamber, where there was one rising out of bed; and as he put on his raiment, he shook and trembled. Then said Christian, Why doth this man thus tremble? The Interpreter then bid him tell to Christian the reason of his so doing. So he began and said, This night, as I was in my sleep, I dreamed, and behold the heavens grew exceeding black; also it thundered and lightened in most fearful wise, that it put me into an agony; so I looked up in my dream, and saw the clouds rack at an unusual rate, upon which I heard a great sound of a trumpet, and saw also a man sit upon a cloud, attended with the thousands of heaven; they were all in flaming fire: also the heavens were in a burning flame.

I heard then a voice saying, "Arise, ye dead, and come to judgment;" and with that the rocks rent, the graves opened, and the dead that were therein came forth. Some of them were exceeding glad, and looked upward; and some sought to hide themselves under the mountains.[63] Then I saw the man that sat upon the cloud open the book and bid the world draw near. Yet there was, by reason of a fierce flame which issued out and came from before him, a convenient distance betwixt him and them, as betwixt the judge and the prisoners at the bar.[64]

I heard it also proclaimed to them that attended on the man that sat on the cloud, "Gather together the tares, the chaff, and stubble, and cast them into the burning lake."[65] And with that, the bottomless pit opened, just whereabout I stood; out of the mouth of which there came, in an abundant manner, smoke and coals of fire, with hideous noises.

THE MAN DREAMS.

It was also said to the same persons, "Gather my wheat into the garner."[66] And with that I saw many catched up and carried away into the clouds, but I was left behind.[67] I also sought to hide myself, but I could not, for the man that sat upon the cloud still kept his eye upon me: my sins also came into my mind; and my conscience did accuse me on every side.[68] Upon this I awaked from my sleep.

CHR. But what was it that made you so afraid of this sight?

MAN. Why, I thought that the day of judgment was come, and that I was not ready for it: but this frighted me most, that the angels gathered up several, and left me behind; also the pit of hell opened her mouth just where I stood. My conscience, too, afflicted me; and, as I thought, the Judge had always his eye upon me showing indignation in his countenance.

Then said the Interpreter to Christian, Hast thou considered all these things?

CHR. Yes, and they put me in hope and fear.

INTER. Well, keep all things so in thy mind that they may be as a goad in thy sides, to prick thee forward in the way thou must go. Then Christian began to gird up his loins, and to address himself to his journey. Then said the Interpreter, The Comforter be always with thee, good Christian, to guide thee in the way that leads to the City. So Christian went on his way, saying—

> "Here I have seen things rare and profitable;
> Things pleasant, dreadful, things to make me stable
> In what I have begun to take in hand;
> Then let me think on them, and understand
> Wherefore they showed me were, and let me be
> Thankful, O good Interpreter, to thee."

CHAPTER III.

NOW I saw in my dream, that the highway up which Christian was to go, was fenced on either side with a wall, and that wall was called Salvation.[69] Up this way therefore did burdened Christian run, but not without great difficulty, because of the load on his back.

He ran thus till he came at a place somewhat ascending, and upon that place stood a cross, and a little below, in the bottom, a sepulchre. So I saw in my dream, that just as Christian came up with the cross, his burden loosened from off his shoulders, and fell from off his back, and began to tumble, and so continued to do, till it came to the mouth of the sepulchre, where it fell in, and I saw it no more.

Then was Christian glad and lightsome, and

CHRISTIAN'S BURDEN FALLS OFF.

said, with a merry heart, He hath given me rest by his sorrow, and life by his death. Then he stood still awhile to look and wonder; for it was very

91

surprising to him that the sight of the cross should thus ease him of his burden. He looked therefore, and looked again, even till the springs that were in his head sent the waters down his cheeks.[70]

Now, as he stood looking and weeping, behold three Shining Ones came to him and saluted him with Peace be to thee. So the first said to him, Thy sins be forgiven thee;[71] the second stripped him of his rags, and clothed him with change of raiment;[72] the third also set a mark on his forehead, and gave him a roll with a seal upon it, which he bade him look on as he ran, and that he should give it in at the Celestial Gate.[73] So they went their way.

Then Christian gave three leaps for joy, and went on singing—

> "Thus far I did come laden with my sin ;
> Nor could aught ease the grief that I was in
> Till I came hither : What a place is this !
> Must here be the beginning of my bliss?
> Must here the burden fall from off my back ?
> Must here the strings that bound it to me crack ?
> Blest cross ! blest sepulchre ! blest rather be
> The Man that there was put to shame for me !"

I saw then in my dream, that he went on thus, even until he came at a bottom, where he saw, a little out of the way, three men fast asleep, with fetters upon their heels. The name of the one was Simple, another Sloth, and the third Presumption.

Christian then seeing them lie in this case went to them, if peradventure he might awake them, and cried, You are like them that sleep on the top of a mast, for the Dead Sea is under you—a gulf that hath no bottom.[74] Awake, therefore, and come away; be willing also, and I will help you off with your irons. He also told them, If he that goeth about like a roaring lion comes by, you will certainly become a prey to his teeth.[75] With that they looked upon him, and began to reply in this sort : Simple said, I see no danger; Sloth said, Yet a little more sleep; and Presumption said, Every vat must stand upon its own bottom; what is the answer else that I should give thee? And so they lay down to sleep again, and Christian went on his way.

Yet was he troubled to think that men in that danger should so little esteem the kindness of him that so freely offered to help them, both by awakening of them, counselling of them, and proffering to help them off with their irons. And as he was troubled thereabout, he espied two men come tumbling over the wall, on the left hand of the narrow way; and they made up apace to him. The name of the one was Formalist, and

THE THREE SHINING ONES.

the name of the other Hypocrisy. So, as I said, they drew up unto him,
who thus entered with them into discourse.

Chr. Gentlemen, whence came you, and whither go you?

Form. and Hyp. We were born in the land of Vainglory, and are going for praise to Mount Zion.

Chr. Why came you not in at the gate which standeth at the beginning of the way? Know you not that it is written, that he that cometh not in by the door, but climbeth up some other way, the same is a thief and a robber?[76]

FORMALIST AND HYPOCRISY COMING INTO THE WAY OVER THE WALL.

Form. and Hyp. They said, That to go to the gate for entrance was, by all their countrymen, counted too far about; and that, therefore, their usual way was to make a short cut of it, and to climb over the wall, as they had done.

Chr. But will it not be counted a trespass against the Lord of the city whither we are bound, thus to violate his revealed will?

Form. and Hyp. They told him, that, as for that, he needed not to trouble his head thereabout; for what they did they had custom for; and could produce, if need were, testimony that would witness it for more than a thousand years.

CHR. But, said Christian, will your practice stand a trial at law?

FORM. and HYP. They told him, That custom, it being of so long a standing as above a thousand years, would, doubtless, now be admitted as a thing legal by any impartial judge; and beside, said they, if we get into the way, what matter is it which way we get in? if we are in, we are in; thou art but in the way, who, as we perceive, came in at the gate; and we are also in the way, that came tumbling over the wall; wherein, now, is thy condition better than ours?

CHR. I walk by the rule of my Master; you walk by the rude working of your fancies. You are counted thieves already, by the Lord of the way; therefore, I doubt you will not be found true men at the end of the way. You come in by yourselves, without his direction; and shall go out by yourselves, without his mercy.

To this they made him but little answer; only they bid him look to himself. Then I saw that they went on every man in his way, without much conference one with another; save that these two men told Christian, that as to laws and ordinances, they doubted not but they should as conscientiously do them as he; therefore, said they, we see not wherein thou differest from us but by the coat that is on thy back, which was, as we trow, given thee by some of thy neighbors, to hide the shame of thy nakedness.

CHR. By laws and ordinances you will not be saved, since you came not in by the door.[77] And as for this coat that is on my back, it was given me by the Lord of the place whither I go; and that, as you say, to cover my nakedness with. And I take it as a token of his kindness to me; for I had nothing but rags before. And besides, thus I comfort myself as I go: Surely, think I, when I come to the gate of the city, the Lord thereof will know me for good, since I have his coat on my back—a coat that he gave me freely in the day that he stripped me of my rags. I have, moreover, a mark in my forehead, of which, perhaps, you have taken no notice, which one of my Lord's most intimate associates fixed there in the day that my burden fell off my shoulders. I will tell you, moreover, that I had then given me a roll, sealed, to comfort me by reading as I go on the way; I was also bid to give it in at the Celestial Gate, in token of my certain going in after it; all which things, I doubt, you want, and want them because you came not in at the gate.

FORMALIST.

To these things they gave him no answer; only they looked upon each other, and laughed. Then I saw that they went on all, save that

HYPOCRISY.

Christian kept before, who had no more talk but with himself, and that
sometimes sighingly, and sometimes comfortably ; also he would be often

7

reading in the roll that one of the Shining Ones gave him, by which he
was refreshed.

I beheld, then, that they all went on till they came to the foot of the
Hill Difficulty; at the bottom of which was a spring.   There were also

CHRISTIAN CLIMBING THE HILL DIFFICULTY.

in the same place two other ways besides that which came straight from
the gate; one turned to the left hand, and the other to the right, at the
bottom of the hill; but the narrow way lay right up the hill, and the

name of the going up the side of the hill is called Difficulty. Christian
now went to the spring, and drank thereof, to refresh himself,[78] and then
began to go up the hill, saying—

> "The hill, though high, I covet to ascend,
>   The difficulty will not me offend ;
>   For I perceive the way to life lies here.
>   Come, pluck up heart, let's neither faint nor fear ;
>   Better, though difficult, the right way to go,
>   Than wrong, though easy, where the end is woe."

The other two also came to the foot of the hill; but when they saw
that the hill was steep and high, and that there were two other ways to
go; and supposing also that these two ways might meet again, with that
up which Christian went, on the other side of the hill : therefore they
were resolved to go in those ways.

Now the name of one of those ways was Danger, and the name of the
other Destruction. So the one took the way which is called Danger,
which led him into a great wood, and the other took directly up the way
to Destruction, which led him into a wide field, full of dark mountains,
where he stumbled and fell and rose no more.

I looked, then, after Christian, to see him go up the hill, where I perceived he fell from running to going, and from going to clambering upon
his hands and his knees, because of the steepness of the place. Now,
about the midway to the top of the hill was a pleasant arbor, made by
the Lord of the hill for the refreshing of weary travellers; thither, therefore, Christian got, where also he sat down to rest him. Then he pulled
his roll out of his bosom, and read therein to his comfort; he also now
began to take a review of the coat or garment that was given him as he
stood by the cross.

Thus pleasing himself a while, he at last fell into a slumber, and
thence into a fast sleep, which detained him in that place until it was
almost night ; and in his sleep his roll fell out of his hand. Now, as
he was sleeping there came one to him, and awaked him, saying, "Go
to the ant, thou sluggard; consider her ways and be wise."[79] And with
that Christian started up, and sped him on his way, and went apace, till
he came to the top of the hill.

Now, when he was got up to the top of the hill, there came two men
coming to meet him amain; the name of the one was Timorous, and of the
other, Mistrust; to whom Christian said, Sirs, what's the matter ? You

run the wrong way. Timorous answered, that they were going to the City of Zion, and had got up that difficult place; but, said he, the further we go the more danger we meet with; wherefore we turned, and are going back again.

Yes, said Mistrust, for just before us lie a couple of lions in the way, whether sleeping or waking we know not, and we could not think, if we came within reach, but they would presently pull us in pieces.

TIMOROUS AND MISTRUST.

CHR. Then said Christian, You make me afraid, but whither shall I fly to be safe? if I go back to mine own country, *that* is prepared for fire and brimstone, and I shall certainly perish there. If I can get to the Celestial City, I am sure to be in safety there. I must venture. To go back is nothing but death; to go forward is fear of death, and life everlasting beyond it. I will yet go forward. So Mistrust and Timorous ran down the hill, and Christian went on his way. But, thinking again of what he

CHRISTIAN MEETS MISTRUST AND TIMOROUS.

had heard from the men, he felt in his bosom for his roll, that he might read therein, and be comforted; but he felt, and found it not. Then was Christian in great distress, and knew not what to do; for he wanted that which used to relieve him, and that which should have been his pass into the Celestial City. Here, therefore, he began to be much perplexed, and knew not what to do.

At last he bethought himself that he had slept in the arbor that is on the side of the hill; and, falling down upon his knees, he asked God's forgiveness for that his foolish act, and then went back to look for his roll. But all the way he went back, who can sufficiently set forth the sorrow of Christian's heart? Sometimes he sighed, sometimes he wept, and oftentimes he chid himself for being so foolish to fall asleep in that place, which was erected only for a little refreshment for his weariness. Thus, therefore, he went back, carefully looking on this side and on that, all the way as he went, if happily he might find his roll, that had been his comfort so many times in his journey.

He went thus, till he came again within sight of the arbor where he sat and slept; but that sight renewed his sorrow the more, by bringing again, even afresh, his evil of sleeping into his mind.[80] Thus, therefore, he now went on bewailing his sinful sleep, saying, "O wretched man that I am!" that I should sleep in the day-time! that I should sleep in the midst of difficulty! that I should so indulge the flesh, as to use that rest for ease to my flesh which the Lord of the hill hath erected only for the relief of the spirits of pilgrims!

How many steps have I took in vain! Thus it happened to Israel, for their sin; they were sent back again by the way of the Red Sea; and I am made to tread those steps with sorrow, which might I have trod with delight, had it not been for this sinful sleep. How far might I have been on my way by this time! I am made to tread those steps thrice over, which I needed not to have trod but once; yea, now also I am like to be benighted, for the day is almost spent. Oh, that I had not slept!

Now, by this time he was come to the arbor again, where for a while he sat down and wept; but at last, as Christian would have it, looking sorrowfully down under the settle, there he espied his roll; the which he, with trembling and haste, catched up, and put it into his bosom. But who can tell how joyful this man was when he had gotten his roll again! for this roll was the assurance of his life and acceptance at the desired haven. Therefore he laid it up in his bosom, gave thanks to God for directing his

CHRISTIAN PASSES THE LIONS.

103

eye to the place where it lay, and with joy and tears betook himself again to his journey. But oh, how nimbly now did he go up the rest of the hill! Yet, before he got up, the sun went down upon Christian; and this made him again recall the vanity of his sleeping to his remembrance; and thus he again began to condole with himself. O thou sinful sleep: how for thy sake am I like to be benighted in my journey! I must walk without the sun; darkness must cover the path of my feet; and I must hear the noise of the doleful creatures, because of my sinful sleep.[81] Now also he remembered the story that Mistrust and Timorous told him of, how they were frighted with the sight of the lions. Then said Christian to himself again, These beasts range in the night for their prey; and if they should meet with me in the dark, how should I shift them? How should I escape being by them torn in pieces? Thus he went on his way. But while he was thus bewailing his unhappy miscarriage, he lift up his eyes, and behold there was a very stately palace before him, the name of which was Beautiful; and it stood just by the highway side.

So I saw in my dream that he made haste and went forward, that if possible he might get lodging there. Now, before he had gone far, he entered into a very narrow passage, which was about a furlong off of the porter's lodge; and looking very narrowly before him as he went, he espied two lions in the way. Now, thought he, I see the dangers that Mistrust and Timorous were driven back by. (The lions were chained, but he saw not the chains.) Then he was afraid, and thought also himself to go back after them, for he thought nothing but death was before him. But the Porter at the lodge, whose name is Watchful, perceiving that Christian made a halt as if he would go back, cried unto him, saying, Is thy strength so small?[82] Fear not the lions, for they are chained, and are placed there for trial of faith, where it is, and for discovery of those that have none. Keep in the midst of the path, and no hurt shall come unto thee.

Then I saw that he went on, trembling for fear of the lions, but taking good heed to the directions of the porter; he heard them roar, but they did him no harm. Then he clapped his hands, and went on till he came and stood before the gate where the porter was. Then said Christian to the porter, Sir, what house is this? And may I lodge here tonight? The porter answered, This house was built by the Lord of the hill, and he built it for the relief and security of pilgrims. The porter also asked whence he was, and whither he was going.

CHR. I am come from the City of Destruction, and am going to Mount Zion; but because the sun is now set, I desire, if I may, to lodge here to-night.

CHRISTIAN IS ASKED ABOUT HIS JOURNEY.

POR. What is your name?

CHR. My name is now Christian, but my name at the first was Graceless; I came of the race of Japheth, whom God will persuade to dwell in the tents of Shem.[83]

Por. But how doth it happen that you come so late? The sun is set.

Chr. I had been here sooner, but that, "wretched man that I am!" I slept in the arbor that stands on the hill-side; nay, I had, notwithstanding that, been here much sooner, but that, in my sleep, I lost my evidence, and came without it to the brow of the hill; and then feeling for it, and finding it not, I was forced, with sorrow of heart, to go back to the place where I slept my sleep, where I found it, and now I am come.

Por. Well, I will call out one of the virgins of this place, who will, if she likes your talk, bring you in to the rest of the family, according to the rules of the house. So Watchful, the porter, rang a bell, at the sound of which came out at the door of the house, a grave and beautiful damsel, named Discretion, and asked why she was called.

The Porter answered, This man is on a journey from the City of Destruction to Mount Zion, but being weary and benighted, he asked me if he might lodge here to-night; so I told him I would call for thee, who, after discourse had with him, mayest do as seemeth thee good, even according to the law of the house.

Then she asked him whence he was, and whither he was going; and he told her. She asked him also how he got into the way; and he told her. Then she asked him what he had seen and met with in the way; and he told her. And last she asked his name; so he said, It is Christian, and I have so much the more a desire to lodge here to-night, because, by what I perceive, this place was built by the Lord of the hill, for the relief and security of Pilgrims. So she smiled, but the water stood in her eyes; and after a little pause, she said, I will call forth two or three more of the family. So she ran to the door, and called out Prudence, Piety, and Charity, who, after a little more discourse with him, had him into the family; and many of them, meeting him at the threshold of the house, said, "Come in, thou blessed of the Lord;" this house was built by the Lord of the hill, on purpose to entertain such pilgrims in. Then he bowed his head, and followed them into the house. So when he was come in and sat down, they gave him something to drink, and consented together, that until supper was ready, some of them should have some particular discourse with Christian, for the best improvement of time; and they appointed Piety, and Prudence, and Charity to discourse with him; and thus they began:

Piety. Come, good Christian, since we have been so loving to you, to receive you in our house this night, let us, if perhaps we may better

THE PORTER CALLS DISCRETION TO THE DOOR OF THE PALACE.

ourselves thereby, talk with you of all things that have happened to you in your pilgrimage.

CHR. With a very good will, and I am glad that you are so well disposed.

PIETY. What moved you at first to betake yourself to a pilgrim's life?

CHR. I was driven out of my native country, by a dreadful sound that was in mine ears: to wit, that unavoidable destruction did attend me, if I abode in that place where I was.

PIETY. But how did it happen that you came out of your country this way?

CHR. It was as God would have it; for when I was under the fears of destruction, I did not know whither to go ; but by chance there came a man even to me, as I was trembling and weeping, whose name is Evangelist, and he directed me to the wicket-gate, which else I should never have found, and so set me into the way that hath led me directly to this house.

PIETY. But did you not come by the house of the Interpreter?

CHR. Yes, and did see such things there, the remembrance of which will stick by me as long as I live; especially three things: to wit, how Christ in despite of Satan maintains his work of grace in the heart; how the man had sinned himself quite out of hopes of God's mercy; and also the dream of him that thought in his sleep the day of judgment was come.

PIETY. Why, did you hear him tell his dream?

CHR. Yes, and a dreadful one it was. I thought it made my heart ache as he was telling of it ; but yet I am glad I heard it.

PIETY. Was that all that you saw at the house of the Interpreter?

CHR. No; he took me and had me where he showed me a stately palace, and how the people were clad in gold that were in it; and how there came a venturous man and cut his way through the armed men that stood in the door to keep him out, and how he was bid to come in, and win eternal glory. Methought those things did ravish my heart! I would have stayed at that good man's house a twelvemonth, but that I knew I had further to go.

PIETY. And what saw you else in the way?

CHR. Saw! why, I went but a little further, and I saw one, as I thought in my mind, hang bleeding upon the tree; and the very sight of him made my burden fall from my back (for I groaned under a very heavy burden), but then it fell down from off me.   It was a strange thing to me, for I never saw such a thing before; yea, and while I stood looking up, for then I could not forbear looking, three Shining Ones came to me.

One of them testified that my sins were forgiven me; another stripped me of my rags, and gave me this broidered coat which you see; and the third set the mark which you see in my forehead, and gave me this sealed roll.   (And with that he plucked it out of his bosom.)

PIETY. But you saw more than this, did you not?

CHR. The things that I have told you were the best; yet some other matters I saw, as, namely: I saw three men, Simple, Sloth, and Presumption, lie asleep a little out of the way, as I came, with irons upon their heels; but do you think I could awake them?   I also saw Formality and Hypocrisy come tumbling over the wall, to go, as they pretended, to Zion, but they were quickly lost, even as I myself did tell them; but they would not believe.

But above all, I found it hard work to get up this hill, and as hard to come by the lions' mouths; and truly, if it had not been for the good man, the porter that stands at the gate, I do not know but that after all I might have gone back again; but now, I thank God I am here, and I thank you for receiving of me.

Then Prudence thought good to ask him a few questions, and desired his answer to them.

PRUD. Do you not think sometimes of the country from whence you came?

CHR. Yes, but with such shame and detestation: "truly, if I had been mindful of that *country* from whence I came out, I might have had an opportunity to have returned; but now I desire a better country, that is, an heavenly."[84]

PRUD. Do you not yet bear away with you some of the things that then you were conversant withal?

CHR. Yes, but greatly against my will; especially my inward and carnal cogitations, with which all my countrymen, as well as myself, were delighted; but now all those things are my grief; and might I but choose mine own things, I would choose never to think of those things more; but when I would be doing that of which is best, that which is worst is with me.[85]

PRUD. Do you not find sometimes as if those things were vanquished, which at other times are your perplexity?

CHRISTIAN ENTERS THE PALACE CALLED BEAUTIFUL.

CHR. Yes, but that is seldom; but they are to me golden hours in which such things happen to me.

PRUD. Can you remember by what means you find your annoyances, at times, as if they were vanquished?

CHR. Yes, when I think what I saw at the cross, that will do it; and

CHRISTIAN IS INSTRUCTED AT THE PALACE BEAUTIFUL.

when I look upon my broidered coat, that will do it; also when I look into the roll that I carry in my bosom, that will do it; and when my thoughts wax warm about whither I am going, that will do it.

PRUD. And what is it that makes you so desirous to go to Mount Zion?

CHR. Why, there I hope to see him alive that did hang dead on the cross; and there I hope to be rid of all those things that to this day are in me an annoyance to me; there, they say, there is no death;[86] and there I shall dwell with such company as I like best.[87] For, to tell you truth, I love him, because I was by him eased of my burden; and I am weary of my inward sickness. I would fain be where I shall die no more, and with the company that shall continually cry, "Holy, Holy, Holy!"

Then said Charity to Christian, have you a family? Are you a married man?

CHR. I have a wife and four small children.

CHAR. And why did you not bring them along with you?

CHR. Then Christian wept, and said, Oh, how willingly would I have done it! but they were all of them utterly averse to my going on pilgrimage.

CHAR. But you should have talked to them, and have endeavored to have shown them the danger of being behind.

CHR. So I did; and told them also what God had shown to me of the destruction of our city; "But I seemed to them as one that mocked," and they believed me not.[88]

CHAR. And did you pray to God that he would bless your counsel to them?

CHR. Yes, and that with much affection: for you must think that my wife and poor children were very dear unto me.

CHAR. But did you tell them of your own sorrow, and fear of destruction? for I suppose that destruction was visible enough to you.

CHR. Yes, over, and over, and over. They might also see my fears in my countenance, in my tears, and also in my trembling under the apprehension of the judgment that did hang over our heads; but all was not sufficient to prevail with them to come with me.

CHAR. But what could they say for themselves, why they came not?

CHR. Why, my wife was afraid of losing this world, and my children were given to the foolish delights of youth: so what by one thing, and what by another, they left me to wander in this manner alone.

CHAR. But did you not, with your vain life, damp all that you by words used by way of persuasion to bring them away with you?

CHR. Indeed, I cannot commend my life; for I am conscious to myself of many failings therein: I know also, that a man by his conversation may soon overthrow what by argument or persuasion he doth labor **to** fasten upon others for their good. Yet this I can say, I was very wary of giving them occasion, by any unseemly action, to make them averse to going on pilgrimage. Yea, for this very thing they would tell me I was too precise, and that I denied myself of things, for their sakes, in which they saw no evil. Nay, I think I may say, that if what they saw in me did hinder them, it was my great tenderness in sinning against God, or of doing any wrong to my neighbor.

CHAR. Indeed Cain hated his brother, "because his own works were evil, and his brother's righteous";[89] and if thy wife and children have been offended with thee for this, they thereby show themselves to be implacable to good, and "thou hast delivered thy soul from their blood".[90]

Now I saw in my dream, that thus they sat talking together until supper was ready. So when they had made ready, they sat down to meat. Now the table was furnished "with fat things, and with wine that was well refined:" and all their talk at the table was about the Lord of the hill; as, namely, about what he had done, and wherefore he did what he did, and why he had builded that house. And by what they said, I perceived that he had been a great warrior, and had fought with and slain "him that had the power of death," but not without great danger to himself, which made me love him the more.[91]

For, as they said, and as I believe (said Christian), he did it with the loss of much blood; but that which put glory of grace into all he did, was, that he did it out of pure love to his country. And besides, there were some of them of the household that said they had been and spoke with him since he did die on the cross; and they have attested that they had it from his own lips, that he is such a lover of poor pilgrims, that the like is not to be found from the east to the west.

They, moreover, gave an instance of what they affirmed, and that was, he had stripped himself of his glory, that he might do this for the poor; and that they heard him say and affirm, "that he would not dwell in the mountain of Zion alone." They said, moreover, that he had made many pilgrims princes, though by nature they were beggars born, and their original had been the dunghill.[92]

Thus they discoursed together till late at night; and after they had committed themselves to their Lord for protection, they betook themselves to rest: the Pilgrim they laid in a large upper chamber, whose window opened toward the sun-rising: the name of the chamber was Peace; where he slept till break of day, and then he awoke and sang—

8

"Where am I now? Is this the love and care
Of Jesus for the men that pilgrims are?
Thus to provide! that I should be forgiven!
And dwell already the next door to heaven!"

So in the morning they all got up: and, after some more discourse, they told him that he should not depart till they had shown him the rarities of that place. And first they had him into the study, where they showed him records of the greatest antiquity; in which, as I remember my dream, they showed him first the pedigree of the Lord of the hill, that he was the son of the Ancient of Days, and came by that eternal generation. Here also was more fully recorded the acts that he had done, and the names of many hundreds that he had taken into his service; and how he had placed them in such habitations, that could neither by length of days, nor decays of nature, be dissolved.

Then they read to him some of the worthy acts that some of his servants had done: as, how they had "subdued kingdoms, wrought righteousness, obtained promises, stopped the mouths of lions, quenched the violence of fire, escaped the edge of the sword, out of weakness were made strong, waxed valiant in fight, and turned to flight the armies of the aliens." [93]

Then they read again, in another part of the records of the house, where it was showed how willing their Lord was to receive into his favor any, even any, though they in time past had offered great affronts to his person and proceedings. Here also were several other histories of many other famous things of all which Christian had a view; as of things both ancient and modern; together with prophecies and predictions of things that have their certain accomplishment, both to the dread and amazement of enemies, and the comfort and solace of pilgrims.

The next day they took him and had him into the armory, where they showed him all manner of furniture, which their Lord had provided for pilgrims, as sword, shield, helmet, breast-plate, *all-prayer*, and shoes that would not wear out. And there was here enough of this to harness out as many men for the service of their Lord as there be stars in the heaven for multitude.

They also showed him some of the engines with which some of his servants had done wonderful things. They showed him Moses' rod; the hammer and nail with which Jael slew Sisera; the pitchers, trumpets, and lamps too, with which Gideon put to flight the armies of Midian.

THEY READ TO CHRISTIAN SOME OF THE WORTHY ACTS THAT SOME OF HIS SERVANTS HAD DONE.

Then they showed him the ox's goad wherewith Shamgar slew six hundred men. They showed him also the jaw-bone with which Samson did such mighty feats. They showed him, moreover, the sling and stone with which David slew Goliath of Gath; and the sword, also, with which their Lord will kill the Man of Sin, in the day that he shall rise up to the prey. They showed him, besides, many excellent things, with which Christian was much delighted. This done, they went to their rest again.

Then I saw in my dream, that on the morrow he got up to go forward; but they desired him to stay till the next day also; and then, said they, we will, if the day be clear, show you the Delectable Mountains, which, they said, would yet further add to his comfort, because they were nearer the desired haven than the place where at present he was; so he consented and stayed.

When the morning was up, they had him to the top of the house, and bid him look south; so he did: and behold, at a great distance, he saw a most pleasant mountainous country, beautified with woods, vineyards, fruits of all sorts, flowers also, with springs and fountains, very delectable to behold.[94] Then he asked the name of the country. They said it was Immanuel's Land; and it is as common, said they, as this hill is, to and for all the pilgrims. And when thou comest there, from thence, said they, thou mayest see to the gate of the Celestial City, as the shepherds that live there will make appear.

Now he bethought himself of setting forward, and they were willing he should. But first, said they, let us go again into the armory. So they did; and when they came there, they harnessed him from head to foot with what was of proof, lest, perhaps, he should meet with assaults in the way. He being, therefore, thus accoutred, walketh out with his friends to the gate, and there he asked the porter if he saw any pilgrims pass by. Then the porter answered, Yes.

CHR. Pray, did you know him, said he.

POR. I asked him his name, and he told me it was Faithful.

CHR. Oh, said Christian, I know him; he is my townsman, my near neighbor; he comes from the place where I was born. How far do you think he may be before?

POR. He is got by this time below the hill.

CHR. Well, said Christian, good Porter, the Lord be with thee, and add to all thy blessings much increase for the kindness that thou hast showed to me.

CHRISTIAN GOES DOWN INTO THE VALLEY OF HUMILIATION.

CHAPTER IV.

THEN he began to go forward; but Discretion, Piety, Charity, and Prudence would accompany him down to the foot of the hill. So they went on together, reiterating their former discourses, till they came to go down the hill. Then said Christian, As it was difficult coming up, so, so far as I can see, it is dangerous going down.

Yes, said Prudence, so it is, for it is a hard matter for a man to go down into the Valley of Humiliation, as thou art now, and to catch no slip by the way; therefore, said they, are we come out to accompany thee down the hill. So he began to go down, but very warily; yet he caught a slip or two.

Then I saw in my dream that these good companions, when Christian was gone to the bottom of the hill, gave him a loaf of bread, a bottle of wine, and a cluster of raisins; and then he went on his way.

But now, in this Valley of Humiliation, poor Christian was hard put to it; for he had gone but a little way before he espied a foul fiend coming over the field to meet him; his name is Apollyon.

Then did Christian begin to be afraid, and to cast in his mind whether to go back or to stand his ground. But he considered again that he had no armor for his back; and therefore thought that to turn the back to him might give him the greater advantage with ease to pierce him with his darts. Therefore he resolved to venture and stand his ground; for, thought he, had I no more in mine eye than the saving of my life, it would be the best way to stand.

So he went on, and Apollyon met him. Now the monster was hideous to behold; he was clothed with scales, like a fish (and they are his pride), he had wings like a dragon, feet like a bear, and out of his belly came fire and smoke, and his mouth was as the mouth of a lion. When he was come up to Christian, he beheld him with a disdainful countenance, and thus began to question him.

Apol. Whence come you? and whither are you bound?

Chr. I am come from the City of Destruction, which is the place of all evil, and am going to the City of Zion.

Apol. By this I perceive thou art one of my subjects, for all that country is mine, and I am the prince and god of it. How is it, then, that thou hast run away from thy king? Were it not that I hope thou mayest do me more service, I would strike thee now, at one blow, to the ground.

Chr. I was born, indeed, in your dominions, but your service was hard, and your wages such as a man could not live on, "for the wages of sin *is* death;"[95] therefore when I was come to years, I did as other considerate persons do, look out, if, perhaps, I might mend myself.

Apol. There is no prince that will thus lightly lose his subjects, neither will I as yet lose thee; but since thou complainest of thy service and wages, be content to go back; what our country will afford, I do here promise to give thee.

Chr. But I have let myself to another; even to the King of Princes; and how can I, with fairness, go back with thee?

Apol. Thou hast done in this according to the proverb, "Changed a bad for worse;" but it is ordinary for those that have professed themselves his servants, after a while to give him the slip, and return again to me. Do thou so too, and all shall be well.

CHR. I have given him my faith, and sworn my allegiance to him; how, then, can I go back from this, and not be hanged as a traitor?

APOL. Thou didst the same to me, and yet I am willing to pass by all, if now thou wilt yet turn again and go back.

CHR. What I promised thee was in my nonage;* and,   *Youth. besides, I count the Prince under whose banner now I stand is able to absolve me; yea, and to pardon also what I did as to my compliance with thee; and, besides, O thou destroying Apollyon! to speak truth, I like his service, his wages, his servants, his government, his company and country, better than thine; and, therefore, leave off to persuade me further: I am his servant, and I will follow him.

APOL. Consider, again, when thou art in cool blood, what thou art like to meet with in the way that thou goest. Thou knowest that, for the most part, his servants come to an ill end, because they are transgressors against me and my ways.

How many of them have been put to shameful deaths; and, besides, thou countest his service better than mine, whereas he never came yet from the place where he is to deliver any that served him out of our hands; but as for me, how many times, as all the world very well knows, have I delivered, either by power, or fraud, those that have faithfully served me, from him and his, though taken by them; and so I will deliver thee.

CHR. His forbearing at present to deliver them is on purpose to try their love, whether they will cleave to him to the end; and as for the ill end thou sayest they come to, that is most glorious in their account; for, for present deliverance, they do not much expect it, for they stay for their glory, and then they shall have it, when their Prince comes in his, and the glory of the angels.

APOL. Thou hast already been unfaithful in thy service to him; and how dost thou think to receive wages of him?

CHR. Wherein, O Apollyon! have I been unfaithful to him?

APOL. Thou didst faint at first setting out, when thou wast almost choked in the Gulf of Despond; thou didst attempt wrong ways to be rid of thy burden, whereas thou shouldest have stayed till thy Prince had taken it off; thou didst sinfully sleep and lose thy choice thing; thou wast, also, almost persuaded to go back at the sight of the lions; and when thou talkest of thy journey, and of what thou hast heard and seen, thou art inwardly desirous of vain-glory in all thou sayest or doest.

Chr. All this is true, and much more which thou hast left out; but the Prince whom I serve and honor is merciful, and ready to forgive; but, besides, these infirmities possessed me in thy country, for there I sucked them in; and I have groaned under them, been sorry for them, and have obtained pardon of my Prince.

Apol. Then Apollyon broke out into a grievous rage, saying, I am an enemy to this Prince; I hate his person, his laws, and people; I am come out on purpose to withstand thee.

Chr. Apollyon, beware what you do; for I am in the king's highway, the way of holiness; therefore take heed to yourself.

Apol. Then Apollyon straddled quite over the whole breadth of the way, and said, I am void of fear in this matter; prepare thyself to die; for I swear by my infernal den, that thou shalt go no further; here will I spill thy soul.

And with that he threw a flaming dart at his breast; but Christian had a shield in his hand with which he caught it, and so prevented the danger of that.

Then did Christian draw, for he saw it was time to bestir him: and Apollyon as fast made at him, throwing darts as thick as hail; by the which, notwithstanding all that Christian could do to avoid it, Apollyon wounded him in his head, his hand, and foot.

This made Christian give a little back; Apollyon, therefore, followed his work amain, and Christian again took courage, and resisted as manfully as he could. This sore combat lasted for above half a day, even till Christian was almost quite spent; for you must know that Christian, by reason of his wounds, must needs grow weaker and weaker.

Then Apollyon, espying his opportunity, began to gather up close to Christian, and wrestling with him, gave him a dreadful fall; and with that Christian's sword flew out of his hand.

Then said Apollyon, I am sure of thee now. And with that he had almost pressed him to death, so that Christian began to despair of life: but as God would have it, while Apollyon was fetching of his last blow thereby to make a full end of this good man, Christian nimbly stretched out his hand for his sword, and caught it, saying, "Rejoice not against me, O mine enemy: when I fall I shall arise," [96] and with that gave him a deadly thrust, which made him give back, as one that had received his mortal wound.

Christian perceiving that, made at him again, saying, "Nay, in all these things we are more than conquerors through him that loved us."[97] And with that Apollyon spread forth his dragon's wings, and sped him away, that Christian for a season saw him no more.[98]

CHRISTIAN DEFEATS APOLLYON.

In this combat no man can imagine, unless he had seen and heard as I did, what yelling and hideous roaring Apollyon made all the time of the fight—he spake like a dragon; and on the other side, what sighs and

CHRISTIAN RETURNS THANKS FOR VICTORY.

groans burst from Christian's heart. I never saw him all the while give so much as one pleasant look, till he perceived he had wounded Apollyon with his two-edged sword; then, indeed, he did smile, and look upward; but it was the dreadfullest sight that ever I saw.

So when the battle was over, Christian said, "I will here give thanks to him that delivered me out of the mouth of the lion, to him that did help me against Apollyon." And so he did, saying,—

Great Beelzebub, the captain of this fiend,
Designed my ruin; therefore to this end
He sent him harness'd out: and he with rage
That hellish was, did fiercely me engage.
But blessed Michael helped me, and I,
By dint of sword, did quickly make him fly.
Therefore to him let me give lasting praise,
And thank and bless his holy name always.

Then there came to him a hand, with some of the leaves of the tree of life, the which Christian took, and applied to the wounds that he had received in the battle, and was healed immediately.

He also sat down in that place to eat bread, and to drink of the bottle that was given him a little before; so, being refreshed, he addressed himself to his journey, with his sword drawn in his hand; for he said, I know not but some other enemy may be at hand. But he met with no other affront from Apollyon quite through this valley.

Now, at the end of this valley was another, called the Valley of the Shadow of Death, and Christian must needs go through it, because the way to the Celestial City lay through the midst of it. Now, this valley is a very solitary place. The prophet Jeremiah thus describes it: "A wilderness, a land of deserts and of pits, a land of drought, and of the shadow of death, a land that no man" (but a Christian) "passed through, and where no man dwelt."[99]

Now here Christian was worse put to it than in his fight with Apollyon; as by the sequel you shall see.

I saw then in my dream, that when Christian was got to the borders of the Shadow of Death, there met him two men, children of them that brought up an evil report of the good land,[100] making haste to go back; to whom Christian spake as follows:—

CHR. Whither are you going?

MEN. They said, Back! back! and we would have you to do so too, if either life or peace is prized by you.

CHR. Why, what's the matter? said Christian.

MEN. Matter, said they; we were going that way as you are going, and went as far as we durst; and indeed we were almost past coming back; for had we gone a little further, we had not been here to bring the news to thee.

CHR. But what have you met with? said Christian.

MEN. Why, we were almost in the Valley of the Shadow of Death; but that, by good hap, we looked before us, and saw the danger before we came to it.[101]

CHR. But what have you seen? said Christian.

MEN. Seen! Why, the Valley itself, which is as dark as pitch; we also saw there the hobgoblins, satyrs, and dragons of the pit; we heard also in that Valley a continual howling and yelling, as of a people under unutterable misery, who there sat bound in affliction and irons; and over that Valley hangs the discouraging clouds of confusion. Death also doth always spread his wings over it. In a word, it is every whit dreadful, being utterly without order.[102]

CHR. Then, said Christian, I perceive not yet, by what you have said, but that this is my way to the desired haven.[103]

MEN. Be it thy way; we will not choose it for ours. So they parted, and Christian went on his way, but still with his sword drawn in his hand, for fear lest he should be assaulted.

I saw then in my dream so far as this valley reached, there was on the right hand a very deep ditch; that ditch is it into which the blind have led the blind in all ages, and have both there miserably perished.[104] Again, behold, on the left hand, there was a very dangerous quag, into which, if

THE VALLEY OF THE SHADOW OF DEATH.

even a good man falls, he can find no bottom for his foot to stand on. Into that quag king David once did fall, and had no doubt therein been smothered, had not HE that is able plucked him out.

The pathway was here also exceeding narrow, and therefore good Christian was the more put to it; for when he sought, in the dark, to shun the ditch on the one hand, he was ready to tip over into the mire on the other; also when he sought to escape the mire, without great carefulness he would be ready to fall into the ditch. Thus he went on, and I heard him here sigh bitterly; for, besides the dangers mentioned above, the pathway was here so dark, that ofttimes, when he lift up his foot to set forward, he knew not where or upon what he should set it next.

About the midst of this valley, I perceived the mouth of hell to be, and it stood also hard by the way-side. Now, thought Christian, what shall I do? And ever and anon the flame and smoke would come out in such abundance, with sparks and hideous noises (things that cared not for Christian's sword, as did Apollyon before), that he was forced to put up his sword, and betake himself to another weapon, called All-prayer.[105] So he cried in my hearing, "O Lord, I beseech thee, deliver my soul!"[106]

Thus he went on a great while, yet still the flames would be reaching towards him. Also he heard doleful voices, and rushings to and fro, so that sometimes he thought he should be torn in pieces, or trodden down like mire in the streets. This frightful sight was seen, and these dreadful noises were heard by him for several miles together; and, coming to a place where he thought he heard a company of fiends coming forward to meet him, he stopped, and began to muse what he had best to do.

Sometimes he had half a thought to go back; then again he thought he might be half way through the valley; he remembered also how he had already vanquished many a danger, and that the danger of going back might be much more than for to go forward; so he resolved to go on. Yet the fiends seemed to come nearer and nearer; but when they were come even almost at him, he cried out with a most vehement voice, "I will walk in the strength of the Lord God!" so they gave back, and came no further.

One thing I would not let slip; I took notice that now poor Christian was so confounded, that he did not know his own voice; and thus I perceived it.

Just when he was come over against the mouth of the burning pit, one of the wicked ones got behind him, and stept up softly to him; and whisperingly suggested many grievous blasphemies to him, which he verily thought had proceeded from his own mind.

This put Christian more to it than anything that he met with before, even to think that he should now blaspheme him that he loved so much before; yet, if he could have helped it, he would not have done it; but he had not the discretion either to stop his ears, or to know from whence these blasphemies came.

When Christian had travelled in this disconsolate condition some considerable time, he thought he heard the voice of a man, as going before him, saying, "Though I walk through the valley of the shadow of death; I will fear no evil, for thou art with me." [107]

Then he was glad, and that for these reasons:

First, Because he gathered from thence, that some who feared God were in this valley as well as himself.

Secondly, For that he perceived God was with them, though in that dark and dismal state; and why not, thought he, with me? though, by reason of the impediment that attends this place, I cannot perceive it. [108]

Thirdly, For that he hoped, could he overtake them, to have company by and by. So he went on, and called to him that was before; but he knew not what to answer; for that he also thought himself to be alone. And by and by the day broke; then said Christian, He hath turned "the shadow of death into morning." [109]

Now morning being come, he looked back, not out of desire to return, but to see, by the light of day, what hazards he had gone through in the dark. So he saw more perfectly the ditch that was on the one hand, and the quag that was on the other; also how narrow the way was which led betwixt them both; also now he saw the hobgoblins, and satyrs, and dragons of the pit, but all afar off (for after break of day, they came not nigh); yet they were discovered to him, according to that which is written, "He discovereth deep things out of darkness, and bringeth out to light the shadow of death. [110]

Now was Christian much affected with his deliverance from all the dangers of his solitary way; which dangers, though he feared them more before, yet he saw them more clearly now, because the light of the day made them conspicuous to him.

And about this time the sun was rising, and this was another mercy to Christian; for you must note, that though the first part of the Valley of the Shadow of Death was dangerous, yet this second part which he was yet to go, was, if possible, far more dangerous: for from the place where he now stood, even to the end of the valley, the way was all along set so full of snares, traps, gins, and nets here, and so full of pits, pitfalls, deep holes, and shelvings down there, that, had it now been dark, as it was when he came the first part of the way, had he had a thousand souls, they had in reason been cast away; but, as I said just now, the sun was rising.

Then, said he, His candle shineth upon my head, and by his light I walk through darkness.

CHRISTIAN ENTERS THE SECOND PART OF THE VALLEY OF THE SHADOW OF DEATH.

In this light, therefore, he came to the end of the valley. Now I saw in my dream, that at the end of this valley lay blood, bones, ashes, and mangled bodies of men, even of pilgrims that had gone this way for-

merly; and while I was musing what should be the reason, I espied a little
before me a cave, where two giants, POPE, and PAGAN, dwelt in old
times; by whose power and tyranny the men whose bones, blood, ashes,
&c., lay there, were cruelly put to death.

But by this place Christian went without much danger, whereat I
somewhat wondered; but I have learnt since, that PAGAN has been dead
many a day; and as for the other, though he be yet alive, he is, by reason
of age, and also of the many shrewd brushes that he met with in his
younger days, grown so crazy and stiff in his joints, that he can now do
little more than sit in his cave's mouth, grinning at pilgrims as they go
by, and biting his nails because he cannot come at them.

GIANT POPE.

So I saw that Christian went on his way; yet, at the sight of the Old
Man that sat in the mouth of the cave, he could not tell what to think,
especially because he spake to him, though he could not go after him,
saying, "You will never mend till more of you be burned." But he held
his peace, and set a good face on it, and so went by, and catched no hurt.
Then sang Christian—

O world of wonders! (I can say no less)
That I should be preserved in that distress
That I have met with here! O blessed be
That hand that from it hath deliver'd me!
Dangers in darkness, devils, hell, and sin,
Did compass me, while I this vale was in:
Yea, snares and pits, and traps, and nets, did lie
My path about, that worthless, silly I
Might have been catch'd, entangled, and cast down;
But since I live, let JESUS wear the crown.

9

CHAPTER V.

NOW, as Christian went on his way, he came to a little ascent, which was cast up on purpose that pilgrims might see before them. Up there, therefore, Christian went, and looking forward, he saw Faithful before him, upon his journey.

Then said Christian aloud, "Ho! Ho! Soho! stay, and I will be your companion!" At that Faithful looked behind him; to whom Christian cried again, "Stay, stay, till I come up to you." But Faithful answered, "No, I am upon my life; and the avenger of blood is behind me."

At this Christian was somewhat moved, and putting to all his strength, he quickly got up with Faithful, and did also overrun him; so the last was first. Then did Christian vain-gloriously smile, because he had gotten the start of his brother; but not taking good heed to his feet, he suddenly stumbled and fell, and could not rise again until Faithful came up to help him.

Then I saw in my dream they went very lovingly on together, and had sweet discourse of all things that had happened to them in their pilgrimage; and thus Christian began:

CHR. My honored and well-beloved brother, Faithful, I am glad that I have overtaken you; and that God has so tempered our spirits, that we can walk as companions in this so pleasant a path.

FAITH. I had thought, dear friend, to have had your company quite from our town; but you did get the start of me, wherefore I was forced to come thus much of the way alone.

CHR. How long did you stay in the City of Destruction, before you set out after me on your pilgrimage?

FAITH. Till I could stay no longer; for there was great talk presently after you were gone out, that our city would, in a short time, with fire from heaven, be burned down to the ground.

CHR. What! did your neighbors talk so?

FAITH. Yes, it was for a while in everybody's mouth.

130

CHR. What! and did no more of them but you come out to escape the danger?

FAITH. Though there was, as I said, a great talk thereabout, yet I do not think they did firmly believe it. For in the heat of the discourse, I heard some of them deridingly speak of you and of your desperate journey

FAITHFUL HELPS CHRISTIAN.

(for so they called this your pilgrimage), but I did believe, and do still, that the end of our city will be with fire and brimstone from above; and therefore I have made my escape.

CHR. Did you hear no talk of neighbor Pliable?

FAITH. Yes, Christian, I heard that he followed you till he came at the Slough of Despond, where, as some said, he fell in; but he would not be known to have so done; but I am sure he was soundly bedabbled with that kind of dirt.

CHR. And what said the neighbors to him?

FAITH. He hath, since his going back, been had greatly in derision, and that among all sorts of people; some do mock and despise him; and scarce will any set him on work. He is now seven times worse than if he had never gone out of the city.

CHR. But why should they be so set against him, since they also despise the way that he forsook?

FAITH. Oh, they say hang him, he is a turn-coat! He was not true to his profession. I think God has stirred up even his enemies to hiss at him, and make him a proverb, because he hath forsaken the way.[112]

PLIABLE IS MOCKED AFTER HIS RETURN.

CHR. Had you no talk with him before you came out?

FAITH. I met him once in the streets, but he sheered away on the other side, as one ashamed of what he had done; so I spake not to him.

CHR. Well, at my first setting out, I had hopes of that man; but now I fear he will perish in the overthrow of the city; for it is happened to him according to the true proverb, "The dog is turned to his own vomit again; and the sow that was washed, to her wallowing in the mire."[113]

FAITH. These are my fears of him too; but who can hinder that which will be?

CHR. Well, neighbor Faithful, said Christian, let us leave him, and talk of things that more immediately concern ourselves. Tell me now, what you have met with in the way as you came: for I know you have met with some things, or else it may be writ for a wonder.

FAITHFUL AND WANTON.

FAITH. I escaped the Slough that I perceived you fell into, and got up to the gate without that danger; only I met with one whose name was Wanton, who had like to have done me a mischief.

CHR. It was well you escaped her net; Joseph was hard put to it by her, and he escaped her as you did; but it had like to have cost him his life.[114] But what did she do to you?

FAITH. You cannot think, but that you know something, what a flattering tongue she had; she lay at me hard to turn aside with her, promising me all manner of content.

CHR. Nay, she did not promise you the content of a good conscience.

FAITH. You know what I mean; all carnal and fleshly content.

CHR. Thank God you have escaped her: "The abhorred of the Lord shall fall into her ditch." [115]

FAITH. Nay, I know not whether I did wholly escape her or no.

CHR. Why, I trow, you did not consent to her desires?

FAITH. No, not to defile myself; for I remembered an old writing that I had seen, which said, "Her steps take hold on hell." [116] So I shut mine eyes, because I would not be bewitched with her looks. [117] Then she railed on me, and I went my way.

CHR. Did you meet with no other assault as you came?

FAITH. When I came to the foot of the hill called Difficulty, I met with a very aged man, who asked me what I was, and whither bound. I told him that I am a pilgrim, going to the Celestial City. Then said the old man, Thou lookest like an honest fellow; wilt thou be content to dwell with me for the wages that I shall give thee? Then I asked him his name, and where he dwelt. He said his name was Adam the First, and that he dwelt in the town of Deceit. [118] I asked him then what was his work, and what the wages that he would give. He told me that his work was many delights; and his wages, that I should be his heir at last. I further asked him what house he kept, and what other servants he had. So he told me, that his house was maintained with all the dainties in the world; and that his servants were those of his own begetting. Then I asked him if he had any children. He said that he had but three daughters: the Lust of the Flesh, the Lust of the Eyes, and the Pride of Life, and that I should marry them all if I would. [119] Then I asked how long time he would have me live with him? And he told me, As long as he lived himself.

CHR. Well, and what conclusion came the old man and you to at last?

FAITH. Why, at first, I found myself somewhat inclinable to go with the man, for I thought he spake very fair; but looking in his forehead, as I talked with him, I saw there written, "Put off the old man with his deeds."

CHR. And how then?

FAITH. Then it came burning hot into my mind, whatever he said, and however he flattered, when he got me home to his house, he would sell

FAITHFUL'S STRUGGLE WITH ADAM THE FIRST.

135

me for a slave. So I bid him forbear to talk, for I would not come near the door of his house. Then he reviled me, and told me that he would send such a one after me, that should make my way bitter to my soul. So I turned to go away from him; but just as I turned myself to go thence, I felt him take hold of my flesh, and give me such a deadly twitch back, that I thought he had pulled part of me after himself. This made me cry, "Oh, wretched man!" [120] So I went on my way up the hill.

Now when I had got about half way up, I looked behind, and saw one coming after me, swift as the wind; so he overtook me just about the place where the settle stands.

CHR. Just there, said Christian, did I sit down to rest me; but being overcome with sleep, I there lost this roll out of my bosom.

FAITH. But, good brother, hear me out. So soon as the man overtook me, he was but a word and a blow, for down he knocked me, and laid me for dead. But when I was a little come to myself again, I asked him wherefore he served me so. He said, because of my secret inclining to Adam the First: and with that he struck me another deadly blow on the breast, and beat me down backward; so I lay at his foot as dead as before. So, when I came to myself again, I cried him mercy; but he said, I know not how to show mercy; and with that knocked me down again. He had doubtless made an end of me, but that one came by and bid him forbear.

CHR. Who was that that bid him forbear?

FAITH. I did not know him at first, but as he went by, I perceived the holes in his hands and in his side; then I concluded that he was our Lord. So I went up hill.

CHR. That man that overtook you was Moses. He spareth none, neither knoweth he how to show mercy to those that transgress his law.

FAITH. I know it very well; it was not the first time that he has met with me. It was he that came to me when I dwelt securely at home, and that told me he would burn my house over my head if I stayed there.

CHR. But did you not see the house that stood there on the top of the hill, on the side of which Moses met you?

FAITH. Yes, and the lions too, before I came at it: but for the lions, I think they were asleep, for it was about noon; and because I had so much of the day before me, I passed by the porter, and came down the hill.

CHR. He told me, indeed, that he saw you go by, but I wish you had called at the house, for they would have showed you so many rarities, that you would scarce have forgot them to the day of your death. But pray tell me, Did you meet nobody in the Valley of Humility?

FAITH. Yes, I met with one Discontent, who would willingly have persuaded me to go back again with him; his reason was, for that the valley was altogether without honor. He told me, moreover, that there to go was the way to disobey all my friends, as Pride, Arrogancy, Self-

FAITHFUL IS DISOWNED BY HIS RELATIVES.

Conceit, Worldly-glory, with others, who, he knew, as he said, would be very much offended, if I made such a fool of myself as to wade through this valley.

CHR. Well, and how did you answer him?

FAITH. I told him that although all these that he named might claim kindred of me, and that rightly, for indeed they were my relations according to the flesh; yet since I became a pilgrim, they have disowned me, as I also have rejected them; and therefore were to me now no more than if they had never been of my lineage.

I told him, moreover, that as to this valley, he had quite misrepresented the thing; "for before honor is humility, and a haughty spirit before a fall." Therefore, said I, I had rather go through this valley to the honor that was so accounted by the wisest, than choose that which he esteemed most worthy our affections.

CHR. Met you with nothing else in that valley?

FAITH. Yes, I met with Shame; but of all the men that I met with in my pilgrimage, he I think bears the wrong name. The others would be said nay, after a little argumentation, and somewhat else; but this boldfaced Shame would never have done.

CHR. Why, what did he say to you?

FAITH. What! why, he objected against religion itself; he said it was a pitiful, low, sneaking business, for a man to mind religion; he said that a tender conscience was an unmanly thing; and that for a man to watch over his words and ways, so as to tie up himself from that hectoring liberty that the brave spirits of the times accustom themselves unto, would make him the ridicule of the times.

He objected also, that but few of the mighty, rich, or wise, were ever of my opinion;[121] nor any of them neither,[122] before they were persuaded to be fools, and to be of a voluntary fondness, to venture the loss of all, for nobody knows what. He, moreover, objected the base and low estate and condition of those that were chiefly the pilgrims, of the times in which they lived: also their ignorance and want of understanding in all natural science.

Yea, he did hold me to it at that rate also, about a great many more things than here I relate; as, that it was a *shame* to sit whining and mourning under a sermon, and a *shame* to come sighing and groaning home; that it was a *shame* to ask my neighbor forgiveness for petty faults, or to make restitution where I have taken from any. He said, also, that religion made a man grow strange to the great, because of a few vices, which he called by finer names; and made him own and respect the base, because of the same religious fraternity. And is not this, said he, a *shame?*

CHR. And what did you say to him?

FAITH. Say! I could not tell what to say at the first. Yea, he put me so to it, that my blood came up in my face; even this Shame fetched it up, and had almost beat me quite off,

But at last I began to consider, that "that which is highly esteemed among men, is had in abomination with God." [123] And I thought again, this Shame tells me what men are; but he tells me nothing what God or the Word of God is. And I thought, moreover, that at the day of doom, we shall not be doomed to death or life according to the hectoring spirits of the world, but according to the wisdom and law of the Highest.

Therefore, thought I, what God says is best, indeed is best, though all the men in the world are against it. Seeing, then, that God prefers his religion; seeing God prefers a tender conscience; seeing they that make themselves fools for the kingdom of heaven are wisest; and that the poor man that loveth Christ is richer than the greatest man in the world that hates him; *Shame*, depart, thou art an enemy to my salvation! Shall I entertain thee against my sovereign Lord? How then shall I look him in the face at his coming? Should I now be ashamed of his ways and servants, how can I expect the blessing? [124]

But, indeed, this Shame was a bold villain: I could scarce shake him out of my company; yea, he would be haunting of me, and continually whispering me in the ear, with some one or other of the infirmities that attend religion; but at last I told him it was but in vain to attempt further in this business; for those things that he disdained, in those did I see most glory; and so at last I got past this importunate one. And when I had shaken him off, then I began to sing—

> The trials that those men do meet withal,
> That are obedient to the heavenly call,
> Are manifold, and suited to the flesh,
> And come, and come, and come again afresh;
> That now, or some time else, we by them may
> Be taken, overcome, and cast away.
> Oh, let the pilgrims, let the pilgrims, then
> Be vigilant, and quit themselves like men.

CHR. I am glad, my brother, that thou didst withstand this villain so bravely: for of all, as thou sayest, I think he has the wrong name; for he is so bold as to follow us in the streets, and to attempt to put us to shame before all men: that is, to make us ashamed of that which is good; but if he was not himself audacious, he would never attempt to do as he does. But let us still resist him; for notwithstanding all his bravadoes, he promoteth the fool and none else. "The wise shall inherit glory," said Solomon; "but shame shall be the promotion of fools." [125]

FAITH. I think we must cry to Him for help against Shame, who would have us to be valiant for the truth upon the earth.

CHR. You say true; but did you meet nobody else in that valley?

FAITH. No, not I; for I had sunshine all the rest of the way through that, and also through the Valley of the Shadow of Death.

CHR. It was well for you. I am sure it fared far otherwise with me; I had for a long season, as soon almost as I entered into that valley, a dreadful combat with that foul fiend Apollyon; yea, I thought verily he would have killed me, especially when he got me down and crushed me under him, as if he would have crushed me to pieces; for as he threw me, my sword flew out of my hand; nay, he told me he was sure of me: but I cried to God, and he heard me, and delivered me out of all my troubles. Then I entered into the Valley of the Shadow of Death, and had no light for almost half the way through it. I thought I should have been killed there, over and over; but at last day brake, and the sun rose, and I went through that which was behind with far more ease and quiet.

Moreover, I saw in my dream, that as they went on, Faithful as he chanced to look on one side, saw a man whose name is Talkative, walking at a distance beside them; for in this place there was room enough for them all to walk. He was a tall man, and something more comely at a distance than at hand. To this man Faithful addressed himself in this manner.

FAITH. Friend, whither away? Are you going to the heavenly country?

TALK. I am going to the same place.

FAITH. That is well; then I hope we may have your good company.

TALK. With a very good will will I be your companion.

FAITH. Come on, then, and let us go together, and let us spend our time in discoursing of things that are profitable.

TALK. To talk of things that are good, to me is very acceptable, with you or with any other; and I am glad that I have met with those that incline to so good a work; for, to speak the truth, there are but few that care thus to spend their time (as they are in their travels), but choose much rather to be speaking of things to no profit; and this hath been a trouble to me.

FAITH. That is indeed a thing to be lamented; for what things so worthy of the use of the tongue and mouth of men on earth, as are the things of the God of heaven?

TALK. I like you wonderful well, for your sayings are full of conviction; and I will add, what thing is so pleasant, and what so profitable, as to talk of the things of God? What things so pleasant (that is, if a man hath any delight in things that are wonderful)? For instance, if a man doth delight to talk of the history or the mystery of things; or if a man doth love to talk of miracles, wonders, or signs, where shall he find things recorded so delightful, and so sweetly penned, as in the Holy Scripture?

FAITH. That is true; but to be profited by such things in our talk should be that which we design.

TALK. That is it that I said; for to talk of such things is most profitable; for by so doing a man may get knowledge of many things; as of the vanity of earthly things, and the benefit of things above. Thus, in general, but more particularly, by this, a man may learn the necessity of the new birth, the insufficiency of our works, the need of Christ's righteousness, &c. Besides, by this a man may learn, by talk, what it is to repent, to believe, to pray, to suffer, or the like; by this also a man may learn what are the great promises and consolations of the gospel, to his own comfort. Further, by this a man may learn to refute false opinions, to vindicate the truth, and also to instruct the ignorant.

FAITH. All this is true, and glad am I to hear these things from you.

TALK. Alas! the want of this is the cause why so few understand the need of faith, and the necessity of a work of grace in their soul, in order to eternal life; but ignorantly live in the works of the law, by which a man can by no means obtain the kingdom of heaven.

FAITH. But, by your leave, heavenly knowledge of these is the gift of God; no man attaineth to them by human industry, or only by the talk of them.

TALK. All this I know very well; for a man can receive nothing, except it be given him from heaven; all is of grace, not of works. I could give you a hundred scriptures for the confirmation of this.

FAITH. Well, then, said Faithful, what is that one thing that we shall at this time found our discourse upon?

TALK. What you will. I will talk of things heavenly, or things earthly; things moral, or things evangelical; things sacred, or things profane; things past, or things to come; things foreign, or things at home; things more essential, or things circumstantial; provided that all be done to our profit.

FAITH. Now did Faithful begin to wonder; and stepping to Christian

(for he walked all this while by himself), he said to him (but softly),
What a brave companion have we got! Surely this man will make a
very excellent pilgrim.

CHR. At this Christian modestly smiled, and said, This man, with
whom you are so taken, will beguile, with that tongue of his, twenty of
them that know him not.

FAITH. Do you know him then?

CHR. Know him! Yes, better than he knows himself.

FAITH. Pray what is he?

CHR. His name is Talkative; he dwelleth in our town. I wonder that
you should be a stranger to him, only I consider that our town is large.

FAITH. Whose son is he? And whereabouts does he dwell?

CHR. He is the son of one Say-well; he dwelt in Prating Row; and is
known of all that are acquainted with him, by the name of Talkative in
Prating Row; and notwithstanding his fine tongue, he is but a sorry
fellow.

FAITH. Well, he seems to be a very pretty man.

CHR. That is, to them who have not thorough acquaintance with him;
for he is best abroad; near home, he is ugly enough. Your saying that
he is a pretty man brings to my mind what I have observed in the work
of the painter, whose pictures show best at a distance, but, very near,
more unpleasing.

FAITH. But I am ready to think you do but jest, because you smiled.

CHR. God forbid that I should jest (although I smiled) in this matter,
or that I should accuse any falsely! I will give you a further discovery
of him. This man is for any company, and for any talk; as he talketh
now with you, so will he talk when he is on the ale-bench; and the more
drink he hath in his crown, the more of these things he hath in his
mouth; religion hath no place in his heart, or house, or conversation; all
he hath, lieth in his tongue, and his religion is, to make a noise therewith.

FAITH. Say you so! then am I in this man greatly deceived.

CHR. Deceived! you may be sure of it; remember the proverb, "They
say and do not." [126] But the "kingdom of God is not in word, but in
power." [127] He talketh of prayer, of repentance, of faith, and of the new
birth; but he knows but only to talk of them. I have been in his family,
and have observed him both at home and abroad, and I know what I say
of him is the truth.

PRATING ROW.

W J LINTON

143

His house is as empty of religion as the white of an egg is of savor. There is there neither prayer, nor sign of repentance for sin; yea, the brute in his kind serves God far better than he. He is the very stain, reproach, and shame of religion, to all that know him; it can hardly have a good word in all that end of the town where he dwells, through him.[128] Thus say the common people that know him, A saint abroad, and a devil at home. His poor family finds it so; he is such a churl, such a railer at, and so unreasonable with his servants,

TALKATIVE AT THE ALEHOUSE.

that they neither know how to do for, or speak to him. Men that have any dealings with him, say it is better to deal with a Turk than with him; for fairer dealing they shall have at their hands. This Talkative (if it be possible) will go beyond them, defraud, beguile, and overreach them.

Besides, he brings up his sons to follow his steps; and if he findeth in any of them a foolish timorousness (for so he calls the first appearance of a tender conscience), he calls them fools and blockheads, and by no means will employ them in much, or speak to their commendations before others. For my part, I am of opinion, that he has, by his wicked life, caused many to stumble and fall; and will be, if God prevent not, the ruin of many more.

FAITH. Well, my brother, I am bound to believe you; not only because you say you know him, but also because, like a Christian, you make your reports of men. For I cannot think that you speak these things of ill-will, but because it is even so as you say.

TALKATIVE AT HOME.

CHR. Had I known him no more than you, I might perhaps have thought of him, as, at the first, you did; yea, had he received this report at their hands only that are enemies to religion, I should have thought it had been a slander—a lot that often falls from bad men's mouths upon good men's names and professions; but all these things, yea, and a great many more as bad, of my own knowledge, I can prove him guilty of.

10

Besides, good men are ashamed of him; they can neither call him brother, nor friend; the very naming of him among them makes them blush, if they know him.

FAITH. Well, I see that saying and doing are two things, and hereafter I shall better observe this distinction.

CHR. They are two things, indeed, and are as diverse as are the soul and the body; for as the body without the soul is but a dead carcass, so saying, if it be alone, is but a dead carcass also. The soul of religion is the practical part: "Pure religion and undefiled, before God and the Father, is this, to visit the fatherless and widows in their affliction, and to keep himself unspotted from the world." [129]

This, Talkative is not aware of; he thinks that hearing and saying will make a good Christian, and thus he deceiveth his own soul. Hearing is but as the sowing of the seed; talking is not sufficient to prove that fruit is indeed in the heart and life; and let us assure ourselves, that at the day of doom men shall be judged according to their fruits. [130]

It will not be said then, Did you believe? but, Were you doers, or talkers only? and accordingly shall they be judged. The end of the world is compared to our harvest; and you know men at harvest regard nothing but fruit. Not that anything can be accepted that is not of faith, but I speak this to show you how insignificant the profession of Talkative will be at that day.

FAITH. This brings to my mind that of Moses, by which he describeth the beast that is clean. [131] He is such a one that parteth the hoof and cheweth the cud; not that parteth the hoof only, or that cheweth the cud only.

The hare cheweth the cud, but is yet unclean, because he parteth not the hoof. And thus truly resembleth Talkative; he cheweth the cud, he seeketh knowledge, he cheweth upon the word; but he divideth not the hoof, he parteth not with the way of sinners; but, as the hare, he retaineth the foot of a dog or bear, and therefore he is unclean.

CHR. You have spoken, for aught I know, the true gospel-sense of those texts. And I will add another thing: Paul calleth some men, yea, and those great talkers, too, "sounding brass and tinkling cymbals," that is, as he expounds them in another place, "things without life, giving sound." [132] Things without life, that is, without the true faith and grace of the gospel; and consequently, things that shall never be placed in the kingdom of heaven among those that are the children of life; though their sound, by their talk, be as if it were the tongue or voice of an angel.

FAITH. Well, I was not so fond of his company at first, but I am as sick of it now. What shall we do to be rid of him?

CHR. Take my advice, and do as I bid you, and you shall find that he will soon be sick of your company too, except God shall touch his heart and turn it.

FAITH. What would you have me to do?

CHR. Why, go to him, and enter into some serious discourse about the power of religion; and ask him plainly (when he has approved of it, for that he will) whether this thing be set up in his heart, house, or conversation.

FAITH. Then Faithful stepped forward again, and said to Talkative, Come, what cheer? How is it now?

TALK. Thank you well. I thought we should have had a great deal of talk by this time.

FAITH. Well, if you will, we will fall to it now; and since you left it with me to state the question, let it be this: How doth the saving grace of God discover itself, when it is in the heart of man?

TALK. I perceive, then, that our talk must be about the power of things. Well, it is a very good question, and I shall be willing to answer you. And take my answer in brief, thus: First, Where the grace of God is in the heart, it causeth there a great outcry against sin. Secondly—

FAITH. Nay, hold, let us consider of one at once. I think you should rather say, It shows itself by inclining the soul to abhor its sin.

TALK. Why, what difference is there between crying out against, and abhorring of sin?

FAITH. Oh, a great deal. A man may cry out against sin of policy, but he cannot abhor it, but by virtue of a godly antipathy against it. I have heard many cry out against sin in the pulpit, who yet can abide it well enough in the heart, house, and conversation. Joseph's mistress cried out with a loud voice, as if she had been very holy; but she would willingly, notwithstanding that, have committed uncleanness with him.[132] Some cry out against sin, even as the mother cries out against her child in her lap, when she calleth it slut and naughty girl, and then falls to hugging and kissing it.

TALK. You lie at a catch, I perceive.

FAITH. No, not I; I am only for setting things right. But what is the second thing whereby you would prove a discovery of a work of grace in the heart?

TALK. Great knowledge of gospel mysteries.

FAITH. This sign should have been first; but first or last, it is also false; for knowledge, great knowledge, may be obtained in the mysteries of the gospel, and yet no work of grace in the soul.[134] Yea, if a man have all knowledge, he may yet be nothing, and so consequently be no child of God. When Christ said, "Do you know all these things?" and the disciples had answered, Yes; he addeth, "Blessed are ye if ye do them." He doth not lay the blessing in the knowing of them, but in the doing of them. For there is a knowledge that is not attended with doing: "He that knoweth his master's will, and doeth it not."

A man may know like an angel and yet be no Christian, therefore your sign of it is not true. Indeed, *to know* is a thing that pleaseth talkers and boasters; but *to do* is that which pleaseth God. Not that the heart can be good without knowledge; for without that the heart is naught.

There is, therefore, knowledge and knowledge. Knowledge that resteth in the bare speculation of things; and knowledge that is accompanied with the grace of faith and love; which puts a man upon doing even the will of God from the heart: the first of these will serve the talker; but without the other the true Christian is not content. "Give me understanding, and I shall keep thy law; yea, I shall observe it with my whole heart." [135]

TALK. You lie at the catch again; this is not for edification.

FAITH. Well, if you please, propound another sign how this work of grace discovereth itself where it is.

TALK. Not I, for I see we shall not agree.

FAITH. Well, if you will not, will you give me leave to do it?

TALK. You may use your liberty.

FAITH. A work of grace in the soul discovereth itself, either to him that hath it, or to standers by.

To him that hath it thus: It gives him conviction of sin, especially of the defilement of his nature and the sin of unbelief (for the sake of which he is sure to be damned, if he findeth not mercy at God's hand, by faith in Jesus Christ).[136]

This sight and sense of things worketh in him sorrow and shame for sin; he findeth, moreover, revealed in him the Saviour of the world, and the absolute necessity of closing with him for life, at the which he findeth hungerings and thirstings after him; to which hungerings, &c., the promise is made.[137]

Now, according to the strength or weakness of his faith in his Saviour, so is his joy and peace, so is his love to holiness, so are his desires to know him more, and also to serve him in this world. But though I say it discovereth itself thus unto him, yet it is but seldom that he is able to conclude that this is a work of grace; because his corruption now, and his abused reason, make his mind to misjudge in this matter; therefore, in him that hath this work, there is required a very sound judgment before he can, with steadiness, conclude that this is a work of grace.

To others, it is thus discovered:

1. By an experimental confession of his faith in Christ.[138]

2. By a life answerable to that confession; to wit, a life of holiness, heart-holiness, family-holiness (if he hath a family), and by conversation-holiness in the world; which, in the general, teacheth him, inwardly, to abhor his sin, and himself for that, in secret; to suppress it in his family, and to promote holiness in the world; not by talk only, as a hypocrite or talkative person may do, but by a practical subjection, in faith and love, to the power of the Word.[139] And now, Sir, as to this brief description of the work of grace, and also the discovery of it, if you have aught to object, object; if not, then give me leave to propound to you a second question.

TALK. Nay, my part is not now to object, but to hear; let me, therefore, have your second question.

FAITH. It is this: Do you experience this first part of this description of it? and doth your life and conversation testify the same? or standeth your religion in word or in tongue, and not in deed and truth? Pray, if you incline to answer me in this, say no more than you know the God above will say Amen to; and also nothing but what your conscience can justify you in; "for, not he that commendeth himself is approved, but whom the Lord commendeth." Besides, to say I am thus and thus, when my conversation, and all my neighbors, tell me I lie, is great wickedness.

TALK. Then Talkative at first began to blush; but, recovering himsel, thus he replied: You come now to experience, to conscience, and God; and to appeal to him for justification of what is spoken. This kind of discourse I did not expect; nor am I disposed to give an answer to such questions, because I count not myself bound thereto, unless you take upon you to be a catechiser, and, though you should so do, yet I may refuse to make you my judge. But, I pray, will you tell me why you ask me such questions?

FAITH. Because I saw you forward to talk, and because I knew not that you had aught else but notion. Besides, to tell you all the truth, I have heard of you, that you are a man whose religion lies in talk, and that your conversation gives this, your mouth-profession, the lie. They say you are a spot among Christians; and that religion fareth the worse for your ungodly conversation; that some have already stumbled at your wicked ways, and that more are in danger of being destroyed thereby; your religion, and an ale-house, and covetousness, and uncleanness, and swearing, and lying, and vain-company keeping, &c., will stand together.

TALK. Since you are ready to take up reports and to judge so rashly as you do, I cannot but conclude you are some peevish or melancholy man, not fit to be discoursed with; and so farewell.

CHR. Then came up Christian and said to his brother, I told you how it would happen: your words and his lusts could not agree; he had rather leave your company than reform his life. But he is gone, as I said; let him go, the loss is no man's but his own; he has saved us the trouble of going from him; for he continuing (as I suppose he will do) as he is, he would have been but a blot in our company: besides, the Apostle says, "From such withdraw thyself."

FAITH. But I am glad we had this little discourse with him; it may happen that he will think of it again: however, I have dealt plainly with him, and so am clear of his blood, if he perisheth.

CHR. You did well to talk so plainly to him as you did; there is but little of this faithful dealing with men now-a-days, and that makes religion to stink so in the nostrils of many, as it doth; for they are these talkative fools whose religion is only in word, and are debauched and vain in their conversation, that (being so much admitted into the fellowship of the godly) do puzzle the world, blemish Christianity, and grieve the sincere.

I wish that all men would deal with such as you have done; then should they either be made more comfortable to religion, or the company of saints would be too hot for them. Then did Faithful say

> How Talkative at first lifts up his plumes!
> How bravely doth he speak! How he presumes
> To drive down all before him! But so soon
> As Faithful talks of heart-work, like the moon
> That's past the full, into the wane he goes.
> And so will all, but he that HEART-WORK knows.

Thus they went on talking of what they had seen by the way, and so made that way easy which would otherwise, no doubt, have been tedious to them; for now they went through a wilderness.

CHAPTER VI.

NOW, when they were got almost quite out of this wilderness, Faithful chanced to cast his eye back, and espied one coming after them, and he knew him. Oh! said Faithful to his brother, Who comes yonder?

Then Christian looked, and said, It is my good friend Evangelist. Aye, and my good friend too, said Faithful; for it was he that set me the way to the gate. Now was Evangelist come up to them, and thus saluted them:

EVAN. Peace be with you, dearly beloved, and peace be to your helpers.

CHR. Welcome, welcome, my good Evangelist; the sight of thy countenance brings to my remembrance thy ancient kindness and unwearied laboring for my eternal good.

FAITH. And a thousand times welcome, said good Faithful. Thy company, O sweet Evangelist, how desirable it is to us poor pilgrims!

EVAN. Then said Evangelist, How hath it fared with you, my friends, since the time of our last parting? What have you met with and how have you behaved yourselves?

Then Christian and Faithful told him of all things that had happened to them in the way; and how, and with what difficulty, they had arrived to that place.

EVAN. Right glad am I, said Evangelist, not that you have met with trials, but that you have been victors; and for that you have, notwithstanding many weaknesses, continued in the way to this very day.

I say, right glad am I of this thing, and that for mine own sake and yours. I have sowed and you have reaped: and the day is coming, when both he that sowed and they that reaped shall rejoice together; that is, if you hold out: "for in due season ye shall reap, if ye faint not." [140] The crown is before you, and it is an incorruptible one; "so run, that you may obtain it." [141]

151

Some there be that set out for this crown, and, after they have gone far for it, another comes in, and takes it from them: hold fast therefore that you have; let no man take your crown.[142]   You are not yet out of the gunshot of the devil; you have not resisted unto blood, striving against sin, let the kingdom be always before you, and believe steadfastly concerning things that are invisible.   Let nothing that is on this side the other world get within you, and, above all, look well to your own hearts, and to the lusts thereof, "for they are deceitful above all things, and desperately wicked;" set your faces like a flint; you have all power in heaven and earth on your side.

CHR. Then Christian thanked him for his exhortation; but told him, withal, that they would have him speak further to them for their help the rest of the way, and the rather, for that they well knew that he was a prophet, and could tell them of things that might happen unto them, and also how they might resist and overcome them.   To which request Faithful also consented.   So Evangelist began as followeth:—

EVAN. My sons, you have heard in the words of the truth of the gospel, that you must, through many tribulations, enter into the kingdom of heaven.   And, again, that in every city bonds and afflictions abide in you; and therefore you cannot expect that you should go long on your pilgrimage without them, in some sort or other.

You have found something of the truth of these testimonies upon you already, and more will immediately follow; for now as you see, you are almost out of this wilderness, and therefore you will soon come into a town that you will by-and-by see before you; and in that town you will be hardly beset with enemies, who will strain hard but they will kill you; and be you sure that one or both of you must seal the testimony which you hold, with blood; but be you faithful unto death, and the King will give you a crown of life.

He that shall die there, although his death will be unnatural, and his pain perhaps great, he will yet have the better of his fellow; not only because he will be arrived at the Celestial City soonest, but because he will escape many miseries that the other will meet with in the rest of his journey.   But when you are come to the town, and shall find fulfilled what I have here related, then remember your friend, and quit yourselves like men, and commit the keeping of your souls to your God in well-doing, as unto a faithful Creator.

Then I saw in my dream, that when they were got out of the wilderness, they presently saw a town before them, and the name of that town is Vanity; and at the town there is a fair kept, called Vanity Fair; it is kept all the year long; it beareth the name of Vanity Fair, because the town where it is kept is lighter than vanity; and also because all that is there sold, or that cometh thither, is vanity. As is the saying of the wise, "all that cometh is vanity." [143]

This fair is no new-erected business, but a thing of ancient standing; I will show you the original of it.

Almost five thousand years agone, there were pilgrims walking to the Celestial City, as these two honest persons are: and Beelzebub, Apollyon, and Legion, with their companions, perceiving by the path that the pilgrims made, that their way to the city lay through this town of Vanity, they contrived here to set up a fair; a fair wherein should be sold all sorts of vanity, and that it should last all the year long; therefore at this fair are all such merchandise sold, as houses, lands, trades, places, honors, preferments, titles, countries, kingdoms, lusts, pleasures, and delights of all sorts. Wives, husbands, children, masters, servants, lives, blood, bodies, souls, silver, gold, pearls, precious stones, and what not.

And, moreover, at this fair there is at all times to be seen juggling, cheats, games, plays, fools, apes, knaves, and rogues, and that of every kind.

Here are to be seen, too, and that for nothing, thefts, murders, adulteries, false swearers, and that of a blood-red color.

And as in other fairs of less moment, there are the several rows and streets, under their proper names, where such and such wares are vended; so here likewise you have the proper places, rows, streets (viz. countries and kingdoms), where the wares of this fair are soonest to be found. Here is the Britain Row, the French Row, the Italian Row, the Spanish Row, the German Row, where several sorts of vanities are to be sold. But, as in other fairs, some one commodity is as the chief of all the fair, so the ware of Rome and her merchandise is greatly promoted in this fair; only our English nation, with some others, have taken a dislike thereat.

Now, as I said, the way to the Celestial City lies just through this town where this lusty fair is kept; and he that will go to the City, and yet not go through this town, must needs " go out of the world." [144]

The Prince of princes himself, when here, went through this town to his own country, and that upon a fair-day too; yea, and as I think, it was Beelzebub, the chief lord of this fair, that invited him to buy of his vanities;

VANITY FAIR.

yea, would have made him lord of the fair, would he have but done him reverence as he went through the town. [145]

Yea, because he was such a person of honor, Beelzebub had him from street to street, and showed him all the kingdoms of the world in a little time, that he might, if possible allure the Blessed One to cheapen and buy some of his vanities; but he had no mind to the merchandise, and therefore left the town, without laying out so much as one farthing upon these vanities.

This fair, therefore, is an ancient thing, of long standing, and a very great fair. Now these Pilgrims, as I said, must needs go through this fair. Well, so they did: but, behold, even as they entered into the fair all the people in the fair were moved, and the town itself as it were in a hubbub about them; and that for several reasons: for—

First, The pilgrims were clothed with such kind of raiment as was diverse from the raiment of any that traded in that fair. The people, therefore, of the fair, made a great gazing upon them: some said they were fools, some they were bedlams, and some they are outlandish men.[146]

Secondly, And as they wondered at their apparel, so they did likewise at their speech; for few could understand what they said; they naturally spoke the language of Canaan, but they that kept the fair were the men of this world; so that, from one end of the fair to the other, they seemed barbarians each to the other.

Thirdly, But that which did not a little amuse the merchandisers was, that these pilgrims set very light by all their wares; they cared not so much as to look upon them; and if they called upon them to buy, they would put their fingers in their ears, and cry, "Turn away mine eyes from beholding vanity," and look upwards, signifying that their trade and traffic was in heaven.[147]

One chanced mockingly, beholding the carriage of the men, to say unto them, What will ye buy? But they, looking gravely upon him, answered, "We buy the truth."[148] At that there was an occasion taken to despise the men the more; some mocking, some taunting, some speaking reproachfully, and some calling upon others to smite them.

At last things came to a hubbub and great stir in the fair, insomuch that all order was confounded. Now was word presently brought to the great one of the fair, who quickly came down, and deputed some of his most trusty friends to take these men into examination, about whom the fair was almost overturned.

So the men were brought to examination; and they that sat upon them, asked them whence they came, whither they went, and what they did there, in such an unusual garb? The men told them that they were pilgrims and strangers in the world, and that they were going to their own country, which was the heavenly Jerusalem;[149] and that they had given no occasion to the men of the town, nor yet to the merchandisers, thus to abuse them, and to let them in their journey, except it was for that, when one asked them what they would buy, they said they would buy the truth. But they that were appointed to examine them did not believe

CHRISTIAN AND FAITHFUL ARE BEATEN.

them to be any other than bedlams and mad, or else such as came to put all things into a confusion in the fair.

Therefore they took them and beat them, and besmeared them with dirt, and then put them into the cage, that they might be made a spectacle to all the men of the fair.

There, therefore, they lay for some time, and were made the objects of any man's sport, or malice, or revenge, the great one of the fair laughing still at all that befell them.

But the men being patient, and not rendering railing for railing, but contrariwise, blessing, and giving good words for bad, and kindness for injuries done, some men in the fair that were more observing, and less prejudiced than the rest, began to check and blame the baser sort for their continual abuses done by them to the men; they, therefore, in angry manner, let fly at them again, counting them as bad as the men in the cage, and telling them that they seemed confederates, and should be made partakers of their misfortunes.

The other replied, that for aught they could see, the men were quiet, and sober, and intended nobody any harm; and that there were many that traded in their fair that were more worthy to be put into the cage, yea, and pillory too, than were the men they had abused.

Thus, after divers words had passed on both sides, the men behaving themselves all the while very wisely and soberly before them, they fell to some blows among themselves, and did harm one to another. Then were these two poor men brought before their examiners again, and there charged with being guilty of the late hubbub that had been in the fair.

So they beat them pitifully, and hanged irons upon them, and led them in chains up and down the fair, for an example and a terror to others, lest any should speak in their behalf, or join themselves unto them.

But Christian and Faithful behaved themselves yet more wisely, and received the ignominy and shame that was cast upon them with so much meekness and patience, that it won to their side, though but few in comparison of the rest, several of the men in the fair.

This put the other party into yet greater rage, insomuch that they concluded the death of these two men. Wherefore they threatened, that the cage nor irons should serve their turn, but that they should die, for the abuse they had done, and for deluding the men of the fair.

Then were they remanded to the cage again, until further order should be taken with them. So they put them in, and made their feet fast in the stocks.

Here, therefore, they called again to mind what they had heard from their faithful friend Evangelist, and were the more confirmed in their way and sufferings, by what he told them would happen to them. They also now comforted each other, that whose lot it was to suffer, even he should have the best of it; therefore each man secretly wished that he might have that preferment: but committing themselves to the all-wise disposal of Him that ruleth all things, with much content, they abode in the condition in which they were, until they should be otherwise disposed of.

Then a convenient time being appointed, they brought them forth to their trial, in order to their condemnation. When the time was come,

THE PILGRIMS IN THE CAGE.

they were brought before their enemies and arraigned. The Judge's name was Lord Hate-good. Their indictment was one and the same in substance, though somewhat varying in form, the contents whereof were this:—

"That they were enemies to and disturbers of their trade; that they had made commotions and divisions in the town, and had won a party to their own most dangerous opinions, in contempt of the law of their prince.''

Then Faithful began to answer, that he had only set himself against that which hath set itself against Him that is higher than the highest. And, said he, as for disturbance, I make none, being myself a man of peace; the parties that were won to us, were won by beholding our truth

CHRISTIAN AND FAITHFUL ARE BROUGHT TO TRIAL.

and innocence, and they are only turned from the worse to the better. And as to the king you talk of, since he is Beelzebub, the enemy of our Lord, I defy him and all his angels.

Then proclamation was made, that they that had aught to say for their lord the king against the prisoner at the bar, should forthwith appear and give in their evidence. So there came in three witnesses, to wit, Envy,

Superstition, and Pickthank. They were then asked if they knew the prisoner at the bar; and what they had to say for their lord the king against him.

Then stood forth Envy, and said to this effect: My Lord, I have known this man a long time, and will attest upon my oath before this honorable bench that he is—

JUDGE. Hold! Give him his oath. (So they sware him.) Then he said—

ENVY. My Lord, this man, notwithstanding his plausible name, is one of the vilest men in our country. He neither regardeth prince nor people, law nor custom; but doth all that he can to possess all men with certain of his disloyal notions, which he in the general calls principles of faith and holiness.

And, in particular, I heard him once myself affirm that Christianity and the customs of our town of Vanity were diametrically opposite, and could not be reconciled. By which saying, my Lord, he doth at once not only condemn all our laudable doings, but us in the doing of them.

JUDGE. Then did the Judge say to him, Hast thou any more to say?

ENVY. My Lord, I could say much more, only I would not be tedious to the court. Yet, if need be, when the other gentlemen have given in their evidence, rather than anything shall be wanting that will despatch him, I will enlarge my testimony against him. So he was bid to stand by.

Then they called Superstition, and bid him look upon the prisoner. They also asked, what he could say for their lord the king against him. Then they sware him; so he began.

SUPER. My Lord, I have no great acquaintance with this man, nor do I desire to have further knowledge of him; however, this I know, that he is a very pestilent fellow, from some discourse that, the other day, I had with him in this town; for then, talking with him, I heard him say, that our religion was nought, and such by which a man could by no means please God. Which sayings of his, my Lord, your Lordship very well knows, what necessarily thence will follow, to wit, that we do still worship in vain, are yet in our sins, and finally shall be damned; and this is that which I have to say.

Then was Pickthank sworn, and bid say what he knew, in behalf of their lord the king, against the prisoner at the bar.

PICK. My Lord, and you gentlemen all, This fellow I have known of a long time, and have heard him speak things that ought not to be spoke; for he hath railed on our noble prince Beelzebub, and hath spoken contemptibly of his honorable friends, whose names are the Lord Old Man,

LORD HATE-GOOD.

the Lord Carnal Delight, the Lord Luxurious, the Lord Desire of Vain
Glory, my old Lord Lechery, Sir Having Greedy, with all the rest of our
nobility; and he hath said, moreover, That if all men were of his mind,

11

if possible, there is not one of these noblemen should have any longer a being in this town.

Besides, he hath not been afraid to rail on you, my Lord, who are now appointed to be his judge, calling you an ungodly villain, with many other such like vilifying terms, with which he hath bespattered most of the gentry of this town.

When this Pickthank had told his tale, the Judge directed his speech to the prisoner at the bar, saying, Thou runagate, heretic, and traitor, hast thou heard what these honest gentlemen have witnessed against thee?

FAITH. May I speak a few words in my own defence?

JUDGE. Sirrah! Sirrah! thou deservest to live no longer, but to be slain immediately upon the place; yet, that all men may see our gentleness towards thee, let us hear what thou, vile runagate, hast to say.

FAITH. 1. I say, then, in answer to what Mr. Envy hath spoken, I never said aught but this, That what rule, or laws, or customs, or people, were flat against the Word of God, are diametrically opposite to Christianity. If I have said amiss in this, convince me of my error, and I am ready here before you to make my recantation.

FAITHFUL SPEAKS IN HIS OWN DEFENCE.

2. As to the second, to wit, Mr. Superstition, and his charge against

THE JURY:—Mr. Blind-man, Mr. No-good, Mr. Malice, Mr. Love-lust, Mr. Live-loose, Mr. Heady, Mr. High-mind, Mr. Enmity, Mr. Liar, Mr. Cruelty, Mr. Hate-light, and Mr. Implacable.

163

me, I said only this, That in the worship of God there is required a Divine faith; but there can be no Divine faith without a Divine revelation of the will of God.   Therefore, whatever is thrust into the worship of God that is not agreeable to Divine revelation, cannot be done but by a human faith, which faith will not be profitable to eternal life.

3. As to what Mr. Pickthank hath said, I say (avoiding terms, as that I am said to rail, and the like), that the prince of this town, with all the rabblement, his attendants, by this gentleman named, are more fit for a being in hell, than in this town and country: and so, the Lord have mercy upon me!

Then the Judge called to the jury (who all this while stood by, to hear and observe): Gentlemen of the jury, you see this man about whom so great an uproar hath been made in this town.   You have also heard what these worthy gentlemen have witnessed against him.   Also you have heard his reply and confession.   It lieth now in your breasts to hang him or save his life; but yet I think meet to instruct you into our law.

There was an Act made in the days of Pharaoh the Great, servant to our prince, that, lest those of a contrary religion should multiply and grow too strong for him, their males should be thrown into the river.[150]

There was also an Act made in the days of Nebuchadnezzar the Great, another of his servants, that whosoever would not fall down and worship his golden image, should be thrown into a fiery furnace.[151]

There was also an Act made in the days of Darius, that whoso, for some time, called upon any god but him, should be cast into the lions' den.[152]   Now the substance of these laws this rebel has broken, not only in thought (which is not to be borne), but also in word and deed; which must therefore needs be intolerable.

For that of Pharaoh, his law was made upon a supposition, to prevent mischief, no crime being yet apparent; but here is a crime apparent. For the second and third, you see he disputeth against our religion; and for the treason he hath confessed, he deserveth to die the death.

Then went the jury out, whose names were, Mr. Blind-man, Mr. No-good, Mr. Malice, Mr. Love-lust, Mr. Live-loose, Mr. Heady, Mr. High-mind, Mr. Enmity, Mr. Liar, Mr. Cruelty, Mr. Hate-light, and Mr. Implacable; who every one gave in his private verdict against him among themselves, and afterwards unanimously concluded to bring him in guilty before the Judge.   And first, among themselves, Mr. Blind-man, the fore-man, said, I see clearly that this man is a heretic.

Then said Mr. No-good, Away with such a fellow from the earth. Ay, said Mr. Malice, for I hate the very looks of him. Then said Mr. Love-lust, I could never endure him. Nor I, said Mr. Live-loose, for he would be always condemning my way. Hang him, hang him, said Mr. Heady. A sorry scrub, said Mr. High-mind. My heart riseth against him, said

THE JURY AGREE ON THEIR VERDICT.

Mr. Enmity. He is a rogue, said Mr. Liar. Hanging is too good for him, said Mr. Cruelty. Let us despatch him out of the way, said Mr. Hate-light. Then said Mr. Implacable, Might I have all the world given me, I could not be reconciled to him; therefore, let us forthwith bring him in guilty of death.

FAITHFUL IS BURNED AT VANITY FAIR.

And so they did; therefore he was presently condemned to be had from the place where he was, to the place from whence he came, and there to be put to the most cruel death that could be invented.

They, therefore, brought him out, to do with him according to their law; and, first, they scourged him, then they buffeted him, then they lanced his flesh with knives; after that, they stoned him with stones, then pricked him with their swords; and, last of all they burned him to ashes at the stake. Thus came Faithful to his end.

Now, I saw that there stood behind the multitude a chariot and a couple of horses, waiting for Faithful, who (so soon as his adversaries had despatched him) was taken up into it, and straightway was carried up through the clouds, with sound of trumpet, the nearest way to the celestial gate.

But as for Christian, he had some respite, and was remanded back to prison. So he there remained for a space; but he that overrules all things, having the power of their rage in his own hand, so wrought it about, that Christian for that time escaped them, and went his way; and as he went, he sang, saying—

> Well, Faithful, thou hast faithfully profest
> Unto thy Lord; with whom thou shalt be blest,
> When faithless ones, with all their vain delights,
> Are crying out under their hellish plights:
> Sing, Faithful, sing, and let thy name survive:
> For, though they killed thee, thou art yet alive.

CHAPTER VII.

CHRISTIAN AND HOPEFUL ENTER INTO A BROTHERLY COVENANT.

NOW I saw in my dream, that Christian went not forth alone, for there was one whose name was Hopeful (being made so by the beholding of Christian and Faithful in their words and behavior, in their sufferings at the Fair), who joined himself unto him, and, entering into a brotherly covenant, told him that he would be his companion.

Thus, one died to bear testimony to the truth, and another rises out of his ashes, to be a companion with Christian in his pilgrimage. This Hopeful also told Christian, that there were many more of the men in the Fair, that would take their time and follow after.

So I saw that quickly after they were got out of the Fair, they overtook one that was going before them, whose name was By-ends: so they said to him, What countryman, Sir? and how far go you this way? He told them that he came from the town of Fair-speech, and he was going to the Celestial City, but told them not his name.

From Fair-speech! said Christian.   Is there any good that lives there? [153]

Yes, said By-ends, I hope.

CHR. Pray, Sir, what may I call you? said Christian.

BY-ENDS. I am a stranger to you, and you to me: if you be going this way, I shall be glad of your company; if not, I must be content.

CHR. This town of Fair-speech, said Christian, I have heard of; and as I remember, they say it is a wealthy place.

BY-ENDS. Yes, I will assure you that it is; and I have very many rich kindred there.

CHR. Pray, who are your kindred there? if a man be so bold.

BY-ENDS. Almost the whole town; and in particular, my Lord Turn-about, my Lord Time-server, my Lord Fair-speech (from whose ancestors that town first took its name), also Mr. Smooth-man, Mr. Facing-both-ways, Mr. Any-thing; and the parson of our parish, Mr. Two-tongues, was my mother's own brother by father's side; and to tell you the truth, I am become a gentleman of good quality, yet my great-grandfather was but a waterman, looking one way and rowing another, and I got most of my estate by the same occupation.

CHR. Are you a married man?

BY-ENDS. Yes, and my wife is a very virtuous woman, the daughter of a virtuous woman; she was my Lady Feigning's daughter, therefore she came of a very honorable family, and is arrived to such a pitch of breeding that she knows how to carry it to all, even to prince and peasant.

It is true we somewhat differ in religion from those of the stricter sort, yet but in two small points: first we never strive against wind and tide; secondly, we are always most zealous when Religion goes in his silver slippers; we love much to walk with him in the street, if the sun shines, and the people applaud him.

Then Christian stepped a little aside to his fellow, Hopeful, saying, It runs in my mind that this is one By-ends of Fair-speech; and if it be he, we have as very a knave in our company as dwelleth in all these parts.

Then said Hopeful, Ask him; methinks he should not be ashamed of his name.   So Christian came up with him again, and said, Sir, you talk as if you knew something more than all the world doth; and if I take not my mark amiss, I deem I have half a guess of you: Is not your name Mr. By-ends of Fair-speech?

LADY FEIGNING'S DAUGHTER.

BY-ENDS. This is not my name, but indeed it is a nickname that is given me by some that cannot abide me: and I must be content to bear it as a reproach, as other good men have borne theirs before me.

CHR. But did you never give an occasion to men to call you by this name?

BY-ENDS. Never, never! The worse that ever I did to give them an occasion to give me this name was, that I had always the luck to jump in my judgment with the present way of the times, whatever it was, and my chance was to get thereby; but if things are thus cast upon me, let me count them a blessing; but let not the malicious load me therefore with reproach.

CHR. I thought, indeed, that you were the man that I heard of; and to tell you what I think, I fear this name belongs to you more properly than you are willing we should think it doth.

BY-ENDS. Well, if you will thus imagine, I cannot help it; you shall find me a fair company-keeper, if you will still admit me your associate.

CHR. If you will go with us, you must go against wind and tide; the which, I perceive, is against your opinion; you must also own Religion in his rags, as well as when in his silver slippers; and stand by him, too, when bound in irons, as well as when he walketh the streets with applause.

BY-ENDS. You must not impose, nor lord it over my faith; leave me to my liberty, and let me go with you.

CHR. Not a step further, unless you will do in what I propound as we.

Then, said By-ends, I shall never desert my old principles, since they are harmless and profitable. If I may not go with you, I must do as I did before you overtook me, even go by myself, until some overtake me that will be glad of my company.

Now I saw in my dream, that Christian and Hopeful forsook him, and kept their distance before him; but one of them looking back, saw three men following Mr. By-ends, and behold, as they came up to him, he made them a very low bow; and they also gave him a compliment. The men's names were Mr. Hold-the-world, Mr. Money-love, and Mr. Save-all; men that Mr. By-ends had formerly been acquainted with; for in their minority they were schoolfellows, and were taught by one Mr. Gripe-man, a schoolmaster in Love-gain, which is a market town in the county of Coveting, in the north. This schoolmaster taught them the art of getting, either by violence, cozenage, flattery, lying or by putting on a guise of religion; and these four gentlemen had attained much of the art of their master, so that they could each of them have kept such a school themselves.

Well, when they had, as I said, thus saluted each other, Mr. Money-love said to Mr. By-ends, Who are they upon the road before us? (for Christian and Hopeful were yet within view.)

By-ends. They are a couple of far country men, that, after their mode, are going on pilgrimage.

BY-ENDS AND HIS FRIENDS.

Money-love. Alas! Why did they not stay, that we might have had their good company? for they, and we, and you, Sir, I hope, are all going on a pilgrimage.

By-ends. We are so, indeed; but the men before us are so rigid, and love so much their own notions, and do also so lightly esteem the opinions of others, that let a man be never so godly, yet if he jumps not with them in all things, they thrust him quite out of their company.

SAVE-ALL. That is bad, but we read of some that are righteous overmuch; and such men's rigidness prevails with them to judge and condemn all but themselves. But I pray, what, and how many, were the things wherein you differed?

BY-ENDS. Why, they, after their headstrong manner, conclude that it is duty to rush on their journey all weathers; and I am for waiting for wind and tide.

They are for hazarding all for God at a clap; and I am for taking all advantages to secure my life and estate.

They are for holding their notions, though all other men are against them; but I am for Religion in what, and so far as the times, and my safety, will bear it.

They are for Religion when in rags and contempt; but I am for him when he walks in his golden slippers, in the sunshine, and with applause.

MR. HOLD-THE-WORLD. Aye, and hold you there still, good Mr. By-ends; for, for my part, I can count him but a fool, that having the liberty to keep what he has, shall be so unwise as to lose it.

Let us be wise as serpents; it is best to make hay when the sun shines; you see how the bee lieth still all winter, and bestirs her only when she can have profit with pleasure. God sends sometimes rain, and sometimes sunshine; if they be such fools to go through the first, yet let us be content to take fair weather along with us.

For my part, I like that religion best that will stand with the security of God's good blessings unto us; for who can imagine, that is ruled by his reason, since God has bestowed upon us the good things of this life, but that he would have us keep them for his sake? Abraham and Solomon grew rich in religion. And Job says, that a good man shall lay up gold as dust. But he must not be such as the men before us, if they be as you have described them.

MR. SAVE-ALL. I think that we are all agreed in this matter, and therefore there needs no more words about it.

MR. MONEY-LOVE. No, there needs no more words about this matter, indeed; for he that believes neither Scripture nor reason (and you see we have both on our side), neither knows his own liberty, nor seeks his own safety.

MR. BY-ENDS. My brethren, we are, as you see, going all on pilgrimage; and for our better diversion from things that are bad, give me leave to propound unto you this question :—

Suppose a man, a minister, or a tradesman, &c., should have an advantage lie before him, to get the good blessings of this life, yet so as that he can by no means come by them except, in appearance at least, he becomes extraordinarily zealous in some points of religion that he meddled not with before; may he not use these means to attain his end, and yet be a right honest man?

MR. MONEY-LOVE. I see the bottom of your question; and with these gentlemen's good leave, I will endeavor to shape you an answer.

And first, to speak to your question as it concerns a minister himself: Suppose, a minister, a worthy man, possessed but of a very small benefice, and has in his eye a greater, more fat, and plump by far; he has also now an opportunity of getting of it, yet so as by being more studious, by preaching more frequently, and zealously, and, because the temper of the people requires it, by altering of some of his principles; for my part, I see no reason but a man may do this (provided he has a call), aye, and more a great deal besides, and yet be an honest man. For why—

1. His desire of a greater benefice is lawful (this cannot be contradicted), since it is set before him by Providence; so then, he may get it, if he can, making no question for conscience' sake.

2. Besides, his desire after that benefice makes him more studious, a more zealous preacher, &c., and so makes him a better man; yea, makes him better improve his parts, which is according to the mind of God.

3. Now, as for his complying with the temper of his people, by dissenting, to serve them, some of his principles, this argueth—(1) That he is a self-denying temper; (2) Of a sweet and winning deportment; and so (3) more fit for the ministerial function.

4. I conclude, then, that a minister that changes a small for a great, should not for so doing, be judged as covetous; but rather, since he has improved in his parts and industry thereby, be counted as one that pursues his call, and the opportunity put into his hand to do good.

And now to the second part of the question, which concerns the tradesman you mentioned. Suppose such an one to have but a poor employ in the world, but by becoming religious, he may mend his market, perhaps get a rich wife, or more and far better customers to his shop; for my part, I see no reason but that this may be lawfully done. For why—

MR. MONEY-LOVE'S LESSON.

1. To become religious is a virtue, by what means soever a man becomes so.

2. Nor is it unlawful to get a rich wife, or more custom to my shop.

3. Besides, the man that gets these by becoming religious, gets that which is good, of them that are good, by becoming good himself; so then here is a good wife, and good customers, and good gain, and all these by becoming religious, which is good; therefore, to become religious, to get all these, is a good and profitable design.

This answer, thus made by this Mr. Money-love to Mr. By-ends' question, was highly applauded by them all; wherefore they concluded, upon the whole, that it was most wholesome and advantageous. And because, as they thought, no man was able to contradict it, and because Christian and Hopeful were yet within call, they jointly agreed to assault them with the question as soon as they overtook them; and the rather because they had opposed Mr. By-ends before.

So they called after them, and they stopped, and stood still till they came up to them; but they concluded, as they went, that not Mr. By-ends, but old Mr. Hold-the-world, should propound the question to them, because as they supposed, their answer to him would be without the remainder of that heat that was kindled betwixt Mr. By-ends and them, at their parting a little before.

So they came up to each other, and after a short salutation, Mr. Hold-the-world propounded the question to Christian and his fellow, and bid them to answer it if they could.

CHR. Then said Christian, Even a babe in religion may answer ten thousand such questions. For if it be unlawful to follow Christ for loaves (as it is in the sixth of John), how much more abominable is it to make of him and religion a stalking-horse, to get and enjoy the world! Nor do we find any other than heathens, hypocrites, devils, and witches, that are of this opinion.

1. Heathens; for when Hamor and Shechem had a mind to the daughter and cattle of Jacob, and saw that there was no way for them to come at them, but by becoming circumcised; they say to their companions, if every male of us be circumcised, as they are circumcised, shall not their cattle, and their substance, and every beast of theirs, be ours? Their daughter and their cattle were that which they sought to obtain, and their religion the stalking-horse they made use of to come at them. Read the whole story.[154]

2. The hypocritical Pharisees were also of this religion; long prayers were their pretence, but to get widows' houses was their intent; and greater damnation was from God their judgment.[155]

3. Judas the devil was also of this religion; he was religious for the bag, that he might be possessed of what was therein; but he was lost, cast away, and the very son of perdition.

4. Simon the witch was of this religion too; for he would have had the Holy Ghost, that he might have got money therewith; and his sentence from Peter's mouth was according.[156]

5. Neither will it out of my mind, but that that man that takes up

CHRISTIAN ANSWERS BY-ENDS AND HIS FRIENDS.

religion for the world, will throw away religion for the world; for so surely as Judas resigned the world in becoming religious, so surely did he also sell religion and his Master for the same.

To answer the question, therefore, affirmatively, as I perceive you have done, and to accept of, as authentic, such answer, is both heathenish, hypocritical, and devilish; and your reward will be according to your works.

Then they stood staring one upon another, but had not wherewith to answer Christian. Hopeful also approved of the soundness of Christian's answer; so there was a great silence among them. Mr. By-ends and his

12

company also staggered and kept behind, that Christian and Hopeful might outgo them.

Then said Christian to his fellow, If these men cannot stand before the sentence of men, what will they do with the sentence of God? And if they are mute when dealt with by vessels of clay, what will they do when they shall be rebuked by the flames of a devouring fire?

Then Christian and Hopeful outwent them again, and went till they came at a delicate plain called Ease, where they went with much content; but that plain was but narrow, so they were quickly got over it.

Now, at the further side of that plain was a little hill called Lucre, and in that hill a silver mine, which some of them that had formerly gone that way, because of the rarity of it, had turned aside to see; but going too near the brink of the pit, the ground being deceitful under them, broke, and they were slain: some also had been maimed there, and could not, to their dying day, be their own men again.

Then I saw in my dream, that a little off the road, over against the silver mine, stood Demas (gentleman-like) to call to passengers to come and see; who said to Christian and his fellow, Ho! turn aside hither, and I will show you a thing.

CHR. What thing is so deserving as to turn us out of the way to see it?

DEMAS. Here is a silver mine, and some digging in it for treasure. If you will come, with a little pains you may richly provide for yourselves.

HOPE. Then said Hopeful, Let us go see.

CHR. Not I, said Christian, I have heard of this place before now; and how many have there been slain; and besides that, treasure is a snare to those that seek it; for it hindereth them in their pilgrimage. Then Christian called to Demas saying, Is not the place dangerous? Hath it not hindered many in their pilgrimage? [157]

DEMAS. Not very dangerous, except to those that are careless (but withal, he blushed as he spake).

CHR. Then said Christian to Hopeful, Let us not stir a step, but still keep on our way.

HOPE. I will warrant you, when By-ends comes up, if he hath the same invitation as we, he will turn in thither to see.

CHR. No doubt thereof, for his principles lead him that way, and a hundred to one but he dies there.

DEMAS. Then Demas called again, saying, But will you not come over and see?

CHR. Then Christian roundly answered, saying, Demas, thou art an enemy to the right ways of the Lord of this way, and hast been already condemned for thine own turning aside, by one of his Majesty's judges;[158] and why seekest thou to bring us into the like condemnation? Besides, if we at all turn aside, our Lord the King will certainly hear thereof, and will there put us to shame, where we would stand with boldness before him.

DEMAS TEMPTS CHRISTIAN AND HOPEFUL.

Demas cried again that he also was one of their fraternity; and that if they would tarry a little, he also himself would walk with them.

CHR. Then said Christian, What is thy name? Is it not the same by the which I have called thee?

DEMAS. Yes, my name is Demas; I am the son of Abraham.

CHR. I know you; Gehazi was your great-grandfather, and Judas your father; and you have trod in their steps.[159] It is but a devilish prank that

thou usest; thy father was hanged for a traitor, and thou deservest no
better reward.   Assure thyself, that when we come to the King, we will
do him word of this thy behavior.   Thus they went their way.

By this time By-ends and his companions were come again within
sight, and they, at the first beck, went over to Demas.   Now whether they
fell into the pit by looking over the brink thereof, or whether they went
down to dig, or whether they were smothered in the bottom by the damps
that commonly arise, of these things I am not certain; but this I observed,
that they never were seen again in the way.   Then sang Christian—

> By-ends and silver Demas both agree ;
> One calls, the other runs, that he may be
> A sharer in his lucre ; so these do
> Take up in this world, and no further go.

Now I saw that, just on the other side of this plain, the Pilgrims came
to a place where stood an old monument, hard by the highway side, at the
sight of which they were both concerned, because of the strangeness of the
form thereof; for it seemed to them as if it had been a woman transformed
into the shape of a pillar; here therefore they stood looking, and looking
upon it, but could not for a time tell what they should make thereof.

At last Hopeful espied written above the head thereof, a writing in an
unusual hand; but he being no scholar, called to Christian (for he was
learned) to see if he could pick out the meaning; so he came, and after a
little laying of letters together, he found the same to be this, "Remember Lot's wife."

So he read it to his fellow; after which they both concluded that that
was the pillar of salt into which Lot's wife was turned, for her looking
back with a covetous heart, when she was going from Sodom for safety.[160]
Which sudden and amazing sight gave them occasion of this discourse.

CHR. Ah, my brother! this is a seasonable sight; it came opportunely
to us after the invitation which Demas gave us to come over to view
the Hill Lucre; and had we gone over, as he desired us, and as thou
wast inclining to do, my brother, we had, for aught I know, been made
ourselves like this woman, a spectacle for those that shall come after to
behold.

HOPE. I am sorry that I was so foolish, and am made to wonder that
I am not now as Lot's wife; for wherein was the difference betwixt her
sin and mine ?   She only looked back; and I had a desire to go and see.

THE PILLAR OF SALT.

Let grace be adored, and let me be ashamed that ever such a thing should be in mine heart.

CHR. Let us take notice of what we see here, for our help for time to come. This woman escaped one judgment, for she fell not by the destruction of Sodom; yet she was destroyed by another, as we see she is turned into a pillar of salt.

HOPE. True; and she may be to us both caution and example; caution, that we should shun her sin; or a sign of what judgment will overtake such as shall not be prevented by this caution; so Korah, Dathan, and Abiram, with the two hundred and fifty men that perished in their sin, did also become a sign or example to others to beware.[161]

But above all, I muse at one thing, to wit, how Demas and his fellows can stand so confidently yonder to look for that treasure, which this woman, but for looking behind her after (for we read not that she stepped one foot out of the way), was turned into a pillar of salt; especially since the judgment which overtook her did make her an example, within sight of where they are; for they cannot choose but see her, did they but lift up their eyes.

CHR. It is a thing to be wondered at, and it argueth that their hearts are grown desperate in the case; and I cannot tell who to compare them to so fitly, as to them that pick pockets in the presence of the judge, or that will cut purses under the gallows.

It is said of the men of Sodom, that they were sinners exceedingly, because they were sinners before the Lord, that is, in his eyesight, and notwithstanding the kindness that he had showed them;[162] for the land of Sodom was now like the garden of Eden heretofore.[163] This, therefore, provoked him the more to jealousy, and made their plague as hot as the fire of the Lord out of heaven could make it.

And it is most rationally to be concluded, that such, even such as these are, that shall sin in the sight, yea, and that too in despite of such examples that are set continually before them, to caution them to the contrary, must be partakers of severest judgments.

HOPE. Doubtless thou hast said the truth; but what a mercy is it, that neither thou, but especially I, am not made myself this example! This ministereth occasion to us to thank God, to fear before him, and always to remember Lot's wife.

I saw, then, that they went on their way to a pleasant river; which David the king called "the river of God," but John, "the river of the water of life."[164]

Now their way lay just upon the bank of the river; here, therefore, Christian and his companion walked with great delight; they drank also of the water of the river, which was pleasant, and enlivening to their weary spirits; besides, on the banks of this river, on either side were green trees, that bore all manner of fruit; and the leaves of the trees were good for medicine; with the fruit of these trees they were also much delighted: and the leaves they eat to prevent surfeits, and other diseases that are incident to those that heat their blood by travels.

REMEMBER LOT'S WIFE.

On either side of the river was also a meadow, curiously beautified with lilies, and it was green all the year long. In this meadow they lay down, and slept; for here they might lie down safely. When they awoke, they gathered again of the fruit of the trees, and drank again of the water of the river, and then lay down again to sleep.[165] Thus they did several days and nights. Then they sang—

> Behold ye how these crystal streams do glide,
> To comfort pilgrims by the highway side;
> The meadows green, beside their fragrant smell,
> Yield dainties for them: and he that can tell

What pleasant fruit, yea, leaves, these trees do yield,
Will soon sell all, that he may buy this field.

So when they were disposed to go on (for they were not, as yet, at their journey's end), they ate and drank, and departed.

Now, I beheld in my dream, that they had not journeyed far, but the river and the way for a time parted; at which they were not a little sorry; yet they durst not go out of the way.

THE PILGRIMS REST BY THE RIVER OF THE WATER OF LIFE.

Now the way from the river was rough, and their feet tender, by reason of their travels; "so the souls of the pilgrims were much discouraged because of the way." [166] Wherefore, still as they went on, they wished for better way. Now, a little before them, there was on the left hand of the road a meadow, and a stile to go over into it; and that meadow is called By-path Meadow.

Then said Christian to his fellow, If this meadow lieth along by our way-side, let us go over into it. Then he went to the stile to see, and behold, a path lay along by the way, on the other side of the fence. It is according to my wish, said Christian. Here is the easiest going; come good Hopeful, and let us go over.

HOPE. But how if this path should lead us out of the way?

That is not likely, said the other. Look, doth it not go along by the way-side? So Hopeful, being persuaded by his fellow, went after him over the stile.

CHRISTIAN AND HOPEFUL AT THE STILE LEADING INTO BY-PATH MEADOW.

When they were gone over, and were got into the path, they found it very easy for their feet; and, withal, they, looking before them, espied a man walking as they did, (and his name was Vain-confidence); so they called after him, and asked him whither that way led. He said, To the Celestial Gate. Look, said Christian, did not I tell you so? By this you may see we are right. So they followed, and he went before them. But, behold the night came on, and it grew very dark; so that they that were behind lost the sight of him that went before.

He, therefore, that went before (Vain-confidence by name), not seeing the way before him, fell into a deep pit,[167] which was on purpose there made, by the Prince of those grounds, to catch vain-glorious fools withal, and was dashed in pieces with his fall.

Now Christian and his fellow heard him fall. So they called to know the matter, but there was none to answer, only they heard a groaning. Then said Hopeful, Where are we now? Then was his fellow silent, as mistrusting that he had led him out of the way; and now it began to rain, and thunder, and lighten in a very dreadful manner; and the water rose amain.

Then Hopeful groaned in himself, saying, Oh, that I had kept on my way!

CHR. Who could have thought that this path should have led us out of the way?

HOPE. I was afraid on it at the very first, and therefore gave you that gentle caution. I would have spoken plainer, but that you are older than I.

CHR. Good brother, be not offended; I am sorry I have brought thee out of the way, and that I have put thee into such imminent danger; pray, my brother, forgive me; I did not do it of an evil intent.

HOPE. Be comforted, my brother, for I forgive thee; and believe, too, that this shall be for our good.

CHR. I am glad I have with me a merciful brother; but we must not stand thus: let us try to go back again.

HOPE. But, good brother, let me go before.

CHR. No, if you please, let me go first, that if there be any danger, I may be first therein, because by my means we are both gone out of the way.

HOPE. No, said Hopeful, you shall not go first; for your mind being troubled may lead you out of the way again. Then, for their encouragement, they heard the voice of one saying, "Set thine heart toward the highway, even the way which thou wentest; turn again." [168]

But by this time the waters were greatly risen, by reason of which the way of going back was very dangerous. (Then I thought that it is easier going out of the way, when we are in, than going in when we are out.) Yet they adventured to go back, but it was so dark, and the flood was so high, that in their going back they had like to have been drowned nine or ten times.

Neither could they, with all the skill they had, get again to the stile that night. Wherefore, at last, lighting under a little shelter, they sat down there until the daybreak; but, being weary, they fell asleep.

Now there was, not far from the place where they lay, a castle called Doubting Castle; the owner whereof was Giant Despair; and it was in his grounds they now were sleeping: wherefore he, getting up in the morning early, and walking up and down in his fields, caught Christian and Hopeful asleep in his grounds. Then, with a grim and surly voice, he bid them awake; and asked them whence they were. and what they did in his grounds.

They told him they were pilgrims, and that they had lost their way. Then said the Giant, You have this night trespassed on me, by tram-

THE PILGRIMS FOUND ASLEEP BV GIANT DESPAIR.

pling in, and lying on my grounds, and therefore you must go along with me.

So they were forced to go, because he was stronger than they. They also had but little to say, for they knew themselves in a fault.

The Giant, therefore, drove them before him, and put them into his castle, into a very dark dungeon, nasty and stinking to the spirits of these two men.[169] Here, then, they lay from Wednesday morning till Saturday night, without one bit of bread, or drop of drink, or light, or any to ask how they did; they were, therefore, here in evil case, and were far from friends and acquaintance.

Now in this place Christian had double sorrow, because it was through his unadvised counsel that they were brought into this distress.

Now Giant Despair had a wife, and her name was Diffidence. So when he was gone to bed, he told his wife what he had done; to wit, that he had taken a couple of prisoners and cast them into his dungeon, for trespassing on his grounds.

Then he asked her also what he had best to do further to them. So she asked him what they were, whence they came, and whither they were bound; and he told her. Then she counselled him that when he arose in the morning he should beat them without any mercy.

So, when he arose, he getteth him a grievous crab-tree cudgel, and goes down into the dungeon to them, and there first falls to rating of them as if they were dogs, although they never gave him a word of distaste. Then he falls upon them, and beats them fearfully, in such sort, that they were not able to help themselves, or to turn them upon the floor. This done, he withdraws and leaves them, there to condole their misery, and to mourn under their distress. So all that day they spent the time in nothing but sighs and bitter lamentations. The next night, she, talking with her husband about them further, and understanding they were yet alive, did advise him to counsel them to make away with themselves.

So when morning was come, he goes to them in a surly manner as before, and perceiving them to be very sore with the stripes that he had given them the day before, he told them, that since they were never like to come out of that place, their only way would be forthwith to make an end of themselves, either with knife, halter, or poison, for why, said he, should you choose life, seeing it is attended with so much bitterness? But they desired him to let them go.

With that he looked ugly upon them, and, rushing to them, had doubtless made an end of them himself, but that he fell into one of his fits (for he sometimes, in sunshiny weather, fell into fits), and lost for a time the use of his hands; wherefore he withdrew, and left them as before, to consider what to do. Then did the prisoners consult between themselves, whether it was best to take his counsel or no; and thus they began to discourse:—

CHR. Brother, said Christian, what shall we do? The life that we

CHRISTIAN AND HOPEFUL IN THE CASTLE OF GIANT DESPAIR.

189

now live is miserable. For my part I know not which is best, to live thus, or to die out of hand. "My soul chooseth strangling rather than life," [170] and the grave is more easy for me than this dungeon. Shall we be ruled by the Giant?

HOPE. Indeed, our present condition is dreadful, and death would be far more welcome to me than thus for ever to abide; but yet, let us consider, the Lord of the country to which we are going hath said, Thou shalt do no murder: no, not to another man's person; much more, then, are we forbidden to take his counsel to kill ourselves.

Besides, he that kills another, can but commit murder upon his body; but for one to kill himself is to kill body and soul at once. And, moreover, my brother, thou talkest of ease in the grave; but hast thou forgotten the hell, whither for certain the murderers go? For "no murderer hath eternal life," &c. And let us consider, again, that all the law is not in the hand of Giant Despair.

Others, so far as I can understand, have been taken by him, as well as we; and yet have escaped out of his hand. Who knows, but that God, who made the world, may cause that Giant Despair may die? or that, at some time or other, he may forget to lock us in? or that he may, in a short time, have another of his fits before us, and may lose the use of his limbs? and if ever that should come to pass again, for my part, I am resolved to pluck up the heart of a man, and to try my utmost to get from under his hand.

I was a fool that I did not try to do it before; but, however, my brother, let us be patient, and endure a while. The time may come that may give us happy release; but let us not be our own murderers. With these words, Hopeful at present did moderate the mind of his brother; so they continued together (in the dark) that day, in their sad and doleful condition.

Well, towards evening, the Giant goes down into the dungeon again, to see if his prisoners had taken his counsel; but when he came there he found them alive; and truly, alive was all; for now, what for want of bread and water, and by reason of the wounds they received when he beat them, they could do little but breathe. But, I say, he found them alive; at which he fell into a grievous rage, and told them that, seeing they had disobeyed his counsel, it should be worse with them than if they had never been born.

At this they trembled greatly, and I think that Christian fell into a

CASTLE OF GIANT DESPAIR.

swoon; but, coming a little to himself again, they renewed their discourse about the Giant's counsel; and whether yet they had best to take it or no. Now Christian again seemed to be for doing it, but Hopeful made his second reply as followeth:—

THE GIANT GOES DOWN INTO THE DUNGEON TO SEE THE PILGRIMS.

HOPE. My brother, said he, rememberest thou not how valiant thou hast been heretofore? Apollyon could not crush thee, nor could all that thou didst hear, or see, or feel in the Valley of the Shadow of Death. What hardship, terror, and amazement hast thou already gone through! And art thou now nothing but fear? Thou seest that I am in the dungeon with thee, a far weaker man by nature than thou art; also, this Giant has wounded me as well as thee, and hath also cut off the bread and water from my mouth; and with thee I mourn without the light. But let us exercise a little more patience; remember how thou playedst the man at Vanity Fair, and wast neither afraid of the chain, nor cage, nor yet of bloody death. Wherefore let us (at least to avoid the shame, that becomes not a Christian to be found in) bear up with patience as well as we can.

Now, night being come again, and the Giant and his wife being in bed, she asked him concerning the prisoners, and if they had taken his counsel. To which he replied, They are sturdy rogues, they choose rather to bear all hardship, than to make away with themselves.

Then said she, Take them into the castle-yard to-morrow, and show them the bones and skulls of those that thou hast already despatched, and make them believe, ere a week comes to an end, thou also wilt tear them in pieces, as thou hast done their fellows before them.

So when the morning was come, the Giant goes to them again, and takes them into the castle-yard, and shows them, as his wife had bidden him.

These, said he, were pilgrims as you are, once, and they trespassed in my grounds, as you have done; and when I thought fit, I tore them in pieces, and so, within ten days, I will do you. Go, get you down to your den again; and with that he beat them all the way thither.

They lay, therefore, all day on Saturday in a lamentable case, as before. Now, when night was come, and when Mrs. Diffidence and her husband, the Giant, were got to bed, they began to renew their discourse of their prisoners; and withal the old Giant wondered, that he could neither by his blows nor his counsel bring them to an end. And with that his wife replied, I fear, said she, that they live in hope that some will come to relieve them, or that they have picklocks about them, by the means of which they hope to escape. And sayest thou so, my dear? said the Giant; I will, therefore, search them in the morning.

Well, on Saturday, about midnight, they began to pray, and continued in prayer till almost break of day.

Now, a little before it was day, good Christian, as one half amazed, brake out in this passionate speech: What a fool, quoth he, am I, thus to lie in a stinking dungeon, when I may as well walk at liberty! I have a key in my bosom, called Promise, that will, I am persuaded, open any lock in Doubting Castle. Then said Hopeful, That is good news, good brother; pluck it out of thy bosom, and try.

13

Then Christian pulled it out of his bosom, and began to try at the dungeon door, whose bolt (as he turned the key) gave back, and the door flew open with ease, and Christian and Hopeful both came out.

Then he went to the outward door that leads into the castle-yard, and with his key, opened that door also. After that, he went to the iron gate, for that must be opened too; but that lock went desperately hard, yet the key did open it.

CHRISTIAN FINDS THE KEY CALLED PROMISE.

Then they thrust open the gate to make their escape with speed, but that gate, as it opened, made such a creaking, that it waked Giant Despair, who hastily rising to pursue his prisoners, felt his limbs to fail, for his fits took him again, so that he could by no means go after them. Then they went on, and came to the King's highway, and so were safe, because they were out of his jurisdiction.

Now, when they were gone over the stile, they began to contrive with themselves what they should do at that stile, to prevent those that should come after, from falling into the hands of Giant Despair. So they consented to erect there a pillar, and to engrave upon the side thereof this sentence—"Over this stile is the way to Doubting Castle, which is kept by Giant Despair, who despiseth the King of the Celestial Country, and seeks to destroy his holy pilgrims." Many, therefore, that followed after, read what was written, and escaped the danger. This done, they sang as follows:

Out of the way we went, and then we found
What 'twas to tread upon forbidden ground ;
And let them that come after have a care,
Lest heedlessness makes them, as we, to fare.
Lest they for trespassing his prisoners are,
Whose castle's Doubting, and whose name's Despair.

CHRISTIAN AND HOPEFUL ESCAPE FROM DOUBTING CASTLE.

CHAPTER VIII.

HEY went then till they came to the Delectable Mountains, which mountains belong to the Lord of that hill of which we have spoken before; so they went up to the mountains, to behold the gardens and orchards, the vineyards and fountains of water; where also they drank and washed themselves, and did freely eat of the vineyards.

THE PILGRIMS WELCOMED BY THE SHEPHERDS ON THE DELECTABLE MOUNTAINS.

Now there were on the tops of these mountains shepherds feeding their flocks, and they stood by the highway side. The Pilgrims therefore went to them, and leaning upon their staves (as is common with weary pilgrims, when they stand to talk with any by the way), they asked, Whose Delectable Mountains are these? And whose be the sheep that feed upon them?

SHEP. These mountains are Immanuel's Land, and they are within sight of his city; and the sheep also are his, and he laid down his life for them.[171]

CHR. Is this the way to the Celestial City?

SHEP. You are just in your way.

CHR. How far is it thither?

SHEP. Too far for any but those that shall get thither indeed.

CHR. Is the way safe or dangerous?

SHEP. Safe for those for whom it is to be safe; "but the transgressors shall fall therein."[172]

CHR. Is there, in this place, any relief for pilgrims that are weary and faint in the way?

SHEP. The Lord of these mountains hath given us a charge not to be "forgetful to entertain strangers,"[173] therefore the good of the place is before you.

I saw also in my dream, that when the Shepherds perceived that they were wayfaring men, they also put questions to them, to which they made answer as in other places; as, Whence came you? and, How got you into the way? and, By what means have you so persevered therein? For but few of them that begin to come hither do show their face on these mountains.

But when the Shepherds heard their answers, being pleased therewith, they looked very lovingly upon them, and said, Welcome to the Delectable Mountains.

The Shepherds, I say, whose names were Knowledge, Experience, Watchful, and Sincere, took them by the hand, and had them to their tents, and made them partake of that which was ready at present. They said, moreover, We would that ye should stay here a while, to be acquainted with us; and yet more to solace yourselves with the good of these Delectable Mountains. Then they told them, that they were content to stay; so they went to their rest that night, because it was very late.

Then I saw in my dream, that in the morning the Shepherds called up Christian and Hopeful to walk with them upon the mountains; so they went forth with them, and walked a while, having a pleasant prospect on every side.   Then said the Shepherds one to another, Shall we show these pilgrims some wonders?   So when they had concluded to do it, they had them first to the top of a hill called Error, which was very steep on the furthest side, and bid them look down to the bottom.

So Christian and Hopeful looked down, and saw at the bottom several men dashed all to pieces by a fall that they had from the top.   Then said Christian, What meaneth this?   The Shepherds answered, Have you not

THE SHEPHERDS SHOW THE PILGRIMS THE HILL ERROR.

heard of them that were made to err, by hearkening to Hymeneus and Philetus, as concerning the faith of the resurrection of the body?[174]

They answered, Yes.   Then said the Shepherds, Those that you see lie dashed in pieces at the bottom of this mountain are they; and they have continued to this day unburied, as you see, for an example to others to take heed how they clamber too high, or how they come too near the brink of this mountain.

Then I saw that they had them to the top of another mountain, and the name of that is Caution, and bid them look afar off; which, when they did, they perceived, as they thought, several men walking up and down among the tombs that were there: and they perceived that the men were blind, because they stumbled sometimes upon the tombs, and because they could not get out from among them. Then said Christian, What means this?

The Shepherds then answered, Did you not see a little below these mountains a stile that led into a meadow, on the left hand of this way? They answered, Yes.

THE VICTIMS OF GIANT DESPAIR AMONG THE TOMBS.

Then said the Shepherds, From that stile there goes a path that leads directly to Doubting Castle, which is kept by Giant Despair, and these (pointing to them among the tombs) came once on pilgrimage, as you do now, even till they came to that same stile; and because the right way was rough in that place, they chose to go out of it into that meadow, and there were taken by Giant Despair, and cast into Doubting Castle; where, after they had been a while kept in the dungeon, he at last did put out their eyes, and led them among those tombs, where he has left them to wander to this very day, that the saying of the wise man might be fulfilled, "He that wandereth out of the way of understanding, shall remain in the congregation of the dead." [175]

Then Christian and Hopeful looked upon one another, with tears gushing out, but yet said nothing to the Shepherds.

Then I saw in my dream, that the Shepherds had them to another place, in a valley, where was a door in the side of a hill, and they opened the door, and bid them look in. They looked in, therefore, and saw that within it was very dark and smoky; they also thought that they heard there a rumbling noise as of fire, and a cry of some tormented, and that they smelt the scent of brimstone.

Then said Christian, What means this? The Shepherds told them, This is a by-way to hell, a way that hypocrites go in at; namely, such as sell their birthright, with Esau; such as sell their master, with Judas; such as blaspheme the gospel, with Alexander; and that lie and dissemble, with Ananias and Sapphira his wife. Then said Hopeful to the Shepherds, I perceive that these had on them, even every one, a show of pilgrimage, as we have now; had they not?

Shep. Yes, and held it a long time too.

Hope. How far might they go on in pilgrimage in their day, since they notwithstanding were thus miserably cast away?

Shep. Some further, and some not so far, as these mountains.

Then said the Pilgrims one to another, We have need to cry to the Strong for strength.

Shep. Aye, and you will have need to use it, when you have it, too.

By this time the Pilgrims had a desire to go forward, and the Shepherds a desire they should; so they walked together towards the end of the mountains. Then said the Shepherds one to another, Let us here show to the Pilgrims the gates of the Celestial City, if they have skill to look through our perspective glass. The Pilgrims then lovingly accepted the motion; so they had them to the top of a high hill, called Clear, and gave them their glass to look.

Then they essayed to look, but the remembrance of that last thing that the Shepherds had shown them, made their hands shake; by means of which impediment, they could not look steadily through the glass; yet they thought they saw something like the gate, and also some of the glory of the place. Then they went away, and sang this song—

Thus, by the Shepherds, secrets are reveal'd,
Which from all other men are kept conceal'd.
Come to the Shepherds, then, if you would see
Things deep, things hid, and that mysterious be.

When they were about to depart, one of the Shepherds gave them a note of the way. Another of them bid them beware of the Flatterer. The third bid them take heed that they sleep not upon the Enchanted Ground. And the fourth bid them God-speed. So I awoke from my dream.

CHAPTER IX.

AND I slept, and dreamed again, and saw the same two Pilgrims going down the mountains along the highway towards the city. Now, a little below these mountains, on the left hand, lieth the country of Conceit; from which country there comes into the way in which the Pilgrims walked, a little crooked lane.

Here, therefore, they met with a very brisk lad, that came out of that country; and his name was Ignorance. So Christian asked him from what parts he came, and whither he was going.

IGNOR. Sir, I was born in the country that lieth off there a little on the left hand, and I am going to the Celestial City.

CHR. But how do you think to get in at the gate? for you may find some difficulty there.

IGNOR. As other good people do, said he.

CHR. But what have you to show at that gate, that may cause that the gate should be opened to you?

IGNOR. I know my Lord's will, and I have been a good liver; I pay every man his own; I pray, fast, pay tithes, and give alms, and have left my country for whither I am going.

CHR. But thou camest not in at the wicket-gate that is at the head of this way; thou camest in hither through that same crooked lane, and therefore, I fear, however thou mayest think of thyself, when the reckoning day shall come, thou wilt have laid to thy charge that thou art a thief and a robber, instead of getting admittance into the city.

IGNOR. Gentlemen, ye be utter strangers to me, I know you not; be content to follow the religion of your country, and I will follow the religion of mine. I hope all will be well. And as for the gate that you talk of, all the world knows that that is a great way off of our country. I cannot think that any man in all our parts doth so much as know the way to it, nor need they care whether they do or no, since we have, as you see, a fine, pleasant green lane, that comes down from our country, the next way into the way.

202

IGNORANCE.

When Christian saw that the man was "wise in his own conceit," he said to Hopeful whisperingly, "There is more hope of a fool than of him."[176] And said, moreover, "When he that is a fool walketh by the way, his wisdom faileth him, and he saith to every one that he is a fool."[177] What, shall we talk further with him, or out-go him at present, and so leave him to think of what he hath heard already, and then stop again for him afterwards, and see if by degrees we can do any good to him? Then said Hopeful—

> Let Ignorance a little while now muse
> On what is said, and let him not refuse
> Good counsel to embrace, lest he remain
> Still ignorant of what's the chiefest gain.
> God saith, those that no understanding have,
> Although he made them, them he will not save.

HOPE. He further added, It is not good, I think, to say all to him at once; let us pass him by, if you will, and talk to him anon, even as he is able to bear it.

So they both went on, and Ignorance he came after. Now when they had passed him a little way, they entered into a very dark lane, where they met a man whom seven devils had bound with seven strong cords, and were carrying back to the door that they saw on the side of the hill.[178]

Now good Christian began to tremble, and so did Hopeful his companion; yet as the devils led away the man, Christian looked to see if he knew him; and he thought it might be one Turn-away, that dwelt in the town of Apostasy. But he did not perfectly see his face, for he did hang his head like a thief that is found. But being once past, Hopeful looked after him, and espied on his back a paper with this inscription, "Wanton professor and damnable apostate."

Then said Christian to his fellow, Now I call to remembrance, that which was told me of a thing that happened to a good man hereabout. The name of the man was Little-faith, but a good man, and he dwelt in the town of Sincere.

The thing was this: At the entering in at this passage, there comes down from Broad-way Gate, a lane called Dead Man's Lane; so called because of the murders that are commonly done there; and this Little-faith going on pilgrimage, as we do now, chanced to sit down there, and slept.

Now there happened, at that time, to come down the lane, from Broad-way Gate, three sturdy rogues, and their names were Faint-heart, Mistrust, and Guilt (three brothers), and they, espying Little-faith, where he was, came galloping up with speed. Now the good man was just awake from his sleep, and was getting up to go on his journey. So they came up all to him, and with threatening language bid him stand.

At this Little-faith looked as white as a sheet, and had neither power to fight nor fly. Then said Faint-heart, Deliver thy purse. But he making no haste to do it (for he was loth to lose his money), Mistrust ran up

LITTLE-FAITH IS ROBBED.

to him, and thrusting his hand into his pocket, pulled out thence a bag of silver.

Then he cried out, Thieves! Thieves!

With that Guilt, with a great club that was in his hand, struck Little-faith on the head, and with that blow, felled him flat to the ground, where he lay bleeding as one that would bleed to death.

All this while the thieves stood by. But, at last, they hearing that some were upon the road, and fearing lest it should be one Great-grace, that dwells in the city of Good-confidence, they betook themselves to their heels, and left this good man to shift for himself. Now, after a while, Little-faith came to himself, and getting up made shift to scrabble on his way. This was the story.

HOPE. But did they take from him all that he ever had?

CHR. No; the place where his jewels were they never ransacked, so those he kept still. But, as I was told, the good man was much afflicted for his loss, for the thieves got most of his spending-money. That which they got not (as I said) were jewels, also he had a little odd money left, but scarce enough to bring him to his journey's end; [179] nay, if I was not misinformed, he was forced to beg as he went, to keep himself alive; for his jewels he might not sell. But beg, and do what he could, he went (as we say) with many a hungry belly the most part of the rest of the way.

HOPE. But is it not a wonder they got not from him his certificate, by which he was to receive his admittance at the Celestial Gate?

CHR. It is a wonder; but they got not that, though they missed it not through any good cunning of his; for he, being dismayed with their coming upon him, had neither power nor skill to hide anything; so it was more by good Providence than by his endeavor, that they missed of that good thing.

HOPE. But it must needs be a comfort to him, that they got not his jewels from him.

CHR. It might have been great comfort to him, had he used it as he should; but they that told me the story said, that he made but little use of it all the rest of the way, and that because of the dismay that he had in the taking away of his money; indeed, he forgot it a great part of the rest of his journey; and besides, when at any time it came into his mind, and he began to be comforted therewith, then would fresh thoughts of his loss come again upon him, and those thoughts would swallow up all. [180]

HOPE. Alas! poor man. This could not but be a great grief to him.

CHR. Grief! ay, a grief indeed. Would it not have been so to any of us, had we been used as he, to be robbed, and wounded too, and that in a strange place, as he was? It is a wonder he did not die with grief, poor heart!

I was told that he scattered almost all the rest of the way with nothing but doleful and bitter complaints; telling also to all that overtook him, or that he overtook in the way as he went, where he was robbed, and how; who they were that did it, and what he lost; how he was wounded, and that he hardly escaped with his life.

HOPE. But it is a wonder that his necessity did not put him upon selling or pawning some of his jewels, that he might have wherewith to relieve himself in his journey.

CHR. Thou talkest like one upon whose head is the shell to this very day; for what should he pawn them, or to whom should he sell them? In all that country where he was robbed, his jewels were not accounted of; nor did he want that relief which could from thence be administered to him.

Besides, had his jewels been missing at the gate of the Celestial City, he had (and that he knew well enough) been excluded from an inheritance there; and that would have been worse to him than the appearance and villany of ten thousand thieves.

LITTLE-FAITH'S GRIEF FOR HIS LOSS.

HOPE. Why art thou so tart, my brother? Esau sold his birthright, and that for a mess of pottage, and that birthright was his greatest jewel; and if he, why might not Little-faith do so too?[181]

CHR. Esau did sell his birthright indeed, and so do many besides, and by so doing exclude themselves from the chief blessing, as also that caitiff did; but you must put a difference betwixt Esau and Little-faith, and also betwixt their estates.

Esau's birthright was typical, but Little-faith's jewels were not so; Esau's belly was his god, but Little-faith's belly was not so; Esau's want lay in his fleshly appetite, Little-faith's did not so.

Besides, Esau could see no further than to the fulfilling of his lusts; "Behold, I am at the point to die (said he), and what profit shall this birthright do me?" [182]   But Little-faith, though it was his lot to have but a little faith, was by his little faith kept from such extravagances, and made to see and prize his jewels more than to sell them, as Esau did his birthright.

You read not anywhere that Esau had faith, no, not so much as a little; therefore no marvel if, where the flesh only bears sway (as it will in that man where no faith is to resist), if he sells his birthright, and his soul and all, and that to the devil of hell; for it is with such, as it is with the ass, who in her occasions cannot be turned away. [183]   When their minds are set upon their lusts, they will have them whatever they cost.

But Little-faith was of another temper, his mind was on things divine; his livelihood was upon things that were spiritual, and from above; therefore, to what end should he that is of such a temper sell his jewels (had there been any that would have bought them) to fill his mind with empty things?   Will a man give a penny to fill his belly with hay; or can you persuade the turtle-dove to live upon carrion like the crow?   Though faithless ones can, for carnal lusts, pawn, or mortgage, or sell what they have, and themselves outright to boot; yet they that have faith, saving faith, though but a little of it, cannot do so.   Here, therefore, my brother, is thy mistake.

HOPE. I acknowledge it; but yet your severe reflection had almost made me angry.

CHR. Why, I did but compare thee to some of the birds that are of the brisker sort, who will run to and fro in untrodden paths, with the shell upon their heads; but pass by that, and consider the matter under debate, and all shall be well betwixt thee and me.

HOPE. But, Christian, these three fellows, I am persuaded in my heart, are but a company of cowards; would they have run else, think you, as they did, at the noise of one that was coming on the road?   Why did not Little-faith pluck up a greater heart?   He might, methinks, have stood one brush with them, and have yielded when there had been no remedy.

CHR. That they are cowards, many have said, but few have found it so in the time of trial. As for a great heart, Little-faith had none; and I perceive by thee, my brother, hadst thou been the man concerned, thou art but for a brush, and then to yield. And, verily, since this is the height of thy stomach, now they are at a distance from us, should they appear to thee as they did to him, they might put thee to second thoughts.

But, consider again, they are but journeymen thieves, they serve under the king of the bottomless pit, who, if need be, will come in to their aid himself, and his voice is as the roaring of a lion.[184] I myself have been engaged as this Little-faith was, and I found it a terrible thing.

These three villains set upon me, and I beginning, like a Christian, to resist, they gave but a call, and in came their master. I would, as the saying is, have given my life for a penny; but that, as God would have it, I was clothed with armor of proof. Ay, and yet, though I was so harnessed, I found it hard work to quit myself like a man. No man can tell what in that combat attends us, but he that hath been in the battle himself.

HOPE. Well, but they ran, you see, when they did but suppose that one Great-grace was in the way.

CHR. True, they have often fled, both they and their master, when Great-grace hath but appeared; and no marvel; for he is the King's Champion. But, I trow, you will put some difference betwixt Little-faith and the King's Champion. All the King's subjects are not his champions, nor can they, when tried, do such feats of war as he.

Is it meet to think that a little child should handle Goliath as David did? Or that there should be the strength of an ox in a wren? Some are strong, some are weak: some have great faith, some have little. This man was one of the weak, and therefore he went to the wall.

HOPE. I would it had been Great-grace for their sakes.

CHR. If it had been, he might have had his hands full; for I must tell you, that though Great-grace is excellent good at his weapons, and has, and can, so long as he keeps them at sword's point, do well enough with them; yet, if they get within him, even Faint-heart, Mistrust, or the other, it shall go hard but they will throw up his heels. And when a man is down, you know, what can he do?

Whoso looks well upon Great-grace's face, shall see those scars and cuts

14

there, that shall easily give demonstration of what I say. Yea, once I heard that he should say (and that when he was in the combat), "We despaired even of life." How did these sturdy rogues and their fellows make David groan, mourn, and roar?

Yea, Heman, and Hezekiah, too, though champions in their day, were forced to bestir them, when by these assaulted; and yet, notwithstanding, they had their coats soundly brushed by them. Peter, upon a time, would go try what he could do; but though some do say of him that he is the prince of the apostles, they handled him so, that they made him at last afraid of a sorry girl.

Besides, their king is at their whistle. He is never out of hearing; and if at any time they be put to the worst, he, if possible, comes in to help them; and of him it is said, "The sword of him that layeth at him cannot hold; the spear, the dart, nor the habergeon: he esteemeth iron as straw, and brass as rotten wood. "The arrow cannot make him flee; sling stones are turned with him into stubble. Darts are counted as stubble: he laugheth at the shaking of a spear."[185]

What can a man do in this case? It is true, if a man could, at every turn, have Job's horse, and had skill and courage to ride him, he might do notable things; "for his neck is clothed with thunder, he will not be afraid of the grasshopper; the glory of his nostrils is terrible: he paweth in the valley, and rejoiceth in his strength, he goeth on to meet the armed men."

"He mocketh at fear, and is not affrighted, neither turneth he back from the sword. The quiver rattleth against him, the glittering spear, and the shield. He swalloweth the ground with fierceness and rage, neither believeth he that it is the sound of the trumpet. He saith among the trumpets, Ha, ha! and he smelleth the battle afar off, the thunder of the captains, and the shouting."[186]

But for such footmen as thee and I are, let us never desire to meet with an enemy, nor vaunt as if we could do better, when we hear of others that they have been foiled, nor be tickled at the thoughts of our own manhood; for such commonly come by the worst when tried.

Witness Peter, of whom I made mention before. He would swagger, ay, he would; he would, as his vain mind prompted him to say, do better, and stand more for his master than all men; but who so foiled, and run down by these villains, as he?

When, therefore, we hear that such robberies are done on the King's highway, two things become us to do: 1. To go out harnessed and to be sure to take a shield with us; for it was for want of that, that he that laid so lustily at Leviathan could not make him yield: for, indeed, if that be wanting, he fears us not at all. Therefore, he that had skill hath said, "Above all, taking the shield of faith, wherewith ye shall be able to quench all the fiery darts of the wicked."[187]

2. It is good, also, that we desire of the King a convoy, yea, that he will go with us himself. This made David rejoice when in the Valley of the Shadow of Death; and Moses was rather for dying where he stood, than to go one step without his God.[188]

Oh, my brother, if he will but go along with us, what need we be afraid of ten thousands that shall set themselves against us?[189] But, without him, the proud helpers "fall under the slain."[190]

I, for my part, have been in the fray before now; and though, through the goodness of him that is best, I am, as you see, alive; yet I cannot boast of my manhood. Glad shall I be, if I meet with no more such brunts; though I fear we are not got beyond all danger.

However, since the lion and the bear have not as yet devoured me, I hope God will also deliver us from the next uncircumcised Philistine. Then sang Christian—

> Poor Little-faith! Hast been among the thieves?
> Wast robb'd? Remember this, whoso believes,
> And gets more faith, shall then a victor be
> Over ten thousand, else scarce over three.

So they went on, and Ignorance followed. They went then till they came at a place where they saw a way put itself into their way, and seemed withal to lie as straight as the way which they should go: and here they knew not which of the two to take, for both seemed straight before them; therefore, here they stood still to consider.

And as they were thinking about the way, behold a man, black of flesh, but covered with a very light robe, came to them, and asked them why they stood there. They answered they were going to the Celestial City, but knew not which of these ways to take. Follow me, said the man, it is thither that I am going.

So they followed him in the way that but now came into the road, which by degrees turned, and turned them so from the city that they desired to go to, that, in a little time, their faces were turned away from it; yet they followed him.

But by and by, before they were aware, he led them both within the compass of a net, in which they were both so entangled, that they knew not what to do; and with that the white robe fell off the black man's back. Then they saw where they were. Wherefore, there they lay crying some time, for they could not get themselves out.

CHRISTIAN AND HOPEFUL ARE LED ASTRAY BY THE FLATTERER.

CHR. Then said Christian to his fellow, Now do I see myself in error. Did not the Shepherds bid us beware of the flatterers? As is the saying of the wise man, so we have found it this day, "A man that flattereth his neighbor spreadeth a net for his feet."[191]

HOPE. They also gave us a note of directions about the way, for our more sure finding thereof; but therein we have also forgotten to read, and have not kept ourselves from the paths of the destroyer. Here David was

CHRISTIAN AND HOPEFUL DELIVERED FROM THE NET.

wiser than we; for, saith he, "Concerning the works of men, by the word of thy lips, I have kept me from the paths of the destroyer."[192] Thus they lay bewailing themselves in the net.

At last they espied a Shining One coming towards them with a whip of small cord in his hand. When he was come to the place where they were, he asked them whence they came, and what they did there. They told him that they were poor pilgrims going to Zion, but were led out of their way by a black man, clothed in white, who bid us, said they, follow him, for he was going thither too.

Then said he with the whip, It is Flatterer, a false apostle, that hath transformed himself into an angel of light.[193] So he rent the net, and let the men out.

Then said he to them, Follow me, that I may set you in your way again. So he led them back to the way which they had left to follow the Flatterer. Then he asked them, saying, Where did you lie the last night? They said, With the Shepherds upon the Delectable Mountains.

He asked them then, if they had not of those Shepherds a note of direction for the way. They answered, Yes. But did you, said he, when you were at a stand, pluck out and read your note? They answered, No. He asked them, Why? They said, they forgot. He asked, moreover, if the Shepherds did not bid them beware of the Flatterer. They answered, Yes, but we did not imagine, said they, that this fine-spoken man had been he.[194]

Then I saw in my dream, that he commanded them to lie down; which, when they did, he chastised them sore, to teach them the good way wherein they should walk;[195] and as he chastised them he said, "As many as I love, I rebuke and chasten; be zealous, therefore, and repent."[196]

This done, he bid them go on their way, and take good heed to the other directions of the Shepherds. So they thanked him for all his kindness, and went softly along the right way singing—

> Come hither, you that walk along the way;
> See how the pilgrims fare that go astray!
> They catched are in an entangling net,
> 'Cause they good counsel lightly did forget:
> 'Tis true they rescued were, but yet you see,
> They're scourged to boot. Let this your caution be.

Now, after a while, they perceived, afar off, one coming softly and alone, all along the highway to meet them. Then said Christian to his fellow, Yonder is a man with his back towards Zion, and he is coming to meet us.

HOPE. I see him; let us take heed to ourselves now, lest he should prove a flatterer also. So he drew nearer and nearer, and at last came up unto them. His name was Atheist, and he asked them whither they were going.

CHR. We are going to Mount Zion.

Then Atheist fell into a very great laughter.

CHR. What is the meaning of your laughter?

ATHEIST. I laugh to see what ignorant persons you are, to take upon you so tedious a journey, and you are like to have nothing but your travel for your pains.

CHR. Why, man, do you think we shall not be received?

ATHEIST. Received! There is no such place as you dream of in all this world.

CHR. But there is in the world to come.

ATHEIST. When I was at home in mine own country, I heard as you now affirm, and from that hearing went out to see, and have been seeking this city this twenty years; but find no more of it than I did the first day I set out.[197]

CHR. We have both heard and believe that there is such a place to be found.

ATHEIST. Had not I, when at home, believed, I had not come thus far to seek; but finding none (and yet I should, had there been such a place to be found, for I have gone to seek it further than you), I am going back again, and will seek to refresh myself with the things that I then cast away, for hopes of that which, I now see, is not.

CHR. Then said Christian to Hopeful his fellow, Is it true which this man hath said?

HOPE. Take heed, he is one of the flatterers; remember what it hath cost us once already for our hearkening to such kind of fellows. What! no Mount Zion? Did we not see, from the Delectable Mountains, the gate of the city? Also, are we not now to walk by faith? Let us go on, said Hopeful, lest the man with the whip overtake us again.[198]

You should have taught me that lesson, which I will round you in the ears withal: "Cease, my son, to hear the instruction that causeth to err from the words of knowledge."[199] I say, my brother, cease to hear him, and let us "believe to the saving of the soul."[200]

ATHEIST.

CHR. My brother, I did not put the question to thee for that I doubted of the truth of our belief myself, but to prove thee, and to fetch from thee a fruit of the honesty of thy heart. As for this man, I know that he is blinded by the god of this world. Let thee and I go on, knowing that we have belief of the truth, "and no lie is of the truth."[201]

HOPE. Now do I rejoice in hope of the glory of God. So they turned away from the man; and he, laughing at them, went his way.

I saw then in my dream, that they went till they came into a certain country, whose air naturally tended to make one drowsy, if he came a stranger into it. And here Hopeful began to be very dull and heavy with sleep; wherefore he said unto Christian, I do now begin to grow so drowsy that I can scarcely hold up mine eyes; let us lie down here and take one nap.

CHR. By no means, said the other; lest sleeping, we never awake more.

HOPE. Why, my brother? Sleep is sweet to the laboring man; we may be refreshed if we take a nap.

CHR. Do you not remember that one of the Shepherds bid us beware of the Enchanted Ground? He meant by that, that we should beware of sleeping; "Therefore let us not sleep, as do others, but let us watch and be sober."[202]

HOPE. I acknowledge myself in a fault; and had I been here alone, I had by sleeping run the danger of death. I see it is true that the wise man saith, "Two are better than one." Hitherto hath thy company been my mercy, and thou shalt have a good reward for thy labor.[203]

CHR. Now then, said Christian, to prevent drowsiness in this place, let us fall into good discourse.

HOPE. With all my heart, said the other.

CHR. Where shall we begin?

HOPE. Where God began with us. But do you begin, if you please.

CHR. I will sing you first this song:—

> When saints do sleepy grow, let them come hither,
> And hear how these two pilgrims talk together:
> Yea, let them learn of them, in any wise,
> Thus to keep ope their drowsy slumbering eyes.
> Saints' fellowship, if it be managed well,
> Keeps them awake, and that in spite of hell.

CHR. Then Christian began and said, I will ask you a question. How came you to think at first of so doing as you do now?

Hope. Do you mean, how came I at first to look after the good of my soul?

Chr. Yes, that is my meaning.

Hope. I continued a great while in the delight of those things which were seen and sold at our fair; things which I believe now, would have, had I continued in them still, drowned me in perdition and destruction.

HOPEFUL TELLS CHRISTIAN HIS EXPERIENCE.

Chr. What things are they?

Hope. All the treasures and riches of the world. Also I delighted much in rioting, reveling, drinking, swearing, lying, uncleanness, Sabbath-breaking, and what not, that tended to destroy the soul. But I found at last, by hearing and considering of things that are Divine, which indeed I heard of you, as also of beloved Faithful, that was put to death for his faith and good living in Vanity Fair, that "the end of these things is death." [204] And that for these things' sake "cometh the wrath of God upon the children of disobedience." [205]

CHR. And did you presently fall under the power of this conviction?

HOPE. No, I was not willing presently to know the evil of sin, nor the damnation that follows upon the commission of it; but endeavored, when my mind at first began to be shaken with the Word, to shut mine eyes against the light thereof.

CHR. But what was the cause of your carrying of it thus to the first workings of God's blessed Spirit upon you?

HOPE. The causes were, 1. I was ignorant that this was the work of God upon me. I never thought that, by awakenings for sin, God at first begins the conversion of a sinner. 2. Sin was yet very sweet to my flesh, and I was loath to leave it. 3. I could not tell how to part with mine old companions, their presence and actions were so desirable unto me. 4. The hours in which convictions were upon me, were such troublesome and such heart-affrighting hours, that I could not bear, no not so much as the remembrance of them upon my heart.

CHR. Then, as it seems, sometimes you got rid of your trouble.

HOPE. Yes, verily, but it would come into my mind again, and then I should be as bad, nay, worse, than I was before.

CHR. Why, what was it that brought your sins to mind again?

HOPE. Many things; as,

1. If I did but meet a good man in the streets; or,
2. If I have heard any read in the Bible; or,
3. If mine head did begin to ache; or,
4. If I were told that some of my neighbors were sick; or,
5. If I heard the bell toll for some that were dead; or,
6. If I thought of dying myself; or,
7. If I heard that sudden death happened to others;
8. But especially when I thought of myself, that I must quickly come to judgment.

CHR. And could you at any time, with ease, get off the guilt of sin, when by any of these ways it came upon you?

HOPE. No, not I, for then they got faster hold of my conscience; and then, if I did but think of going back to sin (though my mind was turned against it), it would be double torment to me.

CHR. And how did you do then?

HOPE. I thought I must endeavor to mend my life; for else, thought I, I am sure to be damned.

CHR. And did you endeavor to mend?

HOPE. Yes; and fled from not only my sins, but sinful company too; and betook me to religious duties, as prayer, reading, weeping for sin, speaking truth to my neighbors, &c. These things did I, with many others, too much here to relate.

CHR. And did you think yourself well then?

HOPEFUL'S SINS BROUGHT TO MIND.

HOPE. Yes, for a while; but at the last my trouble came tumbling upon me again, and that over the neck of all my reformations.

CHR. How came that about, since you were now reformed?

HOPE. There were several things brought it upon me, especially such sayings as these: " All our righteousnesses are as filthy rags." [206] " By the works of the law shall no flesh be justified." [207] " When ye shall have done all those things, say, We are unprofitable;" [208] with many more such like.

From whence I began to reason with myself thus: If ALL my righteousnesses are filthy rags; if, by the deeds of the law, NO man can be justified; and if, when we have done ALL, we are yet unprofitable, then it is but a folly to think of heaven by the law.

I further thought thus: If a man runs a hundred pounds into the shopkeeper's debt, and after that shall pay for all that he shall fetch; yet, if this old debt stands still in the book uncrossed, for that, the shopkeeper may sue him, and cast him into prison till he shall pay the debt.

CHR. Well, and how did you apply this to yourself?

HOPE. Why, I thought thus with myself: I have, by my sins, run a great way into God's book, and that my now reforming will not pay off that score; therefore I should think still, under all my present amendments, But how shall I be freed from that damnation that I have brought myself in danger of, by my former transgressions?

CHR. A very good application: but, pray, go on.

HOPE. Another thing that hath troubled me, even since my late amendments, is, that if I look narrowly into the best of what I do now, I still see sin, new sin, mixing itself with the best of that I do; so that now I am forced to conclude, that notwithstanding my former fond conceits of myself and duties, I have committed sin enough in one day to send me to hell, though my former life had been faultless.

CHR. And what did you do then?

HOPE. Do! I could not tell what to do, until I brake my mind to Faithful, for he and I were well acquainted. And he told me, that unless I could obtain the righteousness of a man that never had sinned, neither mine own, nor all the righteousness of the world could save me.

CHR. And did you think he spake true?

HOPE. Had he told me so when I was pleased and satisfied with mine own amendment, I had called him fool for his pains; but now, since I see mine own infirmity, and the sin that cleaves to my best performance, I have been forced to be of his opinion.

CHR. But did you think, when at first he suggested it to you, that there was such a man to be found, of whom it might justly be said, that he never committed sin?

HOPE. I must confess the words at first sounded strangely, but after a little more talk and company with him, I had full conviction about it.

CHR. And did you ask him what man this was, and how you must be justified by him?

HOPE. Yes, and he told me it was the Lord Jesus, that dwelleth on the right hand of the Most High. And thus, said he, you must be justified by him, even by trusting to what he hath done by himself, in the days of his flesh, and suffered when he did hang on the tree.

I asked him further, how that man's righteousness could be of that efficacy to justify another before God? And he told me he was the mighty

FAITHFUL INSTRUCTS HOPEFUL.

God, and did what he did, and died the death also, not for himself, but for me; to whom his doings, and the worthiness of them, should be imputed, if I believed on Him.[209]

CHR. And what did you do then?

HOPE. I made my objections against my believing, for that I thought he was not willing to save me.

CHR. And what said Faithful to you then?

HOPE. He bid me go to him and see. Then I said it was presumption; but he said, No, for I was invited to come.[210] Then he gave me a book of Jesus, his inditing, to encourage me the more freely to come; and he said, concerning that book, that every jot and tittle thereof stood firmer than heaven and earth.[211]

Then I asked him, What I must do when I came; and he told me I must entreat upon my knees, with all my heart and soul, the Father to reveal him to me.[212]

Then I asked him further, how I must make my supplication to him? And he said, Go, and thou shalt find him upon a mercy-seat, where he sits all the year long, to give pardon and forgiveness to them that come.

I told him that I knew not what to say when I came. And he bid me say to this effect: God be merciful to me a sinner, and make me to know and believe in Jesus Christ; for I see, that if his righteousness had not been, or I have not faith in that righteousness, I am utterly cast away. Lord, I have heard that thou art a merciful God, and hast ordained that thy Son Jesus Christ should be the Saviour of the world; and moreover, that thou art willing to bestow him upon such a poor sinner as I am (and I am a sinner indeed); Lord, take therefore this opportunity, and magnify thy grace in the salvation of my soul, through thy Son Jesus Christ. Amen.[213]

CHR. And did you do as you were bidden?

HOPE. Yes; over, and over, and over.

CHR. And did the Father reveal his Son to you?

HOPE. Not at the first, nor second, nor third, nor fourth, nor fifth; no, nor at the sixth time neither.

CHR. What did you do then?

HOPE. What! why I could not tell what to do.

CHR. Had you not thoughts of leaving off praying?

HOPE. Yes; an hundred times twice told.

CHR. And what was the reason you did not?

HOPE. I believed that that was true which had been told me, to wit, that without the righteousness of this Christ, all the world could not save me; and therefore, thought I with myself, if I leave off I die, and I can but die at the throne of grace. And withal, this came into my mind, "Though it tarry, wait for it; because it will surely come, it will not tarry."[214] So I continued praying until the Father showed me his Son.

CHR. And how was he revealed unto you?

HOPE. I did not see him with my bodily eyes, but with the eyes of my understanding;[215] and thus it was: One day I was very sad, I think sadder than at any one time in my life, and this sadness was through a fresh sight of the greatness and vileness of my sins. And as I was then looking for nothing but hell, and the everlasting damnation of my soul, suddenly, as I thought, I saw the Lord Jesus Christ look down from heaven upon me, and saying, "Believe on the Lord Jesus Christ, and thou shalt be saved."[216]

But I replied, Lord, I am a great, a very great sinner. And he answered, "My grace is sufficient for thee."[217] Then I said, But, Lord, what is believing? And then I saw from that saying, "He that cometh to me shall never hunger, and he that believeth on me shall never thirst," that believing and coming was all one; and that he that came, that is, ran out in his heart and affections after salvation by Christ, he indeed believed in Christ.[218]

Then the water stood in mine eyes, and I asked further, But, Lord, may such a great sinner as I am be indeed accepted of thee, and be saved by thee? And I heard him say, "And him that cometh to me, I will in no wise cast out."[219] Then I said, But how, Lord, must I consider of thee in my coming to thee, that my faith may be placed aright upon thee? Then he said, "Christ Jesus came into the world to save sinners."[220] "He is the end of the law for righteousness to every one that believeth."[221] "He died for our sins, and rose again for our justification."[222] "He loved us, and washed us from our sins in his own blood."[223] "He is mediator betwixt God and us."[224] "He ever liveth to make intercession for us."[225]

From all which I gathered, that I must look for righteousness in his person, and for satisfaction for my sins by his blood; that what he did in obedience to his Father's law, and in submitting to the penalty thereof, was not for himself, but for him that will accept it for his salvation, and be thankful. And now was my heart full of joy, mine eyes full of tears, and mine affections running over with love to the name, people, and ways of Jesus Christ.

CHR. This was a revelation of Christ to your soul indeed; but tell me particularly what effect this had upon your spirit.

HOPE. It made me see that all the world, notwithstanding all the righteousness thereof, is in a state of condemnation. It made me see that God the Father, though he be just, can justly justify the coming sinner.

It made me greatly ashamed of the vileness of my former life, and confounded me with the sense of mine own ignorance; for there never came
thought into my heart before now. that showed me so the beauty of Jesus
Christ.   It made me love a holy life, and long to do something for the
honor and glory of the name of the Lord Jesus; yea, I thought that had
I now a thousand gallons of blood in my body, I could spill it all for the
sake of the Lord Jesus.

I saw then in my dream that Hopeful looked back and saw Ignorance,
whom they had left behind, coming after.   Look, said he to Christian,
how far yonder youngster loitereth behind.

CHR. Ay, ay, I see him; he careth not for our company.

HOPE. But I trow it would not have hurt him, had he kept pace with
us hitherto.

CHR. That is true; but I warrant you, he thinketh otherwise.

HOPE. That, I think, he doth; but, however, let us tarry for him.   So
they did.

Then Christian said to him, Come away, man, why do you stay so
behind ?

IGNOR. I take my pleasure in walking alone, even more a great deal
than in company, unless I like it the better.

Then said Christian to Hopeful (but softly), Did I not tell you he
cared not for our company ?   But, however, said he, come up, and let us
talk away the time in this solitary place.

Then directing his speech to Ignorance, he said, Come, how do you ?
How stands it between God and your soul now ?

IGNOR. I hope well ; for I am always full of good motions, that come
into my mind to comfort me as I walk. [226]

CHR. What good motions ? pray, tell us.

IGNOR. Why, I think of God and heaven.

CHR. So do the devils and damned souls.

IGNOR. But I think of them and desire them.

CHR. So do many that are never like to come there.   "The soul of
the sluggard desireth, and hath nothing." [227]

IGNOR. But I think of them and leave all for them.

CHR. That I doubt ; for leaving all is a hard matter: yea, a harder
matter than many are aware of.   But why, or by what, art thou persuaded
that thou hast left all for God and heaven ?

IGNOR. My heart tells me so.

15

CHR. The wise man says, " He that trusts his own heart is a fool."[228]

IGNOR. This is spoken of an evil heart, but mine is a good one.

CHR. But how dost thou prove that?

IGNOR. It comforts me in hopes of heaven.

CHR. That may be through its deceitfulness; for a man's heart may minister comfort to him in the hopes of that thing for which he yet has no ground to hope.

IGNOR. But my heart and life agree together, and therefore my hope is well grounded.

CHR. Who told thee that thy heart and life agree together?

IGNOR. My heart tells me so.

CHR. Ask my fellow if I be a thief! Thy heart tells thee so! Except the Word of God beareth witness in this matter, other testimony is of no value.

IGNOR. But is it not a good heart that hath good thoughts? and is not that a good life that is according to God's commandments?

CHR. Yes, that is a good heart that hath good thoughts, and that is a good life that is according to God's commandments; but it is one thing, indeed, to have these, and another thing only to think so.

IGNOR. Pray, what count you good thoughts, and a life according to God's commandments?

CHR. There are good thoughts of divers kinds; some respecting ourselves, some God, some Christ, and some other things.

IGNOR. What be good thoughts respecting ourselves?

CHR. Such as agree with the Word of God.

IGNOR. When do our thoughts of ourselves agree with the Word of God?

CHR. When we pass the same judgment upon ourselves which the Word passes. To explain myself—the Word of God saith of persons in a natural condition, "There is none righteous, there is none that doeth good."[229] It saith also, that "every imagination of the heart of man is only evil, and that continually."[230] And again, "The imagination of man's heart is evil from his youth."[231] Now, then, when we think thus of ourselves, having sense thereof, then are our thoughts good ones, because according to the Word of God.

IGNOR. I will never believe that my heart is thus bad.

CHR. Therefore thou never hadst one good thought concerning thyself in thy life. But let me go on. As the Word passeth a judgment upon our heart, so it passeth a judgment upon our ways; and when OUR thoughts of our hearts and ways agree with the judgment which the Word giveth of both, then are both good because agreeing thereto.

IGNOR. Make out your meaning.

CHR. Why, the Word of God saith that man's ways are crooked ways; not good, but perverse.[232] It saith they are naturally out of the good way, that they have not known it.[233] Now, when a man thus thinketh of his ways, I say, when he doth sensibly, and with heart-humiliation, thus think, then hath he good thoughts of his own ways, because his thoughts now agree with the judgment of the Word of God.

IGNOR. What are good thoughts concerning God?

CHR. Even as I have said concerning ourselves, when our thoughts of God do agree with what the Word saith of him; and that is, when we think of his being and attributes as the Word hath taught, of which I cannot now discourse at large; but to speak of him with reference to us: Then we have right thoughts of God, when we think that he knows us better than we know ourselves, and can see sin in us when and where we can see none in ourselves; when we think he knows our inmost thoughts, and that our heart, with all its depths, is always open unto his eyes; also, when we think that all our righteousness stinks in his nostrils, and that, therefore, he cannot abide to see us stand before him in any confidence, even in all our best performances.

IGNOR. Do you think that I am such a fool as to think God can see no further than I? or, that I would come to God in the best of my performances?

CHR. Why, how dost thou think in this matter?

IGNOR. Why, to be short, I think I must believe in Christ for justification.

CHR. How! think thou must believe in Christ, when thou seest not thy need of him! Thou neither seest thy original nor actual infirmities; but hast such an opinion of thyself, and of what thou dost, as plainly renders thee to be one that did never see a necessity of Christ's personal righteousness to justify thee before God. How, then, dost thou say, I believe in Christ?

IGNOR. I believe well enough for all that.

CHR. How dost thou believe?

IGNOR. I believe that Christ died for sinners; and that I shall be justified before God from the curse, through his gracious acceptance of my obedience to his law. Or thus, Christ makes my duties, that are religious, acceptable to his Father, by virtue of his merits; and so shall I be justified.

CHR. Let me give an answer to this confession of thy faith.

1. Thou believest with a fantastical faith; for this faith is nowhere described in the Word.

2. Thou believest with a false faith; because it taketh justification from the personal righteousness of Christ, and applies it to thy own.

3. This faith maketh not Christ a justifier of thy person, but of thy actions; and of thy person for thy actions' sake, which is false.

4. Therefore, this faith is deceitful, even such as will leave thee under wrath, in the day of God Almighty; for true justifying faith puts the soul, as sensible of its condition by the law, upon flying for refuge unto Christ's righteousness, (which righteousness of his is not an act of grace, by which he maketh, for justification, thy obedience accepted with God; but his personal obedience to the law, in doing and suffering for us what that required at our hands;) this righteousness, I say, true faith accepteth; under the skirt of which, the soul being shrouded, and by it presented as spotless before God, it is accepted, and acquit from condemnation.

IGNOR. What! would you have us trust to what Christ, in his own person, has done without us? This conceit would loosen the reins of our lust, and tolerate us to live as we list; for what matter how we live, if we may be justified by Christ's personal righteousness from all, when we believe it?

CHR. Ignorance is thy name, and as thy name is, so art thou; even this thy answer demonstrateth what I say. Ignorant thou art of what justifying righteousness is, and as ignorant how to secure thy soul, through the faith of it, from the heavy wrath of God. Yea, thou also art ignorant of the true effects of saving faith in this righteousness of Christ, which is, to bow and win over the heart to God in Christ, to love his name, his word, ways, and people, and not as thou ignorantly imaginest.

HOPE. Ask him if ever he had Christ revealed to him from heaven.

IGNOR. What! you are a man for revelations! I believe that what both you, and all the rest of you, say, about that matter, is but the fruit of distracted brains.

HOPE. Why, man! Christ is so hid in God from the natural apprehensions of the flesh, that he cannot by any man be savingly known, unless God the Father reveals him to them.

CHRISTIAN INSTRUCTS IGNORANCE.

IGNOR. That is your faith, but not mine; yet mine, I doubt not, is as good as yours, though I have not in my head so many whimsies as you.

CHR. Give me leave to put in a word. You ought not so slightly to speak of this matter; for this I will boldly affirm, even as my good companion hath done, that no man can know Jesus Christ but by the revelation of the Father;[234] yea, and faith too, by which the soul layeth hold upon Christ, (if it be right,) must be wrought by the exceeding greatness of his mighty power; the working of which faith, I perceive, poor Ignorance, thou art ignorant of.[235] Be awakened, then, see thine own wretchedness, and fly to the Lord Jesus; and by his righteousness, which is the righteousness of God, for he himself is God, thou shalt be delivered from condemnation.

IGNOR. You go so fast, I cannot keep pace with you. Do you go on before; I must stay a while behind.

Then they said—

> Well, Ignorance, wilt thou yet foolish be,
> To slight good counsel, ten times given thee?
> And if thou yet refuse it, thou shalt know,
> Ere long the evil of thy doing so.
> Remember, man, in time, stoop, do not fear;
> Good counsel taken well, saves: therefore hear;
> But if thou yet shall slight it, thou wilt be
> The loser (Ignorance), I'll warrant thee.

CHAPTER X.

THEN Christian addressed himself thus to his fellow:—

CHR. Well, come, my good Hopeful, I perceive that thou and I must walk by ourselves again.

So I saw in my dream that they went on apace before, and Ignorance he came hobbling after. Then said Christian to his companion, It pities me much for this poor man, it will certainly go ill with him at last.

HOPE. Alas! there are abundance in our town in his condition, whole families, yea, whole streets, and that of pilgrims too; and if there be so many in our parts, how many, think you, must there be in the place where he was born?

CHR. Indeed the Word saith, "He hath blinded their eyes, lest they should see," &c. But now we are by ourselves, what do you think of such men? Have they at no time, think you, convictions of sin, and so consequently fears that their state is dangerous?

HOPE. Nay, do you answer that question yourself, for you are the elder man.

CHR. Then I say, sometimes (as I think) they may; but they being naturally ignorant, understand not that such convictions tend to their good; and therefore they do desperately seek to stifle them, and presumptuously continue to flatter themselves in the way of their own hearts.

HOPE. I do believe, as you say, that fear tends much to men's good, and to make them right, at their beginning to go on pilgrimage.

CHR. Without all doubt it doth, if it be right; for so says the Word, "The fear of the Lord is the beginning of wisdom." [236]

HOPE. How will you describe right fear?

CHR. True or right fear is discovered by three things:—

1. By its rise; it is caused by saving convictions for sin.

2. It driveth the soul to lay fast hold of Christ for salvation.

3. It begetteth and continueth in the soul a great reverence of God, his Word, and ways, keeping it tender, and making it afraid to turn from

them, to the right hand or to the left, to anything that may dishonor God, break its peace, grieve the Spirit, or cause the enemy to speak reproachfully.

HOPE. Well said; I believe you have said the truth. Are we now almost got past the Enchanted Ground?

CHR. Why, art thou weary of this discourse?

HOPE. No, verily, but that I would know where we are.

CHR. We have not now above two miles further to go thereon. But let us return to our matter. Now the ignorant know not that such convictions as tend to put them in fear are for their good, and therefore they seek to stifle them.

HOPE. How do they seek to stifle them?

CHR. 1. They think that those fears are wrought by the devil (though indeed they are wrought of God); and, thinking so, they resist them as things that directly tend to their overthrow.

2. They also think that these fears tend to the spoiling of their faith, when, alas for them, poor men that they are, they have none at all! and therefore they harden their hearts against them.

3. They presume they ought not to fear; and therefore, in despite of them, wax presumptuously confident.

4. They see that those fears tend to take away from them their pitiful old self-holiness, and therefore they resist them with all their might.

HOPE. I know something of this myself; for, before I knew myself, it was so with me.

CHR. Well, we will leave, at this time, our neighbor Ignorance by himself, and fall upon another profitable question.

HOPE. With all my heart, but you shall still begin.

CHR. Well then, did you not know, about ten years ago, one Temporary in your parts, who was a forward man in religion then?

HOPE. Know him! yes, he dwelt in Graceless, a town about two miles off of Honesty, and he dwelt next door to one Turnback.

CHR. Right, he dwelt under the same roof with him. Well, that man was much awakened once; I believe that then he had some sight of his sins, and of the wages that were due thereto.

HOPE. I am of your mind, for, my house not being above three miles from him, he would ofttimes come to me, and that with many tears. Truly I pitied the man, and was not altogether without hope of him; but one may see, it is not every one that cries, Lord, Lord.

CHR. He told me once that he was resolved to go on pilgrimage, as we do now; but all of a sudden he grew acquainted with one Save-self, and then he became a stranger to me.

HOPE. Now, since we are talking about him, let us a little inquire into the reason of the sudden blacksliding of him and such others.

CHR. It may be very profitable, but do you begin.

HOPE. Well, then, there are in my judgment four reasons for it:—

1. Though the consciences of such men are awakened, yet their minds are not changed; therefore, when the power of guilt weareth away, that which provoked them to be religious ceaseth, wherefore they naturally turn to their own course again, even as we see the dog that is sick of what he has eaten, so long as his sickness prevails, he vomits and casts up all; not that he doth this of a free mind (if we may say a dog has a mind), but because it troubleth his stomach; but now, when his sickness is over, and so his stomach eased, his desire being not at all alienate from his vomit, he turns him about and licks up all, and so it is true which is written, "The dog is turned to his own vomit again." [237]

Thus, I say, being hot for heaven, by virtue only of the sense and fear of the torments of hell, as their sense of hell, and the fears of damnation, chills and cools, so their desires for heaven and salvation cool also. So then it comes to pass, that when their guilt and fear is gone, their desires for heaven and happiness die, and they return to their course again.

2. Another reason is, they have slavish fears that do overmaster them; I speak now of the fears that they have of men, for "the fear of man bringeth a snare." [238] So then, though they seem to be hot for heaven, so long as the flames of hell are about their ears, yet when that terror is a little over, they betake themselves to second thoughts; namely, that it is good to be wise, and not to run (for they know not what) the hazard of losing all, or, at least, of bringing themselves into unavoidable and unnecessary troubles, and so they fall in with the world again.

3. The shame that attends religion lies also as a block in their way; they are proud and haughty, and religion in their eye is low and contemptible; therefore, when they have lost their sense of hell and wrath to come, they return again to their former course.

4. Guilt, and to meditate terror are grievous to them. They like not to see their misery before they come into it; though perhaps the sight of it first, if they loved that sight, might make them fly whither the righteous fly and are safe.

But because they do, as I hinted before, even shun the thoughts of guilt and terror, therefore, when once they are rid of their awakenings about the terrors and wrath of God, they harden their hearts gladly, and choose such ways as will harden them more and more.

CHR. You are pretty near the business, for the bottom of all is, for want of a change in their mind and will. And therefore they are but like the felon that standeth before the judge, he quakes and trembles, and seems to repent most heartily, but the bottom of all is the fear of the halter; not that he hath any detestation of the offence, as is evident, because, let but this man have his liberty, and he will be a thief, and so a rogue still, whereas, if his mind was changed, he would be otherwise.

HOPE. Now I have showed you the reasons of their going back, do you show me the manner thereof.

CHR. So I will willingly.

1. They draw off their thoughts, all that they may from the remembrance of God, death, and judgment to come.

2. Then they cast off by degrees private duties, as closet prayer, curbing their lusts, watching, sorrow for sin, and the like.

3. Then they shun the company of lively and warm Christians.

4. After that they grow cold to public duty, as hearing, reading, godly conference, and the like.

5. Then they begin to pick holes, as we say, in the coats of some of the godly; and that devilishly, that they may have a seeming color to throw religion (for the sake of some infirmity they have espied in them) behind their backs.

6. Then they begin to adhere to, and to associate themselves with, carnal, loose, and wanton men.

7. Then they give way to carnal and wanton discourses in secret; and glad are they if they can see such things in any that are counted honest, that they may the more boldly do it through their example.

8. After this they begin to play with little sins openly.

9. And then, being hardened, they show themselves as they are. Thus, being launched again into the gulf of misery, unless a miracle of grace prevent it, they everlastingly perish in their own deceivings.

Now I saw in my dream, that by this time the Pilgrims were got over the Enchanted Ground, and entering into the country of Beulah, whose air was very sweet and pleasant, the way lying directly through it, they solaced themselves there for a season.[239] Yea, here they heard continually the singing of birds, and saw every day the flowers appear in the earth, and heard the voice of the turtle-dove in the land.[240]

In this country the sun shineth night and day; wherefore this was beyond the Valley of the Shadow of Death, and also out of the reach of Giant Despair, neither could they from this place so much as see Doubting Castle.

Here they were within sight of the city they were going to, also here met them some of the inhabitants thereof; for in this land the Shining

THE PILGRIMS IN SIGHT OF THE HOLY CITY.

Ones commonly walked, because it was upon the borders of Heaven. In this land also, the contract between the bride and the bridegroom was renewed; yea, here, "As the bridegroom rejoiceth over the bride, so did their God rejoice over them."[241] Here they had no want of corn and wine; for in this place they met with abundance of what they had sought for in all their pilgrimage.[242] Here they heard voices from out of the city, loud voices saying, "Say ye to the daughter of Zion, Behold, thy salvation cometh! Behold his reward is with him!"[243] Here all the inhabitants of the country called them, "The holy people, The redeemed of the Lord sought out," &c.[244]

Now, as they walked in this land, they had more rejoicing than in parts more remote from the kingdom to which they were bound; and drawing near to the city, they had yet a more perfect view thereof. It was builded of pearls and precious stones, also the street thereof was paved with gold; so that by reason of the natural glory of the city and the reflection of the sunbeams upon it, Christian with desire fell sick; Hopeful also had a fit or two of the same disease. Wherefore, here they lay by it a while, crying out, because of their pangs, "If ye find my beloved, tell him that I am sick of love."[245]

But, being a little strengthened, and better able to bear their sickness, they walked on their way, and came yet nearer and nearer, where were orchards, vineyards, and gardens, and their gates opened into the highway.

Now, as they came up to these places, behold the gardener stood in the way, to whom the Pilgrims said, Whose goodly vineyards and gardens are these? He answered they are the King's, and are planted here for his own delight, and also for the solace of pilgrims. So the gardener had them into the vineyards, and bid them refresh themselves with the dainties.[246] He also showed them there the King's walks, and the arbors where he delighted to be; and here they tarried and slept.

Now I beheld in my dream, that they talked more in their sleep at this time than ever they did in all their journey; and being in a muse thereabout, the gardener said even to me, Wherefore musest thou at the matter? It is the nature of the fruit of the grapes of these vineyards to go down so sweetly as to cause the lips of them that are asleep to speak.

So I saw that when they awoke they addressed themselves to go up to the city; but, as I said, the reflection of the sun upon the city (for "the city was pure gold,"[247]) was so extremely glorious that they could not, as yet, with open face behold it, but through an instrument made for that purpose.[248] So I saw, that as I went on, there met them two men, in raiment that shone like gold; also their faces shone as the light.

These men asked the Pilgrims whence they came, and they told them. They also asked them where they had lodged, what difficulties and dangers, what comforts and pleasures, they had met in the way; and they told them. Then said the men that met them, You have but two difficulties more to meet with, and then you are in the city.

Christian then, and his companion, asked the men to go along with

CHRISTIAN AND HOPEFUL MEET TWO MEN OF THE LAND OF BEULAH.

them; so they told them they would. But, said they, you must obtain it by your own faith. So I saw in my dream that they went on together, until they came in sight of the gate.

Now, I further saw, that betwixt them and the gate was a river, but there was no bridge to go over: the river was very deep. At the sight, therefore, of this river, the Pilgrims were much stunned; but the men that went with them said, You must go through, or you cannot come at the gate.

The Pilgrims then began to inquire if there was no other way to the gate; to which they answered, Yes; but there hath not any, save two, to wit, Enoch and Elijah, been permitted to tread that path, since the foundation of the world, nor shall, until the last trumpet shall sound.[249] The Pilgrims then, especially Christian, began to despond in their minds, and looked this way and that, but no way could be found by them, by which they might escape the river. Then they asked the men if the waters were all of a depth. They said, No; yet they could not help them in that case; for, said they, you shall find it deeper or shallower, as you believe in the King of the place.

They then addressed themselves to the water; and entering, Christian began to sink, and crying out to his good friend Hopeful, he said, I sink in deep waters; the billows go over my head, all his waves go over me! Selah.

Then said the other, Be of good cheer, my brother, I feel the bottom, and it is good. Then said Christian, Ah! my friend, "the sorrows of death have compassed me about;" I shall not see the land that flows with milk and honey.

And with that a great darkness and horror fell upon Christian, so that he could not see before him. Also here he in a great measure lost his senses, so that he could neither remember, nor orderly talk of any of those sweet refreshments that he had met with in the way of his pilgrimage. But all the words that he spake still tended to discover that he had horror of mind, and heart fears that he should die in that river, and never obtain entrance in at the gate.

Here also, as they that stood by perceived, he was much in the troublesome thoughts of the sins that he had committed, both since and before he began to be a pilgrim. It was also observed that he was troubled with apparitions of hobgoblins and evil spirits, for ever and anon he would intimate so much by words.

Hopeful, therefore, here had much ado to keep his brother's head above water; yea, sometimes he would be quite gone down, and then, ere a while, he would rise up again half dead. Hopeful also would endeavor to comfort him, saying, Brother, I see the gate, and men standing by to receive us; but Christian would answer, It is you, it is you they wait for; you have been Hopeful ever since I knew you. And so have you, said he to Christian. Ah, brother! said he, surely if I was right he would now arise to help me; but for my sins he hath brought me into the snare, and hath left me.

THE PILGRIMS CROSS THE RIVER OF DEATH.

Then said Hopeful, My brother, you have quite forgot the text, where it is said of the wicked, "There are no bands in their death, but their strength is firm. They are not troubled as other men, neither are they plagued like other men." [250] These troubles and distresses that you go through in these waters are no sign that God hath forsaken you; but are sent to try you, whether you call to mind that which heretofore you have received of his goodness, and live upon him in your distresses.

Then I saw in my dream, that Christian was as in a muse a while. To whom also Hopeful added this word, Be of good cheer, Jesus Christ maketh thee whole; and with that Christian brake out with a loud voice, Oh! I see him again, and he tells me, "When thou passest through the waters, I will be with thee; and through the rivers, they shall not overflow thee." [251]

Then they both took courage, and the enemy was after that as still as a stone, until they were gone over. Christian therefore presently found ground to stand upon, and so it followed that the rest of the river was but shallow. Thus they got over.

Now, upon the bank of the river, on the other side, they saw the two shining men again, who there waited for them; wherefore, being come out of the river, they saluted them saying, We are ministering spirits, sent forth to minister for those that shall be heirs of salvation. Thus they went along towards the gate.

Now you must note that the city stood upon a mighty hill, but the Pilgrims went up that hill with ease, because they had these two men to lead them up by the arms; also, they had left their mortal garments behind them in the river, for though they went in with them, they came out without them.

They, therefore, went up here with much agility and speed, though the foundation upon which the city was framed was higher than the clouds. They therefore went up through the regions of the air, sweetly talking as they went, being comforted, because they safely got over the river, and had such glorious companions to attend them.

The talk they had with the Shining Ones was about the glory of the place; who told them that the beauty and glory of it was inexpressible. There, said they, is the "Mount Zion, the heavenly Jerusalem, the innumerable company of angels, and the spirits of just men made perfect." [252]

You are going now, said they, to the paradise of God, wherein you shall see the tree of life, and eat of the never-fading fruits thereof; and when you come there, you shall have white robes given you, and your walk and talk shall be every day with the King, even all the days of eternity. [252]

There you shall not see again such things as you saw when you were in the lower region upon the earth, to wit, sorrow, sickness, affliction, and death, "for the former things are passed way."

You are now going to Abraham, to Isaac, and Jacob, and to the prophets—men that God hath taken away from the evil to come, and that are now resting upon their beds, each one walking in his righteousness. [254]

The men then asked, What must we do in the holy place? To whom it was answered, You must there receive the comforts of all your toil, and have joy for all your sorrow; you must reap what you have sown, even the fruit of all your prayers, and tears, and sufferings for the King by the way.[255] In that place you must wear crowns of gold, and enjoy the perpetual sight and vision of the Holy One, for "there you shall see him as he is."[256]

There also you shall serve him continually with praise, with shouting, and thanksgiving, whom you desired to serve in the world, though with much difficulty, because of the infirmity of your flesh.

There your eyes shall be delighted with seeing, and your ears with hearing the pleasant voice of the Mighty One. There you shall enjoy your friends again, that are gone thither before you; and there you shall with joy receive, even every one that follows into the holy place after you.

There also shall you be clothed with glory and majesty, and put into an equipage fit to ride out with the King of Glory. When he shall come with sound of trumpet in the clouds, as upon the wings of the wind, you shall come with him; and when he shall sit upon the throne of judgment, you shall sit by him; yea, and when he shall pass sentence upon all the workers of iniquity, let them be angels or men, you also shall have a voice in that judgment, because they were his and your enemies.[257] Also, when he shall again return to the city, you shall go too, with sound of trumpet, and be ever with him.

Now while they were thus drawing towards the gate, behold a company of the heavenly host came out to meet them; to whom it was said by the other two Shining Ones, These are the men that have loved our Lord when they were in the world, and that have left all for his holy name; and he hath sent us to fetch them, and we have brought them thus far on their desired journey, that they may go in and look their Redeemer in the face with joy.

Then the heavenly host gave a great shout, saying, "Blessed are they which are called into the marriage supper of the Lamb."[258]

There came out also at this time to meet them, several of the King's trumpeters, clothed in white and shining raiment, who, with melodious noises, and loud, made even the heavens to echo with their sound.

These trumpeters saluted Christian and his fellow with ten thousand welcomes from the world; and this they did with shouting, and sound of trumpet.

This done they compassed them round on every side; some went before,

16

some behind, and some on the right hand, some on the left (as it were to guard them through the upper regions), continually sounding as they went, with melodious noise, in notes on high; so that the very sight was to them that could behold it as if heaven itself was come down to meet them.

THE PILGRIMS APPROACH THE GATE OF THE HOLY CITY.

Thus, therefore, they walked on together; and as they walked ever and anon these trumpeters, even with joyful sound, would, by mixing their music with looks and gestures, still signify to Christian and his brother, how welcome they were into their company, and with what gladness they came to meet them; and now were these two men, as it were, in heaven, before they came at it, being swallowed up with the sight of angels, and with hearing of their melodious notes.

Here also they had the city itself in view, and they thought they heard all the bells therein to ring, to welcome them thereto. But above all, the warm and joyful thoughts that they had about their own dwelling there, with such company, and that for ever and ever. Oh, by what tongue or pen can their glorious joy be expressed! And thus they came up to the gate.

Now, when they were come up to the gate, there was written over it in letters of gold, "Blessed are they that do his commandments, that they may have right to the tree of life, and may enter in through the gates into the city."[259]

Then I saw in my dream, that the Shining Men bid them call at the gate; the which, when they did, some looked from above over the gate, to wit, Enoch, Moses, and Elijah, &c., to whom it was said, These pilgrims are come from the City of Destruction, for the love that they bear to the King of this place.

And then the Pilgrims gave in unto them each man his certificate, which they had received in the beginning; those, therefore, were carried in to the King, who, when he had read them, said, Where are the men? To whom it was answered, They are standing without the gate. The King then commanded to open the gate, "That the righteous nation," said he "which keepeth the truth, may enter in."[260]

Now I saw in my dream that these two men went in at the gate: and lo, as they entered, they were transfigured, and they had raiment put on that shone like gold. There were also that met them with harps and crowns, and gave them to them—the harps to praise withal, and the crowns in token of honor. Then I heard in my dream that all the bells in the city rang again for joy, and that it was said unto them, "ENTER YE INTO THE JOY OF YOUR LORD." I also heard the men themselves, that they sang with a loud voice, saying, "BLESSING AND HONOR, AND GLORY, AND POWER, BE UNTO HIM THAT SITTETH UPON THE THRONE, AND UNTO THE LAMB, FOR EVER AND EVER."[261]

Now just as the gates were opened to let in the men, I looked in after them, and, behold, the City shone like the sun; the streets also were paved with gold, and in them walked many men, with crowns on their heads, palms in their hands, and golden harps to sing praises withal.

There were also of them that had wings, and they answered one another without intermission, saying, "Holy, holy, holy is the Lord." [262] And after that they shut up the gates; which, when I had seen, I wished myself among them.

Now while I was gazing upon all these things, I turned my head to look

IGNORANCE THRUST INTO HELL.

back, and saw Ignorance come up to the river side; but he soon got over, and that without half that difficulty which the other two men met with.

For it happened that there was then in that place one Vain-hope, a ferryman, that with his boat helped him over; so he, as the others I saw, did ascend the hill, to come up to the gate, only he came alone; neither did any man meet him with the least encouragement.

When he was come up to the gate, he looked up to the writing that was above, and then began to knock, supposing that entrance should have been quickly administered to him; but he was asked by the men that looked over the top of the gate, Whence came you? and what would you have?

He answered, I have ate and drank in the presence of the King, and he has taught in our streets. Then they asked him for his certificate, that they might go in and show it to the King; so he fumbled in his bosom for one, and found none.

Then said they, Have you none? But the man answered never a word. So they told the King, but he would not come down to see him, but commanded the two Shining Ones that conducted Christian and Hopeful to the City, to go out and take Ignorance, and bind him hand and foot, and have him away.

Then they took him up, and carried him through the air, to the door that I saw in the side of the hill, and put him in there. Then I saw that there was a way to hell, even from the gates of heaven, as well as from the City of Destruction. So I awoke, and behold it was a dream.

THE CONCLUSION.

Now, READER, I have told my dream to thee;
See if thou canst interpret it to me,
Or to thyself, or neighbor; but take heed
Of misinterpreting; for that, instead
Of doing good, will but thyself abuse:
By misinterpreting, evil ensues.

Take heed, also, that thou be not extreme,
In playing with the outside of my dream:
Nor let my figure or similitude
Put thee into a laughter or a feud.
Leave this for boys and fools; but as for thee,
Do thou the substance of my matter see.

Put by the curtains, look within my veil,
Turn up my metaphors, and do not fail,
There, if thou seekest them, such things to find,
As will be helpful to an honest mind.

What of my dross thou findest there, be bold
'To throw away, but yet preserve the gold ;
What if my gold be wrapped up in ore ?—
None throws away the apple for the core.
But if thou shalt cast all away as vain,
I know not but 'twill make me dream again

END OF THE FIRST PART.

THE PILGRIM'S PROGRESS

FROM

THIS WORLD TO THAT WHICH IS TO COME.

THE SECOND PART.

247

THE AUTHOR'S WAY

OF

SENDING FORTH HIS SECOND PART OF THE PILGRIM.

Go now, my little book, to every place
Where my first Pilgrim has but shown his face,
Call at their door. If any say, Who's there?
Then answer thou, CHRISTIANA is here.
If they bid thee come in, then enter thou,
With all thy boys ; and then, as thou know'st how,
Tell who they are, also from whence they came ;
Perhaps they'll know them by their looks or name.
But if they should not, ask them yet again
If formerly they did not entertain
One CHRISTIAN, a Pilgrim ? If they say
They did; and were delighted in his way:
Then let them know, that those related were
Unto him ; yea, his wife and children are.

Tell them that they have left their house and home,
Are turned Pilgrims, seek a world to come ;
That they have met with hardships in the way,
That they do meet with troubles night and day,
That they have trod on serpents, fought with devils,
Have also overcome a many evils.
Yea, tell them also of the next, who have,
Of love to pilgrimage, been stout and brave
Defenders of that way, and how they still
Refuse this world, to do their Father's will.

Go, tell them also of those dainty things,
That pilgrimage unto the Pilgrim brings.
Let them acquainted be, too, how they are
Beloved of their King, under his care ;
What goodly mansions for them he provides,
Though they meet with rough winds and swelling tides,

How brave a calm they will enjoy at last,
Who to their Lord, and by his ways hold fast.
  Perhaps with heart and hand they will embrace
Thee, as they did my firstling, and will grace
Thee, and thy fellows, with such cheer and fare,
As show well they of Pilgrims lovers are.

OBJECTION I.

  But how, if they will not believe of me
That I am truly thine ; 'cause some there be
That counterfeit the Pilgrim and his name,
Seek by disguise to seem the very same :
And by that means have wrought themselves into
The hands and houses of I know not who ?

ANSWER.

  'Tis true, some have of late, to counterfeit
My Pilgrim, to their own my title set ;
Yea others, half my name and title too
Have stitched to their books, to make them do ;
But yet they, by their features, do declare
Themselves not mine to be, whose e'er they are.
  If such thou meet'st with, then thine only way
Before them all, is, to say out thy say,
In thine own native language, which no man
Now useth, nor with ease dissemble can.
If, after all, they still of you shall doubt,
Thinking that you, like gipsies, go about
In naughty wise, the country to defile,
Or that you seek good people to beguile
With things unwarrantable ; send for me,
And I will testify you PILGRIMS be.
Yea, I will testify that only you
My Pilgrims are ; and that alone will do.

OBJECTION II.

  But yet, perhaps, I may inquire for him,
Of those that wish him damned, life and limb.
What shall I do, when I at such a door
For Pilgrims ask, and they shall rage the more ?

ANSWER.

Fright not thyself, my book for such bugbears
Are nothing else but ground for groundless fears.

My Pilgrim's book has travell'd sea and land,
Yet could I never come to understand
That it was slighted, or turn'd out of door
By any kingdom, were they rich or poor.

  In France, and Flanders, where men kill each other,
My Pilgrim is esteem'd a friend, a brother.

  In Holland, too, 'tis said, as I am told,
My Pilgrim is with some worth more than gold.

  Highlanders and wild Irish can agree
My Pilgrim should familiar with them be.

  'Tis in New England under such advance,
Receives there so much loving countenance,
As to be trimm'd, new clothed, and deck'd with gems
That it may show its features and its limbs.
Yet more ; so comely doth my Pilgrim walk,
That of him thousands daily sing and talk.

  If you draw nearer home it will appear,
My Pilgrim knows no ground of shame or fear ;
City and country will him entertain
With, Welcome, Pilgrim ; yea, they can't refrain
From smiling, if my Pilgrim be but by,
Or shows his head in any company.

  Brave gallants do my Pilgrim hug and love,
Esteem it much, yea, value it above
Things of a greater bulk : yea, with delight,
Say, My lark's leg is better than a kite.

  Young ladies, and young gentlewomen, too,
Do no small kindness to my Pilgrim show.
Their cabinets, their bosoms, and their hearts,
The Pilgrim has, 'cause he to them imparts
His pretty riddles in such wholesome strains,
As yields them profit double to their pains
Of reading ; yea, I think, I may be bold
To say, some prize him far above their gold.
The very children that do walk the street,
If they do but my holy Pilgrim meet,
Salute him will, will wish him well, and say,
He is the only stripling of the day.

  They have never seen him, yet admire
What they have heard of him, and much desire
To have his company, and hear him tell
Those pilgrim stories which he knows so well.

  Yea, some who did not love him at the first,
But call'd him fool and noddy, say they must,

Now they have seen and heard him, him commend,
And to those whom they love they do him send.
　Wherefore, my Second Part, thou need'st not be
Afraid to show thy head; none can hurt thee,
That wish but well to him that went before,
'Cause thou com'st after with a second store
Of things as good, as rich, as profitable,
For young, for old, for stagg'ring, and for stable.

OBJECTION III.

　But some there be that say, He laughs too loud;
And some do say, His head is in a cloud.
Some say, His words and stories are so dark,
They know not how, by them, to find his mark.

ANSWER.

　One may, I think, say, Both his laughs and cries
May well be guess'd at by his watery eyes.
Some things are of that nature, as to make
One's fancy chuckle, while his heart doth ache.
When Jacob saw his Rachel with the sheep,
He did at the same time both kiss and weep.
　Whereas some say, A cloud is in his head,
That doth but show how wisdom's covered
With its own mantles, and to stir the mind
To a search after what it fain would find.
Things that seem to be hid in words obscure,
Do but the godly mind the more allure
To study what those sayings should contain
That speak to us in such a cloudy strain.
　I also know a dark similitude
Will on the fancy more itself intrude,
And will stick faster in the heart and head,
Than things from similes not borrowed.
　Wherefore, my book, let no discouragement
Hinder thy travels.　Behold thou art sent
To friends, not foes; to friends that will give place
To thee, thy pilgrims, and thy words embrace.
　Besides, what my first Pilgrim left conceal'd,
Thou, my brave second Pilgrim, hast reveal'd;
What CHRISTIAN left locked up, and went his way,
Sweet CHRISTIANA opens with her key.

OBJECTION IV.

But some love not the method of your first;
Romance they count it, throw't away as dust,
If I should meet with such, what should I say?
Must I slight them as they slight me, or nay?

ANSWER.

My CHRISTIANA, if with such thou meet,
By all means, in all loving-wise, them greet;
Render them not reviling for revile;
But if they frown, I prithee on them smile;
Perhaps 'tis nature, or some ill-report,
Has made them thus despise, or thus retort.
Some love no cheese, some love no fish, and some
Love not their friends, nor their own house or home.
Some start at pig, slight chicken, love not fowl
More than they love a cuckoo, or an owl;
Leave such, my CHRISTIANA, to their choice,
And seek those who to find thee will rejoice;
By no means strive, but in humble-wise
Present thee to them in thy Pilgrim's guise.
Go, then, my little book, and show to all
That entertain, and bid thee welcome, shall,
What thou shalt keep close, shut up from the rest,
And wish what thou shalt show them may be blest
To them for good, may make them choose to be
Pilgrims better by far than thee or me.
Go, then, I say, tell all men who thou art;
Say I am CHRISTIANA, and my part
Is now, with my four sons, to tell you what
It is for men to take a Pilgrim's lot.
Go also, tell them who and what they be,
That now do go on Pilgrimage with thee;
Say, Here's my neighbor, Mercy, she is one
That has long time with me a Pilgrim gone.
Come, see her in her virgin face, and learn
'Twixt idle ones and Pilgrims to discern.
Yea, let young damsels learn of her to prize
The world which is to come, in any wise.
When little tripping maidens follow God,
And leave old doting sinners to his rod;
'Tis like those days wherein the young ones cried
Hosanna! to whom old ones did deride.

Next, tell them of old Honest, whom you found
With his white hairs, treading the Pilgrim's ground.
Yea, tell them how plain-hearted this man was,
How after his good Lord he bare his cross;
Perhaps with some grey head this may prevail
With Christ to fall in love, and sin bewail.
  Tell them also, how Master Fearing went
On pilgrimage, and how the time he spent
In solitariness, with fears and cries;
And how, at last, he won the joyful prize.
He *was* a good man, though much down in spirit,
He *is* a good man, and doth life inherit.
  Tell them of Master Feeble-mind also,
Who, not before, but still behind would go.
Show them also, how he had like been slain,
And how one Great-heart did his life regain.
This man was true of heart, though weak in grace,
One might true godliness read in his face.
  Then tell them of Master Ready-to-halt,
A man with crutches, but much without fault;
Tell them how Master Feeble-mind and he
Did love, and in opinions much agree.
And let all know, though weakness was their chance,
Yet sometimes one could sing, the other dance.
  Forget not Master Valiant-for-the-truth,
That man of courage, though a very youth.
Tell every one his spirit was so stout,
No man could ever make him face about;
And how Great-heart and he could not forbear,
But put down Doubting Castle, slay Despair.
  Overlook not Master Despondency,
Nor Much-afraid, his daughter, though they lie
Under such mantles, as may make them look
(With some) as if their God had them forsook.
They softly went, but sure, and at the end
Found that the Lord of Pilgrims was their friend.
  When thou hast told the world of all these things,
Then turn about, my book, and touch these strings,
Which, if but touched, will such music make,
They'll make a cripple dance, a giant quake.
  These riddles that lie couch'd within thy breast,
Freely propound, expound; and for the rest
Of thy mysterious lines, let them remain
For those whose nimble fancies shall them gain.

Now may this *little book* a blessing be
To those who love this *little book* and me,
And may its buyer have no cause to say,
His money is but lost or thrown away;
Yea, may this Second Pilgrim yield that fruit,
As may with each good Pilgrim's fancy suit;
And may it persuade some that go astray,
To turn their feet and heart to the right way,
        Is the hearty prayer of
                The Author,
                        JOHN BUNYAN.

THE PILGRIM'S PROGRESS

PART II

W.L. THOMAS. Sc

258

THE PILGRIM'S PROGRESS.

THE SECOND PART.

CHAPTER I.

COURTEOUS COMPANIONS,
    SOME time since, to tell you my dream that I had of Christian the Pilgrim, and of his dangerous journey towards the Celestial Country, was pleasant to me, and profitable to you.

I told you then, also, what I saw concerning his wife and children, and how unwilling they were to go with him on pilgrimage, insomuch that he was forced to go on his progress without them; for he durst not run the danger of that destruction which he feared would come by staying with them in the City of Destruction. Wherefore, as I then showed you, he left them and departed.

Now it hath so happened, through the multiplicity of business, that I have been much hindered and kept back from my wonted travels into those parts from whence he went, and so could not, till now, obtain an opportunity to make further inquiry after whom he left behind, that I might give you an account of them.

But having had some concerns that way of late, I went down again thitherward. Now, having taken up my lodgings in a wood, about a mile off the place, as I slept I dreamed again.

And as I was in my dream, behold, an aged gentleman came by where I lay; and because he was to go some part of the way that I was travelling, methought I got up and went with him.

So as we walked, and as travellers usually do, I was as if we fell into discourse, and our talk happened to be about Christian and his travels; for thus I began with the old man:—

17   257

Sir, said I, what town is that there below, that lieth on the left hand of our way?

Then said Mr. Sagacity (for that was his name), It is the City of Destruction, a populous place, but possessed with a very ill-conditioned and idle sort of people.

I thought that was that city, quoth I; I went once myself through that town, and, therefore, know that this report you give of it is true.

SAG. Too true; I wish I could speak truth in speaking better of them that dwell therein.

Well, Sir, quoth I, then I perceive you to be a well-meaning man; and so one that takes pleasure to hear and tell of that which is good. Pray, did you never hear what happened to a man some time ago in this town, whose name was Christian, that went on pilgrimage up towards the higher regions?

SAG. Hear of him! Aye, and I also heard of the molestations, troubles, wars, captivities, cries, groans, frights, and fears that he met with and had in his journey; besides, I must tell you, all our country rings of him.

There are but few houses that have heard of him and his doings but have sought after and got the records of his pilgrimage; yea, I think I may say that his hazardous journey has got many well-wishers to his ways; for though, when he was here, he was *fool* in every man's mouth, yet, now he is gone, he is highly commended of all. For, it is said, he lives bravely where he is, yea, many of them that are resolved never to run his hazards, yet have their mouths water at his gains.

They may, quoth I, well think, if they think anything that is true, that he liveth well where he is; for he now lives at and in the Fountain of Life, and has what he has without labor and sorrow, for there is no grief mixed therewith. But, pray, what talk have the people about him?

SAG. Talk; the people talk strangely about him; some say that he now walks in white;[1] that he has a chain of gold about his neck; that he has a crown of gold, beset with pearl, upon his head.

Others say that the Shining Ones, that sometimes showed themselves to him in his journey, are become his companions, and that he is as familiar with them in the place where he is, as here one neighbor is with another.

Besides, it is confidently affirmed, concerning him, that the King of the place where he is has bestowed upon him already a very rich and pleasant dwelling at court;[2] and that he every day eateth,[3] and drinketh,

THE AUTHOR AND MR. SAGACITY.

and walketh, and talketh with him; and receiveth of the smiles and favors of him that is Judge of all there.

Moreover, it is expected of some, that his Prince, the Lord of that country, will shortly come into these parts, and will know the reason, if they can give any, why his neighbors set so little by him, and had him so much in derision, when they perceived that he would be a pilgrim.[4] For, they say, that now he is so in the affections of his Prince, and that his Sovereign is so much concerned with the indignities that were cast upon Christian, when he became a pilgrim, that he will look upon all as if done unto himself; and no marvel, for it is for the love that he had to his Prince that he ventured as he did.[5]

I dare say, quoth I, I am glad on it; I am glad for the poor man's sake, for that he now has rest from his labor;[6] and for that he now reapeth the benefit of his tears with joy;[7] and for that he has got beyond the gunshot of his enemies, and is out of the reach of them that hate him.

I also am glad, for that a rumor of these things is noised abroad in this country; who can tell but that it may work some good effect on some that are left behind? But, pray Sir, while it is fresh in my mind, do you hear anything of his wife and children? Poor hearts! I wonder in my mind what they do.

SAG. Who! Christiana and her sons? They are like to do as well as did Christian himself; for though they all played the fool at the first, and would by no means be persuaded by either the tears or entreaties of Christian, yet second thoughts have wrought wonderfully with them; so they have packed up, and are also gone after him.

Better and better, quoth I. But what! wife and children, and all?

SAG. It is true; I can give you an account of the matter, for I was upon the spot at the instant, and was thoroughly acquainted with the whole affair.

Then, said I, a man, it seems, may report it for a truth?

SAG. You need not fear to affirm it; I mean that they are all gone on pilgrimage, both the good woman and her four boys. And being (we are, as I perceive) going some considerable way together, I will give you an account of the whole of the matter.

This Christiana (for that was her name from the day that she, with her children, betook themselves to a pilgrim's life), after her husband was gone over the river, and she could hear of him no more, her thoughts began to work in her mind.

First, for that she had lost her husband, and for that the loving bond of that relation was utterly broken betwixt them. For you know, said he to me, nature can do no less but entertain the living with many a heavy cogitation in the remembrance of the loss of loving relations.

This, therefore, of her husband did cost her many a tear. But this was not all; for Christiana did also begin to consider with herself, whether her

CHRISTIANA'S THOUGHTS BEGAN TO WORK IN HER MIND.

unbecoming behavior towards her husband was not one cause that she saw him no more; and that in such sort he was taken away from her.

And upon this, came into her mind, by swarms, all her unkind, unnatural, and ungodly carriages to her dear friend; which also clogged her conscience, and did load her with guilt.

She was, moreover, much broken with calling to remembrance the restless groans, brinish tears, and self-bemoanings of her husband, and how she did harden her heart against all his entreaties, and loving persuasions, of her and her sons, to go with him; yea, there was not anything that Christian either said to her or did before her all the while that his burden did hang on his back, but it returned upon her like a flash of lightning, and rent her heart in sunder.

Specially that bitter outcry of his, " What shall I do to be saved?" did ring in her ears most dolefully.

Then said she to her children, Sons, we are all undone. I have sinned away your father, and he is gone; he would have had us with him, but I would not go myself. I also have hindered you of life.

With that the boys fell all into tears, and cried out to go after their father. O! said Christiana, that it had been but our lot to go with him, then had it fared well with us, beyond what it is like to do now; for though I formerly foolishly imagined, concerning the troubles of your father, that they proceeded of a foolish fancy that he had, or for that he was overrun with melancholy humors; yet now it will not out of my mind, but that they sprang from another cause, to wit, for that the Light of light was given him;[8] by the help of which, as I perceived, he has escaped the snares of death. Then they all wept again, and cried out, " O woe worth the day!"

The next night Christiana had a dream; and, behold, she saw as if a broad parchment was opened before her, in which were recorded the sum of her ways;[9] and the times, as she thought, looked very black upon her. Then she cried out aloud in her sleep, " Lord have mercy upon me a sinner!" and the little children heard her.

After this she thought she saw two very ill-favored ones standing by her bed-side, and saying, What shall we do with this woman? for she cries out for mercy waking and sleeping; if she be suffered to go on as she begins, we shall lose her as we have lost her husband. Wherefore we must, by one way or other, seek to take her off from the thoughts of what shall be hereafter, else all the world cannot help it but she will become a pilgrim.

Now she awoke in a great sweat, also a trembling was upon her; but after a while she fell to sleeping again. And then she thought she saw Christian her husband in a place of bliss, among many immortals, with a harp in his hand, standing and playing upon it before one that sat on a throne, with a rainbow about his head. She saw also as if he bowed his head, with his face to the paved work that was under the Prince's feet,

CHRISTIANA TALKS WITH HER SONS.

263

saying, I heartily thank my Lord and King, for bringing of me into this place.

Then shouted a company of them that stood round about, and harped with their harps; but no man living could tell what they said, but Christian and his companions.

Next morning, when she was up, had prayed to God, and talked with

CHRISTIANA'S DREAM.

her children a while, some one knocked hard at the door, to whom she spake out, saying, If thou comest in God's name, come in.

So he said, Amen, and opened the door, and saluted her with "Peace be to this house." The which, when he had done, he said, Christiana, knowest thou wherefore I am come?

Then she blushed and trembled, also her heart began to wax warm with desires to know whence he came, and what was his errand to her.

So he said unto her, my name is Secret; I dwell with those that are high. It is talked of where I dwell, as if thou hadst a desire to go thither; also, there is a report, that thou art aware of the evil thou hast formerly done to thy husband, in hardening of thy heart against his way, and in keeping of these thy babes in their ignorance. Christiana, the Merciful One has sent me to tell thee, that he is a God ready to forgive, and that he taketh delight to multiply the pardon of offences.

He would also have thee know, that he inviteth thee to come into his presence, to his table, and that he will feed thee with the fat of his house, and with the heritage of Jacob thy father.

There is Christian thy husband (that was), with legions more, his companions, ever beholding that face that doth minister life to beholders; and they will all be glad when they shall hear the sound of thy feet step over thy Father's threshold.

Christiana at this was greatly abashed in herself, and bowing her head to the ground, this Visitor proceeded, and said, Christiana, here is also a letter for thee, which I have brought from thy husband's King.

So she took it, and opened it, but it smelt after the manner of the best perfume;[10] also it was written in letters of gold. The contents of the letter was, That the King would have her do as did Christian her husband; for that was the way to come to his city, and to dwell in his presence with joy for ever.

At this the good woman was quite overcome; so she cried out to her visitor, Sir, will you carry me and my children with you, that we also may go and worship this King?

Then said the visitor, Christiana, the bitter is before the sweet. Thou must through troubles, as did he that went before thee, enter this Celestial City. Wherefore I advise thee to do as did Christian thy husband.

Go to the wicket-gate yonder, over the plain, for that stands in the head of the way up which thou must go, and I wish thee all good speed. Also I advise that thou put this letter in thy bosom; that thou read therein to thyself, and to thy children, until you have got it by rote of heart, for it is one of thy songs that thou must sing while thou art in this house of thy pilgrimage;[11] also this thou must deliver in at the further gate.

Now I saw in my dream, that this old gentleman, as he told me this story, did himself seem to be greatly affected therewith.

He, moreover, proceeded and said, So Christiana called her sons together, and began thus to address herself unto them: My sons, I have, as you may perceive, been of late under much exercise in my soul, about the

CHRISTIANA PROPOSES TO HER CHILDREN THAT THEY SHOULD GO ON PILGRIMAGE.

death of your father, not for that I doubt at all of his happiness, for I am satisfied now that he is well.

I have been also much affected with the thoughts of mine own state and yours; which I verily believe is by nature miserable. My treatment also, of your father in his distress is a great load to my conscience; for I hardened both my own heart and yours against him, and refused to go with him on pilgrimage.

The thoughts of these things would now kill me outright, but that for a dream which I had last night, and but for the encouragement that this stranger has given me this morning.

Come, my children, let us pack up and begone to the gate that leads

MRS. TIMOROUS AND MERCY FIND CHRISTIANA PACKING UP.

to the Celestial Country, that we may see your father, and be with him and his companions in peace, according to the laws of that land.

Then did her children burst out into tears for joy, that the heart of their mother was so inclined. So their visitor bade them farewell; and they began to prepare to set out on their journey.

But while they were thus about to be gone, two of the women, that were Christiana's neighbors, came up to her house, and knocked at her door. To whom she said as before, If you come in God's name come in.

At this the women were stunned; for that kind of language they used not to hear, or to perceive to drop from the lips of Christiana. Yet they came in: but, behold, they found the good woman a-preparing to be gone from her house.

So they began and said, Neighbor, pray what is your meaning by this?

Christiana answered and said to the eldest of them, whose name was Mrs. Timorous, I am preparing for a journey. (This Timorous was daughter to him that met Christian upon the Hill Difficulty, and would have had him go back for fear of the lions.)

TIM. For what journey, I pray you?

CHRIS. Even to go after my good husband. And with that she fell a-weeping.

TIM. I hope not so, good neighbor; pray, for your poor children's sakes, do not so unwomanly cast away yourself.

CHRIS. Nay, my children shall go with me, not one of them is willing to stay behind.

TIM. I wonder, in my very heart, what, or who has brought you into this mind.

CHRIS. Oh! neighbor, knew you but as much as I do, I doubt not but that you would go with me.

TIM. Prithee, what new knowledge hast thou got, that so worketh off thy mind from thy friends, and that tempteth thee to go, nobody knows where?

CHRIS. Then Christiana replied, I have been sorely afflicted since my husband's departure from me; but especially since he went over the river. But that which troubleth me most, is my churlish manner to him, when he was under his distress.

Besides, I am now as he was then; nothing will serve me but going on pilgrimage. I was a-dreaming last night that I saw him. Oh that my soul was with him! He dwelleth in the presence of the King of the country; he sits and eats with him at his table; he is become a companion of immortals;[12] and has a house now given him to dwell in, to which the best palaces on earth, if compared, seem to me but as a dunghill.

The Prince of the place has also sent for me, with promise of entertainment if I shall come to him; his messenger was here even now, and has brought me a letter, which invites me to come. And with that she plucked out her letter, and read it, and said to them, What now will ye say to this?

Tim. Oh the madness that has possessed thee and thy husband, to run yourselves upon such difficulties! You have heard, I am sure, what your husband did meet with, even, in a manner, at the first step he took on his way, as our neighbor Obstinate can yet testify, for he went along with them; yea, and Pliable too, until they, like wise men, were afraid to go any further.

We also heard, over and above, how he met with the lions, Apollyon, the Shadow of Death, and many other things. Nor is the danger that he met with at Vanity Fair to be forgotten by thee; for if he, though a man, was so hard put to it, what canst thou, being but a poor woman, do? Consider, also, that these four sweet babes are thy children, thy flesh and thy bones. Wherefore, though thou shouldest be so rash as to cast away thyself; yet, for the sake of the fruit of thy body, keep thou at home.

But Christiana said unto her, Tempt me not, my neighbor. I have now a price put into my hand to get gain, and I should be a fool of the greatest size, if I should have no heart to strike in with the opportunity.

And for that you tell me of all these troubles that I am like to meet with in the way, they are so far off from being to me a discouragement, that they show I am in the right. "The bitter must come before the sweet," and that also will make the sweet the sweeter. Wherefore, since you came not to my house in God's name, as I said, I pray you be gone, and not disquiet me further.

Then Timorous also reviled her, and said to her fellow, Come, neighbor Mercy, let us leave her in her own hands, since she scorns our counsel and company.

But Mercy was at a stand, and could not so readily comply with her neighbor, and that for a two-fold reason. First, her bowels yearned over Christiana. So she said within herself, If my neighbor will needs be gone, I will go a little way with her and help her.

Secondly, her bowels yearned over her own soul, for what Christiana had said had taken some hold upon her mind. Wherefore she said within herself again, I will yet have more talk with this Christiana, and if I find truth and life in what she shall say, myself with my heart shall also go with her.   Wherefore Mercy began thus to reply to her neighbor Timorous.

MERCY. Neighbor, I did, indeed, come with you to see Christiana this

morning; and since she is, as you see, a-taking of her last farewell of her country, I think to walk, this sun-shiny morning, a little way with her, to help her on the way.   But she told her not of the second reason, but kept that to herself.

TIM. Well, I see you have a mind to go a-fooling too, but take heed in time, and be wise. While we are out of danger we are out; but when we are in, we are in.

So Mrs. Timorous returned to her house, and Christiana betook herself to her journey.

But when Timorous was got home to her house, she sends for some of her neighbors, to wit, Mrs. Bat's-eyes, Mrs. Inconsiderate, Mrs. Light-mind, and Mrs. Know-nothing. So when they were come to her house, she falls to

MERCY DESIRES TO GO WITH CHRISTIANA.

telling of the story of Christiana, and of her intended journey.   And thus she began her tale.

TIM. Neighbors, having had little to do this morning, I went to give Christiana a visit; and when I came at the door, I knocked, as you know it is our custom.   And she answered, If you come in God's name, come in.

So in I went, thinking all was well. But when I came in, I found her preparing herself to depart the town, she and also her children.

So I asked her what was her meaning by that. And she told me, in short, that she was now of a mind to go on pilgrimage, as did her hus-

MRS. TIMOROUS AND HER NEIGHBORS.

band. She told me also a dream that she had, and how the King of the country where her husband was, had sent her an inviting letter to come thither.

Then said Mrs. Know-nothing, And what! do you think she will go?

TIM. Aye, go she will, whatever come on't; and methinks I know it by this; for that which was my great argument to persuade her to stay at home (to wit, the troubles she was like to meet with in the way) is one great argument with her to put her forward on her journey.

For she told me in so many words, "The bitter goes before the sweet." Yea, and forasmuch as it so doth, it makes the sweet the sweeter.

MRS. BAT'S-EYES. Oh, this blind and foolish woman! will she not take warning by her husband's afflictions? For my part, I see, if he was here again, he would rest him content in a whole skin, and never run so many hazards for nothing.

MRS. INCONSIDERATE also replied, saying, Away with such fantastical fools from the town! a good riddance, for my part, I say, of her. Should she stay where she dwells, and retain this her mind, who could live quietly by her? for she will either be dumpish or unneighborly, or talk of such matters as no wise body can abide; wherefore, for my part, I shall never be sorry for her departure. Let her go, and let better come in her room. It was never a good world since these whimsical fools dwelt in it.

Then MRS. LIGHT-MIND added as followeth:—Come, put this kind of talk away. I was yesterday at Madame Wanton's, where we were as merry as the maids. For who do you think should be there, but I and Mrs. Love-the-flesh, and three or four more, with Mr. Lechery, Mrs. Filth, and some others. So there we had music and dancing, and what else was meet to fill up the pleasure. And, I dare say, my lady herself is an admirably well-bred gentlewoman, and Mr. Lechery is as pretty a fellow.

CHAPTER II.

B Y this time, Christiana was got on her way, and Mercy went along with her. So as they went, her children being there also, Christiana began to discourse. And, Mercy, said Christiana, I take this as an unexpected favor, that thou shouldst set foot out of doors with me, to accompany me a little in my way.

MERCY. Then said young Mercy (for she was but young), If I thought it would be of any purpose to go with you, I would never go near the town more.

CHRIS. Well, Mercy, said Christiana, cast in thy lot with me; I well know what will be the end of our pilgrimage.

My husband is where he would not but be for all the gold in the Spanish mines. Nor shalt thou be rejected, though thou goest but upon my invitation.

The King who has sent for me and my children is one that delighteth in mercy. Besides, if thou wilt, I will hire thee, and thou shalt go along with me as my servant; yet we will have all things in common betwixt thee and me; only, go along with me.

MERCY. But how shall I be certain that I also shall be entertained? Had I this hope but from one that can tell, I would make no stick at all, but would go, being helped by him that can help, though the way was never so tedious.

CHRIS. Well, loving Mercy, I will tell thee what thou shalt do. Go with me to the wicket-gate, and there I will further inquire for thee; and if there thou shalt not meet with encouragement, I will be content that thou shalt return to thy place. I also will pay thee for thy kindness which thou showest to me and my children, in thy accompanying us in our way, as thou dost.

MERCY. Then will I go thither, and will take what shall follow; and the Lord grant that my lot may there fall, even as the King of Heaven shall have his heart upon me.

Christiana then was glad at her heart, not only that she had a com-

CHRISTIANA AND HER FAMILY, WITH MERCY, SET OUT.

panion, but also for that she had prevailed with this poor maid to fall in love with her own salvation. So they went on together, and Mercy began to weep. Then said Christiana, Wherefore weepeth my sister so?

MERCY. Alas! said she, who can but lament, that shall but rightly consider, what a state and condition my poor relations are in that yet remain in our sinful town? and that which makes my grief the more heavy is, because they have no instructor nor any to tell them what is to come.

CHRIS. Pity becometh pilgrims; and thou dost for thy friends as my good Christian did for me when he left me; he mourned for that I would not heed nor regard him; but his Lord and ours did gather up his tears, and put them into his bottle; and now both I and thou, and these my sweet babes, are reaping the fruit and benefit of them. I hope, Mercy, these tears of thine will not be lost; for the truth hath said, that, "They that sow in tears shall reap in joy," in singing. And "he that goeth forth and weepeth, bearing precious seed, shall doubtless come again with rejoicing, bringing his sheaves with him." [13]

Then said Mercy—

> Let the Most Blessed be my guide,
>   If't be his blessed will;
> Unto his gate, into his fold,
>   Up to his holy hill.
>
> And let him never suffer me
>   To swerve or turn aside
> From his free grace, and holy ways,
>   Whate'er shall me betide.
>
> And let him gather them of mine,
>   That I have left behind;
> Lord, make them pray they may be thine,
>   With all their heart and mind.

Now my old friend proceeded and said: But when Christiana came up to the Slough of Despond, she began to be at a stand; for, said she, this is the place in which my dear husband had like to have been smothered with mud.

She perceived, also, that notwithstanding the command of the King to make this place for pilgrims good, yet it was rather worse than formerly. So I asked if that was true. Yes, said the old gentleman, too true; for that many there be that pretend to be the King's laborers, and that say they are for mending the King's highway, that bring dirt and dung instead of stones, and so mar instead of mending. Here, Christiana, therefore, with her boys, did make a stand; but, said Mercy, Come, let us venture, only let us be wary. Then they looked well to the steps, and made a shift to get staggeringly over.

Yet Christiana had like to have been in, and that not once or twice. Now they had no sooner got over, but they thought they heard words that said unto them, "Blessed is she that believed: for there shall be a performance of those things which were told her from the Lord." [14]

Then they went on again; and said Mercy to Christiana, Had I as good ground to hope for a loving reception at the wicket-gate as you, I think no Slough of Despond would discourage me.

Well, said the other, you know your sore, and I know mine; and, good friend, we shall all have enough evil before we come at our journey's end.

For can it be imagined, that the people that design to attain such excellent glories as we do, and that are so envied that happiness as we are; but that we shall meet with what fears and scares, with what troubles and afflictions they can possibly assault us with, that hate us?

And now Mr. Sagacity left me to dream out my dream by myself. Wherefore, methought I saw Christiana and Mercy, and the boys, go all of them up to the gate; to which, when they were come they betook themselves to a short debate about how they must manage their calling at the gate, and what should be said to him that did open to them.

So it was concluded, since Christiana was the eldest, that she should knock for entrance, and that she should speak to him that did open, for the rest. So Christiana began to knock; and, as her poor husband did, she knocked, and knocked again. But, instead of any that answered, they all thought that they heard as if a dog came barking upon them; a dog, and a great one too, and this made the women and children afraid: nor durst they, for a while, to knock any more, for fear the mastiff should fly upon them.

Now, therefore, they were greatly tumbled up and down in their minds, and knew not what to do; knock they durst not for fear of the dog; go back they durst not, for fear the Keeper of that gate should espy them as they so went, and should be offended with them; at last they thought of knocking again, and knocked more vehemently than they did at the first. Then said the Keeper of the gate, Who is there? So the dog left off to bark, and he opened unto them.

Then Christiana made low obeisance, and said, Let not our Lord be offended with his handmaidens, for that we have knocked at his princely

THE KING'S TRUMPETER.

gate. Then said the Keeper, Whence come ye, and what is it that you would have?

Christiana answered, We are come from whence Christian did come, and upon the same errand as he; to wit, to be, if it shall please you, graciously admitted by this gate into the way that leads to the Celestial City. And I answer, my Lord, in the next place, that I am Christiana, once the wife of Christian, that now has gone above.

With that the Keeper of the gate did marvel, saying, What, is she become now a pilgrim, that, but a while ago, abhorred that life? Then she bowed her head, and said, Yes, and so are these my sweet babes also.

Then he took her by the hand, and let her in, and said also, "Suffer the little children to come unto me;" and with that he shut up the gate.

This done, he called to a trumpeter that was above, over the gate, to entertain Christiana with shouting and sound of trumpet for joy. So he obeyed, and sounded, and filled the air with his melodious notes. [15]

Now, all this while poor Mercy did stand without, trembling and crying, for fear that she was rejected. But when Christiana had gotten admittance for herself and her boys, then she began to make intercession for Mercy.

And she said, My Lord, I have a companion of mine that stands yet without, that is come hither upon the same account as myself; one that is much dejected in her mind, for that she comes, as she thinks, without sending for; whereas I was sent to by my husband's King to come.

Now Mercy began to be very impatient, for each minute was as long to her as an hour; wherefore she prevented Christiana from a fuller interceding for her, by knocking at the gate herself. And she knocked then so loud that she made Christiana to start. Then said the Keeper of the gate, Who is there? and said Christiana, It is my friend.

So he opened the gate, and looked out, but Mercy was fallen down without in a swoon, for she fainted, and was afraid that no gate would be opened to her.

Then he took her by the hand, and said, Damsel, I bid thee arise.

Oh, Sir, said she, I am faint; there is scarce life left in me. But he answered, That one once said, "When my soul fainted within me, I remembered the Lord; and my prayer came in unto thee, into thine holy temple." [16] Fear not, but stand upon thy feet, and tell me wherefore thou art come.

THE KEEPER OF THE GATE FINDS MERCY FAINTING OUTSIDE.

MERCY. I am come for that unto which I was never invited, as my friend Christiana was. Hers was from the King, and mine was but from her. Wherefore I fear I presume.

KEEP. Did she desire thee to come with her to this place?

MERCY. Yes; and, as my Lord sees, I am come. And, if there is any grace or forgiveness of sins, to spare, I beseech that I, thy poor hand-maiden, may be partaker thereof.

MERCY AT THE GATE.

Then he took her again by the hand, and led her gently in, and said, I pray for all them that believe on me, by what means soever they come unto me.

Then said he to those that stood by, Fetch something, and give it to Mercy to smell on, thereby to stay her fainting. So they fetched her a bundle of myrrh; and a while after, she was revived.

And now was Christiana and her boys, and Mercy, received of the Lord at the head of the way, and spoken kindly unto by him. Then said they yet further unto him, We are sorry for our sins, and beg of our Lord his pardon, and further information what we must do.

I grant pardon, said he, by word and deed; by word, in the promise of forgiveness; by deed, in the way I obtained it. Take the first from my lips with a kiss; and the other as it shall be revealed.[17]

Now, I saw in my dream, that he spake many good words unto them, whereby they were greatly gladdened. He also had them up to the top of the gate, and showed them by what deed they were saved; and told them withal, That that sight they would have again, as they went along in the way, to their comfort.

So he left them a while in a summer parlor below, where they entered into talk by themselves; and thus Christiana began: O Lord! how glad am I that we are got in hither.

MERCY. So, you well may; but I of all have cause to leap for joy.

CHRIS. I thought one time, as I stood at the gate (because I had knocked, and none did answer), that all our labor had been lost, especially when that ugly cur made such a heavy barking against us.

MERCY. But my worse fear was after I saw that you were taken into his favor, and that I was left behind. Now, thought I, it is fulfilled which is written, "Two women shall be grinding together, the one shall be taken and the other left."[18] I had much ado to forbear crying out, Undone! undone!

And afraid I was to knock any more; but when I looked up to what was written over the gate, I took courage. I also thought that I must either knock again, or die; so I knocked, but I cannot tell how, for my spirit now struggled betwixt life and death.

CHRIS. Can you not tell how you knocked? I am sure your knocks were so earnest, that the very sound of them made me start; I thought I never heard such knocking in all my life; I thought you would have come in by violent hands, or have taken the kingdom by storm.[19]

MERCY. Alas! to be in my case, who that so was could but have done so? You saw that the door was shut upon me, and that there was a most cruel dog thereabout. Who, I say, that was so faint-hearted as I, that would not have knocked with all their might? But, pray, what said my Lord to my rudeness? Was he not angry with me?

CHRIS. When he heard your lumbering noise, he gave a wonderful, innocent smile; I believe what you did pleased him well enough, for he showed no sign to the contrary.

But I marvel in my heart why he keeps such a dog; had I known that before, I fear I should not have had heart enough to have ventured myself in this manner. But now we are in, we are in: and I am glad with all my heart.

MERCY. I will ask, if you please, next time he comes down, why he keeps such a filthy cur in his yard; I hope he will not take it amiss.

Aye, do, said the children, and persuade him to hang him; for we are afraid he will bite us when we go hence.

So at last he came down to them again, and Mercy fell to the ground on her face before him, and worshipped, and said, Let my Lord accept of the sacrifice of praise which I now offer unto him with the "calves of my lips."

So he said unto her, "Peace be to thee, stand up." But she continued upon her face, and said, "Righteous art thou, O Lord, when I plead with thee: yet let me talk with thee of thy judgments." [20] Wherefore dost thou keep so cruel a dog in thy yard, at the sight of which such women and children as we, are ready to fly from thy gate for fear?

He answered and said, That dog has another owner, he also is kept close in another man's ground, only my pilgrims hear his barking; he belongs to the castle which you see there at a distance, but can come up to the walls of this place.

He has frighted many an honest pilgrim from worse to better, by the great voice of his roaring. Indeed, he that owneth him doth not keep him of any good will to me or mine, but with intent to keep the pilgrims from coming to me, and that they may be afraid to knock at this gate for entrance.

Sometimes also he has broken out, and has worried some that I loved; but I take all at present patiently. I also give my pilgrims timely help, so they are not delivered up to his power, to do to them what his doggish nature would prompt him to. But what! my purchased one, I trow, hadst thou known never so much beforehand, thou wouldst not have been afraid of a dog.

The beggars that go from door to door will, rather than they will lose a supposed alms, run the hazard of the bawling, barking, and biting too, of a dog; and shall a dog—a dog in another man's yard, a dog whose barking I turn to the profit of pilgrims—keep any from coming to me? I deliver them from the lions, their darling from the power of the dog.

MERCY. Then said Mercy, I confess my ignorance; I spake what I understood not; I acknowledge that thou dost all things well.

CHRIS. Then Christiana began to talk of their journey, and to inquire after the way. So he fed them, and washed their feet, and set them in the way of his steps, according as he had dealt with her husband before.

CHAPTER III.

SO I saw in my dream, that they walked on in their way, and had the weather very comfortable to them.

Then Christiana began to sing, saying,

> Bless'd be the day that I began
> A pilgrim for to be;
> And blessed also be that man
> That thereto moved me.
>
> 'Tis true 'twas long ere I began
> To seek to live for ever:
> But now I run fast as I can:
> 'Tis better late than never.
>
> Our tears to joy, our fears to faith,
> Are turned, as we see,
> That our beginning as one saith,
> Shows what our end will be.

Now there was, on the other side of the wall that fenced in the way up which Christiana and her companions were to go, a garden, and that garden belonged to him whose was that barking dog of whom mention was made before.

And some of the fruit-trees that grew in that garden shot their branches over the wall; and being mellow, they that found them did gather them up, and oft eat of them to their hurt.

So Christiana's boys, as boys are apt to do, being pleased with the trees, and with the fruit that did hang thereon, did pluck them, and began to eat. Their mother did also chide them for so doing, but still the boys went on.

Well, said she, my sons, you transgress, for that fruit is none of ours; but she did not know that they did belong to the enemy; I will warrant you, if she had, she would have been ready to die for fear. But that passed, and they went on their way.

Now, by the time they were gone about two bow-shots from the place that

284

let them into the way, they espied two very ill-favored ones coming down apace to meet them. With that Christiana, and Mercy, her friend, covered themselves with their veils, and so kept on their journey; the children also went on before; so that at last they met together. Then they that came down to meet them, came just up to the women, as if they would embrace them; but Christiana said, Stand back, or go peaceably by, as you should.

THE CHILDREN EAT OF THE ENEMY'S FRUIT.

Yet these two, as men that are deaf, regarded not Christiana's words, but began to lay hands upon them. At that Christiana, waxing very wroth, spurned at them with her feet. Mercy also, as well as she could, did what she could to shift them. Christiana again said to them, Stand back, and begone; for we have no money to lose, being pilgrims, as you see, and such, too, as live upon the charity of our friends.

ILL-FAVORED ONES. Then said one of the two men, We make no assault upon you for money, but are come out to tell you, that if you will but grant one small request, which we shall ask, we will make women of you for ever.

CHRIS. Now Christiana, imagining what they should mean, made answer again, We will neither hear, nor regard, nor yield to what you shall ask. We are in haste, cannot stay; our business is a business of life and death. So, again, she and her companions made a fresh essay to go past them; but they hindered them in their way.

ILL-FAV. And they said, We intend no hurt to your lives; it is another thing we would have.

CHRIS. Ah, quoth Christiana, you would have us body and soul, for I know it is for that you are come; but we will die rather upon the spot, than suffer ourselves to be brought into such snares as shall hazard our well-being hereafter.

And with that they both shrieked out, and cried, Murder! murder! and so put themselves under those laws that are provided for the protection of women.[21]

But the men still made their approach upon them, with design to prevail against them. They, therefore, cried out again.

Now, they being, as I said, not far from the gate in at which they came, their voices were heard from where they were thither; wherefore some of the house came out, and knowing that it was Christiana's tongue, they made haste to her relief.

But by the time they were got within sight of them, the women were in a very great scuffle, the children also stood crying by. Then did he that came in for their relief call out to the ruffians, saying, What is that thing that you do? Would you make my Lord's people to transgress? He also attempted to take them, but they did make their escape over the wall into the garden of the man to whom the great dog belonged; so the dog became their protector.

This Reliever then came up to the women, and asked them how they did. So they answered, We thank thy Prince, pretty well; only we have been somewhat affrighted; we thank thee also, for that thou camest in to our help, for otherwise we had been overcome.

So after a few more words this Reliever said as followeth: I marvelled much, when you were entertained at the gate above, being, as ye knew, but weak women, that you petitioned not the Lord there for a conductor; then might you have avoided these troubles and dangers, for he would have granted you one.

Alas! said Christiana, we were so taken with our present blessing, that dangers to come were forgotten by us; besides, who could have thought, that so near the King's palace, there should have lurked such naughty ones? Indeed, it had been well for us, had we asked our Lord for one; but, since our Lord knew it would be for our profit, I wonder he sent not one along with us!

REL. It is not always necessary to grant things not asked for, lest, by so doing, they become of little esteem; but when the want of a thing is felt, it then comes under, in the eyes of him that feels it, that estimate that properly is its due, and so, consequently, will be thereafter used.

Had my Lord granted you a conductor, you would not neither so have bewailed that oversight of yours, in not asking for one, as now you have occasion to do. So all things work for good, and tend to make you wary.

CHRIS. Shall we go back again to my Lord, and confess our folly and ask one?

REL. Your confession of your folly I will present him with. To go back again you need not: for in all places where you shall come, you will find no want at all; for in every one of my Lord's lodgings which he has prepared for the reception of his pilgrims, there is sufficient to furnish them against all attempts whatsoever. But, as I said, "He will be inquired of by them to do it for them." [22] And it is a poor thing that is not worth asking for. When he had thus said, he went back to his place, and the pilgrims went on their way.

Then said Mercy, What a sudden blank is here! I made account we had now been past all danger, and that we should never see sorrow more.

Thy innocency, my sister, said Christiana to Mercy, may excuse thee much; but as for me, my fault is so much the greater, for that I saw this danger before I came out of the doors, and yet did not provide for it where provision might have been had. I am therefore much to be blamed.

Then said Mercy, How knew you this before you came from home? Pray open to me this riddle.

CHRIS. Why, I will tell you. Before I set foot out of doors, one night, as I lay in my bed, I had a dream about this; for, methought I saw two men, as like these as ever the world they could look, stand at my bed's feet, plotting how they might prevent my salvation. I will tell you their very words.

They said (it was when I was in my troubles), What shall we do with this woman? for she cries out, waking and sleeping, for forgiveness. If she be suffered to go on as she begins, we shall lose her, as we have lost her husband. This, you know, might have made me take heed, and have provided when provision might have been had.

Well, said Mercy, As by this neglect we have an occasion ministered unto us, to behold our own imperfections; so our Lord has taken occasion thereby to make manifest the riches of his grace; for he, as we see, has followed us with unasked kindness, and has delivered us from their hands that were stronger than we, of his mere good pleasure.

Thus, now, when they had talked away a little more time, they drew nigh to a house which stood in the way, which house was built for the relief of pilgrims; as you will find more fully related in the First Part of these Records of the Pilgrim's Progress. So they drew on towards the house (the House of the Interpreter), and when they came to the door, they heard a great talk in the house.

They then gave ear, and heard, as they thought, Christiana mentioned by name. For you must know that there went along, even before her, a talk of her and her children's going on pilgrimage. And this thing was the more pleasing to them, because they had heard that she was Christian's wife, that woman who was some time ago so unwilling to hear of going on pilgrimage.

Thus, therefore, they stood still, and heard the good people within commending her, who, they little thought, stood at the door. At last Christiana knocked, as she had done at the gate before. Now, when she had knocked, there came to the door a young damsel, named Innocent, and opened the door and looked, and behold two women were there.

Then said the damsel to them, With whom would you speak in this place?

Christiana answered, We understand that this is a privileged place for those that are become pilgrims, and we now at this door are such; wherefore we pray that we may be partakers of that for which we at this time are come; for the day, as thou seest, is very far spent, and we are loath to-night to go any further.

DAMSEL. Pray, what may I call your name, that I may tell it to my Lord within?

CHRIS. My name is Christiana; I was the wife of that pilgrim that some years ago did travel this way, and these be his four children. This maiden also is my companion, and is going on pilgrimage too.

INNOCENT. Then ran Innocent in (for that was her name), and said to those within, Can you think who is at the door? There is Christiana and her children, and her companion, all waiting for entertainment here.

Then they leaped for joy, and went and told their master. So he came to the door, and looking upon her he said, Art thou that Christiana whom Christian, the good man, left behind him, when he betook himself to a pilgrim's life?

CHRIS. I am that woman that was so hard-hearted as to slight my husband's troubles, and that left him to go on his journey alone, and these are his four children; but now I also am come, for I am convinced that no way is right but this.

INTER. Then is fulfilled that which also is written of the man that said to his son, "Go, work to-day in my vineyard. He answered and said, I will not: but afterwards he repented and went." [23]

Then said Christiana, So be it, Amen. God make it a true saying upon me, and grant that I may be found at the last of him in peace, without spot, and blameless!

INTER. But why standest thou thus at the door? Come in, thou daughter of Abraham. We were talking of thee but now, for tidings have come to us before, how thou art become a pilgrim. Come, children, come in; come, maiden, come in. So he had them all into the house.

So, when they were within, they were bid sit down and rest them; the which when they had done, those that attended upon the pilgrims in the house, came into the room to see them. And one smiled, another smiled, and they all smiled, for joy that Christiana was become a pilgrim.

They also looked upon the boys. They stroked them over the faces with the hand, in token of their kind reception of them. They also carried it lovingly to Mercy, and bid all welcome into their Master's house.

After a while, because supper was not ready, the Interpreter took them into his significant rooms, and showed them what Christian, Christiana's husband, had seen some time before.

Here, therefore, they saw the man in the cage, the man and his dream, the man that cut his way through his enemies, and the picture of the greatest of them all, together with the rest of those things that were then so profitable to Christian.

19

"THE MAN COULD LOOK NO WAY·BUT DOWNWARDS, AT THE MUCK·RAKE IN HIS HAND."

This done, after these things had been somewhat digested by Christiana and her company, the Interpreter takes them apart again, and has them first into a room where was a man that could look no way but downwards, with a muck-rake in his hand.

There stood also one over his head, with a celestial crown in his hand, and proffered him that crown for his muck-rake; but the man did neither look up, nor regard, but raked to himself the straws, the small sticks, and dust of the floor.

Then said Christiana, I persuade myself that I know somewhat the meaning of this; for this is a figure of a man of this world, is it not, good Sir?

INTER. Thou hast said the right, said he, and his muck-rake doth show his carnal mind. And whereas thou seest him rather give heed to rake up straws and sticks, and the dust of the floor, than to what he says that calls to him from above, with the celestial crown in his hand, it is to show that heaven is but as a fable to some, and that things here are counted the only things substantial. Now, whereas it was also showed thee, that the man could look no way but downwards, it is to let thee know that earthly things, when they are with power upon men's minds, quite carry their hearts away from God.

Then said Christiana, Oh, deliver me from this muck-rake!

That prayer, said the Interpreter, has lain by till it is almost rusty. "Give me not riches," is scarce the prayer of one of ten thousand.[24] Straws, and sticks, and dust, with most, are the great things now looked after.

With that Mercy and Christiana wept, and said, It is, alas! too true.

When the Interpreter had shown them this, he had them into the very best room in the house; a very brave room it was. So he bid them look round about, and see if they could find anything profitable there. Then they looked round and round; for there was nothing there to be seen but a very great spider on the wall: and that they overlooked.

MERCY. Then said Mercy, Sir, I see nothing, but Christiana held her peace.

INTER. But, said the Interpreter, look again; and she therefore looked again, and said, Here is not anything but an ugly spider, who hangs by her hands upon the wall. Then said he, Is there but one spider in all this spacious room?

Then the water stood in Christiana's eyes, for she was a woman of quick apprehension; and she said, Yea, Lord, there is here more than one. Yea, and spiders whose venom is far more destructive than that which is in her. The Interpreter then looked pleasantly upon her, and said, Thou hast said the truth. This made Mercy blush, and the boys to cover their faces, for they all began now to understand the riddle.

Then said the Interpreter again, "The spider taketh hold with her hands (as you see), and is in King's palaces." [25] And wherefore is this recorded, but to show you, that how full of the venom of sin soever you be, yet you may, by the hand of faith, lay hold of, and dwell in the best room that belongs to the King's house above!

I thought, said Christiana, of something of this; but I could not imagine it all. I thought that we were like spiders, and that we looked like ugly creatures, in what fine room soever we were; but that by this spider, this venomous and ill-favored creature, we were to learn how to act faith, that came not into my mind. And yet she has taken hold with her hands, as I see, and dwells in the best room in the house. God has made nothing in vain.

Then they seemed all to be glad; but the water stood in their eyes; yet they looked one upon another, and also bowed before the Interpreter.

He had them into another room, where was a hen and chickens, and bid them observe a while. So one of the chickens went to the trough to drink, and every time she drank she lifted up her head and her eyes towards heaven. See, said he, what this little chick doth, and learn of her to acknowledge whence your mercies come, by receiving them with looking up. Yet again, said he, observe and look; so they gave heed and perceived that the hen did walk in a four-fold method towards her chickens. 1. She had a common call, and that she hath all day long. 2. She had a special call, and that she had but sometimes. 3. She had a brooding note. And 4. She had an outcry. [26]

Now, said he, compare this hen to your King, and these chickens to his obedient ones. For, answerable to her, himself hath his methods, which he walketh in towards his people; by his common call, he gives nothing; by his special call, he always has something to give; he has also a brooding voice, for them that are under his wing; and he has an outcry to give the alarm when he seeth the enemy come. I chose, my darlings, to lead you into the room where such things are, because you are women, and they are easy for you.

And, Sir, said Christiana, pray let us see some more. So he had

THE INTERPRETER'S GARDEN.

them into the slaughter-house, where was a butcher killing of a sheep; and behold the sheep was quiet, and took her death patiently.

Then said the Interpreter, You must learn of this sheep to suffer, and to bear wrongs without murmurings and complaints. Behold how quietly she taketh her death, and without objecting, she suffereth her skin to be pulled over her ears. Your King doth call you his sheep.

After this, he led them into his garden, where was great variety of flowers; and he said, Do you see all these? So Christiana said, Yes. Then said he again, Behold the flowers are diverse in stature, in quality, and color, and smell, and virtue; and some are better than others; also where the gardener hath set them, there they stand, and quarrel not with one another.

Again, he had them into his field, which he had sowed with wheat and corn; but when they beheld, the tops of all were cut off, only the straw remained; he said again, This ground was dunged, and ploughed, and sowed; but what shall we do with the crop?

Then said Christiana, Burn some, and make muck of the rest. Then said the Interpreter again, Fruit, you see, is that thing you look for, and for want of that you condemn it to the fire, and to be trodden under foot of men: beware that in this you condemn not yourselves.

Then, as they were coming in from abroad, they espied a little robin with a great spider in his mouth; so the Interpreter said, Look here. So they looked, and Mercy wondered; but Christiana said, What a disparagement it is to such a pretty little bird as the robin-red-breast is, being also a bird above many, that loveth to maintain a kind of sociableness with man; I had thought they had lived upon crumbs of bread, or upon other such harmless matter. I like him less than I did.

The Interpreter then replied, This robin is an emblem, very apt to set forth some professors by; for to sight, they are, as this robin, pretty of note, color, and carriage. They seem also to have a very great love for professors that are sincere; and above all other, to desire to associate with them, and to be in their company, as if they could live upon the good man's crumbs.

They pretend also, that therefore it is that they frequent the house of the godly and the appointments of the Lord; but, when they are by themselves, as the robin, they can catch and gobble up spiders, they can change their diet, drink iniquity, and swallow down sin like water.

So, when they were come again into the house, because supper as yet was not ready, Christiana again desired that the Interpreter would either show or tell of some other things that are profitable.

Then the Interpreter began, and said, The fatter the sow is, the more she desires the mire; the fatter the ox is, the more gamesomely he goes to the slaughter; and the more healthy the lusty man is, the more prone he is unto evil.

There is a desire in women to go neat and fine, and it is a comely thing to be adorned with that which in God's sight is of great price.

It is easier watching a night or two, than to sit up a whole year together. So it is easier for one to begin to profess well, than to hold out as he should to the end.

Every shipmaster, when in a storm, will willingly cast that overboard which is of the smallest value in the vessel; but who will throw the best out first? None but he that feareth not God.

One leak will sink a ship; and one sin will destroy a sinner.

He that forgets his friend, is ungrateful unto him; but he that forgets his Saviour, is unmerciful to himself.

He that lives in sin, and looks for happiness hereafter, is like him that soweth cockle, and thinks to fill his barn with wheat or barley.

If a man would live well, let him fetch his last day to him, and make it always his company keeper.

Whispering, and change of thoughts, prove that sin is in the world.

If the world, which God sets light by, is counted a thing of that worth with men, what is heaven, which God commandeth?

If the life that is attended with so many troubles, is so loath to be let go by us, what is the life above?

Everybody will cry up the goodness of men; but who is there that is, as he should be, affected with the goodness of God?

We seldom sit down to meat, but we eat and yet leave some; so there is in Jesus Christ more merit and righteousness than the whole world has need of.

When the Interpreter had done, he takes them out into his garden again, and had them to a tree, whose inside was all rotten and gone, and yet it grew and had leaves.

Then said Mercy, What means this? This tree, said he, whose outside is fair, and whose inside is rotten, it is to which many may be compared that are in the garden of God; who with their mouths speak high in behalf of God, but indeed will do nothing for him; whose leaves are fair, but their heart good for nothing but to be tinder for the devil's tinder-box.

Now supper was ready, the table spread, and all things set on the board; so they sat down and did eat, when one had given thanks. And the Interpreter did usually entertain those that lodged with him, with music at meals; so the minstrels played. There was also one that did sing, and a very fine voice he had. His song was this:

> The Lord is only my support,
> And he that doth me feed;
> How can I then want anything
> Whereof I stand in need?

When the song and music was ended, the Interpreter asked Christiana what it was that at first did move her to betake herself to a Pilgrim's life.

Christiana answered, First the loss of my husband came into my mind, at which I was heartily grieved; but all that was but natural affection. Then, after that, came the troubles and pilgrimage of my husband into my mind, and also how like a churl I had carried it to him as to that.

So guilt took hold of my mind, and would have drawn me into the pond; but that opportunely I had a dream of the well-being of my husband, and a letter sent me by the King of that country where my husband dwells, to come to him. The dream and the letter together so wrought upon my mind, that they forced me to this way.

INTER. But met you with no opposition before you set out of doors?

CHRIS. Yes, a neighbor of mine, one Mrs. Timorous (she was akin to him that would have persuaded my husband to go back, for fear of the lions). She called me fool for, as she thought it, my intended desperate adventure; she also urged what she could to dishearten me to it; the hardship and troubles that my husband met with in the way: but all this I got over pretty well.

But a dream that I had of two ill-looking ones, that I thought did plot how to make me miscarry in my journey, that hath troubled me much; yea, it still runs in my mind, and makes me afraid of every one that I meet, lest they should meet me to do me a mischief, and to turn me out of the way. Yea, I may tell my Lord, though I would not have everybody know it, that between this and the gate by which we got into the way, we were both so sorely assaulted that we were made to cry out, Murder! and the two that made this assault upon us were like the two that I saw in my dream.

Then said the Interpreter, Thy beginning is good, thy latter end shall greatly increase. So he addressed himself to Mercy, and said unto her, And what moved thee to come hither, sweet heart?

Then Mercy blushed and trembled, and for a while continued silent.

Then said he, Be not afraid, only believe, and speak thy mind.

So she began, and said, Truly, Sir, my want of experience is that which makes me covet to be in silence, and that also that fills me with fears of coming short at last. I cannot tell of visions and dreams as my friend Christiana can; nor know I what it is to mourn for my refusing of the counsel of those that were good relations.

INTER. What was it, then, dear heart, that hath prevailed with thee to do as thou hast done?

MERCY. Why, when our friend here was packing up to be gone from our town, I and another went accidentally to see her; so we knocked at the door and went in.

When we were within, and seeing what she was doing, we asked what was her meaning. She said, she was sent for to go to her husband; and then she up and told us how she had seen him in a dream, dwelling in a curious place, among immortals, wearing a crown, playing upon a harp, eating and drinking at his Prince's table, and singing praises to him for bringing him thither, &c.

Now, methought, while she was telling these things unto us my heart burned within me; and I said in my heart, If this be true, I will leave my father and my mother, and the land of my nativity, and will, if I may, go along with Christiana.

So I asked her further of the truth of these things, and if she would let me go with her; for I saw now that there was no dwelling, but with the danger of ruin, any longer in our town. But yet I came away with a heavy heart, not for that I was unwilling to come away, but for that so many of my relations were left behind.

And I am come, with all the desire of my heart, and will go, if I may, with Christiana, unto her husband, and his King.

INTER. Thy setting out is good, for thou hast given credit to the truth. Thou art a Ruth, who did, for the love she bare to Naomi, and to the Lord her God, leave father and mother, and the land of her nativity, to come out, and go with a people that she knew not heretofore. "The Lord recompense thy work, and a full reward be given thee of the Lord God of Israel, under whose wings thou art come to trust." [27]

Now supper was ended, and preparation was made for bed; the women were laid singly alone, and the boys by themselves. Now when Mercy was in bed, she could not sleep for joy, for that now her doubts of missing at last, were removed further from her than ever they were before. So she lay blessing and praising God, who had had such favor for her.

In the morning they rose with the sun, and prepared themselves for their departure; but the Interpreter would have them tarry awhile, for, said he, you must orderly go from hence. Then said he to the damsel that first opened unto them, Take them and have them into the garden to the bath, and there wash them, and make them clean from the soil which they have gathered by travelling.

Then Innocent the damsel took them, and had them into the garden, and brought them to the bath; so she told them that there they must wash and be clean; for so her master would have the women to do that called at his house, as they were going on pilgrimage.

They then went in and washed, yea, they and the boys and all; and they came out of that bath, not only sweet and clean, but also much enlivened and strengthened in their joints. So when they came in, they looked fairer a great deal than when they went out to the washing.

When they were returned out of the garden from the bath, the Interpreter took them, and looked upon them, and said unto them, Fair as the moon. Then he called for the seal, wherewith they used to be sealed that were washed in his bath.

So the seal was brought, and he set his mark upon them, that they might be known in the places whither they were yet to go. Now the seal was the contents and sum of the passover which the children of Israel did eat when they came out from the land of Egypt, and the mark was set between their eyes.

This seal greatly added to their beauty, for it was an ornament to their faces. It also added to their gravity, and made their countenances more like them of angels.[28]

Then said the Interpreter again to the damsel that waited upon these women, Go into the vestry and fetch out garments for these people; so she went and fetched out white raiment, and laid down before him; so he commanded them to put it on. "It was fine linen, white and clean."

When the women were thus adorned, they seemed to be a terror one to the other; for that they could not see that glory each one on herself which they could see in each other. Now, therefore, they began to esteem each

GREAT-HEART BECOMES THE PILGRIMS' GUIDE.

299

other better than themselves. "For you are fairer than I am," said one; and, "You are more comely than I am," said another. The children also stood amazed to see into what fashion they were brought.

The Interpreter then called for a man-servant of his, one Great-heart, and bid him take sword and helmet and shield; and take these my daughters, said he, and conduct them to the house called Beautiful, at which place they will rest next.

So he took his weapons and went before them; and the Interpreter said, God speed. Those, also, that belonged to the family, sent them away with many a good wish. So they went on their way and sang—

> This place has been our second stage;
> 　Here we have heard and seen
> Those good things that, from age to age,
> 　To others hid have been.
>
> The dung-hill raker, spider, hen,
> 　The chicken, too, to me
> Hath taught a lesson; let me then
> 　Conformed to it be.
>
> The butcher, garden, and the field,
> 　The robin and his bait,
> Also the rotten tree doth yield
> 　Me argument of weight;
>
> To move me for to watch and pray,
> 　To strive to be sincere;
> To take my cross up day by day,
> 　And serve the Lord with fear.

CHAPTER IV.

NOW I saw in my dream, that they went on, and Great-heart went before them: so they went and came to the place where Christian's burden fell off his back, and tumbled into a sepulchre.

Here, then, they made a pause; and here also they blessed God. Now, said Christiana, it comes to my mind, what was said to us at the gate, to wit, that we should have pardon by word and deed; by word, that is, by the promise; by deed, to wit, in the way it was obtained. What the promise is, of that I know something; but what it is to have pardon by deed, or in the way that it was obtained, Mr. Great-heart, I suppose you know; wherefore, if you please, let us hear you discourse thereof.

GREAT-HEART. Pardon by the deed done, is pardon obtained by some one, for another that hath need thereof: not by the person pardoned, but in the way, saith another, in which I have obtained it.

So then, to speak to the question more at large, the pardon that you and Mercy and these boys have attained, was obtained by another, to wit, by him that let you in at the gate; and he hath obtained it in this double way. He has performed righteousness to cover you, and spilt blood to wash you in.

CHRIS. But if he parts with his righteousness to us, what will he have for himself?

GREAT-HEART. He has more righteousness than you have need of, or than he needeth himself.

CHRIS. Pray make that appear.

GREAT-HEART. With all my heart; but first I must premise, that he of whom we are now about to speak is one that has not his fellow.

He has two natures in one person, plain to be distinguished, impossible to be divided. Unto each of these natures a righteousness belongeth, and each righteousness is essential to that nature; so that one may as easily cause the nature to be extinct, as to separate its justice or righteousness from it.

301

Of these righteousnesses, therefore, we are not made partakers, so as that they, or any of them, should be put upon us that we might be made just, and live thereby. Besides these, there is a righteousness which this Person has, as these two natures are joined in one: and this is not the righteousness of the Godhead, as distinguished from the manhood; nor the righteousness of the manhood, as distinguished from the Godhead; but a righteousness which standeth in the union of both natures, and may probably be called, the righteousness that is essential to his being prepared of God to the capacity of the mediatory office which he was to be intrusted with.

If he parts with his first righteousness, he parts with his Godhead; if he parts with his second righteousness, he parts with the purity of his manhood; if he parts with his third, he parts with that perfection that capacitates him to the office of mediation. He has, therefore, another righteousness, which standeth in performance, or obedience to a revealed will; and that is it that he puts upon sinners, and that by which their sins are covered. Wherefore he saith, "As by one man's disobedience many were made sinners, so by the obedience of one shall many be made righteous." [29]

CHRIS. But are the other righteousnesses of no use to us?

GREAT-HEART. Yes; for though they are essential to his natures and office, and so cannot be communicated unto another, yet it is by virtue of them, that the righteousness that justifies, is, for that purpose, efficacious. The righteousness of his Godhead gives virtue to his obedience; the righteousness of his manhood giveth capability to his obedience to justify; and the righteousness that standeth in the union of these two natures to his office, giveth authority to that righteousness to do the work for which it is ordained.

So then, here is a righteousness that Christ, as God, has no need for, for he is God without it; here is a righteousness that Christ, as man, has no need of to make him so, for he is perfect man without it; again, here is a righteousness that Christ, as God-man, has no need of, for he is perfectly so without it.

Here, then, is a righteousness that Christ, as God, as man, as God-man, has no need of, with reference to himself, and therefore he can spare it; a justifying righteousness, that he for himself wanteth not, and therefore he giveth it away; hence it is called "the gift of righteousness." [30] This righteousness, since Christ Jesus the Lord, has made himself under

MR. GREAT-HEART.

the law, must be given away; for the law doth not only bind him that is
under it "to do justly," but to use charity. Wherefore he must, he

ought, by the law, if he hath two coats, to give one to him that hath none.

Now, our Lord, indeed, hath two coats, one for himself, and one to spare; wherefore he freely bestows one upon those that have none. And thus, Christiana and Mercy, and the rest of you that are here, doth your pardon come by deed, or by the work of another man. Your Lord Christ is he that has worked, and has given away what he wrought for to the next poor beggar he meets.

But, again, in order to pardon by deed, there must something be paid to God as a price, as well as something prepared to cover us withal. Sin has delivered us up to the just curse of a righteous law; now, from this curse we must be justified by way of redemption, a price being paid for the harms we have done;[31] and this is by the blood of your Lord, who came and stood in your place and stead, and died your death for your transgressions.[32]

Thus has he ransomed you from your transgressions by blood, and covered your polluted and deformed souls with righteousness. For the sake of which God passeth by you, and will not hurt you when he comes to judge the world.

CHRIS. This is brave. Now, I see there was something to be learned by our being pardoned by word and deed. Good Mercy, let us labor to keep this in mind; and, my children, do you remember it also. But, Sir, was not this it that made my good Christian's burden fall from off his shoulders, and that made him give three leaps for joy?

GREAT-HEART. Yes, it was the belief of this, that cut those strings that could not be cut by other means; and it was to give him a proof of the virtue of this, that he was suffered to carry his burden to the cross.

CHRIS. I thought so; for though my heart was lightful and joyous before, yet it is ten times more lightsome and joyous now. And I am persuaded by what I have felt, though I have felt but little as yet, that if the most burdened man in the world was here, and did see and believe as I now do, it would make his heart the more merry and blithe.

GREAT-HEART. There is not only comfort, and the ease of a burden brought to us, by the sight and consideration of these, but an endeared affection begot in us by it; for who can, if he doth but once think that pardon comes not only by promise, but thus, but be affected by the way and means of his redemption, and so with the man that hath wrought it for him?

CHRIS. True; methinks it makes my heart bleed to think that he should bleed for me. Oh, thou loving One! Oh, thou blessed One! Thou deservest to have me; thou hast bought me; thou deservest to have me all; thou hast paid for me ten thousand times more than I am worth.

No marvel that this made the water stand in my husband's eyes, and that it made him trudge so nimbly on; I am persuaded he wished me with him; but, vile wretch that I was, I let him come all alone. Oh, Mercy, that thy father and mother were here; yea, and Mrs. Timorous also; nay, I wish now with all my heart, that here was Madame Wanton too. Surely, surely their hearts would be affected; nor could the fear of the one, nor the powerful lusts of the other, prevail with them to go home again, and to refuse to become good pilgrims.

GREAT-HEART. You speak now in the warmth of your affections. Will it, think you, be always thus with you? Besides, this is not communicated to every one that did see your Jesus bleed. There were those that stood by, and that saw the blood run from his heart to the ground, and yet were so far off this, that, instead of lamenting, they laughed at him; and, instead of becoming his disciples, did harden their hearts against him.

So that all that you have, my daughters, you have by a peculiar impression made by a divine contemplating upon what I have spoken to you. Remember that it was told you, that the hen, by her common call, gives no meat to her chickens. This you have, therefore, by a special grace.

Now, I saw still in my dream, that they went on until they were come to the place that Simple and Sloth, and Presumption, lay and slept in, when Christian went by on pilgrimage; and, behold, they were hanged up in irons, a little way off on the other side.

Then said Mercy to him that was their guide and conductor, What are those three men? and for what are they hanged there?

GREAT-HEART. These three men were men of very bad qualities. They had no mind to be pilgrims themselves, and whosoever they could they hindered. They were for sloth and folly themselves, and whoever they could persuade with, they made so too; and withal, taught them to presume they should do well at last. They were asleep when Christian went by; and now when you go by, they are hanged.

MERCY. But could they persuade any to be of their opinion?

GREAT-HEART. Yes: they turned several out of the way. There was Slow-pace, that they persuaded to do as they. They also prevailed with one Short-wind, with one No-heart, with one Linger-after-lust, and with

20

one Sleepy-head, and with a young woman, her name was Dull, to turn out of the way, and become as they.

Besides, they brought up an ill report of our Lord, persuading others that he was a taskmaster. They also brought up an evil report of the good land, saying it was not half so good as some pretend it was. They also began to vilify his servants, and to count the very best of them meddlesome, troublesome, busybodies. Further they could call the bread of God husks; the comforts of his children, fancies; the travel and labour of pilgrims, things to no purpose.

Nay, said Christiana, if they were such, they shall never be bewailed by me. They have but what they deserve; and I think it is well that they hang so near the highway, that others may see and take warning. But had it not been well if their crimes had been engraven on some plate of iron or brass, and left here, even where they did their mischief, for a caution to other bad men?

GREAT-HEART. So it is, as you well may perceive, if you will go a little to the wall.

MERCY. No, no; let them hang, and their names rot, and their crimes live for ever against them. I think it a high favor that they were hanged before we came hither; who knows else what they might have done to such poor women as we are? Then she turned it into a song, saying—

> Now then, you three, hang there, and be a sign
> To all that shall against the truth combine.
> And let him that comes after fear this end,
> If unto pilgrims he is not a friend.
> And thou, my soul, of all such men beware,
> That unto holiness opposers are.

Thus they went on, till they came at the foot of the Hill Difficulty, where, again, their good friend, Mr. Great-heart, took an occasion to tell them of what happened there when Christian himself went by. So he had them first to the spring. Lo, said he, this is the spring that Christian drank of, before he went up this hill; and then it was clear and good, but now it is dirty with the feet of some that are not desirous that pilgrims here should quench their thirst.[33]

Thereat, Mercy said, And why so envious, trow? But, said their guide, it will do, if taken up, and put into a vessel that is sweet and good; for then the dirt will sink to the bottom, and the water will come out by itself more clear.

THE PILGRIMS DRINK OF THE SPRING.

Thus, therefore Christiana and her companions were compelled to do. They took it up, and put it into an earthen pot, and so let it stand till the dirt was gone to the bottom, and then they drank thereof.

Next, he showed them the two by-ways that were at the foot of the hill, where Formality and Hypocrisy lost themselves. And said he, these are dangerous paths. Two were here cast away when Christian came by; and, although, as you see, these ways are since stopped up with chains, posts, and a ditch, yet there are those that will choose to adventure here, rather than take the pains to go up this hill.

CHRIS. "The way of transgressors is hard."[34] It is a wonder that they can get into those ways without danger of breaking their necks.

GREAT-HEART. They will venture. Yea, if at any time any of the King's servants do happen to see them, and do call unto them, and tell them that they are in the wrong ways, and do bid them beware the danger, then they will railingly return them answer, and say, "As for the word that thou hast spoken unto us in the name of the Lord, we will not hearken unto thee; but we will certainly do whatsoever thing goeth forth out of our own mouth," &c.[35]

Nay, if you look a little further, you shall see that these ways are made cautionary enough, not only by these posts, and ditch, and chain, but also by being hedged up, yet they will choose to go there.

CHRIS. They are idle; they love not to take pains; up-hill way is unpleasant to them. So it is fulfilled unto them as it is written, "The way of the slothful man is as an hedge of thorns."[36] Yea, they will rather choose to walk upon a snare than to go up this hill, and the rest of this way to the city.

Then they set forward, and began to go up the hill, and up the hill they went; but before they got to the top, Christiana began to pant; and said, I dare say this is a breathing hill. No marvel if they that love their ease more than their souls, choose to themselves a smoother way. Then said Mercy, I must sit down; also the least of the children began to cry. Come, come, said Great-heart, sit not down here, for a little above is the Prince's arbor. Then took he the little boy by the hand, and led him up thereto.

When they were come to the arbor, they were very willing to sit down, for they were all in a pelting heat. Then said Mercy, How sweet is rest to them that labor.[37] And how good is the Prince of pilgrims to provide such resting-places for them. Of this arbor I have heard much;

but I never saw it before. But here let us beware of sleeping; for, as I have heard, it cost poor Christian dear.

Then said Mr. Great-heart to the little ones, Come, my pretty boys, how do you do? What think you now of going on pilgrimage? Sir, said the least, I was almost beat out of heart; but I thank you for lending me a hand at my need.

GREAT-HEART HELPS THE PILGRIMS TO CLIMB THE HILL DIFFICULTY.

And I remember now what my mother hath told me, namely, that the way to heaven is as up a ladder, and the way to hell is as down a hill. But I had rather go up the ladder to life, than down the hill to death.

Then said Mercy, But the proverb is, To go down the hill is easy. But James said (for that was his name), The day is coming when, in my opinion, going down hill will be the hardest of all. 'Tis a good boy, said his Master, thou hast given her a right answer. Then Mercy smiled; but the little boy did blush.

Come, said Christiana, will you eat a bit, a little to sweeten your mouths, while you sit here to rest your legs? For I have here a piece of pomegranate, which Mr. Interpreter put in my hand, just when I came out of his doors.

He gave me also a piece of a honeycomb, and a little bottle of spirits. I thought he gave you something, said Mercy, because he called you aside. Yes: so he did, said the other. But, said Christiana, it shall still be, as I said it should, when at first we came from home, thou shalt be a sharer in all the good that I have, because thou so willingly didst become my companion.

Then she gave to them, and they did eat; both Mercy and the boys. And, said Christiana to Mr. Great-heart, Sir, will you do as we? But he answered, You are going on pilgrimage, and presently I shall return. Much good may what you have do to you. At home I eat the same every day.

Now, when they had eaten and drank, and had chatted a little longer, their guide said to them, The day wears away, if you think good, let us prepare to be going. So they got up to go, and the little boys went before. But Christiana forgot to take her bottle of spirits with her; so she sent her little boy back to fetch it. Then said Mercy, I think this is a losing place. Here Christian lost his roll; and here Christiana left her bottle behind her. Sir, what is the cause of this?

So their guide made answer, and said, The cause is sleep or forgetfulness. Some sleep when they should keep awake; and some forget when they should remember; and this is the very cause why, often at the resting-places, some pilgrims, in some things, come off losers.

Pilgrims should watch, and remember what they have already received under their greatest enjoyments; but for want of doing so, ofttimes their rejoicing ends in tears, and their sunshine in a cloud. Witness the story of Christian at this place.

When they were come to the place where Mistrust and Timorous met Christian to persuade him to go back for fear of the lions, they perceived as it were a stage, and before it, towards the road, a broad plate, with a copy of verses written thereon, and underneath, the reason of raising up that stage in that place, given. The verses were these:—

> Let him who sees this stage take heed
> Unto his heart and tongue;
> Lest if he do not, here he speed,
> As some have long agone.

The words underneath the verses were, "This stage was built to punish such upon, who, through Timorousness or Mistrust, shall be afraid to go further on pilgrimage; also, on this stage, both Mistrust and Timorous were burned through the tongue with a hot iron, for endeavoring to hinder Christian in his journey."

Then said Mercy, This is much like to the saying of the Beloved, "What shall be given unto thee? or what shall be done unto thee, thou false tongue? Sharp arrows of the mighty, with coals of juniper." [38]

So they went on, till they came within sight of the lions.

Now Mr. Great-heart was a strong man, so he was not afraid of a lion; but yet when they were come up to the place where the lions were, the boys that went before were glad to cringe behind, for they were afraid of the lions; so they stepped back, and went behind.

At this their guide smiled, and said, How now, my boys, do you love to go before, when no danger doth approach, and love to come behind so soon as the lions appear?

Now, as they went up, Mr. Great-heart drew his sword, with intent to make a way for the pilgrims, in spite of the lions.

Then there appeared one, that it seems had taken upon him to back the lions; and he said to the Pilgrims' guide, What is the cause of your coming hither? Now the name of that man was Grim, or Bloody-man, because of his slaying of pilgrims, and he was of the race of the giants.

Then said the Pilgrims' guide, These women and children are going on pilgrimage; and this is the way they must go, and go it they shall, in spite of thee and the lions.

GRIM. This is not their way, neither shall they go therein. I am come forth to withstand them and to that end will back the lions.

Now, to say truth, by reason of the fierceness of the lions, and of the grim carriage of him that did back them, this way had of late lain much unoccupied, and was almost all grown over with grass.

Then said Christiana, Though the highways have been unoccupied heretofore, and though the travellers have been made in time past to walk through by-paths, it must not be so now I am risen. Now, "I am risen a mother in Israel." [39]

GRIM. Then he swore by the lions, but it should; and therefore bid them turn aside, for they should not have passage there.

GREAT-HEART. But their guide made first his approach unto Grim, and laid so heavily at him with his sword, that he forced him to a retreat.

GRIM. Then said he that attempted to back the lions, Will you slay me upon mine own ground?

GREAT-HEART. It is the king's highway that we are in, and in his way it is that thou hast placed thy lions; but these women and these children, though weak, shall hold on their way in spite of thy lions. And with that he gave him again a downright blow and brought him upon his knees.

With this blow he also broke his helmet, and with the next cut off an arm. Then did the giant roar so hideously that his voice frightened the women, and yet they were glad to see him lie sprawling upon the ground.

Now the lions were chained, and so of themselves could do nothing. Wherefore, when old Grim, that intended to back them, was dead, Mr. Great-heart said to the Pilgrims, "Come now, and follow me, and no hurt shall happen to you from the lions."

They therefore went on, but the women trembled as they passed by them; the boys also looked as if they would die, but they all got by without further hurt.

Now then they were within sight of the Porter's Lodge, and they soon came up unto it; but they made the more haste after this to go thither, because it is dangerous travelling there in the night. So when they were come to the gate, the guide knocked, and the Porter cried, Who is there? But as soon as the guide had said, It is I, he knew his voice, and came down (for the guide had oft before that, come thither as a conductor of pilgrims).

When he was come down, he opened the gate, and seeing the guide standing just before it (for he saw not the women, for they were behind him), he said unto him, How now, Mr. Great-heart, what is your business here so late to-night? I have brought, said he, some Pilgrims hither, where, by my Lord's commandment, they must lodge; I had been here some time ago, had I not been opposed by the giant that did use to back the lions; but I, after a long and tedious combat with him, have cut him off, and have brought the pilgrims hither in safety.

DEATH OF GIANT GRIM.

Porter. Will you not go in and stay till morning!

Great-heart. No, I will return to my Lord to-night.

Chris. Oh, Sir, I know not how to be willing you should leave us in our pilgrimage, you have been so faithful and so loving to us, you have fought so stoutly for us, you have been so hearty in counselling of us, that I shall never forget your favor towards us.

Then said Mercy, O that we might have thy company to our journey's

THE PILGRIMS ENTREAT GREAT-HEART TO STAY WITH THEM.

end! How can such poor women as we hold out in a way so full of troubles as this way is, without a friend and defender?

Then said James, the youngest of the boys, Pray, Sir, be persuaded to go with us, and help us, because we are so weak, and the way so dangerous as it is.

Great-heart. I am at my Lord's commandment; if he shall allot me to be your guide quite through, I will willingly wait upon you. But here you failed at first; for, when he bid me come thus far with you, then you should have begged me of him to have gone quite through with you, and he would have granted your request. However, at present, I must withdraw; and so, good Christiana, Mercy, and my brave children, Adieu.

Then the Porter, Mr. Watchful, asked Christiana of her country, and of her kindred; and she said, I came from the City of Destruction; I am a widow woman, and my husband is dead; his name was Christian, the Pilgrim.

How! said the Porter, was He your husband? Yes, said she, and these are his children; and this, pointing to Mercy, is one of my townswomen. Then the Porter rang his bell, as at such times he is wont, and there came to the door one of the damsels, whose name was Humblemind; and to her the Porter said, Go tell it within, that Christiana, the wife of Christian, and her children, are come hither on pilgrimage.

She went in, therefore, and told it. But O what noise for gladness was there within, when the damsel did but drop that word out of her mouth!

So they came with haste to the Porter, for Christiana stood still at the door. Then some of the most grave said unto her, Come in, Christiana, come in, thou wife of that good man; come in, thou blessed woman; come in, with all that are with thee.

So she went in, and they followed her that were her children and her companions. Now when they were gone in, they were taken into a very large room, where they were bidden to sit down; so they sat down, and the chief of the house was called to see and welcome the guests. Then they came in, and understanding who they were, did salute each other with a kiss, and said, Welcome, ye vessels of the grace of God; welcome to us your friends.

Now, because it was somewhat late, and because the Pilgrims were weary with their journey, and also made faint with the sight of the fight, and of the terrible lions, therefore they desired, as soon as might be, to prepare to go to rest. Nay, said those of the family, refresh yourselves first with a morsel of meat; for they had prepared for them a lamb, with the accustomed sauce belonging thereto;[40] for the Porter had heard before of their coming, and had told it to them within. So when they had supped, and ended their prayer with a psalm, they desired they might go to rest. But let us, said Christiana, if we may be so bold to choose, be in that chamber that was my husband's when he was here. So they had

THE WELCOME AT THE PALACE BEAUTIFUL.

them up thither, and they lay all in a room. When they were at rest, Christiana and Mercy entered into discourse about things that were convenient.

CHRIS. Little did I think once, that when my husband went on pilgrimage, I should ever have followed.

MERCY. And you as little thought of lying in his bed, and in his chamber to rest, as you do now.

CHRIS. And much less did I ever think of seeing his face with comfort, and of worshipping the Lord the King with him, and yet now I believe I shall.

MERCY. Hark! Don't you hear a noise?

CHRIS. Yes; it is, as I believe, a noise of music, for joy that we are here.

MERCY. Wonderful! music in the house, music in the heart, and music also in heaven, for joy that we are here!

Thus they talked a while, and then betook themselves to sleep. So, in the morning, when these were awake, Christiana said to Mercy:

CHRIS. What was the matter that you did laugh in your sleep tonight? I suppose you were in a dream.

MERCY. So I was, and a sweet dream it was; but are you sure I laughed?

CHRIS. Yes; you laughed heartily; but, prithee, Mercy, tell me thy dream.

MERCY. I dreamed that I sat all alone in a solitary place, and was bemoaning of the hardness of my heart.

Now, I had not sat there long, but methought many were gathered about me to see me, and to hear what it was that I said. So they hearkened, and I went on bemoaning the hardness of my heart At this, some of them laughed at me, some called me fool, and some began to thrust me about.

With that, methought I looked up, and saw one coming with wings towards me. So he came directly to me, and said, Mercy, what aileth thee? Now, when he had heard me make my complaint, he said, "Peace be to thee." He also wiped mine eyes with his handkerchief, and clad me in silver and gold. He put a chain about my neck, and ear-rings in mine ears, and a beautiful crown upon my head.[41]

Then he took me by the hand, and said, Mercy, come after me. So he went up, and I followed, till we came at a golden gate. Then he knocked; and when they within had opened, the man went in, and I followed him up to a throne, upon which one sat, and he said to me, Welcome, daughter. The place looked bright and twinkling, like the stars, or rather like the sun; and I thought that I saw your husband there. So I awoke from my dream. But did I laugh?

CHRIS. Laugh! ay, and well you might, to see yourself so well. For

MERCY'S DREAM.

you must give me leave to tell you, that I believe it was a good dream; and that, as you have begun to find the first part true, so you will find the second at last. "God speaketh once, yea, twice, *yet man* perceiveth it not. In a dream, in a vision of the night, when deep sleep falleth upon men, in slumberings upon the bed." [42]

We need not, when a-bed, lie awake to talk with God. He can visit us while we sleep, and cause us then to hear his voice. Our heart oft-times wakes when we sleep; and God can speak to that, either by words, by proverbs, by signs and similitudes, as well as if one was awake.

MERCY. Well, I am glad of my dream; for I hope, ere long, to see it fulfilled, to the making me laugh again.

CHRIS. I think it is now high time to rise, and to know what we must do.

MERCY. Pray, if they invite us to stay a while, let us willingly accept of the proffer. I am the more willing to stay a while here, to grow better acquainted with these maids. Methinks Prudence, Piety, and Charity have very comely and sober countenances.

CHRIS. We shall see what they will do. So when they were up and ready, they came down, and they asked one another of their rest, and if it was comfortable or not.

Very good, said Mercy; it was one of the best night's lodgings that ever I had in my life.

Then said Prudence and Piety, If you will be persuaded to stay here a while, you shall have what the house will afford.

CHAR. Ay, and that with a very good will, said Charity. So they consented, and stayed there about a month or above, and became very profitable one to another.

And because Prudence would see how Christiana had brought up her children, she asked leave of her to catechise them. So she gave her free consent. Then she began at the youngest, whose name was James.

And she said, Come, James, canst thou tell me who made thee?

JAMES. God the Father, God the Son, and God the Holy Ghost.

PRUD. Good boy. And canst thou tell me who saves thee?

JAMES. God the Father, God the Son, and God the Holy Ghost.

PRUD. Good boy still. But how doth God the Father save thee?

JAMES. By his grace.

PRUD. How doth God the Son save thee?

JAMES. By his righteousness, death, and blood, and life.

PRUD. And how doth God the Holy Ghost save thee?

JAMES. By his illumination, by his renovation, and by his preser-vation.

Then said Prudence to Christiana, You are to be commended for thus bringing up your children. I suppose I need not ask the rest these questions, since the youngest of them can answer them so well. I will therefore now apply myself to the next youngest.

PRUD. Then she said, Come, Joseph (for his name was Joseph), will you let me catechise you?

JOSEPH. With all my heart.

PRUD. What is man?

JOSEPH. A reasonable creature, so made by God, as my brother said.

PRUD. What is supposed by this word "saved"?

JOSEPH. That man, by sin, has brought himself into a state of captivity and misery.

PRUD. What is supposed by his being saved by the Trinity?

JOSEPH. That sin is so great and mighty a tyrant, that none can pull us out of its clutches, but God; and that God is so good and loving to man, as to pull him indeed out of this miserable state.

PRUD. What is God's design in saving of poor men?

JOSEPH. The glorifying of his name, of his grace and justice, &c., and the everlasting happiness of his creature.

PRUD. Who are they that must be saved?

JOSEPH. Those that accept of his salvation.

PRUD. Good boy, Joseph; thy mother has taught thee well, and thou hast hearkened to what she hath said unto thee.

Then said Prudence to Samuel, who was the eldest but one,

PRUD. Come, Samuel, are you willing that I should catechise you, also?

SAMUEL. Yes, forsooth, if you please.

PRUD. What is heaven?

SAM. A place and state most blessed, because God dwelleth there.

PRUD. What is hell?

SAM. A place and state most woeful, because it is the dwelling-place of sin, the devil, and death.

PRUD. Why wouldst thou go to heaven?

SAM. That I may see God, and serve him without weariness; that I may see Christ, and love him everlastingly; that I may have that fulness of the Holy Spirit in me that I can by no means here enjoy.

PRUD. A very good boy also, and one that has learned well.

Then she addressed herself to the eldest, whose name was Matthew; and she said to him, Come, Matthew, shall I also catechise you?

MATTHEW. With a very good will.

PRUDENCE ASKS THE BOYS SOME QUESTIONS.

321

21

PRUD. I ask, then, if there was ever anything that had a being antecedent to, or before God?

MATT. No; for God is eternal; nor is there anything excepting himself, that had a being until the beginning of the first day. "For in six days the Lord made heaven and earth, the sea; and all that in them is."

PRUD. What do you think of the Bible?

MATT. It is the holy Word of God.

PRUD. Is there nothing written therein but what you understand?

MATT. Yes; a great deal.

PRUD. What do you do when you meet with such places therein that you do not understand?

MATT. I think God is wiser than I. I pray also that he will please to let me know all therein that he knows will be for my good.

PRUD. How believe you as touching the resurrection of the dead?

MATT. I believe they shall rise, the same that was buried: the same in nature, though not in corruption. And I believe this upon a double account: First, because God has promised it; secondly, because he is able to perform it.

Then said Prudence to the boys, You must still hearken to your mother, for she can learn you more. You must also diligently give ear to what good talk you shall hear from others; for, for your sakes do they speak good things. Observe, also, and that with carefulness, what the heavens and the earth do teach you; but especially be much in the meditation of that Book that was the cause of your father's becoming a pilgrim. I, for my part, my children, will teach you what I can while you are here, and shall be glad if you will ask me questions that tend to godly edifying.

Now, by the time these Pilgrims had been at this place a week, Mercy had a visitor that pretended some goodwill unto her, and his name was Mr. Brisk, a man of some breeding, and that pretended to religion: but a man that stuck very close to the world. So he came once or twice, or more, to Mercy, and offered love unto her. Now Mercy was of a fair countenance, and therefore the more alluring.

Her mind also was, to be always busying of herself in doing; for when she had nothing to do for herself, she would be making of hose and garments for others, and would bestow them upon them that had need.

And Mr. Brisk, not knowing where or how she disposed of what she made, seemed to be greatly taken, for that he found her never idle. I will warrant her a good housewife, quoth he to himself.

MR. BRISK.

Mercy then revealed the business to the maidens that were of the house, and inquired of them concerning him, for they did know him better than she. So they told her, that he was a very busy young man, and one that pretended to religion; but was, as they feared, a stranger to the power of that which was good.

Nay then, said Mercy, I will look no more on him; for I purpose never to have a clog to my soul.

Prudence then replied that there needed no great matter of discouragement to be given to him, her continuing so as she had begun to do, for the poor, would quickly cool his courage.

So the next time he comes, he finds her at her old work, a-making of things for the poor. Then said he, What! always at it? Yes, said she, either for myself or for others. And what canst thou earn a-day? quoth he. I do these things, said she, "that I may be rich in good works, laying up in store a good foundation against the time to come, that I may lay hold on eternal life." [43]

Why, prithee, what dost thou with them? Clothe the naked, said she. With that his countenance fell. So he forbore to come at her again; and when he was asked the reason why, he said, that Mercy was a pretty lass, but troubled with ill conditions.

When he had left her, Prudence said, Did I not tell thee, that Mr. Brisk would soon forsake thee? yea, he will raise up an ill report of thee; for, notwithstanding his pretence to religion, and his seeming love to Mercy, yet Mercy and he are of tempers so different, that I believe they will never come together.

MERCY. I might have had husbands afore now, though I spake not of it to any; but they were such as did not like my conditions, though never did any of them find fault with my person. So they and I could not agree.

PRUD. Mercy in our days is little set by, any further than as to its name; the practice, which is set forth by thy conditions, there are but few that can abide.

Well, said Mercy, if nobody will have me, I will die a maid, or my conditions shall be to me as a husband; for I cannot change my nature; and to have one that lies cross to me in this, that I purpose never to admit of as long as I live. I had a sister named Bountiful, that was married to one of these churls; but he and she could never agree; but because my sister was resolved to do as she had begun, that is, to show kindness to the poor, therefore her husband first cried her down at the cross, and then turned her out of his doors.

PRUD. And yet he was a professor, I warrant you.

MERCY. Yes, such a one as he was, and of such as he the world is now full; but I am for none of them all.

Now Matthew, the eldest son of Christiana, fell sick, and his sickness was sore upon him, for he was much pained in his bowels, so that he was with it, at times, pulled as it were both ends together.

There dwelt also not far from thence, one Mr. Skill, an ancient and well-approved physician. So Christiana desired it, and they sent for him and he came. When he was entered the room, and had a little observed the boy, he concluded that he was sick of the gripes. Then he said to his mother, What diet has Matthew of late fed upon? Diet! said Christiana, nothing but that which is wholesome.

The physician answered, This boy has been tampering with something that lies in his maw undigested, and that will not away without means. And I tell you he must be purged, or else he will die.

Then said Samuel, Mother, mother, what was that which my brother did gather up and eat, so soon as we were come from the gate that is at the head of this way? You know that there was an orchard on the left hand, on the other side of the wall, and some of the trees hung over the wall, and my brother did pluck and did eat.

True, my child, said Christiana, he did take thereof, and did eat; naughty boy as he was, I did chide him, and yet he would eat thereof.

SKILL. I knew he had eaten something that was not wholesome food; and that food, to wit, that fruit, is even the most hurtful of all. It is the fruit of Beelzebub's orchard. I do marvel that none did warn you of it; many have died thereof.

Then Christiana began to cry; and she said, O naughty boy! and O careless mother! What shall I do for my son?

SKILL. Come, do not be too much dejected; the boy may do well again, but he must purge and vomit.

CHRIS. Pray, Sir, try the utmost of your skill with him, whatever it costs.

SKILL. Nay, I hope I shall be reasonable. So he made him a purge, but it was too weak; it was said it was made of the blood of a goat, the ashes of a heifer, and with some of the juice of hyssop, &c.[44] When Mr. Skill had seen that that purge was too weak, he made him one to the purpose; it was made *ex carne et sanguine Christi.*[45] (You know physicians give strange medicines to their patients.) And it was made up into pills, with a promise or two, and a proportionable quantity of salt.[46]

DR. SKILL.

Now he was to take them three at a time fasting, in half a quarter of
a pint of the tears of repentance. When this potion was prepared, and
brought to the boy, he was loath to take it, though torn with the gripes as

if he should be pulled in pieces. Come, come, said the physician, you must take it. It goes against my stomach, said the boy.[47] I must have you take it, said his mother. I shall vomit it up again, said the boy. Pray, Sir, said Christiana to Mr. Skill, how does it taste? It has no ill taste, said the doctor; and with that she touched one of the pills with the tip of her tongue. Oh, Matthew, said she, this potion is sweeter than honey. If thou lovest thy mother, if thou lovest thy brothers, if thou lovest Mercy, if thou lovest thy life, take it.

So with much ado, after a short prayer for the blessing of God upon it, he took it, and it wrought kindly with him. It caused him to purge, it caused him to sleep and rest quietly; it put him into a fine heat and breathing sweat, and did quite rid him of his gripes. So in little time he got up, and walked about with a staff, and would go from room to room, and talk with Prudence, Piety, and Charity, of his distemper, and how he was healed.

So when the boy was healed, Christiana asked Mr. Skill, saying, Sir, what will content you for your pains and care to and of my child? And he said, You must pay the Master of the College of Physicians, according to rules made in that case and provided.[48]

But, Sir, said she, what is this pill good for else?

SKILL. It is an universal pill; it is good against all the diseases that pilgrims are incident to; and when it is well prepared, it will keep good, time out of mind.

CHRIS. Pray, Sir, make me up twelve boxes of them; for if I can get these, I will never take other physic.

SKILL. These pills are good to prevent diseases, as well as to cure when one is sick. Yea, I dare say it, and stand to it, that if a man will but use this physic as he should, it will make him live for ever.[49] But, good Christiana, thou must give these pills no other way but as I have prescribed; for, if you do, they will do no good.

So he gave unto Christiana physic for herself, and her boys, and for Mercy; and bid Matthew take heed how he ate any more green plums, and kissed them, and went his way.

It was told you before, that Prudence bid the boys, that if at any time they would, they should ask her some questions that might be profitable, and she would say something to them.

MATT. Then Matthew, who had been sick, asked her, Why, for the most part, physic should be bitter to our palates?

PRUD. To show how unwelcome the Word of God, and the effects thereof, are to a carnal heart.

MATT. Why does physic, if it does good, purge, and cause that we vomit?

PRUD. To show that the Word, when it works effectually, cleanseth the heart and mind. For look, what the one doth to the body, the other doth to the soul.

MATT. What should we learn by seeing the flame of our fire go up-

MATTHEW AND PRUDENCE.

wards? and by seeing the beams and sweet influences of the sun strike downwards?

PRUD. By the going up of the fire we are taught to ascend to heaven by fervent and hot desires; and by the sun's sending his heat, beams, and sweet influences downwards, we are taught that the Saviour of the world, though high, reacheth down with his grace and love to us below.

MATT. Whence have the clouds their water?

PRUD. Out of the sea.

MATT. What may we learn from that?

PRUD. That ministers should fetch their doctrine from God.

MATT. Why do they empty themselves upon the earth?

PRUD. To show that ministers should give out what they know of God to the world.

MATT. Why is the rainbow caused by the sun?

PRUD. To show that the covenant of God's grace is confirmed to us in Christ.

MATT. Why do the springs come from the sea to us, through the earth?

PRUD. To show that the grace of God comes to us through the body of Christ.

MATT. Why do some of the springs rise out of the tops of high hills?

PRUD. To show that the spirit of grace shall spring up in some that are great and mighty, as well as in many that are poor and low.

MATT. Why doth the fire fasten upon the candle-wick?

PRUD. To show that unless grace doth kindle upon the heart there will be no true light of life in us.

MATT. Why is the wick, and tallow, and all, spent to maintain the light of the candle?

PRUD. To show that body and soul, and all, should be at the service of, and spend themselves to maintain in good condition, that grace of God that is in us.

MATT. Why doth the pelican pierce her own breast with her bill?

PRUD. To nourish her young ones with her blood, and thereby to show that Christ the blessed so loveth his young, his people, as to save them from death by his blood.

MATT. What may one learn by hearing the cock crow?

PRUD. Learn to remember Peter's sin, and Peter's repentance. The cock's crowing shows also that day is coming on; let then the crowing of the cock put thee in mind of that last and terrible day of judgment.

Now, about this time, their month was out; wherefore they signified to those of the house that it was convenient for them to be up and going. Then said Joseph to his mother, It is convenient that you forget not to send to the house of Mr. Interpreter, to pray him to grant that Mr. Greatheart should be sent unto us, that he may be our conductor the rest of our way. Good boy, said she, I had almost forgot.

So she drew up a petition, and prayed Mr. Watchful, the Porter, to send it by some fit man, to her good friend Mr. Interpreter; who, when it was come, and he had seen the contents of the petition, said to the messenger, Go tell them that I will send him.

When the family, where Christiana was, saw that they had a purpose to go forward, they called the whole house together, to give thanks to their King for sending of them such profitable guests as these. Which done, they said to Christiana, And shall we not show thee something, according as our custom is to do to pilgrims, on which thou mayest meditate when thou art upon the way?

So they took Christiana, her children, and Mercy, into the closet, and showed them one of the apples that Eve did eat of, and that she also did give to her husband, and that for the eating of which they both were turned out of Paradise, and asked her what she thought that was? Then Christiana said, It is food or poison, I know not which. So they opened the matter to her, and she held up her hands and wondered.[50]

Then they had her to a place, and showed her Jacob's ladder. Now at that time there were some angels ascending upon it. So Christiana looked, and looked, to see the angels go up; and so did the rest of the company.

Then they were going into another place, to show them something else; but James said to his mother, Pray bid them stay here a little longer, for this is a curious sight. So they turned again, and stood feeding their eyes with this so pleasant a prospect.[51]

After this, they had them into a place where did hang up a golden anchor, so they bid Christiana take it down; for, said they, you shall have it with you, for it is of absolute necessity that you should, that you may lay hold of that within the veil, and stand steadfast, in case you should meet with turbulent weather; so they were glad thereof.[52]

Then they took them, and had them to the mount upon which Abraham our father had offered up Isaac his son, and showed them the altar, the wood, the fire, and the knife, for they remain to be seen to this very day.[53] When they had seen it, they held up their hands and blessed themselves, and said, Oh, what a man for love to his Master, and for denial to himself, was Abraham!

After they had showed them all these things, Prudence took them into the dining-room, where stood a pair of excellent virginals; so she played upon them, and turned what she had showed them into this excellent song, saying—

JACOB'S LADDER.

Eve's apple we have showed you,
    Of that be you aware;
You have seen Jacob's ladder too,
    Upon which angels are;

An anchor you received have;
    But let not these suffice,
Until, with Abr'am, you have gave
    Your best a sacrifice.

Now, about this time, one knocked at the door; so the Porter opened, and behold Mr. Great-heart was there; but when he was come in, what joy was there! For it came now fresh again into their minds, how but a while ago he had slain old Grim Bloody-man the giant, and had delivered them from the lions.

Then said Mr. Great-heart to Christiana, and to Mercy, My Lord hath sent each of you a bottle of wine, and also some parched corn, together with a couple of pomegranates; he has also sent the boys some figs and raisins, to refresh you in your way.

Then they addressed themselves to their journey; and Prudence and Piety went along with them. When they came at the gate, Christiana asked the Porter if any of late went by? He said, No; only one some time since, who also told me, that of late there had been a great robbery committed on the King's highway, as you go; but, he said, the thieves are taken, and will shortly be tried for their lives.

Then Christiana and Mercy were afraid; but Matthew said, Mother, fear nothing, as long as Mr. Great-heart is to go with us and to be our conductor.

Then said Christiana to the Porter, Sir, I am much obliged to you for all the kindnesses that you have shown me since I came hither; and also for that you have been so loving and kind to my children; I know not how to gratify your kindness. Wherefore, pray, as a token of my respects to you, accept of this small mite; so she put a gold angel* in his hand, and he made her a low obeisance, and   *Piece of money. said, Let thy garments be always white, and let thy head want no ointment. Let Mercy live and not die, and let not her works be few.

And to the boys he said, Do you fly youthful lusts, and follow after godliness with them that are grave and wise; so shall you put gladness into your mother's heart, and obtain praise of all that are sober-minded. So they thanked the Porter and departed.

CHAPTER V.

NOW I saw in my dream, that they went forward until they were come to the brow of the hill, where Piety, bethinking herself, cried out, Alas! I have forgot what I intended to bestow upon Christiana and her companions; I will go back and fetch it. So she ran and fetched it.

While she was gone, Christiana thought she heard in a grove, a little way off, on the right hand, a most curious and melodious note, with words much like these—

> Through all my life thy favor is
> So frankly show'd to me,
> That in thy house for evermore
> My dwelling-place shall be.

And, listening still, she thought she heard another answer it, saying—

> For why? The Lord our God is good,
> His mercy is for ever sure.
> His truth at all times firmly stood,
> And shall from age to age endure.

So Christiana asked Prudence what it was that made those curious notes? They are, she said, our country birds; they sing these notes but seldom, except it be at the spring, when the flowers appear, and the sun shines warm, and then you may hear them all day long.[54] I often, said she, go out to hear them; we also ofttimes keep them tame in our house. They are very fine company for us when we are melancholy; also they make the woods, and groves, and solitary places, places desirous to be in.

By this time Piety was come again; so she said to Christiana, Look here, I have brought thee a record of all those things that thou hast seen at our house, upon which thou mayest look when thou findest thyself forgetful, and call those things again to remembrance for thy edification and comfort.

Now they began to go down the hill into the Valley of Humiliation. It was a steep hill, and the way was slippery; but they were very careful, so they got down pretty well.   When they were down in the valley, Piety said to Christiana, This is the place where Christian your husband met with the foul fiend Apollyon, and where they had that dreadful fight that they had; I know you cannot but have heard thereof.   But be of good courage; as long as you have here Mr. Great-heart to be your guide and conductor, we hope you will fare the better.   So when these two had committed the Pilgrims unto the conduct of their guide, he went forward, and they went after.

Then said Mr. Great-heart, We need not to be so afraid of this Valley, for here is nothing to hurt us, unless we procure it to ourselves. It is true, Christian did here meet with Apollyon, with whom he also had a sore combat; but that fray was the fruit of those slips that he got in his going down the hill; for they that get slips there must look for combats here.

And hence it is that this Valley has got so hard a name; for the common people, when they hear that some frightful thing has befallen such a one in such a place, are of an opinion, that that place is haunted with some foul fiend or evil spirit; when, alas! it is for the fruit of their doing, that such things do befall them there.

This Valley of Humiliation is of itself as fruitful a place as any the crow flies over; and I am persuaded, if we could hit upon it, we might find, somewhere hereabouts, something that might give us an account why Christian was so hardly beset in this place.

Then James said to his mother, Lo, yonder stands a pillar, and it looks as if something was written thereon; let us go and see what it is.   So they went, and found there written, "Let Christian's slips, before he came hither, and the battles that he met with in this place, be a warning to those that come after."

Lo, said their guide, did not I tell you that there was something hereabouts that would give intimation of the reason why Christian was so hard beset in this place?   Then turning himself to Christiana, he said, No disparagement to Christian, more than to many others whose hap and lot his was; for it is easier going up than down this hill, and that can be said of but few hills in all these parts of the world.   But we will leave the good man, he is at rest, he also had a brave victory over his enemy; let Him grant that dwelleth above, that we fare no worse, when we come to be tried, than he.

But we will come again to this Valley of Humiliation. It is the best and most useful piece of ground in all these parts. It is fat ground, and, as you see, consisteth much in meadows; and if a man was to come here in the summer-time, as we do now, if he knew not anything before thereof, and if he also delighted himself in the sight of his eyes, he might see that which would be delightful to him.

Behold how green this Valley is, also how beautified with lilies.[55] I

THE PILLAR IN THE VALLEY OF HUMILIATION.

have also known many laboring men that have got good estates in this Valley of Humiliation ("for God resisteth the proud, but giveth more grace unto the humble"[56]), for indeed it is a very fruitful soil, and doth bring forth by handfuls.

Some also have wished that the next way to their Father's house were here, that they might be troubled no more with either hills or mountains to go over, but the way is the way, and there is an end.

Now, as they were going along, and talking, they espied a boy feeding his father's sheep. The boy was in very mean clothes, but of a very

THE SHEPHERD BOY.

fresh and well-favored countenance; and as he sat by himself, he sang. Hark, said Mr. Great-heart, to what the shepherd's boy saith. So they hearkened, and he said—

> He that is down needs fear no fall;
>   He that is low no pride;
> He that is humble, ever shall
>   Have God to be his guide.
>
> I am content with what I have,
>   Little be it, or much:
> And, Lord, contentment still I crave,
>   Because thou savest such.

Fullness to such a burden is,
    That go on pilgrimage ;
Here little, and hereafter bliss,
    Is best from age to age.

Then said the guide, Do you hear him ? I will dare to say, that this boy lives a merrier life, and wears more of that herb called heart's-ease in his bosom, than he that is clad in silk and velvet; but we will proceed in our discourse.

In this Valley our Lord formerly had his country-house; he loved much to be here; he loved also to walk these meadows, for he found the air was pleasant. Besides, here a man shall be free from the noise, and from the hurryings of this life.

All states are full of noise and confusion, only the Valley of Humiliation is that empty and solitary place. Here a man shall not be so let and hindered in his contemplation, as in other places he is apt to be. This is a Valley that nobody walks in, but those that love a pilgrim's life.

And though Christian had the hard hap to meet here with Apollyon, and to enter with him into a brisk encounter, yet I must tell you that in former times men have met with angels here, have found pearls here, and have in this place found the words of life.[57]

Did I say, our Lord had here in former days his country-house, and that he loved here to walk ? I will add, in this place, and to the people that live, and trace these grounds, he has left a yearly revenue, to be faithfully paid them at certain seasons, for their maintenance by the way, and for their further encouragement to go on their pilgrimage.[58]

Now, as they went on, Samuel said to Mr. Great-heart, Sir, I perceive that in this Valley my father and Apollyon had their battle; but where about was the fight? for I perceive this Valley is large.

GREAT-HEART. Your father had that battle with Apollyon at a place yonder before us, in a narrow passage, just beyond Forgetful Green. And indeed, that place is the most dangerous place in all these parts. For if at any time the pilgrims meet with any brunt, it is when they forget what favors they have received, and how unworthy they are of them.

This is the place also, where others have been hard put to it; but more of the place when we are come to it; for I persuade myself, that to this day there remains either some sign of the battle, or some monument to testify that such a battle there was fought.

MERCY. Then said Mercy, I think I am as well in this Valley as I have

22

been anywhere else in all our journey; the place, methinks, suits with my spirit.

I love to be in such places where there is no rattling with coaches, nor rumbling with wheels; methinks, here one may, without much molestation, be thinking what he is, whence he came, what he has done, and to what the King has called him; here one may think, and break at heart, and melt in one's spirit until one's eyes become like "the fish-pools of Heshbon." [59]

They that go rightly through this Valley of Baca, make it a well, the rain that God sends down from heaven upon them that are here, also filleth the pools. [60] This Valley is that from whence also the King will give to his their vineyards; [61] and they that go through it shall sing, as Christian did, for all he met with Apollyon.

GREAT-HEART. It is true, said their guide, I have gone through this Valley many a time, and never was better than when here.

I have also been a conductor to several pilgrims, and they have confessed the same. "To this *man* will I look (saith the King), *even* to *him that is* poor and of a contrite spirit, and trembleth at my word." [62]

Now they were come to the place where the afore-mentioned battle was fought. Then said the guide to Christiana, her children, and Mercy, This is the place, on this ground Christian stood, and up there came Apollyon against him.

And look, did I not tell you? Here is some of your husband's blood upon these stones to this day; behold, also, how here and there are yet to be seen upon the place, some of the shivers of Apollyon's broken darts; see also how they did beat the ground with their feet as they fought, to make good their places against each other; how also, with their by-blows, they did split the very stones in pieces.

Verily, Christian did here play the man, and showed himself as stout, as could, had he been there, even Hercules himself. When Apollyon was beat, he made his retreat to the next Valley, that is called the Valley of the Shadow of Death, unto which we shall come anon.

Lo, yonder also stands a monument, on which is engraven this battle, and Christian's victory, to his fame throughout all ages.

So, because it stood just on the wayside before them, they stepped to it, and read the writing, which word for word was this—

> Hard by, here was a battle fought,
> Most strange, and yet most true;

Christian and Apollyon sought
Each other to subdue.

The man so bravely play'd the man,
He made the fiend to fly ;
Of which a monument I stand,
The same to testify.

When they had passed by this place, they came upon the borders of the Shadow of Death; and this Valley was longer than the other; a place, also, most strangely haunted with evil things, as many are able to testify; but these women and children went the better through it because they had day-light, and because Mr. Great-heart was their conductor.

When they were entered upon this Valley, they thought that they heard a groaning, as of dying men, a very great groaning. They thought, also, they did hear words of lamentation spoken, as of some in extreme torment. These things made the boys to quake, the women also looked pale and wan; but their guide bid them be of good comfort.

So they went on a little further, and they thought that they felt the ground begin to shake under them, as if some hollow place was there; they heard also a kind of a hissing, as of serpents, but nothing as yet appeared.

Then said the boys, Are we not yet at the end of this doleful place? But the guide also bid them be of good courage, and look well to their feet, lest haply, said he, you be taken in some snare.

Now James began to be sick, but I think the cause thereof was fear; so his mother gave him some of that glass of spirits that she had given her at the Interpreter's house, and three of the pills that Mr. Skill had prepared, and the boy began to revive.

Thus they went on, till they came to about the middle of the Valley, and then Christiana said, Methinks I see something yonder upon the road before us, a thing of a shape such as I have not seen.

Then said Joseph, Mother, what is it? An ugly thing, child; an ugly thing, said she. But, mother, what is it like? said he. It is like I can-not tell what, said she. And now it was but a little way off; then said she, It is nigh.

Well, well, said Mr. Great-heart, Let them that are most afraid, keep close to me. So the fiend came on, and the conductor met it; but when it was just come to him, it vanished to all their sights. Then remembered they what had been said some time ago, " Resist the devil, and he will flee from you."[63]

They went therefore on as being a little refreshed; but they had not gone far, before Mercy, looking behind her, saw, as she thought, something most like a lion, and it came a great padding pace after; and it had a hollow voice of roaring; and at every roar that it gave, it made all the Valley echo, and their hearts to ache, save the heart of him that was their guide.

So it came up; and Mr. Great-heart went behind, and put the pilgrims all before him. The lion also came on apace, and Mr. Great-heart addressed himself to give him battle. But when he saw that it was determined that resistance should be made, he also drew back, and came no further.[64]

Then they went on again, and their conductor did go before them, till they came at a place where was cast up a pit the whole breadth of the way; and, before they could be prepared to go over that, a great mist and darkness fell upon them, so that they could not see.

Then said the Pilgrims, Alas! now what shall we do? But their guide made answer, Fear not, stand still, and see what an end will be put to this also. So they stayed there, because their path was marred. They then also thought that they did hear more apparently the noise and rushing of the enemies; the fire, also, and the smoke of the pit, was much easier to be discerned.

Then said Christiana to Mercy, Now I see what my poor husband went through; I have heard much of this place, but I never was here before now. Poor man, he went here all alone in the night; he had night almost quite through the way; also, these fiends were busy about him, as if they would have torn him in pieces. Many have spoken of it, but none can tell what the Valley of the Shadow of Death should mean, until they come in it themselves. "The heart knows its own bitterness, and a stranger intermeddleth not with its joy." To be here is a fearful thing.

GREAT-HEART. This is like doing business in great waters, or like going down into the deep; this is like being in the heart of the sea, and like going down to the bottoms of the mountains; now it seems as if the earth, with its bars, were about us for ever. But let them that walk in darkness, and have no light, trust in the name of the Lord, and stay upon their God.[65]

For my part, as I have told you already, I have gone often through this Valley, and have been much harder put to it than now I am, and yet you see I am alive. I would not boast, for that I am not mine own saviour; but I trust we shall have a good deliverance. Come, let us pray for light to him that can lighten our darkness, and that can rebuke not only these, but all the Satans in hell.

So they cried and prayed, and God sent light and deliverance, for there was now no let in their way; no not there, where but now they were stopped with a pit. Yet they were not got through the Valley; so they went on still, and behold great stinks and loathsome smells, to the great annoyance of them. Then said Mercy to Christiana, It is not so pleasant being here as at the gate, or at the Interpreter's, or at the house where we lay last.

Oh, but, said one of the boys, it is not so bad to go through here as it is to abide here always; and for aught I know, one reason why we must go this way to the house prepared for us, is, that our home might be made the sweeter to us.

Well said, Samuel, quoth the guide, thou hast now spoke like a man. Why, if ever I get out here again, said the boy, I think I shall prize light and good way better than ever I did in all my life. Then said the guide, We shall be out by and by.

So on they went, and Joseph said, Cannot we see to the end of this Valley as yet? Then said the guide, Look to your feet, for you shall presently be among the snares. So they looked to their feet, and went on; but they were troubled much with the snares.

Now, when they were come among the snares, they espied a man cast into the ditch on the left hand, with his flesh all rent and torn. Then said the guide, That is one Heedless, that was agoing this way; he has lain there a great while. There was one Take-heed with him, when he was taken and slain, but he escaped their hands. You cannot imagine how many are killed hereabout, and yet men are so foolishly venturous, as to set out lightly on pilgrimage, and to come without a guide. Poor Christian! it was a wonder that he here escaped; but he was beloved of his God: also, he had a good heart of his own, or else he could never have done it.

Now they drew towards the end of the way; and just there where Christian had seen the cave when he went by, out thence came forth Maul, a giant.

This Maul did use to spoil young pilgrims with sophistry; and he called Great-heart by his name, and said unto him, How many times have you been forbidden to do these things?

Then said Mr. Great-heart, What things? What things? quoth the giant; you know what things: but I will put an end to your trade.

But pray, said Mr. Great-heart, before we fall to it, let us understand wherefore we must fight. Now the women and children stood trembling, and knew not what to do.

Quoth the giant, You rob the country, and rob it with the worst of thefts. These are but generals, said Mr. Great-heart; come to particulars, man.

Then said the giant, Thou practisest the craft of a kidnapper; thou gatherest up women and children, and carriest them into a strange country, to the weakening of my master's kingdom.

But now Great-heart replied, I am a servant of the God of heaven; my business is to persuade sinners to repentance; I am commanded to do my endeavor to turn men, women, and children, "from darkness to light, and from the power of Satan unto God;" and if this be indeed the ground of thy quarrel, let us fall to it as soon as thou wilt.

Then the giant came up, and Mr. Great-heart went to meet him; and as he went, he drew his sword, but the giant had a club. So without more ado, they fell to it, and at the first blow the giant struck Mr. Great-heart down upon one of his knees; with that the women and children cried out: but Mr. Great-heart recovering himself, laid about him in full lusty manner, and gave the giant a wound in his arm; thus he fought for the space of an hour, to that height of heat, that the breath came out of the giant's nostrils, as the heat doth out of a boiling caldron.

Then they sat down to rest them, but Mr. Great-heart betook him to prayer; also the women and children did nothing but sigh and cry all the time that the battle did last.

When they had rested them, and taken breath, they both fell to it again, and Mr. Great-heart, with a full blow, fetched the giant down to the ground.

Nay, hold, and let me recover, quoth he; so Mr. Great-heart fairly let him get up. So to it they went again, and the giant missed but little of all-to-breaking Mr. Great-heart's skull with his club.

Mr. Great-heart seeing that, runs to him in the full heat of his spirit, and pierceth him under the fifth rib; with that the giant began to faint, and could hold his club no longer.

Then Mr. Great-heart seconded his blow, and smote the head of the giant from his shoulders. Then the women and children rejoiced, and Mr. Great-heart also praised God, for the deliverance he had wrought.

GREAT-HEART KILLS GIANT MAUL.

When this was done, they among them erected a pillar, and fastened the giant's head thereon, and wrote underneath in letters, that passers-by might read—

He that did wear this head was one
    That pilgrims did misuse;
He stopp'd their way, he spared none,
    But did them all abuse;

Until that I, Great-heart arose,
    The pilgrims' guide to be;
Until that I did him oppose
    That was their enemy.

THE PILGRIMS ERECT A PILLAR.

CHAPTER VI.

NOW I saw, that they went to the ascent that was a little way off, cast up to be a prospect for pilgrims (that was the place from whence Christian had the first sight of Faithful his brother); wherefore here they sat down and rested; they also here did eat and drink and make merry, for that they had gotten deliverance from this so dangerous an enemy.

As they sat thus, and did eat, Christiana asked the guide if he had caught no hurt in the battle.

Then said Mr. Great-heart, No, save a little on my flesh; yet that also shall be so far from being to my detriment, that it is at present a proof of my love to my Master and you, and shall be a means, by grace, to increase my reward at last.[66]

CHRIS. But were not you afraid, good Sir, when you saw him come out with his club?

GREAT-HEART. It is my duty to distrust my own ability, that I may have reliance on Him that is stronger than all.

CHRIS. But what did you think when he fetched you down to the ground at the first blow?

GREAT-HEART. Why, I thought that so my Master himself was served, and yet he it was that conquered at the last.

MATT. When you all have thought what you please, I think God has been wonderful good unto us, both in bringing us out of this valley, and in delivering us out of the hand of this enemy; for my part, I see no reason why we should distrust our God any more, since he has now, and in such a place as this, given us such testimony of his love as this.

Then they got up and went forward. Now a little before them stood an oak; and under it, when they came to it, they found an old pilgrim fast asleep; they knew that he was a pilgrim by his clothes, and his staff, and his girdle.

So the guide, Mr. Great-heart, awaked him, and the old gentleman, as he lifted up his eyes, cried out, What's the matter? Who are you? and what is your business here?

GREAT-HEART. Come, man, be not so hot, here are none but friends. Yet the old man gets up, and stands upon his guard, and will know of them what they were. Then said the guide, My name is Great-heart; I am the guide of these pilgrims, which are going to the Celestial Country.

Then said Mr. Honest, I cry you mercy; I feared that you had been of the company of those that some time ago did rob Little-faith of his money; but now I look better about me, I perceive you are honester people.

GREAT-HEART. Why, what would, or could you have done, to have helped yourself, if we indeed had been of that company?

HON. Done! why I would have fought as long as breath had been in me; and had I so done, I am sure you could never have given me the worst on it; for a Christian can never be overcome, unless he should yield of himself.

GREAT-HEART. Well said, father Honest, quoth the guide; for by this I know thou art a cock of the right kind, for thou hast said the truth.

HON. And by this, also, I know that thou knowest what true pilgrimage is; for all others do think that we are the soonest overcome of any

GREAT-HEART. Well, now we are so happily met, pray let me crave your name, and the name of the place you came from.

HON. My name I cannot; but I came from the town of Stupidity; it lieth about four degrees beyond the City of Destruction.

GREAT-HEART. Oh! are you that countryman, then? I deem I have half a guess of you; your name is Old Honesty, is it not? So the old gentleman blushed, and said, Not Honesty, in the abstract, but Honest is my *name;* and I wish that my *nature* shall agree to what I am called.

HON. But, Sir, said the old gentleman, how could you guess that I am such a man, since I came from such a place?

GREAT-HEART. I had heard of you before, by my Master; for he knows all things that are done on the earth; but I have often wondered that any should come from your place, for your town is worse than is the City of Destruction itself.

HON. Yes, we lie more off from the sun, and so are more cold and senseless; but was a man in a mountain of ice, yet if the Sun of Righteousness will arise upon him his frozen heart shall feel a thaw; and thus it hath been with me.

OLD HONEST IS FOUND ASLEEP UNDER THE OAK.

OLD HONEST.

GREAT-HEART. I believe it, father Honest, I believe it; for I know the thing is true.

Then the old gentleman saluted all the Pilgrims with a holy kiss of charity; and asked them of their names, and how they had fared since they set out on their pilgrimage.

Then said Christiana, My name, I suppose, you have heard of; good Christian was my husband, and these four were his children. But can you think how the old gentleman was taken, when she told him who she was! He skipped, he smiled, and blessed them with a thousand good wishes, saying:

HON. I have heard much of your husband, and of his travels and wars, which he underwent in his days. Be it spoken to your comfort, the name of your husband rings over all these parts of the world: his faith, his courage, his enduring, and his sincerity under all, has made his name famous.

Then he turned him to the boys, and asked them of their names, which they told him. And then said he unto them: Matthew, be thou like Matthew the publican, not in vice, but in virtue.[67] Samuel, said he, be thou like Samuel the prophet, a man of faith and prayer.[68] Joseph, said he, be thou like Joseph in Potiphar's house, chaste, and one that flies from temptation.[69] And James, be thou like James the Just, and like James the brother of our Lord.[70]

Then they told him of Mercy and how she had left her town and her kindred to come along with Christiana and her sons. At that the old honest man said, Mercy is thy name; by Mercy shalt thou be sustained, and carried through all those difficulties that shall assault thee in thy way, till thou shalt come thither, where thou shalt look the Fountain of Mercy in the face with comfort.

All this while the guide, Mr. Great-heart, was very much pleased, and smiled upon his companion.

Now, as they walked along together, the guide asked the old gentleman if he did not know one Mr. Fearing, that came on pilgrimage out of his parts?

HON. Yes, very well, said he. He was a man that had the root of the matter in him; but he was one of the most troublesome pilgrims that ever I met with in all my days.

GREAT-HEART. I perceive you knew him; for you have given a very right character of him.

HON. Knew him! I was a great companion of his; I was with him most an end; when he first began to think of what would come upon us hereafter, I was with him.

GREAT-HEART. I was his guide from my Master's house to the gates of the Celestial City.

HON. Then you knew him to be a troublesome one.

GREAT-HEART. I did so, but I could very well bear it; for men of my calling are oftentimes intrusted with the conduct of such as he was.

HON. Well then, pray let us hear a little of him, and how he managed himself under your conduct.

GREAT-HEART. Why, he was always afraid that he should come short of whither he had a desire to go.

Everything frightened him that he heard anybody speak of, that had but the least appearance of opposition in it. I hear that he lay roaring at the Slough of Despond for about a month together; nor durst he, for all he saw several go over before him, venture, though they, many of them offered to lend him their hand. But he would not go back again neither. The Celestial City, he said, he should die if he came not to it; and yet was dejected at every difficulty, and stumbled at every straw that anybody cast in his way.

Well, after he had lain at the Slough of Despond a great while, as I have told you, one sunshiny morning, I do not know how, he ventured, and so got over; but when he was over he could scarce believe it. He had, I think a Slough of Despond in his mind; a slough that he carried everywhere with him, or else he could never have been as he was.

So he came up to the gate, you know what I mean, that stands at the head of this way; and there also he stood a good while, before he would adventure to knock.

When the gate was opened, he would give back, and give place to others, and say that he was not worthy. For, although he got before some to the gate, yet many of them went in before him

There the poor man would stand, shaking and shrinking. I dare say it would have pitied one's heart to have seen him; nor would he go back again. At last he took the hammer, that hanged on the gate, in his hand, and gave a small rap or two; then one opened to him, but he shrank back as before. He that opened stepped out after him, and said, Thou trembling one, what wantest thou?

With that he fell down to the ground. He that spoke to him wondered to see him so faint. So he said to him, Peace be to thee; up, for I have set open the door to thee. Come in, for thou art blessed. With that he got up, and went in trembling; and when he was in, he was ashamed to show his face.

Well, after he had been entertained there a while, as you know how the manner is, he was bid go on his way, and also told the way he should take. So he went on till he came to our house. But as he behaved himself at the gate, so he did at my master the Interpreter's door.

He lay thereabout in the cold a good while, before he would adventure to call; yet he would not go back, and the nights were long and cold then. Nay, he had a note of necessity in his bosom to my master, to receive him and grant him the comfort of his house, and also to allow him a stout and valiant conductor, because he was himself so chicken-hearted a man; and yet, for all that, he was afraid to call at the door.

So he lay up and down hereabouts, till, poor man! he was almost starved. Yea, so great was his dejection, that though he saw several others, for knocking, get in, yet he was afraid to venture. At last, I think, I looked out of the window, and perceiving a man to be up and down about the door, I went out to him, and asked what he was; but,

MR. FEARING AT THE GATE.

poor man! the water stood in his eyes; so I perceived what he wanted. I went, therefore, in and told it in the house, and we showed the thing to our Lord.

So he sent me out again, to entreat him to come in; but, I dare say, I had hard work to do it. At last he came in; and I will say that for my Lord, he carried it wonderfully lovingly to him. There were but few good bits at the table, but some of it was laid upon his trencher.

Then he presented the note, and my Lord looked thereon, and said his desire should be granted So when he had been there a good while, he seemed to get some heart, and to be a little more comfortable; for my master, you must know, is one of very tender bowels, especially to them that are afraid; wherefore he carried it so towards him as might tend most to his encouragement.

Well, when he had had a sight of the things of the place, and was ready to take his journey to go to the City, my Lord, as he did to Christian before, gave him a bottle of spirits, and some comfortable things to eat. Thus we set forward, and I went before him; but the man was but of few words, only he would sigh aloud.

When we were come to where the three fellows were hanged, he said that he doubted not but that would be his end also. Only he seemed glad when he saw the Cross and the Sepulchre.

There, I confess, he desired to stay a little to look, and he seemed, for a while after, to be a little cheery. When we came at the Hill Difficulty, he made no stick at that, nor did he much fear the lions; for you must know that his trouble was not about such things as those: his fear was about his acceptance at last.

I got him in at the House Beautiful, I think, before he was willing. Also, when he was in, I made him acquainted with the damsels that were of the place; but he was ashamed to make himself much for company. He desired much to be alone, yet he always loved good talk, and often would get behind the screen to hear it.

He also loved much to see ancient things, and to be pondering them in his mind. He told me afterwards that he loved to be in those two houses from which he came last, to wit, at the gate, and that of the Interpreter, but that he durst not be so bold as to ask.

When we went also from the House Beautiful, down the hill, into the Valley of Humiliation, he went down as well as ever I saw a man in my life; for he cared not how mean he was, so he might be happy at last. Yea, I think there was a kind of a sympathy betwixt that valley and him; for I never saw him better in all his pilgrimage than when he was in that valley.

MR. FEARING IN THE VALLEY OF HUMILIATION.

Here he would lie down, embrace the ground, and kiss the very flowers that grew in this valley.[71] He would now be up every morning by break of day, tracing and walking to and fro in this valley.

But when he was come to the entrance of the Valley of the Shadow of Death, I thought I should have lost my man; not for that he had any inclination to go back; that he always abhorred; but he was ready to die for fear.

Oh! the hobgoblins will have me! the hobgoblins will have me! cried he, and I could not beat him out of it. He made such a noise and such an outcry here, that had they but heard him, it was enough to encourage them to come and fall upon us.

But this I took very great notice of, that this valley was as quiet while he went through it, as ever I knew it before or since. I suppose these enemies here had now a special check from our Lord, and a command not to meddle until Mr. Fearing was passed over it.

It would be too tedious to tell you of all. We will, therefore, only mention a passage or two more. When he was come at Vanity Fair, I thought he would have fought with all the men at the fair.

I feared there we should both have been knocked on the head, so hot was he against their fooleries. Upon the Enchanted Ground he was also very wakeful. But when he was come at the river, where was no bridge, there again he was in a heavy case. Now, now, he said, he should be drowned for ever, and so never see that face with comfort that he had come so many miles to behold.

And here, also, I took notice of what was very remarkable; the water of that river was lower at this time than ever I saw it in all my life. So he went over at last, not much above wet-shod.

When he was going up to the gate, I began to take my leave of him, and to wish him a good reception above. So he said, I shall, I shall. Then parted we asunder, and I saw him no more.

HON. Then, it seems, he was well at last.

GREAT-HEART. Yes, yes; I never had doubt about him; he was a man of a choice spirit, only he was always kept very low, and that made his life so burdensome to himself, and so troublesome to others.[72] He was, above many, tender of sin. He was so afraid of doing injuries to others, that he often would deny himself of that which was lawful, because he would not offend.[73]

HON. But what should be the reason that such a good man should be all his days so much in the dark?

GREAT-HEART. There are two sorts of reasons for it: One is the wise God will have it so; some must pipe and some must weep. [74] Now Mr. Fearing was one that played upon this bass; he and his fellows sound the sackbut, whose notes are more doleful than the notes of other music are; though, indeed, some say the bass is the ground of music.

And, for my part, I care not at all for that profession that begins not in heaviness of mind. The first string that the musician usually touches is the bass when he intends to put all in tune. God always plays upon this string first, when he sets the soul in tune for himself. Only here was the imperfection of Mr. Fearing, he could play upon no other music but this, till towards his latter end.

I make bold to talk thus metaphorically, for the ripening of the wits of young readers; and because, in the book of the Revelations, the saved are compared to a company of musicians that play upon their trumpets and harps, and sing their songs before the throne. [75]

HON. He was a very zealous man, as one may see by what relation you have given of him; difficulties, lions, or Vanity Fair, he feared not at all. It was only sin, death, and hell that was to him a terror, because he had some doubts about his interest in that celestial country.

GREAT-HEART. You say right. Those were the things that were his troublers, and they, as you have well observed, arose from the weakness of his mind thereabout, not from weakness of spirit as to the practical part of a pilgrim's life. I dare believe that, as the proverb is, " he could have bit a firebrand, had it stood in his way;" but the things with which he was oppressed, no man ever yet could shake off with ease.

Then said Christiana, This relation of Mr. Fearing has done me good. I thought nobody had been like me; but I see there was some semblance betwixt this good man and I; only we differed in two things: his troubles were so great they brake out; but mine I kept within. His, also, lay so hard upon him, they made him that he could not knock at the houses provided for entertainment; but my trouble was always such as made me knock the louder.

MERCY. If I might also speak my heart, I must say, that something of him has also dwelt in me; for I have ever been more afraid of the lake, and the loss of a place in Paradise, than I have been of the loss of other things. Oh, thought I, may I have the happiness to have a habitation there, it is enough, though I part with all the world to win it!

MATT. Then said Matthew, Fear was one thing that made me think that I was far from having that within me which accompanies salvation; but if it was so with such a good man as he, why may it not also go well with me?

JAMES. No fears, no grace, said James. Though there is not always grace where there is the fear of hell, yet, to be sure, there is no grace where there is no fear of God.

GREAT-HEART. Well said, James, thou hast hit the mark; for the fear of God is the beginning of wisdom; and, to be sure, they that want the beginning have neither middle nor end. But we will here conclude our discourse of Mr. Fearing, after we have sent after him this farewell.

> Well, Master Fearing, thou didst fear
>   Thy God, and wast afraid
> Of doing anything, while here,
>   That would have thee betrayed.
>
> And didst thou fear the lake and pit?
>   Would others did so too!
> For, as for them that want thy wit,
>   They do themselves undo.

Now I saw that they still went on in their talk; for after Mr. Great-heart had made an end with Mr. Fearing, Mr. Honest began to tell them of another, but his name was Mr. Self-will. He pretended himself to be a pilgrim, said Mr. Honest; but I persuade myself he never came in at the gate that stands at the head of the way.

GREAT-HEART. Had you ever any talk with him about it?

HON. Yes, more than once or twice; but he would always be like himself, self-willed. He neither cared for man, nor argument, nor yet example; what his mind prompted him to do, that he would do, and nothing else could he be got to do.

GREAT-HEART. Pray, what principles did he hold? for I suppose you can tell.

HON. He held that a man might follow the vices as well as the virtues of the pilgrims; and that if he did both, he should be certainly saved.

GREAT-HEART. Now, if he had said, It is possible for the best to be guilty of the vices, as well as to partake of the virtues of pilgrims, he could not much have been blamed; for indeed we are exempted from no vice absolutely, but on condition that we watch and strive. But this, I perceive, is not the thing; but if I understand you right, your meaning is, that he was of the opinion, that it was allowable so to be.

HON. Aye, aye, so I mean; and so he believed and practised.

GREAT-HEART. But what ground had he for his so saying?

HON. Why, he said he had the Scripture for his warrant.

GREAT-HEART. Prithee, Mr. Honest, present us with a few particulars.

HON. So I will. He said, To have to do with other men's wives had been practised by David, God's beloved; and therefore he could do it. He said, To have more women than one, was a thing that Solomon practised;

HONEST TELLS ABOUT ONE SELF-WILL.

and therefore he could do it. He said, That Sarah and the godly midwives of Egypt lied, and so did save Rahab; and therefore he could do it. He said, That the disciples went at the bidding of their Master, and took away the owner's ass; and therefore he could do so too. He said, That Jacob got the inheritance of his father in the way of guile and dissimulation; and therefore he could do so too.

GREAT-HEART. Highly base, indeed. And you are sure he was of this opinion?

HON. I have heard him plead for it, bring Scripture for it, bring argument for it, &c.

GREAT-HEART. An opinion that is not fit to be with any allowance in the world.

HON. You must understand me rightly. He did not say that any man might do this; but that those that had the virtues of those that did such things might also do the same.

GREAT-HEART. But what more false than such a conclusion? for this is as much as to say, that because good men heretofore have sinned of infirmity, therefore he had allowance to do it of a presumptuous mind; or if, because a child by the blast of the wind, or for that it stumbled at a stone, fell down, and defiled itself in mire, therefore he might wilfully lie down and wallow like a boar therein. Who could have thought that any one could so far have been blinded by the power of lust? But what is written must be true: They "stumble at the word, being disobedient; whereunto also they were appointed." [76]

His supposing that such may have the godly man's virtues, who addict themselves to their vices, is also a delusion as strong as the other. It is just as if the dog should say, I have, or may have, the qualities of the child, because I lick up its stinking excrements. To eat up the sin of God's people is no sign that one is possessed with their virtues. [77] Nor can I believe, that one who is of this opinion can at present have faith or love in him. But I know you have made strong objections against him: prithee, what can he say for himself?

HON. Why, he says, To do this by way of opinion, seems abundantly more honest than to do it, and yet hold contrary to it in opinion.

GREAT-HEART. A very wicked answer; for though to let loose the bridle to lusts, while our opinions are against such things, is bad; yet, to sin, and plead a toleration so to do, is worse. The one stumbles beholders accidentally, the other leads them into the snare.

HON. There are many of this man's mind, that have not this man's mouth; and that make going on pilgrimage of so little esteem as it is.

GREAT-HEART. You have said the truth, and it is to be lamented; but he that feareth the King of Paradise shall come out of them all.

CHRIS. There are strange opinions in the world; I know one that said, It was time enough to repent when they come to die.

GREAT-HEART. Such are not over wise. That man would have been loath, might he have had a week to run twenty miles for his life, to have deferred that journey to the last hour of that week.

HON. You say right; and yet the generality of them, that count themselves pilgrims, do indeed do thus. I am, as you see, an old man, and have been a traveller in this road many a day; and I have taken notice of many things.

I have seen some that have set out as if they would drive all the world afore them, who yet have, in few days, died as they in the wilderness, and so never got sight of the promised land.

I have seen some that have promised nothing at first setting out to be pilgrims, and that one would have thought could not have lived a day, that have yet proved very good pilgrims.

I have seen some who have run hastily forward, that again have after a little time, run just as fast back again.

I have seen some who have spoken very well of a pilgrim's life at first, that, after a while, have spoken as much against it.

I have heard some, when they first set out for Paradise, say positively there is such a place; who, when they have been almost there, have come back again, and said there is none.

I have heard some vaunt what they would do, in case they should be opposed, that have, even at a false alarm fled faith, the pilgrim's way and all.

Now, as they were thus in their way, there came one running to meet them, and said, Gentlemen, and you of the weaker sort, if you love life, shift for yourselves, for the robbers are before you.

Then said Mr. Great-heart, they be the three that set upon Little-faith heretofore. Well, said he, we are ready for them; so they went on their way. Now they looked at every turning, when they should have met with the villains; but whether they heard of Mr. Great-heart, or whether they had some other game, they came not up to the pilgrims.

Christiana then wished for an inn for herself and her children, because they were weary. Then said Mr. Honest, There is one a little before us, where a very honorable disciple, one Gaius, dwells.[78]

So they all concluded to turn in thither, and the rather, because the old gentleman gave him so good a report. So when they came to the door, they went in, not knocking, for folks use not to knock at the door of an inn. Then they called for the master of the house, and he came to them. So they asked if they might lie there that night.

GAIUS. Yes, gentlemen, if ye be true men, for my house is for none but pilgrims. Then was Christiana, Mercy, and the boys, the more glad, for that the Innkeeper was a lover of Pilgrims. So they called for rooms, and he showed them one for Christiana and her children, and Mercy, and another for Mr. Great-heart and the old gentleman.

Then said Mr. Great-heart, Good Gaius, what hast thou for supper? for these pilgrims have come far to-day, and are weary.

It is late, said Gaius, so we cannot conveniently go out to seek food; but such as we have, you will be welcome to, if that will content.

GREAT-HEART. We will be content with what thou hast in the house; forasmuch as I have proved thee. thou art never destitute of that which is convenient.

Then he went down and spake to the cook, whose name was Taste-that-which-is-good, to get ready supper for so many pilgrims.

This done, he comes up again, saying, Come, my good friends, you are welcome to me, and I am glad that I have a house to entertain you; and while supper is making ready, if you please, let us entertain one another with some good discourse. So they all said, Content.

Then said Gaius, Whose wife is this aged matron? and whose daughter is this young damsel?

GREAT-HEART. The woman is the wife of one Christian, a Pilgrim of former times; and these are his four children. The maid is one of her acquaintance; one that she hath persuaded to come with her on pilgrimage. The boys take all after their father, and covet to tread in his steps; yea, if they do but see any place where the old Pilgrim hath lain, or any print of his foot, it ministereth joy to their hearts, and they covet to lie or tread in the same.

Then said Gaius, Is this Christian's wife? and are these Christian's children? I knew your husband's father, yea, also his father's father. Many have been good of this stock; their ancestors dwelt first at Antioch.[79] Christian's progenitors (I suppose you have heard your husband talk of them) were very worthy men. They have, above any that I know, showed themselves men of great virtue and courage, for the Lord of the Pilgrims, his ways, and them that loved him.

I have heard of many of your husband's relations, that have stood all trials for the sake of the truth. Stephen, that was one of the first of the family from whence your husband sprang, was knocked on the head with stones.[80] James, another of this generation, was slain with the edge of the

GAIUS RECEIVES THE PILGRIMS.

361

sword.[81] To say nothing of Paul and Peter, men anciently of the family from whence your husband came, there was Ignatius, who was cast to the lions; Romanus, whose flesh was cut by pieces from his bones, and Polycarp, that played the man in the fire.

There was he that was hanged up in a basket in the sun, for the wasps to eat; and he whom they put into a sack, and cast into the sea to be drowned. It would be utterly impossible to count up all of that family that have suffered injuries and death, for the love of a pilgrim's life. Nor can I but be glad to see that thy husband has left behind him four such boys as these. I hope they will bear up their father's name, and tread in their father's steps, and come to their father's end.

GREAT-HEART. Indeed, Sir, they are likely lads; they seem to choose heartily their father's ways.

GAIUS. That is it that I said; wherefore Christian's family is like still to spread abroad upon the face of the ground, and yet to be numerous upon the face of the earth; wherefore let Christiana look out some damsels for her sons, to whom they may be betrothed, &c., that the name of their father and the house of his progenitors may never be forgotten in the world.

HON. It is a pity this family should fall and be extinct.

GAIUS. Fall it cannot, but be diminished it may; but let Christiana take my advice, and that is the way to uphold it.

And, Christiana, said this Innkeeper, I am glad to see thee and thy friend Mercy together here, a lovely couple. And may I advise, take Mercy into a nearer relation to thee; if she will, let her be given to Matthew, thy eldest son; it is the way to preserve you a posterity in the earth. So this match was concluded, and in process of time they were married; but more of that hereafter.

Gaius also proceeded, and said, I will now speak on the behalf of women, to take away their reproach. For as death and the curse came into the world by a woman,[82] so also did life and health: "God sent forth his Son, made of a woman."[83] Yea, to show how much those that came after did abhor the act of the mother, this sex, in the Old Testament, coveted children, if happily this or that woman might be the mother of the Saviour of the world.

I will say again, that when the Saviour was come, women rejoiced in him before either man or angel.[84] I read not, that ever any man did give unto Christ so much as one groat; but the women followed him, and ministered to him of their substance.[85]

It was a woman that washed his feet with tears, and a woman that anointed his body to the burial.[86] They were women that wept, when he was going to the cross, and women that followed him from the cross, and that sat by his sepulchre, when he was buried.[87]

They were women that were first with him at his resurrection-morn; and women that brought tidings first to his disciples, that he was risen

GAIUS PROPOSES MARRIAGE FOR MATTHEW AND MERCY.

from the dead.[88] Women, therefore, are highly favored, and show by these things that they are sharers with us in the grace of life.

Now the cook sent up to signify that supper was almost ready, and sent one to lay the cloth, the trenchers, and to set the salt and bread in order.

Then said Matthew, The sight of this cloth, and of this fore-runner of the supper, begetteth in me a greater appetite for my food than I had before.

GAIUS. So let all ministering doctrines to thee, in this life, beget in thee a greater desire to sit at the supper of the great King in his kingdom; for all preaching, books, and ordinances here, are but as the laying of the trenchers, and as setting of salt upon the board, when compared with the feast that our Lord will make for us when we come to his house.

So supper came up; and first, a heave-shoulder and a wave-breast[89] were set on the table before them, to show that they must begin their meal with prayer and praise to God.[90] The heave-shoulder David lifted his heart up to God with; and with the wave-breast, where his heart lay, with that he used to lean upon his harp when he played. These two dishes were very fresh and good, and they all ate heartily well thereof.

The next they brought up was a bottle of wine, red as blood.[91] So Gaius said to them, Drink freely; this is the juice of the true vine, that makes glad the heart of God and man.[92] So they drank and were merry.

The next was a dish of milk well crumbed; but Gaius said, Let the boys have that, that they may grow thereby.[93]

Then they brought up in course a dish of butter and honey. Then said Gaius, Eat freely of this; for this is good to cheer up, and strengthen your judgments and understandings. This was our Lord's dish when he was a child; "Butter and honey shall he eat, that he may know to refuse the evil and choose the good."[94]

Then they brought them up a dish of apples, and they were very good tasted fruit. Then said Matthew, May we eat apples, since it was they, by and with which the serpent beguiled our first mother?

Then said Gaius—

> Apples were they with which we were beguiled:
> Yet sin, not apples, hath our souls defiled.
> Apples forbid, if eat, corrupt the blood;
> To eat such, when commanded, does us good.
> Drink of his flagons, then, thou church, his dove,
> And eat his apples, who are sick of love.

Then said Matthew, I made the scruple, because I a while since was sick with eating of fruit.

GAIUS. Forbidden fruit will make you sick, but not what our lord has tolerated.

While they were thus talking, they were presented with another dish, and it was a dish of nuts.[95] Then said some at the table, Nuts spoil tender teeth, especially the teeth of children; which when Gaius heard, he said—

> Hard texts are nuts (I will not call them cheaters),
> Whose shells do keep their kernels from the eaters.
> Open then the shells, and you shall have the meat;
> They here are brought for you to crack and eat.

Then were they very merry, and sat at the table a long time, talking

OLD HONEST PROPOSES A RIDDLE.

of many things. Then said the old gentleman, My good landlord, while we are cracking your nuts, if you please, do you open this riddle:

> A man there was, though some did count him mad,
> The more he cast away, the more he had.

Then they all gave good heed, wondering what good Gaius would say; so he sat still a while, and then thus replied:—

> He that bestows his goods upon the poor,
> Shall have as much again, and ten times more.

Then said Joseph, I dare say, Sir, I did not think you could have found it out.

Oh! said Gaius, I have been trained up in this way a great while; nothing teaches like experience; I have learned of my lord to be kind; and have found by experience, that I have gained thereby. "There is that scattereth, and yet increaseth; and there is that withholdeth more than is meet; but it tendeth to poverty."[96] "There is that maketh him-

MERCY CLOTHES THE POOR.

self rich, yet hath nothing; there is that maketh himself poor, yet hath great riches."[97]

Then Samuel whispered to Christiana, his mother, and said, Mother, this is a very good man's house, let us stay here a good while, and let my brother Matthew be married to Mercy before we go any further.

The which Gaius the host overhearing said, With a very good will, my child.

So they staid there more than a month, and Mercy was given to Matthew to wife.

While they staid here, Mercy, as her custom was, would be making coats and garments to give to the poor, by which she brought up a very good report upon the Pilgrims.

But to return again to our story.   After supper the lads desired a bed; for that they were weary with travelling: then Gaius called to show them their chamber; but said Mercy, I will have them to bed.   So she had them to bed, and they slept well; but the rest sat up all night; for Gaius and they were such suitable company, that they could not tell how to part.

Then after much talk of their Lord, themselves, and their journey, old Mr. Honest, he that put forth the riddle to Gaius, began to nod.   Then said Great-heart, What, Sir, you begin to be drowsy; come, rub up; now here is a riddle for you.   Then said Mr. Honest, let us hear it.

Then said Mr. Great-heart—

> He that will kill, must first be overcome,
> Who live abroad would, first must die at home.

Ha! said Mr. Honest, it is a hard one to expound, and harder to practise.   But come, landlord, said he, I will, if you please, leave my part to you; do you expound it, and I will hear what you say.

No, said Gaius, it was put to you, and it is expected that you should answer it.

Then said the old gentleman—

> He first by grace must conquered be,
> That sin would mortify;
> And who, that lives, would convince me,
> Unto himself must die.

It is right, said Gaius; good doctrine and experience teaches this. For, first, until grace displays itself, and overcomes the soul with its glory, it is altogether without heart to oppose sin; besides, if sin is Satan's cords, by which the soul lies bound, how should it make resistance, before it is loosed from that infirmity?

Secondly, nor will any, that knows either reason or grace, believe that such a man can be a living monument of grace that is a slave to his own corruptions.

And now it comes to my mind, I will tell you a story worth the hearing.   There were two men that went on pilgrimage: the one began when he was young, the other when he was old.   The young man had strong corruptions to grapple with; the old man's were decayed with the decays of nature.   The young man trod his steps as carefully as did the old one,

and was every way as light as he.   Who now, or which of them, had their graces shining clearest, since both seemed to be alike?

HON.   The young man's, doubtless.   For that which heads it against the greatest opposition, gives best demonstration that it is strongest, especially when it also holdeth pace with that which meets not with half so much; as, to be sure, old age does not.

Besides, I have observed that old men have blessed themselves with this mistake, namely, taking the decays of nature for a gracious conquest over corruptions, and so have been apt to beguile themselves.

Indeed, old men that are gracious, are best able to give advice to them that are young, because they have seen most of the emptiness of things.   But yet, for an old and a young man to set out

JAMES READS THE BIBLE AT GAIUS'S HOUSE.

both together, the young man has the advantage of the fairest discovery of a work of grace within him, though the old man's corruptions are naturally the weakest.

Thus they sat talking till break of day.   Now, when the family was up, Christiana bid her son James that he should read a chapter; so he read the fifty-third of Isaiah. When he had done, Mr. Honest asked, why it was said that the Saviour is to come " out of a dry ground;" and also, that " he had no form or comeliness in him ?"

Then said Mr. Great-heart, To the first, I answer, Because the church of the Jews, of which Christ came, had then lost almost all the sap and spirit of religion.

To the second, I say, The words are spoken in the person of the unbelievers, who, because they want that eye that can see into our Prince's heart, therefore they judge of him by the meanness of his outside. Just like those that know not that precious stones are covered over with a homely crust; who, when they have found one, because they know not what they have found cast it away again, as men do a common stone.

Well, said Gaius, now you are here, and since, as I know, Mr. Great-heart is good at his weapons, if you please, after we have refreshed ourselves, we will walk into the fields to see if we can do any good. About a mile from hence, there is one Slay-good, a giant that does much annoy the King's highway in these parts; and I know whereabout his haunt is. He is master of a number of thieves. It would be well if we could clear these parts of him.

So they consented, and went, Mr. Great-heart with his sword, helmet, and shield, and the rest with spears and staves.

When they came to the place where he was, they found him with one Feeble-mind in his hands, whom his servants had brought unto him, having taken him in the way. Now the Giant was rifling him, with a purpose, after that, to pick his bones, for he was of the nature of flesh-eaters.

Well, so soon as he saw Mr. Great-heart and his friends at the mouth of his cave, with their weapons, he demanded what they wanted.

GREAT-HEART. We want thee; for we are come to revenge the quarrel of the many that thou hast slain of the pilgrims, when thou hast dragged them out of the King's highway; wherefore, come out of thy cave.

So he armed himself and came out; and to a battle they went, and fought for above an hour, and then stood still to take wind.

Then said the giant, Why are you here on my ground ?

GREAT-HEART. To revenge the blood of pilgrims, as I also told thee before. So they went to it again, and the giant made Mr. Great-heart give back; but he came up again, and, in the greatness of his mind, he let fly with such great stoutness at the giant's head and sides, that he

24

made him let his weapon fall out of his hand; so he smote him, and slew him, and cut off his head, and brought it away to the inn.

He also took Feeble-mind, the pilgrim, and brought him with him to his lodgings. When they were come home, they showed his head to the family, and then set it up, as they had done others before, for a terror to those that shall attempt to do as he hereafter.

Then they asked Mr. Feeble-mind how he fell into his hands?

FEEBLE-MIND. Then said the poor man, I am a sickly man, as you

THE PILGRIMS BRING THE HEAD OF GIANT SLAY-GOOD TO THE INN.

see; and, because death did usually once a-day knock at my door, I thought I should never be well at home; so I betook myself to a pilgrim's life, and have travelled here from the town of Uncertain, where I and my father were born.

I am a man of no strength at all of body, nor yet of mind; but would, if I could, though I can but crawl, spend my life in the pilgrim's way. When I came at the gate that is at the head of the way, the Lord of that place did entertain me freely; neither objected he against my weak looks, nor against my feeble-mind; but gave me such things that were necessary for my journey, and bid me hope to the end.

When I came to the house of the Interpreter, I received much kindness there; and because the Hill Difficulty was judged too hard for me, I was carried up that by one of his servants. Indeed, I have found much relief from pilgrims, though none were willing to go so softly as I am forced to do; yet still, as they came on, they bid me be of good cheer, and said that it was the will of their Lord that comfort should be given to the feeble-minded, and so went on their own pace.[98]

When I was come up to Assault Lane, then this giant met with me, and bid me prepare for an encounter; but, alas! feeble one that I was, I had more need of a cordial. So he came up and took me. I had hopes he would not kill me.

Also, when he had got me into his den, since I went not with him willingly, I believed I should come out alive again; for I have heard that not any pilgrim that is taken captive by violent hands, if he keeps heart-whole towards his Master, is, by the laws of Providence, to die by the hand of the enemy.

Robbed I looked to be, and robbed to be sure I am; but I am, as you see, escaped with life; for the which I thank my King as author, and you as the means. Other brunts I also look for; but this I have resolved on, to wit, to run when I can, to go when I cannot run, and to creep when I cannot go.

As to the main, I thank him that loves me, I am fixed. My way is before me, my mind is beyond the river that has no bridge, though I am, as you see, but of a feeble mind.

Then said old Mr. Honest, Have you not, some time ago, been acquainted with one Mr. Fearing, a pilgrim?

FEEBLE. Acquainted with him! Yes; he came from the town of Stupidity, which lieth four degrees to the northward of the City of Destruction, and as many off of where I was born: yet we were well acquainted, for, indeed, he was my father's brother. He and I have been much of a temper. He was a little shorter than I, but yet we were much of a complexion.

HON. I perceive you know him; and I am apt to believe also that you were related one to another; for you have his whitely look, a cast like his with your eye, and your speech is much alike.

FEEBLE. Most have said so that have known us both; and besides, what I have noticed in him, I have, for the most part, found in myself.

Come, Sir, said good Gaius, be of good cheer, you are welcome to me, and to my house, and what thou hast a mind to, call for freely;

and what thou wouldst have my servants do for thee, they will do it with a ready mind.

Then said Mr. Feeble-mind, This is unexpected favor, and as the sun shining out of a very dark cloud. Did Giant Slay-good intend me this favor when he stopped me, and resolved to let me go no further? Did he intend, that after he had rifled my pockets, I should go to Gaius, mine host? Yet so it is.

Now, just as Mr. Feeble-mind and Gaius were thus in talk, there comes one running, and called at the door, and told that, about a mile and a half off, there was one Mr. Not-right, a pilgrim, struck dead upon the place where he was, with a thunder-bolt.

Alas! said Mr. Feeble-mind, is he slain? He overtook me some days before I came so far as hither, and would be my company-keeper. He also was with me when Slay-good, the giant, took me; but he was nimble of his heels, and escaped. But, it seems, he escaped to die, and I was took to live.

> What, one would think, doth seek to slay outright,
> Ofttimes delivers from the saddest plight.
> That very providence, whose face is death,
> Doth ofttimes, to the lowly, life bequeath.
> I taken was, he did escape and flee;
> Hands cross'd gives death to him, and life to me.

Now, about this time, Matthew and Mercy were married. Also Gaius gave his daughter Phebe to James, Matthew's brother, to wife; after which time they yet staid above ten days at Gaius's house, spending their time, and the seasons, like as pilgrims used to do.

When they were to depart, Gaius made them a feast, and they did eat and drink, and were merry. Now the hour was come that they must be gone; wherefore Mr. Great-heart called for a reckoning; but Gaius told him, that at his house it was not the custom for pilgrims to pay for their entertainment. He boarded them by the year, but looked for his pay from the good Samaritan, who had promised him, at his return, whatsoever charge he was at with them, faithfully to repay him.[99]

Then said Mr. Great-heart to him, "Beloved, thou dost faithfully whatsoever thou dost to the brethren, and to strangers, which have borne witness of thy charity before the church; whom if thou yet bring forward on their journey after a godly sort thou shalt do well."[100]

Then Gaius took his leave of them all, and of his children, and particularly of Mr. Feeble-mind. He also gave him something to drink by the way.

Now Mr. Feeble-mind, when they were going out of the door, made as if he intended to linger; the which when Mr. Great-heart espied, he said, Come, Mr. Feeble-mind, pray do you go along with us, I will be your conductor, and you shall fare as the rest.

THE MARRIAGE OF MATTHEW AND MERCY.

FEEBLE. Alas! I want a suitable companion; you are all lusty and strong; but I, as you see, am weak; I choose, therefore, rather to come behind, lest, by reason of my many infirmities, I shall be both a burden to myself and to you.

I am, as I said, a man of a weak and feeble mind, and shall be offended and made weak at that which others can bear. I shall like no laughing; I shall like no gay attire; I shall like no unprofitable questions. Nay, I am so weak a man as to be offended with that which others have liberty to do.

I do not yet know all the truth. I am a very ignorant Christian man; sometimes if I hear some rejoice in the Lord, it troubles me because I cannot do so too. It is with me as it is with a weak man among the strong, or as with a sick man among the healthy, or as a lamp despised ("He that is ready to slip with his feet, is as a lamp despised in the thought of him that is at ease"[101]), so that I know not what to do.

But, brother, said Mr. Great-heart, I have it in commission to "comfort the feeble-minded," and to "support the weak."[102] You must needs go along with us; we will wait for you; we will lend you our help;[103] we will deny ourselves of some things, both opinionative and practical, for your sake,[104] we will not enter into doubtful disputations before you; we will be made all things to you, rather than you shall be left behind.[105]

Now all this took place while they were at Gaius's door; and behold, as they were thus in the heat of their discourse, Mr. Ready-to-halt came by, with his crutches in his hand;[106] and he also was going on pilgrimage.

Then said Mr. Feeble-mind to him, Man, how camest thou hither? I was but just now complaining, that I had not a suitable companion, but thou art according to my wish. Welcome, welcome, good Mr. Ready-to-halt, I hope thee and I may be some help to each other.

READY-TO-HALT. I shall be glad of thy company, said the other; and good Mr. Feeble-mind, rather than that we should part, since we are thus happily met, I will lend thee one of my crutches.

FEEBLE. Nay, said he, though I thank thee for thy good will, I am not inclined to halt before I am lame. Howbeit, I think, when occasion is, it may help me against a dog.

READY. If either myself or my crutches can do thee a pleasure, we are both at thy command, good Mr. Feeble-mind.

Thus therefore they went on; Mr. Great-heart and Mr. Honest went before, Christiana and her children went next, and Mr. Feeble-mind, and Mr. Ready-to-halt came behind with his crutches.

Then said Mr. Honest, Pray, Sir, now we are upon the road, tell us some profitable things of some that have gone on pilgrimage before us.

GREAT-HEART. With a good will. I suppose you have heard how Christian of old did meet with Apollyon in the Valley of Humiliation;

and also what hard work he had, to go through the Valley of the Shadow of Death. Also I think you cannot but have heard how Faithful was put to it with Madam Wanton, with Adam the First, with one Discontent, and Shame, four as deceitful villains as a man can meet with upon the road.

FEEBLE-MIND WELCOMES READY-TO-HALT.

HON. Yes, I have heard of all this; but indeed, good Faithful was hardest put to it with Shame; he was an unwearied one.

GREAT-HEART. Aye; for as the Pilgrim well said, he of all men had the wrong name.

HON. But pray, Sir, where was it that Christian and Faithful met Talkative? That same was also a notable one.

GREAT-HEART. He was a confident fool, yet many follow his ways.

HON. He had liked to have beguiled Faithful.

GREAT-HEART. Aye, but Christian put him into a way quickly to find him out. Thus they went on till they came at the place where Evangelist met with Christian and Faithful, and prophesied to them of what should befall them at Vanity Fair.

GREAT-HEART. Then said their guide, Hereabouts did Christian and Faithful meet with Evangelist, who prophesied to them of what troubles they should meet with at Vanity Fair.

HON. Say you so? I dare say that it was a hard chapter that then he did read unto them.

GREAT-HEART. It was so: but he gave them encouragement withal. But what do we talk of them? they were a couple of lion-like men; they had set their faces like flint. Don't you remember how undaunted they were when they stood before the judge?

HON. Well, Faithful bravely suffered.

GREAT-HEART. So he did, and as brave things came on it; for Hopeful and some others, as the story relates it, were converted by his death.

HON. Well, but pray go on; for you are well acquainted with things.

GREAT-HEART. Above all that Christian met with after he had passed through Vanity Fair, one By-ends was the arch one.

HON. By-ends! What was he?

GREAT-HEART. A very arch fellow; a downright hypocrite. One that would be religious which way ever the world went; but so cunning that he would be sure neither to lose nor suffer for it.

He had his mode of religion for every fresh occasion; and his wife was as good at it as he. He would turn and change from opinion to opinion; yea, and plead for so doing too. But, so far as I could learn, he came to an ill-end with his by-ends; nor did I ever hear that any of his children were ever of any esteem with those that truly feared God.

Now, by this time, they were come within sight of the town of Vanity, where Vanity Fair is kept. So, when they saw that they were so near the town, they consulted with one another, how they should pass through the town; and some said one thing, and some another.

At last Mr. Great-heart said, I have, as you may understand, often been a conductor of pilgrims through this town; now I am acquainted with one Mr. Mnason, a Cyprusian by nation, an old disciple, at whose house we may lodge.[107] If you think good, said he, we will turn in there.

Content, said old Honest; Content, said Christiana; Content, said Mr. Feeble-mind; and so they said all. Now, you must think, it was eventide by the time they got to the outside of the town; but Mr. Great-heart knew the way to the old man's house.

So thither they came; and he called at the door, and the old man within knew his tongue so soon as ever he heard it; so he opened, and they all came in. Then said Mnason, their host, How far have ye come to-day? So they said, From the house of Gaius our friend. I promise you, said he, you have gone a good stitch, you may well be a-weary; sit down. So they sat down.

GREAT-HEART. Then said their guide, Come, what cheer, Sirs? I dare say you are welcome to my friend.

I also, said Mr. Mnason, do bid you welcome, and whatever you want, do but say, and we will do what we can to get it for you.

HON. Our great want a while since, was harbor and good company, and now I hope we have both.

MNASON. For harbor, you see what it is; but for good company, that will appear in the trial.

Well, said Mr. Great-heart, will you have the Pilgrims up into their lodging?

I will, said Mr. Mnason. So he had them to their respective places; and also showed them a very fair dining-room, where they might be, and sup together, until time was come to go to rest.

Now, when they were set in their places, and were a little cheery after their journey, Mr. Honest asked his landlord, if there were any store of good people in the town?

MNASON. We have a few, for indeed they are but a few, when compared with them on the other side.

HON. But how shall we do to see some of them? for the sight of good men to them that are going on pilgrimage, is like to the appearing of the moon and the stars to them that are sailing upon the seas.

Then Mr. Mnason stamped with his foot, and his daughter Grace came up; so he said unto her, Grace, go you, tell my friends, Mr. Contrite, Mr. Holy-man, Mr. Love-saint, Mr. Dare-not-lie, and Mr. Penitent, that I have a friend or two at my house that have a mind this evening to see them.

So Grace went to call them, and they came; and, after salutation made, they sat down together at the table.

Then said Mr. Mnason, their landlord, My neighbors, I have, as you see, a company of strangers come to my house; they are Pilgrims; they come from afar, and are going to Mount Zion.

But who, quoth he, do you think this is? pointing with his finger to Christiana; it is Christiana, the wife of Christian, that famous Pilgrim, who, with Faithful his brother, were so shamefully handled in our town.

At that they stood amazed, saying, We little thought to see Christiana, when Grace came to call us; wherefore this is a very comfortable surprise.

Then they asked her of her welfare, and if these young men were her husband's sons? And when she had told them they were, they said, The King whom you love and serve, make you as your father, and bring you where he is in peace!

Then Mr. Honest (when they were all sat down) asked Mr. Contrite and the rest, in what posture their town was at present?

CONTRITE. You may be sure we are full of hurry in fair-time. It is

HONEST AND CONTRITE CONVERSE.

hard keeping our hearts and spirits in any good order, when we are in a cumbered condition. He that lives in such a place as this, and that has to do with such as we have, has need of an item, to caution him to take heed, every moment of the day.

HON. But how are your neighbors for quietness?

CONTRITE. They are much more moderate now than formerly. You know how Christian and Faithful were used at our town; but of late, I say, they have been far more moderate. I think the blood of Faithful lieth as a load upon them till now; for since they burned him, they have been ashamed to burn any more.

In those days we were afraid to walk the streets, but now we can show our heads. Then the name of a professor was odious; now, especially in some parts of our town (for you know our town is large), religion is counted honorable.

Then said Mr. Contrite to them, Pray how fareth it with you in your pilgrimage? How stands the country affected towards you?

HON. It happens to us as it happeneth to wayfaring men; sometimes our way is clean, sometimes foul, sometimes up hill, sometimes down hill; we are seldom at a certainty; the wind is not always on our backs, nor is every one a friend that we meet with in the way.

We have met with some notable rubs already; and what are yet ahead we know not; but for the most part, we find it true, that has been talked of, of old, A good man must suffer trouble.

CONTRITE. You talk of rubs; what rubs have you met withal?

HON. Nay, ask Mr. Great-heart, our guide, for he can give the best account of that.

GREAT-HEART. We have been beset three or four times already. First, Christiana and her children were beset with two ruffians, that they feared would have taken away their lives. We were beset with Giant Bloody-man, Giant Maul, and Giant Slay-good.

Indeed we did rather beset the last, than were beset of him. And thus it was: After we had been some time at the house of "Gaius, mine host, and of the whole church,"[108] we were minded upon a time to take our weapons with us, and so go see if we could light upon any of those that were enemies to pilgrims (for we heard that there was a notable one there-abouts). Now Gaius knew his haunt better than I, because he dwelt thereabout, so we looked, and looked, till at last we discerned the mouth of his cave; then we were glad, and plucked up our spirits.

So we approached up to his den, and lo, when we came there, he had dragged, by mere force, into his net, this poor man, Mr. Feeble-mind, and was about to bring him to his end. But when he saw us, supposing, as we thought, he had spied another prey, he left the poor man in his hole, and came out.

So we fell to it full sore, and he lustily laid about him; but in conclusion, he was brought down to the ground, and his head cut off, and set up by the way-side, for a terror to such as should after practise such ungodliness. That I tell you the truth, here is the man himself to affirm it, who was as a lamb taken out of the mouth of the lion.

Then said Mr. Feeble-mind, I found this true, to my cost and comfort; to my cost, when he threatened to pick my bones every moment; and to my comfort, when I saw Mr. Great-heart and his friends, with their weapons, approach so near for my deliverance.

Then said Mr. Holy-man, There are two things that they have need to be possessed with, that go on pilgrimage: courage and an unspotted life. If they have not courage, they can never hold on their way; and if their lives be loose, they will make the very name of a Pilgrim stink.

Then said Mr. Love-saint, I hope this caution is not needful amongst you. But truly there are many that go upon the road, that rather declare themselves strangers to pilgrimage, than strangers and pilgrims in the earth.

Then said Mr. Dare-not-lie, It is true, they neither have the pilgrim's weed, nor the pilgrim's courage; they go not uprightly, but all awry with their feet; one shoe goes inward, another outward, and their hosen out behind; there is here a rag, and there a rent, to the disparagement of their Lord.

These things, said Mr. Penitent, they ought to be troubled for; nor are the pilgrims like to have that grace put upon them and their pilgrim's progress as they desire, until the way is cleared of such spots and blemishes.

Thus they sat talking and spending the time until supper was set upon the table; unto which they went and refreshed their weary bodies; so they went to rest. Now they stayed in this fair a great while, at the house of this Mr. Mnason, who, in process of time, gave his daughter Grace unto Samuel, Christiana's son, to wife, and his daughter Martha to Joseph.

The time, as I said, that they lay here, was long (for it was not now as in former times). Wherefore the Pilgrims grew acquainted with many of the good people of the town, and did them what service they could.

Mercy, as she was wont, labored much for the poor; wherefore their bellies and backs blessed her, and she was there an ornament to her profession. And, to say the truth for Grace, Phebe, and Martha, they were all of a very good nature, and did much good in their place. They were also all of them very fruitful; so that Christian's name, as was said before, was like to live in the world.

While they lay here, there came a monster out of the woods, and slew many of the people of the town. It would also carry away their children, and teach them to suck its whelps. Now no man in the town durst so much as face this monster; but all men fled when they heard of the noise of his coming.

The monster was like unto no one beast upon the earth: its body was like a dragon, and it had seven heads and ten horns.[109] It made great havoc of children, and yet it was governed by a woman. This monster propounded conditions to men, and such men as loved their lives more than their souls, accepted of those conditions. So they came under.

Now this Mr. Great-heart, together with these that came to visit the pilgrims at Mr. Mnason's house, entered into a covenant to go and engage this beast, if perhaps they might deliver the people of this town from the paws and mouth of this so devouring a serpent.

Then did Mr. Great-heart, Mr. Contrite, Mr. Holy-man, Mr. Dare-not-lie, and Mr. Penitent, with their weapons go forth to meet him.

Now the monster, at first, was very rampant, and looked upon these enemies with great disdain; but they so belabored him, being sturdy men at arms, that they made him make a retreat; so they came home to Mr. Mnason's house again.

The monster, you must know, had his certain seasons to come out in, and to make his attempts upon the children of the people of the town; also these seasons did these valiant worthies watch him in, and did still continually assault him; insomuch that in process of time he became not only wounded, but lame; also he has not made that havoc of the townsmen's children, as formerly he has done. And it is verily believed by some, that this beast will die of his wounds.

This, therefore, made Mr. Great-heart and his fellows of great fame in this town; so that many of the people that lacked their taste of things, yet had a reverend esteem and respect for them. Upon this account therefore it was, that these pilgrims got not much hurt here.

True, there were some of the baser sort, that could see no more than a mole, nor understand more than a beast; these had no reverence for these men, nor took they notice of their valor or adventures.

CHAPTER VII.

WELL, the time grew on that the Pilgrims must go on their way, wherefore they prepared for their journey. They sent for their friends; they conferred with them; they had some time set apart, therein to commit each other to the protection of their Prince. There were those also that brought them of such things as they had, that were fit for the weak and the strong, for the women and the men, and so laded them with such things as were necessary.[110]

Then they set forward on their way; and their friends accompanying them so far as was convenient, they again committed each other to the protection of their King, and parted.

They, therefore, that were of the Pilgrim's company went on, and Mr. Great-heart went before them. Now the women and children being weakly, they were forced to go as they could bear; by this means Mr. Ready-to-halt and Mr. Feeble-mind had more to sympathize with their condition.

When they were gone from the townsmen, and when their friends had bid them farewell, they quickly came to the place where Faithful was put to death; there therefore they made a stand, and thanked Him that had enabled him to bear his cross so well; and the rather because they now found that they had a benefit by such a manly suffering as his was.

They went on therefore, after this, a good way further, talking of Christian and Faithful; and how Hopeful joined himself to Christian after that Faithful was dead.

Now they were come up with the Hill Lucre, where the silver mine was, which took Demas off from his pilgrimage, and into which, as some think, By-ends fell and perished; wherefore they considered that.

But when they were come to the old monument that stood over against the Hill Lucre, to wit, to the pillar of salt that stood also within view of Sodom and its stinking lake; they marvelled, as did Christian before, that men of that knowledge and ripeness of wit, as they were, should be so blinded as to turn aside here.

382

THE PILGRIMS AT THE PLACE WHERE FAITHFUL PERISHED.

383

Only they considered again, that nature is not affected with the harms that others have met with, especially if that thing upon which they look has an attracting virtue upon the foolish eye.

I saw now that they went on, till they came at the river that was on this side of the Delectable Mountains. To the river where the fine trees grow on both sides; and whose leaves, if taken inwardly, are good against surfeits, where the meadows are green all the year long, and where they might lie down safely.[111]

By this river side, in the meadow, there were cotes and folds for sheep, a house built for the nourishing and bringing up of those lambs, the babes of those women that go on pilgrimage.[112] Also there was here one that was intrusted with them, who could have compassion, and that could gather these lambs with his arm, and carry them in his bosom, and that could gently lead those that were with young.[113]

Now to the care of THIS MAN, Christiana admonished her four daughters to commit their little ones, that by these waters they might be housed, harbored, succored, and nourished, and that none of them might be lacking in time to come. This Man, if any of them go astray, or be lost, he will bring them again; he will also bind up that which was broken, and will strengthen them that are sick.[114]

Here they will never want meat, and drink, and clothing; here they will be kept from thieves and robbers; for this Man will die before one of those committed to his trust shall be lost.[115] Besides, here they shall be sure to have good nurture and admonition, and shall be taught to walk in right paths, and that you know is a favor of no small account.

Also here, as you see, are delicate waters, pleasant meadows, dainty flowers, variety of trees, and such as bear wholesome fruit; fruit not like that which Matthew ate of, that fell over the wall of Beelzebub's garden; but fruit that procureth health where there is none, and that continueth and increaseth it where it is.

So they were content to commit their little ones to him; and that which was also an encouragement to them so to do, was, for that all this was to be at the charge of the King, and so was as an hospital for young children and orphans.

Now they went on; and when they were come to By-path Meadow, to the stile over which Christian went with his fellow Hopeful, when they were taken by Giant Despair, and put into Doubting Castle; they sat down and consulted what was best to be done; to wit, now they were so strong, and had got such a man as Mr. Great-heart for their conductor, whether they had not best to make an attempt upon the Giant, demolish his castle, and if there were any pilgrims in it, to set them at liberty, before they went any further.

So one said one thing, and another said the contrary. One questioned if it was lawful to go upon unconsecrated ground; another said they might, provided their end was good; but Mr. Great-heart said, Though that assertion offered last cannot be universally true, yet I have a commandment to resist sin, to overcome evil, to fight the good fight of faith; and, I pray, with whom should I fight this good fight, if not with Giant Despair? I will, therefore, attempt the taking away of his life, and the demolishing of Doubting Castle.

Then said he, Who will go with me? Then said old Honest, I will. And so will we too, said Christiana's four sons, Matthew, Samuel, James, and Joseph; for they were young men and strong.[116] So they left the women in the road, and with them Mr. Feeble-mind and Mr. Ready-to-halt with his crutches, to be their guard until they came back; for in that place, though Giant Despair dwelt so near, they, by keeping in the road, a little child might lead them.[117]

So Mr. Great-heart, old Honest, and the four young men, went to go up to Doubting Castle, to look for Giant Despair.

When they came at the Castle-gate, they knocked for entrance with an unusual noise. With that the old Giant comes to the gate, and Diffidence, his wife, follows. Then said he, Who and what is he that is so hardy, as after this manner to molest the Giant Despair?

Mr. Great-heart replied, it is I, Great-heart, one of the King of the Celestial Country's conductors of pilgrims to their place; and I demand of thee that thou open thy gates for my entrance. Prepare thyself also to fight, for I am come to take away thy head, and to demolish Doubting Castle.

Now Giant Despair, because he was a Giant, thought no man could overcome him; and, again, thought he, since heretofore I have made a conquest of angels, shall Great-heart make me afraid! So he harnessed himself, and went out.

He had a cap of steel upon his head, a breast-plate of fire girded to him, and he came out in iron shoes, with a great club in his hand.

Then these six men made up to him, and beset him behind and before. Also when Diffidence, the giantess, came up to help him, old Mr. Honest cut her down at one blow.

25

Then they fought for their lives, and Giant Despair was brought down to the ground, but was very loath to die. He struggled hard, and had, as they say, as many lives as a cat; but Great-heart was his death, for he left him not till he had severed his head from his shoulders.

Then they fell to demolishing Doubting Castle, that you know might with ease be done, since Giant Despair was dead. They were seven days in destroying of that; and in it of pilgrims they found one Mr. Despond-

GREAT-HEART AND THE SONS OF CHRISTIANA DESTROY DOUBTING CASTLE.

ency, almost starved to death, and one Much-afraid, his daughter; these two they saved alive. But it would have made you a-wondered to have seen the dead bodies that lay here and there in the castle-yard, and how full of dead men's bones the dungeon was.

When Mr. Great-heart and his companions had performed this exploit, they took Mr. Despondency, and his daughter Much-afraid, into their protection; for they were honest people, though they were prisoners in Doubting Castle, to that tyrant Giant Despair.

They, therefore, I say, took with them the head of the giant, for his body they had buried under a heap of stones, and down to the road and to their companions they came, and showed them what they had done.

Now when Feeble-mind and Ready-to-halt saw that it was the head of Giant Despair indeed, they were very jocund and merry. Now Christiana, if need was, could play upon the viol, and her daughter Mercy upon the lute; so since they were so merry disposed, she played them a lesson, and Ready-to-halt would dance.

So he took Despondency's daughter, named Much-afraid, by the hand, and to dancing they went in the road. True, he could not dance without one crutch in his hand; but, I promise you, he footed it well. Also the girl was to be commended, for she answered the music handsomely.

As for Mr. Despondency, the music was not much to him; he was for feeding rather than dancing, for that he was almost starved.

MUCH-AFRAID.

So Christiana gave him some of her bottle of spirits, for present relief, and then prepared him something to eat; and, in a little time, the old gentleman came to himself, and began to be finely revived.

Now I saw in my dream when all these things were finished, Mr. Great-heart took the head of Giant Despair, and set it upon a pole by the highway side, right over against the pillar that Christian erected for a caution to pilgrims that came after, to take heed of entering into his grounds.

Then he writ under it, upon a marble stone, these verses following:—

> This is the head of him, whose name only
> In former times did pilgrims terrify.
> His Castle's down; and Diffidence his wife,
> Brave Master Great-heart has bereft of life.
> Despondency, his daughter Much-afraid,
> Great-heart for them also the man has play'd;
> Who hereof doubts, if he'll but cast his eye
> Up hither, may his scruples satisfy:
> This head also, when doubting cripples dance,
> Doth show from fears they have deliverance.

When these men had thus bravely showed themselves against Doubting Castle, and had slain Giant Despair, they went forward; and went on till they came to the Delectable Mountains, where Christian and Hopeful refreshed themselves with the varieties of the place.

They also acquainted themselves with the Shepherds there, who welcomed them, as they had done Christian before, unto the Delectable Mountains.

Now the Shepherds, seeing so great a train follow Mr. Great-heart, for with him they were well acquainted, they said unto him, Good Sir, you have got a goodly company here. Pray, where did you find all these?

Then Mr. Great-heart replied—

> First, here is Christiana, and her train,
> Her sons, and her sons' wives, who like the wain,
> Keep by the pole, and do by compass steer,
> From sin to grace, else they had not been here;
> Next, here's old Honest come on pilgrimage,
> Ready-to-halt, too, who, I dare engage
> True-hearted is, and so is Feeble-mind,
> Who willing was not to be left behind;
> Despondency, good man, is coming after,
> And so also is Much-afraid his daughter.
> May we have entertainment here, or must
> We further go? Let's know whereon to trust.

Then said the Shepherds, This is a comfortable company. You are welcome to us, for we have comfort for the feeble as for the strong. Our Prince has an eye to what is done to the least of these; therefore infirmity must not be a block to our entertainment.[118]

So they had them to the palace door, and then said unto them, Come in, Mr. Feeble-mind; Come in, Mr. Ready-to-halt; Come in, Mr. Despondency; and Mistress Much-afraid, his daughter.

These, Mr. Great-heart, said the Shepherds to the guide, we call in by name, for that they are most subject to draw back; but as for you, and the rest that are strong, we leave you to your wonted liberty.

Then said Mr. Great-heart, This day I see that grace doth shine in your faces, and that you are my Lord's shepherds indeed; for that you have not pushed these diseased ones, neither with side nor shoulder, but have rather strewed their way into the palace with flowers, as you should.[119]

So the feeble and weak went in, and Mr. Great-heart and the rest did follow. When they were also set down, the Shepherds said to those of the weaker sort, What is it that you would have? for, said they, all things must be managed here to the supporting of the weak, as well as the warning of the unruly.

So they made them a feast of things easy of digestion, and that were pleasant to the palate and nourishing; the which, when they had received, they went to their rest, each one respectively unto his proper place.

When morning was come, because the mountains were high and the day clear, and because it was the custom of the Shepherds to show to the Pilgrims, before their departure, some rarities; therefore, after they were ready, and had refreshed themselves, the Shepherds took them out into the fields, and showed them first what they had shown to Christian before.

Then they had them to some new places. The first was to Mount Marvel, where they looked, and beheld a man at a distance, that tumbled the hills about with words.

Then they asked the Shepherds what that should mean? So they told them, that that man was the son of one Great-grace, of whom you read in the First Part of the Records of the Pilgrim's Progress. And he is set there to teach pilgrims how to believe down, or to tumble out of their way, what difficulties they shall meet with, by faith.[120] Then said Mr. Great-heart, I know him. He is a man above many.

Then they had them to another place, called Mount Innocent; and there they saw a man clothed all in white, and two men, Prejudice and Ill-will, continually casting dirt upon him. Now, behold, the dirt, whatsoever they cast at him, would in little time fall off again, and his garments would look as clear as if no dirt had been cast thereat.

Then said the Pilgrims, What means this? The Shepherds answered, This man is named Godly-man, and this garment is to show the innocency of his life.

Now, those that throw dirt at him, are such as hate his well-doing; but, as you see the dirt will not stick upon his clothes, so it shall be with him that liveth truly innocently in the world. Whoever they be that would make such men dirty, they labor all in vain; for God, after a little time is spent, will cause that their innocence shall break forth as the light, and their righteousness as the noon-day.

Then they took them, and had them to Mount Charity, where they showed them a man that had a bundle of cloth lying before him, out of which he cut coats and garments for the poor that stood about him; yet his bundle or roll of cloth was never the less.

Then said they, What should this be? This is, said the Shepherds, to show you, that he that has a heart to give of his labor to the poor, shall never want wherewithal. He that watereth shall be watered himself. And the cake that the widow gave to the prophet did not cause that she had ever the less in her barrel.

They had them also to a place where they saw one Fool, and one Want-wit, washing of an Ethiopian, with intention to make him white; but the more they washed him the blacker he was. They then asked the Shepherds what that should mean.

So they told them, saying, Thus shall it be with the vile person. All means used to get such a one a good name shall, in conclusion, tend but to make him more abominable. Thus it was with the Pharisees, and so shall it be with all hypocrites.

Then said Mercy, the wife of Matthew, to Christiana, her mother, Mother, I would, if it might be, see the hole in the hill, or that commonly called the by-way to hell.

So her mother brake her mind to the Shepherds. Then they went to the door. It was in the side of a hill, and they opened it, and bid Mercy hearken a while.

So she hearkened, and heard one saying, Cursed be my father, for holding of my feet back from the way of peace and life; and another said, O that I had been torn in pieces, before I had, to save my life, lost my soul! and another said, If I were to live again, how would I deny myself, rather than come to this place!

Then there was as if the very earth had groaned and quaked under the feet of this young woman for fear. So she looked white, and came trembling away, saying, Blessed be he and she that are delivered from this place.

Now when the Shepherds had shown them all these things, then they had them back to the palace, and entertained them with what the house would afford. But Mercy being a young and breeding woman, longed for something that she saw there, but was ashamed to ask. Her mother-in-law then asked her what she ailed; for she looked as one not well.

Then said Mercy, There is a looking-glass hangs up in the dining-room, off which I cannot take my mind. Then said her mother, I will mention thy want to the Shepherds, and they will not deny it thee. But she said, I am ashamed that these men should know that I longed. Nay, my daughter, said she, it is no shame but a virtue, to long for such a thing as that. So Mercy said, Then, mother, if you please, ask the Shepherds if they are willing to sell it.

MERCY AT THE BY-WAY TO HELL.

Now the glass was one of a thousand. It would represent a man, one way, with his own features exactly;[121] and, turn it but another way, and it would show one the very face and similitude of the Prince of Pilgrims himself.[122]

Yea, I have talked with them that can tell, and they have said that they have seen the very crown of thorns upon his head, by looking in that glass; they have therein also seen the holes in his hands, in his feet, and his side.[123] Yea, such an excellency is there in that glass, that it will show him to one where they have a mind to see him; whether living or dead; whether in earth or heaven; whether in a state of humiliation, or in his exaltation; whether coming to suffer, or coming to reign.

Christiana, therefore, went to the Shepherds apart—now the names of the Shepherds are Knowledge, Experience, Watchful, and Sincere,—and said unto them, There is one of my daughters, a young woman, that I think doth long for something that she hath seen in this house.

EXPERIENCE. Call her, call her; she shall assuredly have what we can help her to. So they called her, and said to her, Mercy, what is that thing thou wouldst have?

Then she blushed, and said, The great glass that hangs up in the dining-room. So Sincere ran and fetched it, and, with a joyful consent, it was given her. Then she bowed her head, and gave thanks, and said, By this I know that I have obtained favor in your eyes.

They also gave to the other young women, such things as they desired, and to their husbands great commendation, for that they had joined with Mr. Great-heart, to the slaying of Giant Despair, and the demolishing of Doubting Castle.

About Christiana's neck the Shepherds put a bracelet, and so they did about the necks of her four daughters; also they put ear-rings in their ears, and jewels on their foreheads.

When they were minded to go hence, they let them go in peace, but gave not to them those certain cautions which before were given to Christian and his companion. The reason was for that these had Great-heart to be their guide, who was one that was well acquainted with things, and so could give them their cautions more seasonably; to wit, even then when the danger was nigh the approaching.

What cautions Christian and his companion had received of the Shepherds, they had also lost, by that the time was come that they had need to put them in practice. Wherefore, here was the advantage that this company had over the other.

From hence they went on singing, and they said,

> Behold, how fitly are the stages set
> For their relief that pilgrims are become!

And how they us receive without one let,
That makes the other life, our mark and home!

What novelties they have, to us they give,
That we, though Pilgrims, joyful lives may live;
They do upon us, too, such things bestow,
That show we Pilgrims are, where'er we go.

When they were gone from the Shepherds, they quickly came to the
place where Christian met with one Turn-away, that dwelt in the town of

THE SHEPHERDS ADORN THE PILGRIMS.

Apostasy.   Wherefore of him Mr. Great-heart, their guide, did now put
them in mind, saying, This is the place where Christian met with one
Turn-away, who carried with him the character of his rebellion at his
back.   And this I have to say concerning this man; he would hearken to
no counsel, but, once falling, persuasion could not stop him.

When he came to the place where the Cross and the Sepulchre were, he did meet with one that did bid him look there, but he gnashed with his teeth, and stamped, and said, he was resolved to go back to his own town.

Before he came to the gate, he met with Evangelist, who offered to lay hands on him, to turn him into the way again. But this Turn-away resisted him, and having done much despite unto him, he got away over the wall and so escaped his hand.[124]

TURN-AWAY WILL NOT LISTEN TO EVANGELIST.

Then they went on; and just at the place where Little-faith formerly was robbed, there stood a man with his sword drawn, and his face all bloody.

Then said Mr. Great-heart, What art thou?

The man made answer, saying I am one whose name is Valiant-for-truth. I am a pilgrim, and am going to the Celestial City. Now, as I was in my way, there were three men did beset me and propounded unto me these three things: 1. Whether I would become one of them. 2. Or go back from whence I came. 3. Or die upon the place.

To the first, I answered, I had been a true man a long season, and therefore it could not be expected that I now should cast in my lot with thieves.[125] Then they demanded what I would say to the second. So I told them that the place from whence I came, had I not found incommodity there, I would not have forsaken it at all; but finding it altogether unsuitable to me, and very unprofitable for me, I forsook it for this way.

Then they asked me what I said to the third. And I told them, My life cost more dear far, than that I should lightly give it away. Besides, you have nothing to do thus to put things to my choice; wherefore, at your peril be it if you meddle.

Then these three, to wit, Wild-head, Inconsiderate, and Pragmatic, drew upon me, and I also drew upon them.

So we fell to it, one against three, for the space of three hours. They have left upon me, as you see, some of the marks of their valor, and have also carried away with them some of mine. They are but just now gone. I suppose they might, as the saying is, hear your horse dash, and so they betook them to flight.

GREAT-HEART. But here was great odds, three against one.

VALIANT. It is true; but little or more are nothing to him that has the truth on his side. "Though an host should encamp against me," said one, "my heart shall not fear; though war should raise against me, in this will I be confident." [126] Besides, saith he, I have read in some records, that one man has fought an army. And how many did Samson slay with the jaw-bone of an ass. [127]

GREAT-HEART. Then said the guide, Why did you not cry out, that some might have come in for your succor?

VALIANT. So I did, to my King, who, I knew could hear, and afford invisible help, and that was sufficient for me.

Then said Great-heart to Mr. Valiant-for-truth, Thou hast worthily behaved thyself. Let me see thy sword. So he showed it him. When he had taken it in his hand, and looked thereon a while, he said, Ha! it is a right Jerusalem blade. [128]

VALIANT. It is so. Let a man have one of these blades, with a hand to wield it and skill to use it, and he may venture upon an angel with it. He need not fear its holding, if he can but tell how to lay on. Its edges will never blunt. It will cut flesh and bones, and soul and spirit, and all. [129]

GREAT-HEART. But you fought a great while; I wonder you were not weary.

VALIANT. I fought till my sword did cleave to my hand; and when

VALIANT-FOR-TRUTH BESET BY THIEVES.

they were joined together, as if a sword grew out of my arm, and when the blood ran through my fingers, then I fought with most courage.[130]

GREAT-HEART. Thou hast done well. Thou hast "resisted unto blood, striving against sin." Thou shalt abide by us, come in and go out with us, for we are thy companions.

Then they took him, and washed his wounds, and gave him of what they had to refresh him; and so they went on together.

Now, as they went on, because Mr. Great-heart was delighted in him, for he loved one greatly that he found to be a man of his hands, and because there were with his company them that were feeble and weak, therefore he questioned with him about many things; as, first, what countryman he was?

VALIANT. I am of Dark-land; for there I was born, and there my father and mother are still.

GREAT-HEART. Dark-land, said the guide; doth not that lie upon the same coast with the City of Destruction?

MR. VALIANT-FOR-TRUTH.

VALIANT. Yes, it doth. Now that which caused me to come on pilgrimage was this; we had one Mr. Tell-true come into our parts, and he told it about what Christian had done, that went from the City of Destruction; namely, how he had forsaken his wife and children, and betaken himself to a pilgrim's life.

It was also confidently reported, how he had killed a serpent that did come out to resist him in his journey, and how he got through to whither he intended. It was also told, what welcome he had at all his Lord's lodgings, especially when he came to the gates of the Celestial City; for there, said the man, he was received, with sound of trumpet, by a company of Shining Ones.

He told it also, how all the bells in the city did ring for joy at his reception, and what golden garments he was clothed with, with many other things that now I shall forbear to relate. In a word, that man so told the story of Christian and his travels, that my heart fell into a burning haste to be gone after him; nor could father or mother stay me! So I got from them, and am come thus far on my way.

GREAT-HEART. You came in at the gate, did you not?

VALIANT. Yes, yes; for the same man also told us that all would be nothing, if we did not begin to enter this way at the gate.

GREAT-HEART. Look you, said the guide to Christiana, the pilgrimage of your husband, and what he has gotten thereby, is spread abroad far and near.

VALIANT. Why, is this Christian's wife?

GREAT-HEART. Yes, that it is; and these are also her four sons.

VALIANT. What! and going on pilgrimage too?

GREAT-HEART. Yes, verily; they are following after.

VALIANT. It gladdens me at heart. Good man! how joyful will he be when he shall see them that would not go with him, yet to enter after him in at the gates into the city.

GREAT-HEART. Without doubt it will be a comfort to him; for, next to the joy of seeing himself there, it will be a joy to meet there his wife and children.

VALIANT. But, now you are upon that, pray let me hear your opinion about it. Some make a question, Whether we shall know one another when we are there.

GREAT-HEART. Do they think they shall know themselves then, or that they shall rejoice to see themselves in that bliss? and if they think they shall know and do these, why not know others, and rejoice in their welfare also?

Again, since relations are our second self, though that state will be dissolved there; yet why may it not be rationally concluded, that we shall be more glad to see them there, than to see they are wanting?

VALIANT. Well, I perceive whereabouts you are as to this. Have you any more things to ask me about my beginning to come on pilgrimage?

GREAT-HEART. Yes. Were your father and mother willing that you should become a pilgrim?

THE PARENTS OF VALIANT-FOR-TRUTH TRY TO DISSUADE HIM FROM GOING ON PILGRIMAGE.

VALIANT. Oh no! They used all means imaginable to persuade me to stay at home.

GREAT-HEART. What could they say against it?

VALIANT. They said it was an idle life; and if I myself were not inclined to sloth and laziness, I would never countenance a pilgrim's condition.

GREAT-HEART. And what did they say else?

VALIANT. Why, they told me that it was a dangerous way; yea, the most dangerous way in the world, said they, is that which the pilgrims go.

GREAT-HEART. Did they show wherein this way is so dangerous?

VALIANT. Yes; and that in many particulars.

GREAT-HEART. Name some of them.

VALIANT. They told me of the Slough of Despond, where Christian was well nigh smothered. They told me that there were archers standing ready in Beelzebub's Castle, to shoot them that should knock at the wicket-gate for entrance.

They told me also of the wood, and dark mountains; of the Hill Difficulty; of the lions; and also of the three giants, Bloody-man, Maul, and Slay-good.

They said moreover, that there was a foul fiend haunted the Valley of Humiliation, and that Christian was by him almost bereft of life. Besides, said they, you must go over the Valley of the Shadow of Death, where the hobgoblins are; where the light is darkness; where the way is full of snares, pits, traps, and gins.

They told me also of Giant Despair, of Doubting Castle, and of the ruin that the Pilgrims met with there. Further, they said I must go over the Enchanted Ground, which was dangerous. And that, after all this, I should find a river, over which I should find no bridge, and that that river did lie betwixt me and the Celestial Country.

GREAT-HEART. And was this all?

VALIANT. No. They also told me that this way was full of deceivers, and of persons that laid in wait there, to turn good men out of the path.

GREAT-HEART. But how did they make that out?

VALIANT. They told me that Mr. Worldly-wise-man did there lie in wait to deceive. They also said, that there was Formality and Hypocrisy continually on the road.

They said, also, that By-ends, Talkative, or Demas would go near to gather me up; that the Flatterer would catch me in his net; or that, with green-headed Ignorance, I would presume to go on to the gate, from whence he always was sent back to the hole that was in the side of the hill, and made to go the by-way to hell.

GREAT-HEART. I promise you this was enough to discourage; but did they make an end here?

VALIANT. No; stay.   They told me also of many that had tried that way of old, and that had gone a great way therein, to see if they could find something of the glory there, that so many had so much talked of from time to time; and how they came back again, and befooled themselves for setting a foot out of doors in that path, to the satisfaction of all the country.

And they named several that did so; as Obstinate and Pliable, Mistrust and Timorous, Turn-away and old Atheist, with several more, who, they said, had some of them gone far, to see if they could find; but not one of them found so much advantage by going as amounted to the weight of a feather.

GREAT-HEART. Said they anything more to discourage you?

VALIANT. Yes. They told me of one Mr. Fearing, who was a pilgrim; and how he found this way so solitary, that he never had a comfortable hour therein.   Also, that Mr. Despondency had like to have been starved therein; yea, and also, which I had almost forgot, that Christian himself, about whom there has been such a noise, after all his ventures for a celestial crown, was certainly drowned in the Black River, and never went foot further, however it was smothered up.

GREAT-HEART. And did none of these things discourage you?

VALIANT. No; they seemed but as so many nothings to me.

GREAT-HEART. How came that about?

VALIANT. Why, I still believed what Mr. Tell-true had said, and that carried me beyond them all.

GREAT-HEART. Then this was your victory, even your faith.

VALIANT. It was so.   I believed, and therefore came out, got into the way, fought all that set themselves against me, and, by believing, am come to this place.

> Who would true valor see,
>   Let him come hither;
> One here will constant be,
>   Come wind, come weather.
> There's no discouragement
> Shall make him once relent
> His first avow'd intent
>   To be a pilgrim.
>
> Who so beset him round
>   With dismal stories,

Do but themselves confound,—
  His strength the more is;
No lion can him fright,
He'll with a giant fight;
But he will have a right
  To be a pilgrim.

Hobgoblin nor foul fiend
  Can daunt his spirit;
He knows he at the end
  Shall life inherit.
Then fancies fly away,
He'll fear not what men say;
He'll labor night and day
  To be a pilgrim.

CHAPTER VIII.

BY this time they were got to the Enchanted Ground, where the air naturally tended to make one drowsy; and that place was all grown over with briars and thorns, excepting here and there, where was Enchanted Arbor, upon which, if a man sits, or in which, if a man sleeps, it is a question, say some, whether ever he shall rise or wake again in this world.

Over this forest, therefore, they went, both one and the other, and Mr. Great-heart went before, for that he was the guide; and Mr. Valiant-for-truth, he came behind, being there a guard, for fear, lest peradventure some fiend, or dragon, or giant, or thief, should fall upon their rear, and so do mischief.

They went on here, each man with his sword drawn in his hand, for they knew it was a dangerous place. Also they cheered up one another as well as they could; Feeble-mind, Mr. Great-heart commanded, should come up after him, and Mr. Despondency was under the eye of Mr. Valiant.

Now they had not gone far, but a great mist and darkness fell upon them all, so that they could scarce for a great while see the one the other; wherefore they were forced for some time to feel for one another by words; for they walked not by sight.

But any one must think that here was but sorry going for the best of them all, but how much worse for the women and children, who both of feet and heart were but tender. Yet so it was, that through the encouraging words of him that led in the front, and of him that brought them up behind, they made a pretty good shift to wag along.

The way also was here very wearisome, through dirt and slabbiness. Nor was there on all this ground so much as one inn or victualling-house, wherein to refresh the feeble sort. Here, therefore, was grunting, and puffing, and sighing. While one tumbleth over a bush, another sticks fast in the dirt; and the children, some of them, lost their shoes in the mire. While one cries out, I am down; and another, Ho! where are you?

and a third, The bushes have got such fast hold on me, I think I cannot get away from them.

Then they came at an arbor, warm, and promising much refreshing to the Pilgrims; for it was finely wrought above head, beautified with greens, furnished with benches and settles. It also had in it a soft couch, whereupon the weary might lean.

This, you must think, all things considered, was tempting; for the Pilgrims already began to be foiled with the badness of the way; but there was not one of them that made so much as a motion to stop there. Yea, for aught I could perceive, they continually gave so good heed to the advice of their guide, and he did so faithfully tell them of dangers, when they were at them, that usually, when they were nearest to them, they did most pluck up their spirits, and hearten one another to deny the flesh. This arbor was called The Slothful's Friend, on purpose to allure, if it might be, some of the pilgrims there to take up their rest when weary.

I saw then in my dream, that they went on in this their solitary ground, till they came to a place at which a man is apt to lose his way.

Now, though when it was light, their guide could well enough tell how to miss those ways that led wrong, yet in the dark he was put to a stand; but he had in his pocket a map of all ways leading to or from the Celestial City; wherefore he struck a light, for he never goes, also, without his tinder-box, and takes a view of his book or map, which bids him be careful, in that place, to turn to the right-hand way.

And had he not here been careful to look in his map, they had, in all probability, been smothered in the mud; for just a little before them, and that at the end of the cleanest way, too, was a pit, none knows how deep, full of nothing but mud, there made on purpose to destroy the Pilgrims in.

Then thought I with myself, who that goeth on pilgrimage, but would have one of these maps about him, that he may look when he is at a stand, which is the way he must take.

They went on, then, in this Enchanted Ground, till they came to where there was another arbor, and it was built by the highway-side. And in that arbor there lay two men, whose names were Heedless and Too-bold.

These two went thus far on pilgrimage; but here, being wearied with their journey, they sat down to rest themselves, and so fell fast asleep.

When the Pilgrims saw them, they stood still, and shook their heads; for they knew that the sleepers were in a pitiful case.

Then they consulted what to do, whether to go on and leave them in their sleep, or to step to them, and try to awake them. So they concluded to go to them, and awake them; that is, if they could; but with this caution, namely, to take heed that themselves did not sit down nor embrace the offered benefit of that arbor.

So they went in, and spake to the men, and called each by his name, for the guide, it seems, did know them; but there was no voice nor answer. Then the guide did shake them, and do what he could to disturb them. Then said one of them, I will pay you when I take my money. At which the guide shook his head. I will fight so long as I can hold my sword in my hand, said the other. At that one of the children laughed.

Then said Christiana, What is the meaning of this? The guide said, They talk in their sleep. If you strike them, beat them, or whatever else you do to them, they will answer you after this fashion; or, as one of them said in old time, when the waves of the sea did beat upon him, and he slept as one upon the mast of a ship, "When shall I awake? I will seek it yet again." [131] You know, when men talk in their sleep, they say anything, but their words are not governed either by faith or reason.

There is an incoherency in their words now, as there was before, betwixt their going on pilgrimage, and sitting down here. This, then, is the mischief of it, when heedless ones go on pilgrimage, it is twenty to one but they are served thus; for this Enchanted Ground is one of the last refuges that the enemy to pilgrims has.

Wherefore it is, as you see, placed almost at the end of the way, and so it standeth against us with the more advantage. For when, thinks the enemy, will these fools be so desirous to sit down, as when they are weary? and when so like to be weary, as when almost at their journey's end? Therefore it is, I say, that the Enchanted Ground is placed so nigh to the land Beulah, and so near the end of their race. Wherefore, let pilgrims look to themselves, lest it happen to them as it has done to these, that, as you see are fallen asleep, none can wake them.

Then the Pilgrims desired, with trembling, to go forward; only they prayed their guide to strike a light, that they might go the rest of their way by the help of the light of a lantern. So he struck a light, and they went by the help of that through the rest of this way, though the darkness was very great. [132]

But the children began to be sorely weary; and they cried out unto him that loveth pilgrims, to make their way more comfortable. So by the time they had gone a little further, a wind arose, that drove away the fog; so the air became more clear.

Yet they were not off, by much, of the Enchanted Ground, only now they could see one another better, and the way wherein they should walk.

Now, when they were almost at the end of this ground, they perceived that, a little before them, was a solemn noise of one that was much concerned. So they went on and looked before them; and behold they saw, as they thought, a man upon his knees, with hands and eyes lifted up, and speaking, as they thought, earnestly to one that was above.

They drew nigh, but could not tell what he said. So they went softly till he had done. When he had done, he got up, and began to run towards the Celestial City. Then Mr. Great-heart called after him, saying, Soho! friend, let us have your company, if you go, as I suppose you do, to the Celestial City.

So the man stopped, and they came up to him. But so soon as Mr. Honest saw him, he said, I know this man. Then said Mr. Valiant-for-truth, Prithee, who is it? It is one, said he, who comes from whereabouts I dwelt. His name is Stand-fast; he is certainly a right good pilgrim.

So they came up to one another; and presently Stand-fast said to old Honest, Ho! father Honest, are you there? Aye, said he, that I am, as sure as you are there. Right glad am I, said Mr. Stand-fast, that I have found you on this road. And as glad am I, said the other, that I espied you upon your knees.

Then Mr. Stand-fast blushed, and said, But why, did you see me? Yes, that I did, quoth the other, and with my heart was glad at the sight.

Why, what did you think? said Stand-fast.

Think! said old Honest, what should I think? I thought we had an honest man upon the road, and therefore should have his company by and by.

If you thought not amiss, said Stand-fast, how happy am I; but if I be not as I should, I alone must bear it.

That is true, said the other; but your fear doth further confirm me, that things are right betwixt the Prince of Pilgrims and your soul; for, saith he, "Blessed is the man that feareth always."

VALIANT. Well, but, brother, I pray thee tell us what was it that was the cause of thy being upon thy knees even now? Was it for that some special mercies laid obligations upon thee, or how?

STAND-FAST. Why, we are, as you see, upon the Enchanted Ground; and as I was coming along, I was musing with myself of what a dangerous road the road in this place was, and how many that had come even thus far on pilgrimage had here been stopped and been destroyed. I thought also of the manner of the death with which this place destroyeth men. Those that die here die of no violent distemper. The death which such die is not grievous to them; for he that goeth away in a sleep, begins that journey with desire and pleasure; yea, such acquiesce in the will of that disease.

Then Mr. Honest, interrupting of him, said, Did you see the two men asleep in the arbor?

STAND-FAST. Aye, aye, I saw Heedless and Too-bold there; and, for aught I know, there they will lie till they rot.[133] But let me go on in my tale. As I was thus musing, as I said, there was one in very pleasant attire, but old, who presented herself unto me, and offered me three things; to wit, her body, her purse, and her bed.

Now the truth is, I was both a-weary and sleepy; I am also as poor as an owlet, and that, perhaps, the witch knew.

Well, I repulsed her once and twice, but she put by my repulses, and smiled. Then I began to be angry; but she mattered that nothing at all. Then she made offers again, and said, If I would be ruled by her, she would make me great and happy; for said she, I am the mistress of the world, and men are made happy by me.

Then I asked her name, and she told me it was Madame Bubble. This set me further from her: but she still followed me with enticements. Then I betook me, as you saw, to my knees; and with hands lift up, and cries, I prayed to him that had said he would help. So, just as you came up, the gentlewoman went her way. Then I continued to give thanks for this my great deliverance; for I verily believe she intended no good, but rather sought to make stop of me in my journey.

HON. Without doubt her designs were bad. But stay, now you talk of her, methinks I either have seen her, or have read some story of her.

STAND-FAST. Perhaps you have done both.

HON. Madame Bubble! is she not a tall, comely dame, something of a swarthy complexion?

STAND-FAST. Right, you hit it, she is just such a one.

HON. Doth she not speak very smoothly, and give you a smile at the end of a sentence?

STAND-FAST. You fall right upon it again, for these are her very actions.

HON. Doth she not wear a great purse by her side; and is not her hand often in it, fingering her money, as if that was her heart's delight?

STAND-FAST AND MADAME BUBBLE.

STAND-FAST. It is just so; had she stood by all this while, you could not more amply have set her forth before me, nor have better described her features.

HON. Then he that drew her picture was a good limner, and he that wrote of her said true.

GREAT-HEART. This woman is a witch, and it is by virtue of her sorceries that this ground is enchanted. Whoever doth lay their head down in her lap, had as good lay it down upon that block over which the axe doth hang; and whoever lay their eyes upon her beauty, are counted the enemies of God.[134]

This is she that maintaineth in their splendor all those that are the enemies of pilgrims. Yea, this is she that hath bought off many a man from a pilgrim's life. She is a great gossipper; she is always, both she and her daughters, at one pilgrim's heels or another, now commending and then preferring the excellencies of this life. She is a bold and impudent slut; she will talk with any man. She always laugheth poor pilgrims to scorn; but highly commends the rich.

If there be one cunning to get money in a place, she will speak well of him from house to house; she loveth banqueting and feasting mainly well; she is always at one full table or another. She has given it out in some places, that she is a goddess, and therefore some do worship her. She has her times and open places of cheating; and she will say and avow it, that none can show a good comparable to hers. She promiseth to dwell with children's children, if they will but love and make much of her. She will cast out of her purse gold like dust, in some places, and to some persons.

She loves to be sought after, spoken well of, and to lie in the bosoms of men. She is never weary of commending her commodities, and she loves them most that think best of her. She will promise to some crowns and kingdoms, if they will but take her advice; yet many hath she brought to the halter, and ten thousand times more to hell.

Oh, said Stand-fast, what a mercy is it that I did resist! for whither might she have drawn me!

GREAT-HEART. Whither! nay, none but God knows whither. But, in general, to be sure, she would have drawn thee into "many foolish and hurtful lusts, which drown men in destruction and perdition."[135]

It was she that set Absalom against his father, and Jeroboam against his master. It was she that persuaded Judas to sell his Lord, and that prevailed with Demas to forsake the godly pilgrims' life; none can tell of the mischief that she doth. She makes variance betwixt rulers and subjects, betwixt parents and children, betwixt neighbor and neighbor, betwixt a man and his wife, betwixt a man and himself, betwixt the flesh and the heart.

Wherefore, good Master Stand-fast, be as your name is, and "when you have done all, Stand."

At this discourse there was, among the Pilgrims, a mixture of joy and trembling; but at length they brake out, and sang—

> What danger is the Pilgrim in,
>   How many are his foes!
> How many ways there are to sin
>   No living mortal knows.
>
> Some of the ditch shy are, yet can
>   Lie tumbling in the mire;
> Some, though they shun the frying-pan,
>   Do leap into the fire.

After this, I beheld until they were come unto the Land of Beulah, where the sun shineth night and day.

Here, because they were weary, they betook themselves awhile to rest; and because this country was common for pilgrims, and because the orchards and vineyards that were here belonged to the King of the Celestial country, therefore they were licensed to make bold with any of his things.

But a little while soon refreshed them here; for the bells did so ring, and the trumpets continually sound so melodiously, that they could not sleep; and yet they received as much refreshing as if they had slept their sleep ever so soundly.

Here also all the noise of them that walked in the streets, was, More pilgrims are come to town. And another would answer, saying, And so many went over the water, and were let in at the golden gates to-day. They would cry again, There is now a legion of Shining Ones just come to town, by which we know that there are more pilgrims upon the road; for here they come to wait for them, and to comfort them after all their sorrow.

Then the Pilgrims got up, and walked to and fro; but how were their ears now filled with heavenly noises, and their eyes delighted with celestial visions! In this land they heard nothing, saw nothing, felt nothing, smelled nothing, tasted nothing, that was offensive to their stomach or mind; only when they tasted of the water of the river over which they were to go, they thought, that tasted a little bitterish to the palate, but it proved sweeter when it was down.

In this place there was a record kept of the names of them that had been pilgrims of old, and a history of all the famous acts that they had done. It was here also much discoursed, how the river to some had had its flowings, and what ebbings it has had while others have gone over. It has been in a manner dry for some, while it has overflowed its banks for others.

In this place the children of the town would go into the King's gardens, and gather nosegays for the Pilgrims, and bring them to them with much affection. Here also grew camphire, with spikenard, and saffron, calamus, and cinnamon, with all its trees of frankincense, myrrh, and aloes, with all chief spices. With these the Pilgrims' chambers were perfumed, while they staid here; and with these were their bodies anointed, to prepare them to go over the river when the time appointed was come.

Now, while they lay here, and waited for the good hour, there was a noise in the town that there was a post come from the Celestial City, with matter of great importance to one Christiana, the wife of Christian the Pilgrim. So inquiry was made for her, and the house was found out where she was; so the post presented her with a letter, the contents whereof were, "Hail, good woman! I bring thee tidings that the Master calleth for thee, and expecteth that thou shouldest stand in his presence, in clothes of immortality, within these ten days."

When he had read this letter to her, he gave her therewith a sure token that he was a true messenger, and was come to bid her make haste to be gone.

The token was an arrow with the point sharpened with love, let easily into her heart, which by degrees wrought so effectually with her, that at the time appointed she must be gone.

When Christiana saw that her time was come, and that she was the first of this company that was to go over, she called for Mr. Great-heart her guide, and told him how matters were.

So he told her he was heartily glad of the news, and could have been glad had the post come for him. Then she bid that he should give advice how all things should be prepared for her journey. So he told her, saying, thus and thus it must be; and we that survive will accompany you to the river side.

Then she called for her children, and gave them her blessing, and told them, that she yet read with comfort the mark that was set in their foreheads, and was glad to see them with her there, and that they had kept their garments so white. Lastly, she bequeathed to the poor that little she had, and commanded her sons and her daughters to be ready against the time when the messenger should come for them.

When she had spoken these words to her guide and to her children, she called for Mr. Valiant-for-truth, and said unto him, Sir, you have in all places showed yourself true-hearted; "be faithful unto death," and my King will give you "a crown of life." I would also entreat you to

CHRISTIANA CALLS HER CHILDREN AND GIVES THEM HER BLESSING.

have an eye to my children; and if at any time you see them faint, speak comfortably to them. For my daughters, my sons' wives, they have been faithful; and a fulfilling of the promise upon them will be their end. But she gave Mr. Stand-fast a ring.

Then she called for old Mr. Honest, and said of him, "Behold an Israelite indeed, in whom is no guile." Then said he, I wish you a fair day when you set out for Mount Zion, and shall be glad to see that you go over the river dry-shod. But she answered, Come wet, come dry, I long to be gone; for, however the weather is in my journey, I shall have time enough when I come there to sit down and rest me and dry me.

Then came in that good man Mr. Ready-to-halt to see her. So she said to him, Thy travel hither has been with difficulty; but that will

CHRISTIANA ENTERS THE RIVER OF DEATH.

make thy rest the sweeter. But watch and be ready; for at an hour when you think not, the messenger may come.

After him came in Mr. Despondency and his daughter Much-afraid, to whom she said, You ought with thankfulness for ever to remember your deliverance from the hands of Giant Despair, and out of Doubting Castle. The effect of that mercy is, that you are brought with safety hither. Be ye watchful, and cast away fear; "be sober, and hope to the end."

Then she said to Mr. Feeble-mind, Thou wast delivered from the mouth of Giant Slay-good, that thou mightest live in the light of the living for ever, and see thy King with comfort; only I advise thee to repent thee of thine aptness to fear and doubt of his goodness, before he sends for thee; lest thou shouldest, when he comes, be forced to stand before him, for that fault, with blushing.

Now the day drew near that Christiana must be gone. So the road was full of people to see her take her journey. But, behold, all the banks beyond the river were full of horses and chariots, which were come down from above to accompany her to the city gate. So she came forth, and entered the river, with a beckon of farewell to those that followed her to the river side. The last words that she was heard to say here were, I come, Lord, to be with thee, and bless thee.

So her children and friends returned to their place, for that those that waited for Christiana had carried her out of their sight. So she went and called, and entered in at the gate with all the ceremonies of joy that her husband Christian had done before her.

At her departure her children wept; but Mr. Great-heart and Mr. Valiant played upon the well-tuned cymbal and harp for joy. So all departed to their respective places.

In process of time there came a post to the town again, and his business was with Mr. Ready-to-halt. So he inquired him out, and said to him, I am come to thee in the name of him whom thou hast loved and followed, though upon crutches; and my message is to tell thee, that he expects thee at his table to sup with him, in his kingdom, the next day after Easter; wherefore prepare thyself for this journey.

Then he also gave him a token that he was a true messenger, saying, I have broken thy golden bowl, and loosed thy silver cord.[136]

After this, Mr. Ready-to-halt called for his fellow-pilgrims, and told them, saying, I am sent for, and God shall surely visit you also. So he desired Mr. Valiant to make his will; and because he had nothing to bequeath to them that should survive him, but his crutches and his good wishes, therefore thus he said, These crutches I bequeath to my son that shall tread in my steps, with a hundred warm wishes that he may prove better than I have done.

Then he thanked Mr. Great-heart for his conduct and kindness, and so addressed himself to his journey. When he came at the brink of the river, he said, Now I shall have no more need of these crutches, since yonder are chariots and horses for me to ride on. The last words he was heard to say were Welcome life! So he went his way.

After this, Mr. Feeble-mind had tidings brought him, that the post sounded his horn at his chamber door. Then he came in, and told him, saying, I am come to tell thee that thy master hath need of thee, and that, in very little time, thou must behold his face in brightness. And take this as a token of the truth of my message, "Those that look out of the windows shall be darkened." [137]

Then Mr. Feeble-mind called for his friends, and told them what errand had been brought unto him, and what token he had received of the truth of the message. Then he said, Since I have nothing to bequeath to any, to what purpose should I make a will? As for my feeble mind, that I will leave behind me, for I have no need of that in the place whither I go. Nor is it worth bestowing upon the poorest pilgrim; wherefore, when I am gone, I desire that you, Mr. Valiant, would bury it in a dunghill.

This done, and the day being come in which he was to depart, he entered the river as the rest. His last words were, Hold out, faith and patience. So he went over to the other side.

When days had many of them passed away, Mr. Despondency was sent for; for a post was come, and brought this message to him: Trembling man, these are to summon thee to be ready with thy King by the next Lord's day, to shout for joy for thy deliverance from all thy doubtings.

And, said the messenger, that my message is true, take this for a proof; so he gave him the grasshopper to be a burden unto him. [138]

Now, Mr. Despondency's daughter, whose name was Much-afraid, said, when she heard what was done, that she would go with her father. Then Mr. Despondency said to his friends, Myself and my daughter, you know what we have been, and how troublesomely we have behaved ourselves in every company. My will and my daughter's is, that our desponds and slavish fears be by no man ever received, from the day of our departure, for ever; for I know that after my death they will offer themselves to others. For, to be plain with you, they are ghosts the which we entertained when we first began to be pilgrims, and could never shake them off after; and they will walk about and seek entertainment of the pilgrims: but, for our sakes, shut ye the doors upon them.

When the time was come for them to depart, they went to the brink of the river. The last words of Mr. Despondency, were, Farewell, night, welcome, day. His daughter went through the river singing, but none could understand what she said.

Then it came to pass, a while after, that there was a post in the town that inquired for Mr. Honest. So he came to his house where he was, and delivered to his hand these lines: Thou art commanded to be ready against this day seven-night, to present thyself before thy Lord, at his Father's house. And for a token that my message is true, "All thy daughters of music shall be brought low." [139]

Then Mr. Honest called for his friends, and said unto them, I die, but shall make no will. As for my honesty, it shall go with me; let him that comes after be told of this. When the day that he was to be gone was come, he addressed himself to go over the river.

Now the river at that time overflowed the banks in some places; but Mr. Honest in his lifetime had spoken to one Good-conscience to meet him there, the which he also did, and lent him his hand, and so helped him over. The last words of Mr. Honest were, Grace reigns. So he left the world.

After this it was noised abroad, that Mr. Valiant-for-truth was taken with a summons by the same post as the other; and had this for a token that the summons was true, "That his pitcher was broken at the fountain." [140] When he understood it, he called for his friends, and told them of it. Then, said he, I am going to my Father's; and though with great difficulty I am got hither, yet now I do not repent me of all the trouble I have been at to arrive where I am. My sword I give to him that shall succeed me in my pilgrimage, and my courage and skill to him that can get it. My marks and scars I carry with me, to be a witness for me, that I have fought his battles who now will be my rewarder.

When the day that he must go hence was come, many accompanied him to the river side, into which as he went he said, "Death, where is thy sting?" And as he went down deeper, he said, "Grave, where is thy victory?" So he passed over, and all the trumpets sounded for him on the other side.

Then there came forth a summons for Mr. Stand-fast—this Mr. Stand-fast was he that the rest of the Pilgrims found upon his knees in the Enchanted Ground—for the post brought it him open in his hands. The contents whereof were, that he must prepare for a change of life, for his Master was not willing that he should be so far from him any longer.

At this Mr. Stand-fast was put into a muse. Nay, said the messenger, you need not doubt the truth of my message, for here is the token of the truth thereof: "Thy wheel is broken at the cistern.[141] Then he called unto him Mr. Great-heart, who was their guide, and said unto him, Sir, although it was not my hap to be much in your good company in the days of my pilgrimage; yet, since the time I knew you, you have been profitable to me.

When I came from home, I left behind me a wife and five small children; let me entreat you, at your return (for I know that you will go and return to your Master's house, in hopes that you may yet be a conductor to more of the holy pilgrims), that you send to my family, and let them be acquainted with all that hath or shall happen unto me.

Tell them, moreover, of my happy arrival to this place, and of the present and late blessed condition that I am in. Tell them also of Christian, and Christiana his wife, and how she and her children came after her husband. Tell them also of what a happy end she made, and whither she has gone. I have little or nothing to send to my family, except it be prayers and tears for them; of which it will suffice if you acquaint them, if peradventure they may prevail.

When Mr. Stand-fast had thus set things in order, and the time being come for him to haste away, he also went down to the river.

Now there was a great calm at that time in the river; wherefore Mr. Stand-fast, when he was about half-way in, stood a while, and talked to his companions that had waited upon him thither; and he said, This river has been a terror to many; yea, the thoughts of it also have often frightened me. Now, methinks, I stand easy, my foot is fixed upon that upon which the feet of the priests that bare the ark of the covenant stood, while Israel went over this Jordan.[142] The waters, indeed, are to the palate bitter, and to the stomach cold; yet the thoughts of what I am going to, and of the conduct that waits for me on the other side, doth lie as a glowing coal at my heart.

I see myself now at the end of my journey, my toilsome days are ended. I am going now to see that head that was crowned with thorns, and that face that was spit upon for me.

I have formerly lived by hearsay and faith; but now I go where I shall live by sight, and shall be with him in whose company I delight myself.

I have loved to hear my Lord spoken of; and wherever I have seen the print of his shoe in the earth, there I have coveted to set my foot too.

27

His name has been to me as a civet-box; yea, sweeter than all perfumes. His voice to me has been most sweet; and his countenance I have more desired than they that have most desired the light of the sun. His word I did use to gather for my food, and for antidotes against my faintings. "He has held me, and hath kept me from mine iniquities; yea, my steps hath he strengthened in his way."

Now, while he was thus in discourse, his countenance changed, his strong man bowed under him; and after he had said, Take me, for I come unto thee, he ceased to be seen of them.

But glorious it was to see how the open region was filled with horses and chariots, with trumpeters and pipers, with singers and players on stringed instruments, to welcome the Pilgrims as they went up, and followed one another in at the beautiful gate of the city.

As for Christian's children, the four boys that Christiana brought with her, with their wives and children, I did not stay where I was till they were gone over. Also, since I came away, I heard one say that they were yet alive, and so would be for the increase of the CHURCH in that place where they were, for a time.

Shall it be my lot to go that way again, I may give those that desire it an account of what I here am silent about. Meantime, I bid my reader

FAREWELL.

THE END.

REFERENCES TO THE BIBLE

CONTAINED IN THE FIRST PART.

[1] Isa. 64 : 6 ; Luke 14 : 33 ; Psalms 38 : 4.
[2] Acts 2 : 37 ; 16 : 30 ; Habak. 1 : 2, 3.
[3] Acts 16 : 30, 31.
[4] Heb. 9 : 27.
[5] Job 10 : 21, 22.
[6] Ezek. 22 : 14.
[7] Isa. 30 : 33.
[8] Matt. 3 : 7.
[9] Matt. 7 : 13, 14.
[10] Psalms 119 : 105 ; 2 Peter 1 : 19.
[11] Luke 14 : 26.
[12] Gen. 19 : 17.
[13] Jer. 20 : 10.
[14] 2 Cor. 4 : 18.
[15] Luke 15 : 17.
[16] 1 Peter 1 : 4.
[17] Heb. 11 : 16.
[18] Luke 9 : 62.
[19] Heb. 9 : 17-21.
[20] Tit. 1 : 2.
[21] Isa. 65 : 17 ; John 10 : 27-29.
[22] 2 Tim. 4 : 8 ; Rev. 22 : 5 ; Matt. 13 : 43.
[23] Isa. 25 : 8 ; Rev. 7 : 16, 17 ; 2 : 4.
[24] Isa. 6 : 2 ; 1 Thess. 4 : 16, 17 ; Rev. 5 : 11.
[25] Rev. 4 : 4.
[26] Rev. 14 : 1-5.
[27] John 12 : 25.
[28] 2 Cor. 5 : 2.
[29] Isa. 55 : 1, 2 ; John 6 : 37 ; 7 : 37 ; Rev. 21 : 6 ; 22 : 17.
[30] Psalms 40 : 2.
[31] Isa. 35 : 3, 4.
[32] 1 Sam. 12 : 23.
[33] 1 Cor. 7 : 29.
[34] Ex. 19 : 16, 18.
[35] Heb. 12 : 21.
[36] Heb. 12 : 25.
[37] Heb. 10 : 38.
[38] Matt. 12 : 31.
[39] John 20 : 27.
[40] 1 John 4 : 5.

[41] Luke 13 : 24.
[42] Matt. 7 : 13, 14.
[43] Heb. 11 : 25, 26.
[44] Mark 8 : 38 ; John 12 : 25 ; Matt. 10 : 39 ; Luke 14 : 26.
[45] Gal. 4 : 21-27.
[46] Gal. 3 : 10.
[47] Psalms 2 : 12.
[48] Matt. 7 : 7.
[49] John 6 : 37.
[50] Matt. 7 : 14.
[51] 1 Cor. 4 : 15.
[52] Gal. 4 : 19.
[53] Rom. 7 : 6 ; 1 Cor. 15 : 56 ; Rom. 5 : 20.
[54] John 15 : 3 ; Eph. 5 : 26 ; Acts 15 : 9, Rom. 16 : 25, 26 ; John 15 : 13.
[55] Luke 16 : 25.
[56] 2 Cor. 4 : 18.
[57] 2 Cor. 12 : 9.
[58] Acts 14 : 22.
[59] Luke 8 : 13.
[60] Heb. 6 : 6.
[61] Luke 19 : 14.
[62] Heb. 10 : 28, 29.
[63] 1 Cor. 15 : 52 ; 1 Thes. 4 : 16 ; Jude 14 ; John 5 : 28, 29 ; 2 Thes. 1 : 7, 8 ; Rev. 20 : 11-14 ; Isa. 26 : 21 ; Micah 7 : 16, 17 ; Ps. 95 : 1-3 ; Dan. 7 : 10.
[64] Mal. 3 : 2, 3 ; Dan 7 : 9, 10.
[65] Matt. 3 : 12 ; 13 : 30 ; Mal. 4 : 1.
[66] Luke 3 : 17.
[67] 1 Thes. 4 : 16, 17.
[68] Rom. 2 : 14, 15.
[69] Isa. 26 : 1.
[70] Zech. 12 : 10.
[71] Mark 2 : 5.
[72] Zech. 3 : 4.
[73] Eph. 1 : 13.
[74] Prov. 23 : 34.
[75] 1 Pet. 5 : 8.
[76] John 10 : 1.

[77] Gal. 2 : 16.
[78] Ps. 49 : 10.
[79] Prov. 6 : 6.
[80] Rev. 2 : 5 ; 1 Thes. 5, 7, 8.
[81] 1 Thes. 5–6–7.
[82] Mark 13 : 34–37.
[83] Gen. 9 : 27.
[84] Heb. 11 : 15, 16.
[85] Rom. 7 : 15, 21.
[86] Isa. 25 : 8.
[87] Rev. 21 : 4.
[88] Gen. 19 : 14.
[89] 1 John 3 : 12.
[90] Ezek. 3 : 19.
[91] Heb. 2 : 14, 15.
[92] 1 Sam. 11 : 8 ; Ps. 113 : 7.
[93] Heb. 11 : 33, 34.
[94] Isa. 33 : 16, 17.
[95] Rom. 4 : 23.
[96] Micah 7 : 8.
[97] Rom. 8 : 37.
[98] James 4 : 7.
[99] Jer. 2 : 6.
[100] Num. 13 : 32.
[101] Ps. 44 : 19 ; 107 : 19.
[102] Job 3 : 5 ; 10 : 26.
[103] Jer. 2 : 6.
[104] Ps. 69 : 14, 15.
[105] Eph. 6 : 18.
[106] Ps. 116 : 4.
[107] Ps. 23 : 4.
[108] Job 9 : 2.
[109] Amos 5 : 8.
[110] Job 12 : 22.
[111] Job 29 : 3.
[112] Jer. 29 : 18, 19.
[113] 2 Peter 2 : 22.
[114] Gen. 39 : 11–13.
[115] Ps. 22 : 14.
[116] Prov. 5 : 5.
[117] Job 31 : 1.
[118] Eph. 4 : 22.
[119] 1 John 2 : 16.
[120] Rom. 7 : 24.
[121] 1 Cor. 1 : 26 ; 3 : 18 ; Phil. 3 : 7, 8.
[122] John 7 : 48.
[123] Luke 16 : 15.
[124] Mark 8 : 38.
[125] Prov. 3 : 35.
[126] Matt. 23 : 3.
[127] 1 Cor. 4 : 20.
[128] Rom. 2 : 24, 25.
[129] James 1 : 27.
[130] Matt. 13 : 25.
[131] Lev. 11 : Deut. 14.
[132] 1 Cor. 13 : 1–3 ; 14 : 7.
[133] Gen. 39 : 15.

[134] 1 Cor. 13 : 2.
[135] Ps. 119 : 34.
[136] John 16 : 8, 9 ; Rom. 7 : 24 ; Mark 16 : 16.
[137] Ps. 38 : 18 ; Jer. 31 : 19 ; Gal. 2 : 16 ; Acts 4 : 12 ; Matt. 5 : 6 ; Rev. 21 : 6.
[138] Rom. 10 : 10 ; Phil. 1 : 27 ; Matt. 5 : 19.
[139] John 14 : 15 ; Ps. 50 : 23 ; Job 43 : 5, 6 ; Ezek. 20 : 43.
[140] John 4 : 36 ; Gal. 6 : 9.
[141] 1 Cor. 9 : 24–27.
[142] Rev. 3 : 2.
[143] Eccles. 1 ; 2 : 11, 17 ; 11 : 8 ; Isa. 11 : 17.
[144] 1 Cor. 5 : 10.
[145] Matt. 4 : 8 ; Luke 4 : 5–7.
[146] 1 Cor. 2 : 7, 8.
[147] Ps. 119 : 37 ; Phil. 3 : 19, 20.
[148] Prov. 23 : 23.
[149] Heb. 9 : 13–16.
[150] Exod. 1 : 22.
[151] Dan. 3 : 6.
[152] Dan. 6 : 7.
[153] Prov. 26 : 25.
[154] Gen. 34 : 20–23.
[155] Luke 20 : 46, 47.
[156] Acts 8 : 19–22.
[157] Hos. 14 : 8.
[158] 2 Tim. 4 : 10.
[159] 2 Kings 5 : 20 ; Matt. 26 : 14, 15 ; 27 : 1–5.
[160] Gen. 19 : 26.
[161] Num. 26 : 9, 10.
[162] Gen. 13 : 13.
[163] Gen. 13 : 10.
[164] Ps. 65 : 9 ; Rev. 22 : 1, 2 ; Ezek. 47.
[165] Ps. 23 : 2 ; Isa. 14 : 30.
[166] Num. 21 : 4.
[167] Isa. 9 : 16.
[168] Jer. 31 : 21.
[169] Ps. 88 : 18.
[170] Job 7 : 15.
[171] John 10 : 11.
[172] Hos. 14 : 9.
[173] Heb. 13 : 2.
[174] 2 Tim. 2 : 17, 18.
[175] Prov. 21 : 16.
[176] Prov. 26 : 12.
[177] Eccles. 10 : 3.
[178] Matt. 12 : 45 ; Prov. 5 : 22.
[179] 1 Peter 4 : 18.
[180] 1 Peter 1 : 9.
[181] Heb. 12 : 16.
[182] Gen. 25 : 32.
[183] Jer. 2 : 24.
[184] Ps. 7 : 2 ; 1 Peter 5 : 8.
[185] Job 41 : 26–29.
[186] Job 39 : 19–25.
[187] Eph. 6 : 16.

[188] Exod. 33 : 15.
[189] Ps. 3 : 5–8 ; 27 : 1–3.
[190] Isa. 10 : 4.
[191] Prov. 29 : 5.
[192] Ps. 17 : 4.
[193] Prov. 29 : 5 ; Dan. 11 : 32 ; 2 Cor. 11 : 13, 14.
[194] Rom. 16 : 18.
[195] Deut. 25 : 2.
[196] Rev. 3 : 19 ; 2 Chron. 6 : 26, 27.
[197] Jer. 22 : 12 ; Eccles. 10 : 15.
[198] 2 Cor. 5 : 7.
[199] Prov. 19 : 27.
[200] Heb. 10 : 39.
[201] 1 John 2 : 21.
[202] 1 Thess. 5 : 6.
[203] Eccles. 4 : 9.
[204] Rom. 6 : 21–23.
[205] Ephes. 5 : 6.
[206] Isa. 64 : 6.
[207] Gal. 2 : 16.
[208] Luke 17 : 10.
[209] Heb. 10 : 12–21 ; Romans 4 : 5 ; Col. 1 : 14 ; 1 Peter 1 : 19.
[210] Matt. 11 : 28.
[211] Matt. 24 : 35.
[212] Ps. 95 : 6 ; Dan. 6 : 10 ; Jer. 29 : 12, 13.
[213] Exod. 25 : 22 ; Lev. 16 : 2 ; Num. 7 : 89 ; Heb. 4 : 16.
[214] Hab. 2 : 3.
[215] Eph. 1 : 18, 10
[216] Acts 16 : 31.
[217] 2 Cor. 12 : 9.
[218] John 6 : 35.
[219] John 6 : 37.
[220] 1 Tim. 1 : 15.
[221] Rom. 10 : 4.
[222] Rom. 4 : 25.
[223] Rev. 1 : 5.
[224] 1 Tim. 2 : 5.

[225] Heb. 7 : 25.
[226] Prov. 28 : 26.
[227] Prov. 13.
[228] Prov. 28 : 26.
[229] Rom. 3 : 10.
[230] Gen. 6 : 5.
[231] Gen. 8 : 21.
[232] Ps. 125 : 5 ; Prov. 2 : 15.
[233] Rom. 3 : 12.
[234] Matt. 11 : 27.
[235] 1 Cor. 12 : 3 ; Eph. 1 : 17–19.
[236] Prov. 1 : 7 ; 9 : 10 ; Ps. 111 : 10 ; Job 28 : 28.
[237] 2 Peter 2 : 22.
[238] Prov. 29 : 25.
[239] Isa. 62 : 4.
[240] Song 2 : 10–12.
[241] Isa. 62 : 5.
[242] Isa. 62 : 8.
[243] Isa. 62 : 11.
[244] Isa. 62 : 12.
[245] Song 5 : 8.
[246] Deut. 23 : 24.
[247] Rev. 21 : 18.
[248] 2 Cor. 3 : 18.
[249] 1 Cor. 15 : 51, 52.
[250] Ps. 73 : 4, 5.
[251] Isa. 43 : 2.
[252] Heb. 12 : 22–24.
[253] Rev. 2 : 7 ; 3 : 4 ; 22 : 5.
[254] Isa. 57 : 1, 2 ; 65 : 17.
[255] Gal. 6 : 7.
[256] 1 John 3 : 2.
[257] 1 Thes. 4 : 13–17 ; Jude 14 ; Dan. 7 : 9, 10 ; 1 Cor. 6 : 2, 3.
[258] Rev. 19 : 9.
[259] Rev. 22 : 14.
[260] Isa. 26 : 2.
[261] Rev. 5 : 13.
[262] Rev. 4 : 8.

REFERENCES TO THE BIBLE

CONTAINED IN THE SECOND PART.

---

[1] Rev. 3 : 4 ; 6 : 11.
[2] Zech. 3 : 7.
[3] Luke 14 : 15.
[4] Jude 14, 15.
[5] Luke 10 : 16.
[6] Rev. 14 : 13.
[7] Ps. 126 : 5, 6.
[8] James 1 : 23–25.
[9] Luke 18 : 13.
[10] Song 1 : 3.
[11] Ps. 119 : 54.
[12] 1 Cor. 5 : 1–4.
[13] Ps. 126 : 5, 6.
[14] Luke 1 : 45.
[15] Luke 15 : 7.
[16] Jonah 2 : 7.
[17] Song 1 : 2 ; John 20 : 20.
[18] Matt. 24 : 41.
[19] Matt. 11 : 12.
[20] Jer. 12 : 1, 2.
[21] Deut. 22 : 23–27.
[22] Ezek. 36 : 37.
[23] Matt. 21 : 29.
[24] Prov. 30 : 8.
[25] Prov. 30 : 28.
[26] Matt. 23 : 37.
[27] Ruth 2 : 12.
[28] Exod. 13 : 8–10.
[29] Rom. 5 : 19.
[30] Rom. 5 : 17.
[31] Rom. 4 : 24.
[32] Gal. 3 : 13.
[33] Ezek. 34 : 18.
[34] Prov. 13 : 15.
[35] Jer. 44 : 16, 17.
[36] Prov. 15 : 19.
[37] Matt. 11 : 28.
[38] Ps. 120 : 3, 4.
[39] Judges 5 : 6, 7.
[40] Exod. 12 : 21, 28 ; John 1 : 29.

[41] Ezek. 16 : 8–11.
[42] Job 33 : 14, 15.
[43] 1 Tim. 6 : 17–19.
[44] Heb. 10 : 1–4.
[45] John 6 : 54–57 ; Heb. 9 : 14
[46] Mark 9 : 49.
[47] Zech. 12 : 10.
[48] Heb. 13 : 11–16.
[49] John 6 : 50.
[50] Gen. 3 : 6 ; Rom. 7 : 24.
[51] Gen. 28 : 12 ; John 1 : 51
[52] Heb. 6 : 19.
[53] Gen. 22 : 9.
[54] Song 2 : 11, 12.
[55] Song 2 : 1.
[56] James 4 : 6 ; 1 Peter 5 : 6.
[57] Hos. 12 : 4, 5.
[58] Matt. 11 : 29.
[59] Song 7 : 4.
[60] Ps. 84 : 6, 7.
[61] Hos. 2 : 15.
[62] Isa. 66 : 2.
[63] James 4 : 7.
[64] 1 Pet. 5 : 8, 9.
[65] Isa. 50 : 10.
[66] 2 Cor. 4.
[67] Matt. 10 : 3.
[68] Ps. 99 : 6.
[69] Gen. 39.
[70] Acts 1 : 13, 14.
[71] Lam. 3 : 27–29.
[72] Ps. 88.
[73] Rom. 14 : 21 ; 1 Cor. 8 : 13.
[74] Matt. 11 : 16–18.
[75] Rev. 8 : 2 ; 14 : 2, 3.
[76] 1 Peter 2 : 8.
[77] Hos. 4 : 8.
[78] Rom. 16 : 23.
[79] Acts 11 : 26.
[80] Acts 7 : 59, 60.

[81] Acts 12 : 2.
[82] Gen. 3.
[83] Gal. 4 : 4.
[84] Luke 2.
[85] Luke 8 : 2, 3.
[86] Luke 7 : 37, 50; John 11 : 2; 12 : 3.
[87] Luke 23 : 27; Matt. 27 : 55, 56, 61.
[88] Luke 24 : 22, 23.
[89] Lev. 7 : 32–34; 10 : 14, 15.
[90] Ps. 25 : 1; Heb. 13 : 15.
[91] Deut. 22 : 14.
[92] Judges 9 : 13; John 15 : 1.
[93] 1 Peter 2 : 1, 2.
[94] Isa. 7 : 15.
[95] Song 6 : 11.
[96] Prov. 11 : 24.
[97] Prov. 13 : 7.
[98] 1 Thes. 5 : 14.
[99] Luke 10 : 34, 35.
[100] 3 John 5, 6.
[101] Job 12 : 5.
[102] 1 Thes. 5 : 14.
[103] Rom. 14 : 1.
[104] 1 Cor. 8.
[105] 1 Cor. 9 : 22.
[106] Ps. 38 : 17.
[107] Acts 21 : 16.
[108] Rom. 16 : 23.
[109] Rev. 17 : 3.
[110] Acts 28 : 10.
[111] Ps. 23.

[112] Heb. 5 : 2.
[113] Isa. 40 : 11.
[114] Ezek. 34 : 11–16.
[115] Jer. 23 : 4.
[116] 1 John 3 : 13, 14.
[117] Isa. 11 : 6.
[118] Matt. 25 : 40.
[119] Ezek. 34 : 21.
[120] Mark 11 : 23, 24.
[121] James 1 : 23.
[122] 1 Cor. 13 : 12.
[123] 2 Cor. 3 : 18.
[124] Heb. 10 : 26–29.
[125] Prov. 1 : 10, 14.
[126] Ps. 27 : 3.
[127] Judg. 15 : 15, 16.
[128] Isa. 2 : 3.
[129] Eph. 6 : 12–17; Heb. 4 : 12.
[130] 2 Sam. 23 : 10.
[131] Prov. 23 : 34, 35.
[132] 2 Pet. 1 : 19.
[133] Prov. 10 : 7.
[134] James 4 : 4; 1 John 2 : 15.
[135] 2 Tim. 6 : 9.
[136] Ec. 12 : 6.
[137] Ec. 12 : 3.
[138] Ec. 12 : 5.
[139] Ec. 12 : 4.
[140] Ec. 12 : 6.
[141] Ec. 12 : 6.
[142] Jos. 3 : 17.

INTERESTING AND POPULAR BOOKS.

Among our publications are many well-known and popular books which are having a large sale, and furnish a desirable assortment to persons wishing to supply their homes and libraries with works of standard merit.

The prices of our books are moderate, and within the reach of all. They are also adapted to readers of various ages, containing useful information and beautiful pictures which are interesting to both old and young. A better knowledge of important historical events can be obtained from them, in a brief time, than by any similar course of reading. Several of these books are printed in short and easy words, to be understood by children, yet in a style also interesting to older persons. In none of them will be found any subject unsuitable to the young or for home reading. Descriptions of historical incidents are given in the form of continuous stories, which hold the attention of the reader and impress events upon the memory.

Introducing these books into the homes of this country is a business which occupies the time of a large number of persons. It is especially suitable for those wishing light, profitable employment, which requires but little capital, is easy to start, and involves no risk of loss. Furthermore, an agency for the sale of good and instructive books is not merely advantageous to the seller—it benefits the community as well. Knowledge is the source of power, and nothing increases knowledge so surely as the introduction of good literature.

Charles Foster Publishing Co., 716 Sansom Street, Philadelphia, Pa.

THE

STORY OF THE BIBLE

FROM GENESIS TO REVELATION.

Told in Simple Language.   Adapted to all Ages, but Especially to the Young.

BY CHARLES FOSTER.

A BOOK OF 704 PAGES.   300 ILLUSTRATIONS.

THE STANDARD EASY VERSION OF THE BIBLE FOR YOUNG AND OLD.

600,000 COPIES SOLD.

———•———

Many books have been written to simplify the Bible, and to present the beautiful stories which it contains in a form attractive to the young.

Books of this class, however, have often failed to support the claims made for them, perhaps owing to the fact that the work was undertaken by persons unfitted for the task of worthily rendering the Holy Scriptures.

From this cause, or others, attempts to present the Bible in simple language and continuous form, have been looked upon with disfavor even by those persons who most value it, and who are most competent to appreciate the beauty of its style and the importance of its teachings.

It is indeed proper that great caution should be exercised in accepting, and placing in the hands of young persons, works of this kind; they should be prepared only by those who from long and reverent study of the Word of God have imbibed something of its spirit.

There is one book which has been proved by the unfailing test of time, and by its very general adoption, not only in families, but in schools and institutions of learning throughout the land, to present the best simple version of the Holy Scriptures ever offered to the public.   It is suitable for children, for adults, or any who desire to acquire, with ease and pleasure, a knowledge of the main portions of the Bible.

Although simplified in language, the spirit of the Scripture narrative is most carefully preserved, and all the thrilling incidents of the Bible Story, from Genesis to Revelation, are told in interesting and continuous form.

This book is the "STORY OF THE BIBLE."   Eminent men, well qualified to judge of such a work, have given it their warmest approval, and the public generally have testified to its interest and merit by adopting it as the standard of its class, and by a demand which requires it to be kept constantly on the printing-press.

Charles Foster Publishing Co., 716 Sansom Street, Philadelphia, Pa.

— THE —

BEAUTIFUL LIFE OF CHRIST.

THE STORY OF THE GOSPEL,

TOLD IN WORDS OF EASY READING.

By CHARLES FOSTER.

PRINTED IN LARGE PLAIN TYPE AND FILLED WITH PICTURES.

Containing a Superb Collection of Views of the Sites and Cities of
the Holy Land. A very large number of Illustrations accurately
representing the Habits and Customs of Eastern Peoples,
their Dress, Manners and Mode of Life.

275 PICTURES. NEARLY 400 PAGES.

In some respects this work possesses greater interest, for readers both old and
young, than any other book belonging to the well-known and popular series.

It contains the STORY OF CHRIST'S LIFE ON EARTH, in such plain and easy words
that young readers can understand it, will enjoy being instructed from it, and can
read it for themselves.

While far superior to any other book of its class in the simplicity of its style, the
well-sustained interest of its continuous story, and the value of its teachings, the
REMARKABLE COLLECTION OF PICTURES which it also contains cannot fail to create
surprise and interest.

It may be confidently asserted that no set of illustrations, equalling in variety
and merit those contained in this volume, has ever before been published in any
book of the price. Not only is the number of these pictures unusual—**275** in all—
but their character is of such interest and value, and they differ so widely from those
contained in most other books of the same class, that the desire to possess them is
sure to be awakened by even the most casual glance at their attractions.

ALL THE PRINCIPAL INCIDENTS OF THE NEW TESTAMENT NARRATIVE are illustrated with a fulness seldom, if ever, before attempted, and accurate views of scenes
in the Bible Lands accompany the text.

These show the aspect at the present day of many of the places mentioned in the
Scriptures, THE DRESS AND APPEARANCE OF EASTERN PEOPLES, NOTED SITES AND
THE REMAINS OF ANCIENT BUILDINGS, the whole forming an inexhaustible store of
amusement and instruction for readers both young and old.

The book is of large size, measuring $7 \times 9\frac{1}{2}$ inches. The wide pages effectively
display the numerous pictures and clear plain type.

An unusually elaborate and beautiful design, stamped upon the side and back,
appropriately ornaments the exterior, and aids in rendering this book one of the
most attractive that has ever been brought before the public.

Charles Foster Publishing Co., 716 Sansom Street, Philadelphia, Pa.

BIBLE PICTURES

AND

WHAT THEY TEACH US.

A Book containing 400 Illustrations from the Old and New
Testaments, with brief descriptions.

BY CHARLES FOSTER, Author of the " Story of the Bible," Etc.

Quarto, 320 Pages, 400 Engravings, printed on extra heavy calendered paper and bound
in English cloth, ornamental side and back stamp.

THE COLLECTION OF BIBLE PICTURES contained in this book is probably one of the most complete that has ever been brought together in one volume.

In preparing the work, the greatest care has been observed to use only such designs as will ADEQUATELY ILLUSTRATE THE BIBLE SCENES and fittingly portray the principal events in Bible history.

It has been a matter of great difficulty to obtain so large a number of pictures of the necessary merit, as illustrations of Bible subjects present peculiar difficulties to the artist. While preserving the freedom of style and vigor of treatment necessary to give life to his designs and reality to the VARIED SCENES OF THE SCRIPTURE NARRATIVE, he must preserve for them a feeling of reverence and endow them with a dignity worthy of their sacred character.

A large number of the pictures in this book are reproduced from designs by foreign artists who have been celebrated for their skill in this branch of art. Others are by artists in this country. Most of the pictures were personally selected by, or else drawn under the direction of, the author, who spent years of labor and thousands of dollars in forming this collection.

The book forms a COMPLETE PICTORIAL HISTORY of the main portion of the Bible. Many parts are so fully illustrated that the narrative can be followed and understood by merely looking at the series of pictures which illustrate them, so that CHILDREN UNABLE TO READ may obtain a fair idea of the nature and sequence of biblical events by simply turning over the pages. The book, however, is by no means merely a picture book. A lucid and brief explanation, written by the author of the "Story of the Bible," accompanies each picture, on the same page, or on the page immediately facing it, so that the picture and the explanation appear simultaneously to the eye. THE LARGE-SIZED PAGES (8 × 9¾ inches) afford an admirable setting for the 400 pictures, displaying their artistic excellence to the best advantage, and furnishing the space necessary for the reading which accompanies them.

Charles Foster Publishing Co., 716 Sansom Street, Philadelphia, Pa.

FIRST STEPS

FOR LITTLE FEET IN GOSPEL PATHS.

BY CHARLES FOSTER, Author of the "Story of the Bible," Etc.

328 Pages, 16mo, with a Colored Frontispiece and 148 Illustrations.

PRINTED IN LARGE, PLAIN TYPE AND FILLED WITH PICTURES.

———•———

This book has been prepared for the little ones in the nursery or infant school. It is arranged on a different plan from any of the author's preceding works. Instead of being divided into chapters, it consists of separate passages or lessons, most of them quite short, and each one complete in itself. Each lesson has at least one illustration, and is followed by questions so simple that the little hearers, if attentive when the passage is read, may readily answer them.

It is no easy matter to write a book for children of five or six years of age. To the author there seemed to be but one way of doing it with any assurance of success, and that was to impart the subject-matter of the intended book to a little child by word of mouth, carefully omitting or amplifying, during the process, any portion of the discourse which failed to interest his hearer.

Accordingly, when preparing "FIRST STEPS," the author had a little child placed before him, to whom he addressed himself, while a short-hand writer at his side took down the words as they were spoken. After these had been carefully written out, they were corrected and re-corrected for the press. The book contains 140 ILLUSTRATIONS.

Charles Foster Publishing Co., 716 Sansom Street, Philadelphia, Pa.

FAMILY BIBLES.